THE
ORACLE

JONATHAN CAHN

FRONT
LINE

Most Charisma House Book Group products are available at special quantity discounts for bulk purchase for sales promotions, premiums, fund-raising, and educational needs. For details, call us at (407) 333-0600 or visit our website at www .charismahouse.com.

THE ORACLE by Jonathan Cahn
Published by FrontLine
Charisma Media/Charisma House Book Group
600 Rinehart Road, Lake Mary, Florida 32746

Visit the author's website at www.jonathancahn.com and cahnbooks.com.

Library of Congress Cataloging-in-Publication Data:
An application to register this book for cataloging has been submitted to the
Library of Congress.
International Standard Book Number: 978-1-62999-629-5
E-book ISBN: 978-1-62999-630-1

19 20 21 22 23 — 987654321
Printed in the United States of America

What you are about to read is presented in the form of a narrative, but what is contained in the story, all that the Oracle reveals, is absolutely real.

CONTENTS

THE FOURTH DOOR

THE FIFTH DOOR

THE SIXTH DOOR

THE SEVENTH DOOR

THE VISION

Chapter 1

THE MYSTERY

W HAT IF I told you of a mystery so vast that it spans the world and the ages, from ancient times to this very moment…a mystery that moves behind and through all human events, directs and turns the paths of leaders, determines the future of nations and empires… and of the world itself…to bring all things to their appointed end?"

"I wouldn't believe it."

"No," he replied, "I wouldn't have either if I hadn't seen it with my own eyes."

"What do you mean, 'seen it with your own eyes'? And what mystery?"

"One made up of many others…a mystery of mysteries."

"OK. What mysteries then?"

"The Jubilean mysteries," he replied.

"I've never heard of them."

"Their origins are ancient. They were birthed in a desert not unlike this one and on a mountaintop not unlike the one on which we sit…thousands of years ago."

"And yet they're determining what's happening now?"

"Yes."

"How could something from ancient times be doing that?"

"That," he said, "is the mystery."

They were silent for a time as a warm desert wind swept across the mountaintop. The traveler laid down his backpack on the ground by the rock on which he was sitting. His boots were covered with sand, his jeans were torn, and he was tired from the journey. But what he was hearing made him forget his weariness. He had set out in search of answers. The one he had come to see, the man on the mountaintop, didn't look as he had imagined he would have. He appeared to be in his early thirties, not much older than the traveler himself, and was without a beard, clean-shaven, ordinary looking. But there was something about him. He spoke with an authority and a sincerity that gave the traveler confidence that his journey may not have been in vain. And yet he was still as puzzled by the man as he was intrigued.

"I don't see how something like that could exist," he said.

"But nevertheless the mysteries have determined the course of empires and superpowers, kings and presidents..."

"Do you mean ancient principles or guiding truths that still have meaning for the modern world?"

"Such things do exist," he replied, "but no. I'm speaking of something much different and much more specific... ancient mysteries that have determined the events of our world so precisely that they tell us not only what must take place... but when."

"But in ancient times they didn't number the years as we do now."

"There are other ways by which the appointed times are marked."

"It doesn't seem possible."

"And yet it is."

"I just don't see how something so ancient could reveal..."

"More than that," he replied, "they contain ancient words and messages appointed to be spoken at specific times, even on the specific days on which the events of which they speak are to take place."

"It sounds so..." the traveler paused, looking for the right word, which never came.

"And the mystery of *the end*."

"The end?"

"The end that was foretold."

"This is so unlike anything I've ever heard."

"Then you've never heard of prophecy?"

"Is this something that requires faith... like faith in God?"

"It requires nothing," he said. "It exists whether you believe or not. Your belief doesn't make it any more real, and your doubt doesn't make it any less so. If you're ever going to find that which you don't already have, then you have to be open to what you've never known... or believed could exist... And I should be the last person telling you this."

"Why is that?"

"I wasn't a believer. I was a skeptic. I didn't believe there was any purpose to life... any significance, any meaning. I saw everything as a series of random events, chance occurrences, accidents... sorrows with no purpose, joys with no meaning. Everything was meaningless. So I'm the last person to be telling you about the fingerprints of God."

"The fingerprints of God?"

"The signs, the markers, the witnesses in this world of the purpose behind everything... that it's not an accident."

"That *what* isn't an accident?"

"History, life, existence... that there's a reason, a purpose, and a plan. The mystery reveals the threads of the master loom."

"You were a skeptic," he said. "So what happened? What changed you? And how did you end up here, in the middle of...?"

"I came as you did in search of answers and in search of one."

"In search of one what?"

"In search of one who."

"Then who?"

It was only after a long pause that the answer came.

"The Oracle."

Chapter 2

THE VISION

I DON'T KNOW HOW I can convey it, how unlikely it was…how unlikely that it happened to me, of all people. I doubted everything except what I could see with my own eyes. And so that's where it began, with my own eyes."

"What do you mean?"

"I saw a vision."

"How?"

"I don't know how," he replied. "I never saw one before. I had no idea what to expect or what was happening."

"How did it happen?"

"I was in my apartment. It was night. I was sitting on the couch, watching television, when the sound of the television began to fade into silence, and then my apartment…faded away…into the vision."

"So what did you see?"

"I'll tell you," he replied, "but not just yet. At this point the main thing is that it made no sense to me. I couldn't explain it."

"You couldn't explain what you saw or the fact that you saw it?"

"Both. There was nothing in it I could relate to or make sense of, and I couldn't explain why I was seeing it in the first place. At first I thought I was going crazy. So I kept it to myself. I went to work, I came home, and I sat in my apartment and hoped it would never happen again. But that wasn't to be. A week later, again at night, again while I was sitting on my couch, it happened…the same exact vision with every detail playing out as if I was watching a recording of the first vision."

"So what did you think?"

"I thought I was crazy but that my insanity was remarkably consistent."

"So what happened?"

"Another week went by, and it happened yet a third time, every detail unfolding exactly as it did before. It was then that I came to the conclusion that it couldn't be me. No matter how crazy I was, there was no way I could have come up with something so detailed, so real, so consistent, and so totally foreign to anything I had ever seen or imagined before."

"So if you weren't going crazy, then what?"

"I didn't *know* what. But if it didn't come from me, then it had to be coming from somewhere else. And if it was coming from somewhere else, then there had to be a reason it was happening. I had to find out why."

"How would you do that?"

"In the vision a name was given, a person called the Oracle. Along with that name, or title, was a directive. I was to find him. If I could find the Oracle, I would find the answer."

"How could you possibly find him…if he even existed to begin with?"

"I didn't know where to begin. I didn't even know if he was real. But I decided the best way was to go to my computer and search the internet."

"And what did you find?"

"A lot of companies and products and services and projects are called Oracle. That didn't help. So I decided to search the meaning of the word. An oracle was one who spoke, and more specifically, one who spoke divine revelation or counsel or prophecy, an authority you went to for revelation and truth. An oracle could also refer to the revelation itself, the truth, the word, the counsel, the prophecy, the message given.

"The ancient world was filled with oracles. As long as people seek revelation and as long as they believe that there are those who can reveal such things, there will always be oracles of one kind or another. The most famous of these was the oracle at Delphi. The seekers would journey to the Temple of Apollo to receive the oracle's revelations. But the oracles were all over…in China, India, Europe, South America, Africa, all over the world, each claiming the powers of revelation and prophecy, each claiming to speak from God or the gods."

"So oracles were a part of pagan religion."

"Pagan oracles were part of pagan religion," he replied. "The Bible speaks of the pagan soothsayers and warns against their practices, the channeling of spirits, the practicing of divination, and the worship of pagan gods. But the Bible is also filled with those called and appointed to bring forth divine messages and revelations, to share divine counsel, to discern and interpret the signs of the times, and to speak of future events before they happen."

"Prophets?" he asked.

"Yes, prophets, seers, priests, messengers of God, those chosen as vessels of divine revelation. In fact the word *oracle* itself appears throughout the Scriptures. It is written that the counsel given by a man named Ahithophel 'was as if one had inquired at *the oracle of God*.'[1] So the apostle Paul wrote that the nation of Israel was entrusted with the 'oracles of God.'"[2]

"So the oracles of God are…"

"His revelations, His words, messages, and prophecies, that which is linked to the prophets. Their prophecies could be called *the oracles*."

"But how did any of this help you in your search for the Oracle?"

"It gave me something to go on. I now at least had some idea of what I was looking for."

"And where did it lead you?" he asked.

"Nowhere…not for some time. But I wasn't going to give up. I kept searching, on the web, in libraries, in history books, in books on religion, in periodicals, on microfilm, everything I could search through, looking for any trace of the Oracle. And then…"

"And then?"

"And then I found it."

Chapter 3

THE JOURNEY

I WAS IN THE library, going through an article preserved on microfilm. It was there that I saw it, in that article. It wasn't even the main point but was a side note. It mentioned how in a certain region the locals told the story of a man who lived in the mountains and only emerged in the villages on the rarest of occasions. They called him the Oracle."

"They called him the Oracle, why?"

"Because they believed he spoke words of divine wisdom and revelation. They sought his counsel. That was pretty much all it said."

"So what did you do?"

"I narrowed down my searching to that region. I retrieved as many pictures as I could find of its landscape. That's how I knew I was on the right track."

"How?"

"The pictures of the region matched the landscape in my vision. It was then that I decided to make the journey. I didn't believe I had a choice. If I didn't go, I would always be haunted by the fact that I never did. So I would go to the land of the Oracle and seek him out.

"I wrapped up my affairs, arranged for an extended absence, and set out on the journey. I ended up in one of the villages spoken about in the article. I stayed in what could only, by the loosest of interpretations, be called an inn but which served its purpose. I figured I would start out by simply asking the locals if they had ever heard of a man called the Oracle. And if they answered yes, I would see if I could get anything more, any clue to his whereabouts."

"Did you?"

"There were those who didn't speak the language. There were others who said they had never heard of him. Then there were those who told me they had heard of him but only through others, who in turn had only heard of him through others. They knew someone who knew someone who had once encountered him. And then there were those eager to speak of him, but what they shared was so fanciful, the stuff of legends, that it was useless.

"Finally I came across the one person who was able to give me something to go on, an old shopkeeper. He didn't claim to know much about the Oracle except for the region in which he was reputed to dwell. He was the one who directed me into the desert and to the most dangerous part of the journey. But he didn't do so without preparing me. He sold me some used paraphernalia of the nomads of the region, survival gear, a small cloth tent, and rations of dried food. I did wonder whether he really knew of the Oracle's whereabouts or if he just wanted to make a sale. But having nothing else to go on, I went with it.

"So I set off in the desert in the direction I was told to go in. I knew it was a risk. In the daytime my chief goal was to find a source of water and to preserve the little I carried. At night it was to stay on guard against the animals of the region and the possibility of robbers. But the greatest danger would become evident on the third day. It was then that I realized I had no idea where I was. Thus I could no longer pace myself. Nor could I tell if it was safer to head back or keep going.

"It was the night of the third day, a cool and windy night. I was sitting on a rock in front of my tent by a small campfire I had, with much effort, managed to ignite. I noticed, in the distance, a dark figure with a long black coat or cloak and a hood covering his head. He made his way over to the fire."

"Might I join you?" he asked.

He was an older man, his features chiseled and desert worn, his voice rich and with a noticeable accent. But I couldn't place its origin.

"Yes," I replied.

He sat down beside me, staring into the fire as he spoke.

"You're on a journey?" he asked.

"Yes."

"You're looking for the Oracle?"

"How did you know that?" I asked.

"I just do. So why do you seek him? What do you want?"

"I need to ask him something…about something I saw. I believe he's the only one who can answer it."

"And are you seeking gain?"

"Just an answer."

"And if you get your answer, what will you do with it?"

"I don't know. I just know that I need to know it."

It was then that he turned away from the fire and gazed directly into my eyes.

"You must keep going, and in the direction in which you've begun. You'll find the remnant of a trail, the caravan path of nomads. Follow it. In a day or two you'll come to their encampment. Don't set up your tent inside the camp but just outside it, at the foot of the nearest mountain."

At that he rose to his feet.

"I wish you well," he said as he walked away from the fire.

"What about the Oracle?" I asked.

"If you are meant to find him," he said, "you'll find him … or he'll find you."

"He disappeared into the darkness as quickly as he had appeared.

"The following day I set out on the next phase of the journey in accordance with what I was told. I found the caravan path, or what remained of it. At times it would disappear in the sand, but there was always just enough to keep me going.

"It was late in the afternoon when I saw the tent encampment. It seemed as if it was from another age. The people of the camp had to have lived much the same way as they would have thousands of years in the past … in a world of their own. Their tents were made of dark brown and black cloth. The men were clothed in similar cloth and colors, but the women were dressed in more varied cloths and colors and patterns.

"I was, of course, a total stranger to them. But they were welcoming. They found me a continual source of fascination. That night I ate a meal prepared by the women. The communication was challenging since there was no common language between us, not even a shared word. So we spoke mostly with our hands. I asked them to point me to the nearest mountain. They did.

"It was now dark, but I was able to discern its outline. They implored me to stay, to spend the night with them. But I insisted on continuing to my destination. It wasn't long before I reached it, and there, a few feet from the rock of the mountain's base, I set up my tent. I was by now beyond exhaustion. I lay down in my tent on the cloths that formed my pillow. I stayed awake for a time. I couldn't stop wondering what lay ahead. I had reached the end of the instructions.

"It was only when I woke up the next morning that the precariousness of my situation dawned on me. My food and water supply was nearly exhausted. It was then that I noticed a covered object by the entrance of my tent. I uncovered it. It was a plate of food. The women from the camp had brought it out to me. After finishing the meal, I placed the plate in the sand outside the tent. Underneath it I left some money. That evening I found another plate by the tent entrance—dinner. After eating, I did the same thing, leaving the plate just outside the entrance with a second payment underneath it. This went on every day. They never announced their coming, as if to make sure they didn't interrupt me. And they never asked me for anything in return, but I felt it right to pay them. The food was different from anything I had been accustomed to. But over time I grew accustomed to it, and it kept me alive."

"That's why he told you to go there, to stay by the camp…so you would survive."

"That was one reason. The next morning, I began exploring the area, being careful to keep my bearings and not wander too far away from the tent."

"Did you find anything?"

"Valleys, plains, and mountains but no sign of anything else. This went on for several days. But then something happened. It was morning. I emerged from my tent to discover I had company."

"Who?"

"A little boy dressed in brown cloth. He was sitting in the distance outside my tent, as if waiting for me to come out."

"Where did he come from?"

"Maybe from the encampment, maybe from another encampment, from a family of nomads. I don't know. As with those in the tent village, we didn't speak the same language. He got up and motioned for me to follow him. I wasn't sure if I should. On the other hand, I didn't think I had anything to lose by doing so. So I began walking behind him. He would occasionally stop and look back, just to make sure I was there or to allow me time to catch up.

"I couldn't tell which was more absurd, the fact that a little boy was leading me or the fact that I was following him. There was always the possibility that I was being led nowhere in the middle of a barren wilderness. All the more, I tried my best to keep track of all the turns and landmarks along the way. But the bottom line was I had nothing else to go on.

"He led me through a valley, a deep, winding ravine, a plain, and finally to the bottom of the mountain, where he paused to allow me to catch up. Then we began the ascent. His steps followed the outline of a winding mountain path. The terrain was such that I often lost sight of the boy before spotting him again on the other side of a bend or ledge.

"Finally we arrived at the top. It was then that I saw the figure of a man sitting on a large rock near the mountain's pinnacle. At first I could only see his outline, a silhouette against the sunlight. The boy receded to the side as if to indicate that I was to approach the man on my own. So I did. When I looked back, the boy had vanished. I continued the approach. The man was turned away from me, looking into the light of the desert landscape. I don't know if he heard me coming or not, but it was just at that moment that he turned around. He said nothing. But I couldn't hold back."

"Are you the one I've been seeking?"

"That would depend," he replied.

"The one who can answer my questions."

"How could I answer before hearing them?"

"Who are you?" I asked.

"I'm known by many names," he replied.

"What do the people of this region call you?"

"Most of them have no idea who I am."

"But those that do, do they have a name for you?"

"I've heard they do."

"What is it?"

"The Oracle."

Chapter 4

THE ORACLE

H E WASN'T YOUNG. That much I expected. The legend of the Oracle had been around for some time. And as I had expected, he had a distinctly mystical appearance. The hair on his head was snow white, as was his beard. He was wearing an off-white robe-like garment on top of an off-white inner garment, what you might expect to see in ancient times or on a member of some religious order.

"There was a rock opposite the one on which he was sitting. He motioned for me to sit there. So I did."

"You've been searching for how long?" he asked.

"On foot," I said, "for several weeks and, before that, several months."

"How did you hear of me?"

"I read about you in an article."

"There couldn't have been much. There isn't much known of me...and I don't give interviews."

"No," I replied, "it wasn't much. It spoke more of your legend than of you."

"So how did you know I was real?"

"I wasn't sure. I believed you were."

"You came all this way because of a legend you read about in an article. Why?"

"Because I thought you could help me."

He was silent.

"Can you?" I asked.

"That depends on what kind of help you need."

"Answers...truth...an explanation."

"It is possible," he replied, "that I could be of some help. But I can't promise you anything without hearing. How serious are you about finding the truth?"

"Would I be sitting here in the middle of the desert if I weren't?"

"And how long do you have?"

"As long as it takes."

There was a long pause.

"So then," he said, "where shall we begin?"

"Where it all began," I replied. "Do you believe in visions?"

"You've seen a vision?"

"I'm not the type to be seeing them."

"Who is the type?" he asked.

"I don't know, but not me. I never had one before. And now I've had three."

"Three different visions?"

"One vision, three times."

"The exact same vision?" he asked.

"The exact same vision."

"So what did you see?"

I paused to collect my thoughts.

"I was standing inside a temple, an ancient-looking temple with large stone pillars, capitals, steps, a roof…everything pure white, more than pure white. Everything was glowing, radiant. I wasn't alone. I could see figures, clothed in white and likewise radiant, moving around me. In front of me was a man clothed, as were the others, in a white robe. I couldn't see his face at first, as he was turned away from me. He opened a white marble chest and retrieved a key."

"A radiant white key?"

"Yes, like everything else. He turned around, placed the key in my hand, then led me outside the temple. We were standing on its marble steps, looking out into a vast desert landscape of valleys, plains, and mountains. He walked down the steps and into the desert. I followed him.

"He led me to a mountain. As we neared its base, I noticed a massive door in the rock face. He motioned for me to approach it. The door had a small keyhole. I looked back. He nodded as if to give me the go-ahead. I placed the key in the hole and turned it. There was a loud rumbling. The massive door began to open inward. We went inside. The door closed behind us. We were now standing in a gigantic chamber of hewn rock, lit up by the light of torches set in holders along the wall. The chamber was circular. Spaced evenly around the chamber were seven doors, each of a slightly different color. On each door was a symbol different from the others. Seeping through the cracks of each door was light of the color and intensity one would expect of the midday sun.

"'Where are we?' I asked the man.

"'In the house of Oracle,' he answered.

"'And this room?'

"'The Hall of the Seven Doors.'

"I stood in front of the first door, wanting to know what was waiting on the other side. I slipped the key into the hole, but it wouldn't turn. I tried again, but nothing.

"'How do I open it?' I asked the man.

"'There's only one way to open the seven doors,' he said. 'You must find the owner of the house. Find the owner, and you will open the mysteries. Find the owner, and you will have your answer.'

"And with that the vision ended...Each time, that's where it ended. And that's why I'm here."

"Did you write down what the symbols on the seven doors looked like?"

"Yes, after seeing the vision for the third time."

"If I give you a piece of paper, can you write them down for me in the order they appeared?"

"I believe I can."

He handed me a piece of paper, and I drew the seven symbols in the order in which they appeared, as best I could remember. I handed him back the paper. He sat there for some time studying it. Then he looked up and stared out into the distance a few more moments.

Finally he spoke.

"Your vision began in a temple where everything was filled with light. Light is a symbol of truth and revelation of divine origin. You were given a key of light. That was to tell you of a revelation, a mystery to be unlocked."

"And the desert?"

"It represented the desert you've journeyed to, *this* desert."

"I had to open the door myself."

"Yes, because you have a part in it. What is to be revealed requires your seeking it, your unlocking it."

"And the mountain...I was told it was the house of the Oracle."

"It signified the place of my dwelling."

"This mountain."

"Whatever mountain, wherever I dwell."

"And the seven doors?"

"The mystery has seven parts, seven streams. Each door will open up one of them."

"But the key I was given couldn't open them."

"You were meant to open them," said the Oracle, "but you would need help."

"So I was told to find the owner of the house. I was told to find you. And here I am. Now what?"

"Do you mean do I have more to tell you?"

"Yes."

"No. It must come from you."

"But I don't have anything else."

"If it's meant for you to be here, then you will. It all began with a vision. There are seven doors. I would suspect there are more visions for you to see."

"So what do I do now?"

"What did you do before the vision came to you?"

"Nothing."

"So that's what you do now. You've come this far. You just need to stay open…"

"Until how long?"

"Until the time."

THE FIRST DOOR

Chapter 5

THE FIRST DOOR

S O WHAT DID you do?"

"I went back to my tent. In the days that followed, I pondered the Oracle's words. I still had no idea what it was all about. And yet the vision had led me to the Oracle. In at least that much it had proved true. The Oracle was real. Beyond that, I could only imagine where it was all going. So I'm in the middle of a desert with no idea what was to happen next...and then it did."

"What happened?"

"I was in my tent. It was night. Outside the wind was howling and beating against the tent curtains. I was afraid at one point that the wooden frame wouldn't hold out. And while I could still see the shaking of the tent curtains, the sound of the wind and the flapping of the curtains began subsiding."

"The wind was lessening."

"No, just the sound of it, until it faded to silence, as when I saw the first vision. I was about to see another. The tent disappeared. I found myself back in the Hall of the Seven Doors."

"Where the last vision left off."

"Yes. I was standing in front of the first door but now aware of a presence to my right. I never turned to look, but I knew intuitively that it wasn't the man I saw in the first vision. It was the Oracle. He placed a key in my right hand. The key I had been given in the other vision was gone. I inserted it into the lock, and it turned. The door opened. What was behind the door was almost blinding until my eyes adjusted to it...the light of a midday sun on a desert landscape. Only after I stepped through the door could I make out what it was.

"I found myself on top of a high mountain overlooking the vast expanse of a desert plain. The plain was filled with multitudes of people, hundreds of thousands of them, maybe more, all dressed in ancient garments. Everyone was looking up to the mountaintop on which I stood. But they weren't looking at me. As far as I know, I was invisible to them. They were looking at an ancient figure who stood in front of me. He had white hair and a flowing white beard and was clothed in a dark red robe. In his arms was a scroll."

21

"What kind of scroll?"

"The kind I would associate with the Jewish people…a parchment covered with writing and wound around two wooden rollers. The man walked over to what looked like some sort of natural lectern formed out of the mountain rock, on which he laid the scroll and rolled it to the section he was looking for. One of the two rolls was now almost completely unrolled. It was either at its beginning or its end.

"The old man lifted up his arms and began chanting the words of the parchment that was spread out before him. The language was foreign, and the melody sounded ancient. As he sang, a transformation began. The sky began to darken. Then the appearance of the people in the plain began changing. Most were now dressed in the garments of varied ages and lands. Some were still dressed in robes as from ancient times, but others were now in medieval dress, some in black jackets and hats; others were wearing the clothes of more modern times, overcoats, dresses, and caps. Nearly all of them had some sort of baggage at their side as diverse as their clothing.

"As the old man continued his chant, a second transformation took place, that of the landscape. The desert plain in which the multitude stood and the mountain on which the man stood remained the same. But everything else changed. The plain and the mountain were now encircled by an immense collage of diverse landscapes from all over the world—hills, farmland, tundras, seas and rivers, harbors, bridges, walls, villages and cities, ancient, medieval, and modern.

"And then came the last change. The multitude began to scatter. Some fled in haste, grabbing their baggage and running as if to escape a calamity. Others left more slowly and as if in mourning. Each headed out to the land and age to which their garments corresponded. Soon, except for a small remnant of those who lagged behind or chose to stay, the plain was devoid of people.

"The chanting ended. The old man now just gazed into the distance as the people wandered farther and farther away from the plain. Then the clouds began to move more and more rapidly across the sky as the day turned to night. And then it was day again and night in rapid succession. Time was accelerating, faster and faster, until days and nights blurred into weeks and years, decades and centuries, ages. And yet through it all the old man remained, standing unchanged on the mountaintop as everything changed around him. And then it all stopped, or resumed back to normal. I knew that many ages had passed since the time of the vision's beginning.

"The old man then ascended a rock that comprised the highest point of the mountain's pinnacle. He reached into his robe and pulled out a ram's horn. He set it to his mouth and blew. What came out of the horn was not in any way natural but something in between the sound of sirens and the sound of thunder and so powerful that it shook not only the mountain on which he stood but all the landscapes that surrounded it.

"He then looked into the distance and spoke as if to the multitudes scattered in the nations.

"'And thus,' he said, 'you shall return.'

"And the vision ended."

Chapter 6

THE BEGINNING OF MYSTERIES

THE NEXT MORNING I returned to the mountain to find the Oracle. He was there on its summit, sitting in the same place, on the rock. He didn't see me as I approached him. His head was turned downward, and his eyes were closed as if in deep thought. Yet he knew I was there."

"You've had another revelation?" he said.

"I have."

"I was expecting it."

He motioned for me to sit down, which I did.

"Tell me."

"I was standing in front of the first of the seven doors. You were there, at my side. You gave me the key. I opened it."

"And what did you see?" he asked.

So I told him of the old man, the multitudes, the scroll, and the chant. He was quiet for a moment.

"What if there was a people," he said, "brought into existence as a sign, as a witness to the existence of God and a vessel to bring about His purposes? If such a people were to exist, what do you think would become of them?"

"I would think they would be different...they would stand out."

"What about the history of such a people?"

"I would think it would be different from that of other peoples."

"If such a people were to exist," said the Oracle, "they already do. They were the people you saw in your vision on the plain in the desert...the nation of Israel, the Jewish people...a people who stand out as different and whose history is unlike that of other peoples."

"But why were they in my vision?"

"Because apparently the mystery begins with them."

"And who was the old man in the red robe?"

"Only once was the entire nation of Israel in a desert as in your vision...in the days of their journeying from Egypt to Israel. The old man in the red robe would be Moses."

"And the scroll?"

"That would be the scroll of Moses, the Torah, the first five books of the Bible."

"So Moses was reading from the books of Moses?"

"He was reading from the scroll just as it has been read by the Jewish people in every age and land."

"And what exactly was he reading?"

"His last words," said the Oracle, "the last words he would ever speak to the nation, the words he gave them at the end of their journeying in the wilderness, just before he died."

"How do you know?"

"Because he was speaking to them from the end of the scroll. The scroll ends with his last words."

"And what did he tell them there?"

"He told them exactly what would happen to them in the centuries and ages to come. He told them their future."

"But how could he have known that?"

"It's another one of the peculiarities about the nation of Israel. At the beginning of its existence, its future was foretold."

"Where?"

"In the Scriptures, in the prophecies. Its history was foretold ages before it happened, from ancient times."

"But it's impossible to foretell that."

"Yes," said the Oracle, "to foretell the intricate courses of human events even days before they happen, much less thousands of years, would be impossible. There's only one way it could be foretold…if the foretelling was from God. If God was real."

"So this would be recorded in the Bible."

"In the Book of Deuteronomy, Moses' last words."

"What exactly did the prophecy foretell?"

"That the land of Israel would be invaded by an enemy people and that the Jewish people would be taken captive into the nations. They would be scattered '*from one end of the earth to the other.*'[1] They would be persecuted from one nation to the next. They would wander the earth."

"That's what happened in my vision; they were scattered to the world. So did it come true?"

"Yes, first when the armies of Babylon invaded the land, destroyed the Holy City of Jerusalem, and took the people captive into exile in Babylon. The exile would last seventy years, until the rise of the Persian king Cyrus, who would allow them to return to their land."

"But you said that the prophecy spoke of their being scattered '*from one end of the earth to the other.*'"

"Yes, that would be fulfilled in its entirety in the second exile. It would begin in the year AD 70. This time it would be the armies of Rome that would destroy Jerusalem and drive the people into exile not to one city or kingdom but to the ends of the earth, and not for seventy years but for ages. They would be persecuted from nation to nation and wander the earth as no people have ever wandered the earth."

"And how long did the second exile last?" I asked.

"Into modern times."

"What about the ram's horn that Moses sounded? He sounded it and said, 'And thus you shall return.' What did it mean?"

"There's only one place in the writings of Moses where the ram's horn, or shofar, is connected to the words *you shall return*. It's in the law of Jubilees."

"The law of Jubilees? I've never heard of it."

"That's where the mystery begins. Apparently the Jubilean mysteries are to be revealed to you."

"I've heard the word before, but what exactly is a Jubilee?"

"Imagine," said the Oracle, "you lost your home, your land, the land of your family, your ancestral possession, your inheritance. In the year of Jubilee you get it all back. In the year of Jubilee that which was lost is restored. As it was written in the Jubilean ordinance:

> Each of you shall return to his possession, and each of you
> shall return to his family.[2]

"In the year of Jubilee you come home. Your family comes home. Your separation from your land is ended. So the Jubilee is the year of return and restoration. The Jubilee is the restoring of that which was lost. The land is restored to its original owner, and the original owner to the land."

"And where is the law of Jubilees in the Bible?"

"In the third book of Moses, the Book of Leviticus."

"And what's the connection between the Jubilee and the ram's horn?"

"The ram's horn, the shofar, the trumpet, was the sign of the Jubilee. It was the ram's horn that ushered it in and proclaimed its coming throughout the land."

"And when exactly did the Jubilee come?"

"Once every fifty years. The Jubilee is the fiftieth year."

"But what if you lost your land and didn't survive to the fiftieth year?"

"Then the land would be restored to your children. Then your children would return to it."

"So what does the Jubilee have to do with what I saw at the beginning of the vision, the multitudes in the desert and their scattering into the world?"

"Everything," he replied. "To whom was the Jubilee given?"

"To Israel," I said, "the Jewish people."

"And what does the Jubilee concern?"

"Returning to your ancestral possession."

"And what is the Promised Land and Jerusalem to the Jewish people?"

"Their ancestral possession?"

"Yes. And for two thousand years, the Jewish people wandered the earth in exile from their land, from their ancestral possession. It's the mystery of the Jubilee playing out before the world. As the age wore on, the connection between the Jewish people and the land appeared increasingly weaker, and the idea that there would ever be a return to the land more and more of an impossibility."

"But in the Jubilee," I said, "the one who has lost his ancestral land returns to it."

"Yes," said the Oracle. "So then what would the mystery ordain?"

"That the Jewish people would return to their ancestral land."

"Yes, and that is exactly what was prophesied in the Scriptures...the Jewish people would return to the land."

"When was that first prophesied?"

"By Moses in his last words to the people of Israel. After foretelling that they would be scattered to the ends of the earth, he said this:

> The LORD your God will bring you back from captivity, and
> have compassion on you, and gather you again from all the
> nations where the LORD your God has scattered you."[3]

"He said that how long ago?"

"Thousands of years ago. It was all there at the beginning of their history. The return of the Jewish people to their ancient land would be the sign of the *end times*."

"But for that to happen," I said, "for a nation to be destroyed, for its people to be scattered to the ends of the earth and then to return to their homeland and come back into history...that would be unprecedented."

"Yes," said the Oracle, "it would go against all odds and would defy the laws of history. For the Jewish people to return to their ancient land would be the mystery of the Jubilee manifesting on a cosmic scale. And if this was to happen, it would mean the hand of God moving in the events of the modern world. It would mean that behind the events of the modern world was an ancient mystery."

"And so what happened?"

"I believe that's where your vision ended."

"But can't you..."

"No," he said, "but from what you've been shown, I'm sure there's more for you to see."

"Another vision?"

"I would think so."

"So I have to wait."

"Yes, but now the stage is set."

Chapter 7

THE DESERT VISIONS

A FEW DAYS HAD passed. It was midday. I was outside my tent, sitting on a rock. The sound around me began to fade away as it had in the previous visions. I didn't notice it at first, because there wasn't much sound to begin with. But soon enough it became obvious. I was back in the desert on the mountaintop with the old man."

"Moses."

"Yes. He had just sounded the ram's horn and was still holding it in his left hand. The vision was beginning exactly where the last one had ended, except now standing by his side was a ram."

"Where was it before?"

"I have no idea. But I believe its appearance was connected to the sounding of the horn. Strapped across the ram's back were sheaves of grain and a cloth bag that hung down on both of its sides. Around its neck was a chain, from which hung a small white object, something of a pendant, on which was a symbol."

"Of what?"

"The same symbol that was on the first of the seven doors. The old man..."

"Moses."

"Yes, he placed his hand on the ram's head and whispered something into its ear. The ram then began descending the mountain into the desert below. I was led to follow it."

"In the previous vision the plain was surrounded by the landscapes of the world. Was that still the case?"

"No. It was now all desert, as it was at the beginning. I followed the ram through plains and valleys, hills and ravines. And then in the midst of an immense valley the ram stopped and turned its gaze to the left. I turned as well. And I saw a vision."

"A vision within the vision?"

"Visions within the vision. I saw several of them. The ram would turn its gaze to the right or left, and when I turned as well to see what he was looking at, I would see another vision. Each vision would represent one of the mysteries that was to be revealed."

"So this was the first."

"Yes."

"So what did you see?"

The Journeyer

"I saw a man in a faraway land put on a hooded robe, take up a walking staff, and set out on a journey. I saw him arrive at a harbor, board a ship, and set off on a voyage across the sea. I then saw him disembark, journey inland, then return to the ship and sail off to the next land, one land after the other until finally he arrived at his destination.

"It was a forbidding land. I saw him journey through it, through barren hills, barren valleys, deserts, and ruins. He seemed astonished by everything he was seeing. He kept a pen and writing pad to jot down notes throughout the journey. Finally he sat down on a rock, took out his pen and pad, and began writing. He wrote slowly in large letters—just one word. At that moment, I was taken back to the mountaintop where I had seen the man in the red robe, Moses. He was still there and now sitting on a rock. In his hand was a parchment, on which he had also written in large letters a word. It was the same word."

"What was it?"

"*Desolation.*"

The Invisible City

"I continued walking behind the ram. It stopped again and turned now to the right. I did likewise. I saw a young man clothed in red military apparel. He appeared to me to be a soldier from the British Empire. I watched as a man in a white robe approached him and gave him an object. It was a measuring line. The soldier then appeared to be measuring structures that weren't there or that were invisible: invisible walls, buildings, and towers. When he finished, the two of them walked away. But then the man in white stopped and turned around. The soldier did likewise. Then they saw it."

"Saw what?"

"On the ground they had just left now stood a city, an ancient city with walls, buildings, and towers, all according to the dimensions the soldier had just measured out."

The Synagogue Scroll

"I turned and saw again the man with the staff and hooded robe, the journeyer. He was now walking the narrow streets of an old city. He came to an ancient-looking synagogue of hewn stone. He went inside. He sat down with the worshippers, bearded men with their heads covered in white shawls. In the front of the synagogue, standing just behind a rolled-up scroll on a stone lectern, was a man with a long white beard and a shawl over his head. But the shawl was more ornate than those of the other men. I took him to be the rabbi. 'Stand,' he said to the congregation. Everyone rose to their feet. Then he motioned to the journeyer to join him by the scroll. So he did. The rabbi then unrolled the scroll and asked the journeyer to read from it. So he did. 'You are standing today, all of you,' said the journeyer, 'before the Lord your God.' The rabbi then placed his right hand on the journeyer's head. 'And this day,' he said, 'it is fulfilled in your coming.'"

THE SHAFT

"I turned again and saw an ancient city filled with life and movement, men, women, and children walking its streets, going about their daily lives. Then suddenly everything froze and every person became as a statue. And then everything and everyone turned to stone. Then the entire city began to sink down into the sand until it disappeared. Time passed. I saw a man in a white robe with a giant pickax. He walked over to where the city had stood. He raised the ax and smashed it down on the sand. A shaft opened up in the ground. Out of the shaft came rays of light and then a rumbling. The city was rising up through the sand. I could now again see the people, still frozen in stone. But then the stone began to give way to the original colors and textures that were there at the beginning. And then everything unfroze. It was as if no time had elapsed, as if all was continuing on its course from the moment the city froze. And then the man in white spoke: 'And that which was,' he said, 'shall be again.'"

THE WOMAN IN THE VINEYARD

"In the next vision I saw a barren vineyard of withered vines. In the midst of the vineyard was a woman imprisoned in a cage of dry branches. She had the appearance of one who had been beaten, abused, and scarred. She sat downcast on the ground of her cage. A man entered the vineyard. His clothing was more modern than that of the woman, outdoor clothing, what one might wear to go hiking or gardening. He approached the cage and opened it and gently helped the woman to her feet. He gave her water to drink. Slowly he led her through the vineyard. Her steps were halting at first, as if she had been crippled. But as she walked, she began changing, the dust coming off her robe until it was pure white, and the scars disappearing from her face until she was beautiful and radiant. The two kept walking until they came to a white canopy. They stepped inside. At that the vineyard was transformed. The vines began putting forth leaves and fruit. The vineyard was alive."

THE MAN IN THE WHITE TURBAN

"In the last vision I saw a man on horseback with a long, drooping mustache in a red cloak and a white turban. He held a red flag in one hand and a curved sword in the other. Behind him was a vast army of similarly dressed soldiers. They swept through the land until arriving on a mountain. On top of the mountain was a city. The man in the white turban dismounted his horse and walked through the city gate. Inside the gate he came to a stone platform, into which he drove the pole with the red flag. The platform began turning red, and then streets around it, and then the city, and then the entire land."

––––––––––––––––––––

"That was the last of the visions within the vision."

"So you were back in the original vision, with the ram."

"I never really left it. The ram resumed its journey. Finally it arrived at a walled city of golden stone set on a mountain, similar to the city I had just seen in the last vision. The ram entered its gate. I entered behind it. As it walked through the cobblestone streets, the bag on its back began leaking. Seeds were pouring out into the cracks between the cobblestones and in the city walls and buildings. The ram then left the city through a gate on the side of the city opposite the gate through which it had entered. Not long after that I noticed the seeds coming into fruition, sprouting plants, blossoms, and flowers everywhere. And then I heard the sound of a faint rumbling, stones shifting against stones. It was subtle. Few noticed it. But a shifting had begun. And then the vision ended."

"And what did it all mean?"

"I had no idea. But I wrote everything down so I wouldn't forget. I would ask the Oracle."

Chapter 8

THE YEAR OF THE ZERAH

T HE NEXT DAY I returned to the mountaintop to find the Oracle. He was standing by a ledge, gazing out into the vast desert landscape. We sat down. I shared the vision."

"In my vision what was the meaning of the ram?" I asked.

"The Jubilee," he said. "The ram's horn is what ushers it in. As Moses sent the ram down the desert mountain, so the Jubilean mysteries begin on a desert mountain with Moses...on Mount Sinai where the law of Jubilees was given."

"So the ram represents all Jubilees?"

"No, just one Jubilee, one year of Jubilee, and the mysteries thereof."

"And the symbol on the ram's neck and on the first door?"

The Oracle took out the piece of paper I had given him with the seven symbols I had seen in my first vision, the vision of seven doors.

"This is the first symbol you wrote down. Is this what you saw on the first door and on the ram?"

"Yes," I replied.

"It's the Hebrew letter *zayin*. *Zayin* begins the word *zerah*. *Zerah* means seed. You saw the Jubilee of seeds, of origins, beginnings, the sowing of purposes. It's the key to everything else you saw, all the other mysteries of the first door."

"And what was the city?"

"Jerusalem."

"At the end of the vision the seeds came to fruition, and there was a rumbling in the city, and the stones began to shift. What did that signify?"

"It signified that what had been planted in the Jubilee of seeds would in time shake the city...and in time the entire earth."

"Did the Oracle tell you the meaning of the other things you saw, the man with the measuring line, the woman in the vineyard..."

"Not then. But he would. Each mystery would be revealed in its time."

"Starting with…"

"The first of the mysteries…the man in the hooded robe…the stranger."

Chapter 9

THE STRANGER

I RETURNED TO THE mountaintop and found the Oracle. It seemed as if he was waiting for me."

"In my vision the man with the hooded robe who journeyed the world...who was he?"

"In ancient times," he said, "the land of Israel was described as flowing with milk and honey, a fertile and fruitful land. But when the Jewish people were driven into exile, the land withered away. Its forests disappeared. Its fields of grain and fruits became desert. Its hallowed cities stood as ghosts of their former glory or else lay in ruins. The Promised Land was now a barren, lifeless, parched, desolate horror of a land. And do you know who first prophesied of the land's desolation?"

"Moses?"

"Yes, in that same farewell address. He prophesied the future of the Jewish people and also of the land...and more than that. He spoke of a specific sign that would appear in the land. He said this:

> ...the stranger that shall come from a far land, shall say, when they see the plagues of that land, and the sicknesses which the LORD has laid on it: "The whole land is brimstone, salt, and burning; it is not sown, nor does it bear, nor does any grass grow there, like the overthrow of Sodom and Gomorrah."[1]

"This," said the Oracle, "is the mystery of the stranger."

"The mystery of the stranger?"

"That one day there will come a stranger, one who will journey from a far-away land. And when he enters the land, he will bear witness of its barrenness, its devastation, and its desolation."

"Is it speaking of one specific person or all who will come?"

"Both. As with many Scriptures, it has more than one level. In a general sense it speaks of all who would come and be stunned by the land's utter desolateness. On the other hand, it speaks of *one*. The original word used in the prophecy to speak of a stranger, an alien, or a foreigner, the Hebrew word *nakri*, is singular."

"The man I saw in the vision, he was the stranger. He bore witness of the land's desolation."

"Yes. Now when would the stranger come, soon after the Jewish people were exiled from their land or at a later time?"

"A later time," I replied, "because it would take time for a land that was once fertile to turn into a total wasteland."

"Yes," said the Oracle. "And the prophecy itself specifies the time. It begins by saying that these things will take place in a generation or age that is 'akharone.' The word *akharone* can speak of a coming generation or time, but it specifically means latter or last. So it would refer to the latter days, the end times, the last days."

"So the stranger will come to the land in the end times?"

"The stranger will come before a specific end-time event takes place. And that event is foretold in the same Scripture passage:

> The LORD your God will bring you back from captivity, and
> have compassion on you, and gather you again from all the
> nations where the LORD your God has scattered you.[2]

"So the prophecy of the stranger leads into the prophecy of the regathering of the Jewish people. The stranger's coming will be the sign that the exile of the Jewish people is about to end and the scattered children of Israel are to return from the ends of the earth."

"So did the prophecy come true?"

"It did and just when the land's devastation was at its most extreme…the nineteenth century. He would come, as was prophesied, 'from a far land.'"

"From where?"

"He would come from America, from San Francisco, from the ends of the earth. It would be from there that he would begin his journey. And since the prophecy required someone to bring forth words of testimony, so he would be a man of words, a writer."

"Have I heard of him?"

"He is considered by many to be the father of American literature."

"Who was the stranger?"

"The stranger was *Mark Twain*."

"Mark Twain? The one who wrote *Tom Sawyer* and *Huckleberry Finn*? I read his books in school. He's part of the mystery?"

"He would become part. Twain was a skeptic and so the most powerful of witnesses, those who bear witness despite themselves. He was working as a journalist on the West Coast when he heard of a journey across the world on a steamship called the *Quaker City*. It would be among the first ships to undertake such a voyage. It would take months, bringing Twain to Europe, the Middle East, and finally to his ultimate destination, the land of Israel…the city of Jerusalem. And as the one appointed to bear witness, he would keep a notebook throughout the journey to record his observations."

"The pen and pad in my vision."

"Yes. According to the prophecy in Deuteronomy, he was to bear witness of '*the plagues of that land*' and all its '*sicknesses*.'[3] Now listen to the words that Mark Twain would write concerning '*the plagues of that land*':

> Rags, wretchedness, poverty and dirt….Lepers, cripples, the blind….To see the numbers of maimed, malformed and diseased humanity that throng the holy places…[4]

"According to Moses' prophecy, the stranger would describe the land as a desolation. He would say,

> The whole land is brimstone, salt…[5]

"So Twain would bear witness:

> …*all desolate* and unpeopled…[6]

> …miles of *desolate* country…[7]

> …the *far-reaching desolation*….the waste of a limitless *desolation*…[8]

"According to ancient prophecy, the stranger will say,

> All its land is…*a burning waste.*[9]

"Or in another translation,

> Your land has become a *scorching desert.*[10]

"So Twain would write:

> It is a *scorching*, arid, repulsive solitude.[11]

> Such *roasting heat,* such oppressive solitude, and such *dismal desolation* cannot surely exist elsewhere on earth.[12]

> Nowhere in all the *waste* around was there a foot of shade, and we were *scorching* to death.[13]

"The prophecy of Deuteronomy foretells that the stranger will bear witness of the land as devoid of anyone to sow it:

> All its land is…unsown.[14]

"So Twain would bear witness of the land's absence of people:

> One may ride ten miles, hereabouts, *and not see ten human beings.*[15]

> ...*these unpeopled deserts*, these rusty mounds of barrenness, that never, never, never do shake the glare from their harsh outlines...[16]

> There is *not a solitary village throughout its whole extent—* not for thirty miles in either direction.[17]

"According to Moses, the stranger will bear witness of the land's inability to produce life:

> ...*nor does it bear*...[18]

"The prophecy's use of the word *tzamach* specifically refers to sprouting. So the stranger will bear witness of the land's incapacity to sprout vegetation. So Twain would specifically bear witness of this phenomenon:

> The valleys are unsightly deserts fringed with *a feeble vegetation.*[19]

> ...a desert, paved with loose stones, *void of vegetation,* glaring in the fierce sun.[20]

> ...this blistering, *naked, treeless land.*[21]

"Even more specifically, the stranger, according to the ancient prophecy, will speak specifically of grass, or the absence of it. He will say,

> ...no grass grows in it.[22]

"Another translation renders it,

> ...not even a blade of grass.[23]

"So Twain would specifically speak of the grass, the ancient virtually word for word:

> No sprig of grass is visible."[24]

"The words of Moses are coming out of the mouth of Mark Twain...As in my vision, they each wrote down the same word."

"Yes," said the Oracle, "the words of Moses from the mouth of Mark Twain...or the words of Mark Twain from the mouth of Moses in the form of prophecy. And yet there are words in that prophecy one might never expect the stranger to utter."

"What do you mean?"

"The Scripture foretells that in that day it will be said,

> The anger of the LORD burned against that land, *to bring upon it every curse* which is written in this book.[25]

"So according to the prophecy, it will be said that a curse rests upon the land, the curse of God. One would not expect Mark Twain, a cynic, to speak of the curse of God. And yet this would be among the final words of his witness:

> Palestine sits in sackcloth and ashes. Over it broods *the spell of a curse*.[26]

"His witness of the land would be summed up with one final question:

> Palestine is desolate and unlovely. And why should it be otherwise? Can the *curse of the Deity* beautify a land?[27]

"The stranger was to bear witness to that generation. So Mark Twain would send his words back to his native land. They would appear in articles across America and beyond. He would bear witness to multitudes of his generation and thus fulfill the prophecy."

"So he accomplished what he was appointed to do."

"What he was born to do," said the Oracle. "The stranger must come before the return of the Jewish people and when the land lies in desolation and utter hopelessness."

"Why utter hopelessness?"

"It is hopelessness that sets the stage for the moving of God's hand and the impossible that sets the stage for a miracle."

"So the stranger would mark the ending of the land's devastation and lead into the beginning of its redemption and the return of its exiles. So did he?"

"He did."

"When did Mark Twain come to the Holy Land?"

"In the year 1867."

"And was that significant?"

"We shall see," said the Oracle. "But that would be another mystery."

"He would reveal it in time. But there was another mystery to be opened."

"From the vision?"

"Yes."

"Which mystery?"

"The man with the measuring line."

Chapter 10

THE MAN WITH THE MEASURING LINE

I RETURNED TO THE mountain and found the Oracle sitting on the same rock on which he sat when I first saw him. I sat down, as before, on the rock facing him."

"The man in my vision with the white robe and the measuring line…what was that about?"

"The prophet Zechariah saw something very similar:

> Then I raised my eyes and looked, and behold, a man with a measuring line in his hand. So I said, "Where are you going?" And he said to me, "To measure Jerusalem, to see what is its width and what is its length."[1]

"The man with the measuring line," said the Oracle, "was an angel."

"What does it mean?"

"The man with the measuring line appeared to Zechariah in the days when the people of Israel had returned from their exile in Babylon to the land but hadn't yet seen the fullness of God's promised restoration."

"But why a measuring line?"

"When," he asked, "does a builder use a measuring line? When he's about to build. So the man with the measuring line is a sign of God's future purposes, in this case that He was about to rebuild Jerusalem.

"In the Jubilee the original owner returns to his land. What happens when you return to a land? What has to be produced in order to take possession of it? A title, a deed, a survey. The land must be defined or re-defined, its length, its breadth, its borders, its parameters. And if there's no existing survey, then a survey must be made. The land must be defined, mapped out…measured—and so the measuring line. So in the days of Zechariah, when the Jewish people were returning to the land, the man with the measuring line comes to the city in a vision. And his appearance is a sign of what is yet to take place. It happened in the ancient world. So too it would happen again in the modern. The ancient sign would again manifest in the world…in modern times. The man with the measuring line would again come to Jerusalem. And his appearance would be a sign of what was yet to come.

"The man you saw in your vision dressed in a red military uniform. His name was Charles Warren. He was a British officer, a member of the Royal Engineers. He was sent to the land of Israel on a mission to survey and map out Jerusalem, to measure the Holy City—as a man with the measuring line.

"But his mission was not just to survey Jerusalem as it was then but as it once was: to measure its ancient parameters, the boundaries of ancient Jerusalem, the biblical city, to locate its ancient walls and borders, to uncover its foundations. In order to do that, he had to dig through centuries of ruins and earth to get to the city's biblical foundations. But the British weren't in control of the land; the Ottoman Turks were. And they were suspicious of his activities. He was always being watched. So he had to tread lightly and often work in secret.

"Warren's work would constitute the first extensive excavation of biblical Jerusalem, the first extensive measuring of the biblical foundations of the Temple Mount and of the city itself. It would usher in a new age of biblical archaeology. Remember what I told you about the Jubilee—the focus returns to what was lost and must be restored, the ancestral possession. Jerusalem is the ancestral possession of the Jewish people. So the focus must return to the ancient city. And so its dimensions, its borders, and its parameters must be measured out."

"But it was only Jerusalem," I said. "The ancestral possession is the entire Promised Land, the land of Israel."

"Yes. And even in that the man with the measuring line would play a pivotal role. His measuring of Jerusalem would usher in the surveying of the entire land, the measuring of the Promised Land in its entirety.

"In the Jubilee the connection between the land and its original owner is restored. And so the consequences of Warren's work were to restore and strengthen the long-lost connection of the Jewish people to the land. And with every restored connection, the idea that the Jewish people, after almost two thousand years, might somehow return to their homeland began to move one more step out of the realm of fantasy."

"And so if the man with the measuring line in ancient times was a sign that God was going to restore them, what about in modern times? What about Charles Warren?" I asked. "Was he also a sign?"

"He was," said the Oracle. "After nearly two thousand years of exile, the man with the measuring line reappeared in Jerusalem as a sign that God was about to bring about a restoration. A measuring line is used when one is about to build something. So then the reappearance of the man with the measuring line in the person of Charles Warren was a sign that God was about to act, to move again, to build something...to rebuild that which once was and had fallen...the nation of Israel. And when else do you use a measuring line?"

"When there's about to be a transference of land."

"So when the man with the measuring line appeared in Jerusalem, it was a sign that the land was going to be transferred...back to the original owner. The land was being prepared for the return. So it was in ancient times when the prophet Zechariah revealed the meaning of the measuring line:

> A measuring line will be stretched over Jerusalem...and the LORD will again comfort Zion and again choose Jerusalem."[2]

"When did Warren come to measure Jerusalem?" I asked.

"In the year 1867."

"1867? The same year that Mark Twain came to bear witness."

"Yes," said the Oracle. "Both were signs of a coming restoration. So the stranger and the man with the measuring line were joined together. In fact the two would dwell inside the walls of the ancient city at the same time...the same month, the same week, the same days. In fact they would dwell together in the same lodging place, the very same building."

"Did they realize it?"

"No, they had no idea...no more than they had any idea of the part they were playing in the mystery."

"The next vision would open up a realm in which ancient words converge with the events of the modern world."

"And how was it revealed to you?"

"Through an ancient scroll."

Chapter 11

NITZAVIM

I RETURNED TO THE mountaintop and found the Oracle sitting on one of the ledges overlooking the desert landscape. I sat down beside him."

"In my vision the journeyer, or stranger, entered a synagogue and read from a scroll. What did it mean?"

"Your vision," he said, "concerns another realm."

"A realm of what?"

"A realm in which all events that take place in time and space are woven together apart from time and space, woven by the hand of God."

At that he reached into his pocket and pulled out a parchment.

"Every Sabbath day, from ancient times, the Jewish people gather in their synagogues, open up the scrolls, and read the ancient Scriptures. Thus on every Sabbath day there is a specific portion of Scripture appointed to be read. The portion is called the *parasha*."

"When were they appointed?"

"In ages past," he said, "and for every week and every Sabbath day of history into modern times. Could it be possible that some of these appointed words were appointed not only to be spoken *on* those days but *of* and *to* those days…to speak of events that would take place in modern times?"

I didn't answer. The Oracle spent a few moments looking over the parchment as if studying its words.

"What you saw in your vision represented the end of the stranger's journey. The city on the mountain was Jerusalem. Jerusalem was the ultimate goal, not only of Twain's pilgrimage in the land but of his entire journey. The journey had begun in June 1867. In the summer months he would travel the cities of Europe. He would reach the Holy Land in mid-September. He would enter the gates of Jerusalem on September 23. On September 27, after an excursion in the desert, he would return to the Holy City for the culmination of his pilgrimage.

"September 28 would constitute his last full day and night in Jerusalem. The following day he would leave the city and head back to the shore to board his ship and begin the journey home to America, stopping several times along the way. September 28 fell on a Saturday. Saturday is the Sabbath. And so on the stranger's last full day in Jerusalem and the last Sabbath of the stranger's journey in the land there was an appointed Scripture…"

"What was it?"

"The appointed Scripture was this:

> …the stranger that shall come from a far land, shall say, when they see the plagues of that land, and the sicknesses which the Lord has laid on it: 'The whole land is brimstone, salt, and burning; it is not sown, nor does it bear, nor does any grass grow there…'"[1]

"The prophecy of the stranger!" I said. "The very prophecy! The word appointed for the end of the stranger's journey in the land…was the very prophecy that speaks of the stranger's journey in the land! The prophecy from ancient times appointed to be spoken at the very moment of its fulfillment!"

"It was on that day that the stranger had accomplished what the prophecy had foretold…on the day the prophecy was read."

"Amazing!"

"Just as amazing," said the Oracle, "is what happened throughout the earth."

"What do you mean?"

"The prophecy was appointed to be read in every synagogue in the world. So all across the earth, in every synagogue from San Francisco to Siberia, they were reciting and chanting the prophecy of the stranger, who would come from far away to the land of Israel to bear witness of the desolation. And so the prophecy of the stranger was being proclaimed throughout the earth at the very moment the stranger was in the land fulfilling its words."

"And they had no idea."

"Nor did the stranger."

"In the vision the stranger told the men in the synagogue that they were standing before the Lord. Why?"

"In Hebrew the word *standing* would be *nitzavim*. *Nitzavim* is the name of the appointed word in the scrolls that prophesies of the stranger coming to the land. It begins with those same words as Moses tells the children of Israel they are standing before the Lord."

"So all this was taking place, and nobody knew it."

"Ponder this," said the Oracle. "On that Sabbath day, Mark Twain walked through the ancient city. And within the city was a remnant of Jewish people. They would have been observing the Sabbath, reciting the appointed Scripture of the stranger's visit, proclaiming it, chanting it…as the stranger walked in their midst."

"So it's possible that Twain actually heard the words of the prophecy that day."

"It is completely possible. He would have known that they were reading from the ancient Scriptures, but he would have had no idea that it was about him. The mystery manifests regardless of anyone realizing it."

"But everything is like that," I said, "and part of it. Twain just happened to have heard of that particular voyage. Had he not, it never would have happened as it did. Or if he hadn't become a journalist in the first place... And he didn't plan the timing of the voyage. Someone else did. So if they didn't happen to plan it to begin on that date and the rest of the voyage on the other dates, it never would have coincided with the appointed day of the reading of the prophecy of the stranger."

"Yes," said the Oracle, "it was all woven together, every part, every detail, everything falling into its exact place for the mystery to be fulfilled... the convergence of time and space with the eternal. And this is just the beginning, the time of sowing.

"And as the mystery continues to manifest, the dynamic will increase so that it will determine not only the course of such people as the stranger but the course of world wars and the rise and fall of empires and superpowers."

"So Mark Twain, the skeptic, would never know how he was drawn into the mystery and fulfilled the words of the prophecy."

"No, but he was always part of the mystery."

"What do you mean?"

"Since ancient times the scattered children of Israel would pray to God to have mercy on Jerusalem, to restore the city and bring them home:

> Have mercy, Lord, our God... on Jerusalem, Your city; and
> on Zion, the resting place of Your glory... Rebuild Jerusalem,
> the city of holiness, speedily in our days. Bring us up into it
> and gladden us in its rebuilding and let us eat from its fruit
> and be satisfied with its goodness and bless You upon it in
> holiness and purity.[2]

"They prayed that prayer, seeking God's mercy, virtually every day of their exile for two thousand years. And for two thousand years it seemed to them as if God wasn't hearing their prayers. But the stranger would be the sign that their exile was about to end. God had heard their prayers."

"But how was he *always* part of the mystery?"

"The stranger's real name was not Mark Twain. At his birth he was given the name *Samuel*. *Samuel* is a Hebrew name. So he was given a name that came from the land of Israel, the land he would one day visit. And in Hebrew his name contained a message."

"What?"

"*God has heard.*"

"*Samuel* means God has heard?"

"Yes. For God had heard the prayers of His people. He would fulfill His purposes for Jerusalem and the Promised Land. And what were the prayers that His ancient people prayed, that He heard and would soon answer? They were that He would restore the land and that He would bring them back, that He would have mercy, that He would be merciful to them. The stranger's real last name was not Twain; it was Clemens. *Clemens* also holds a mystery and a message. Do you know what *Clemens* means?"

"No, what does *Clemens* mean?"

"Merciful...the quality of showing mercy. The stranger was a sign. Samuel—God had heard their prayers; Clemens—and was about to show them mercy."

"So Mark Twain never realized the part he played in the mystery."

"He never did."

"And the man with the measuring line?"

"Warren came to the land of Israel believing the Bible. But he had no idea what was waiting to be revealed—and waiting from ancient times."

Chapter 12

THE LOST CITY

I RETURNED TO THE Oracle to inquire into the meaning of the next vision."

"I saw a city become stone and sink into the ground. Then it rose up from the earth and became alive again. What was I seeing?"

"In the Jubilee," he said, "the connection between the land and its owner is restored. Up until then the original owner has no right concerning the land. He can't even walk on it without the permission of the one now occupying it. But when the Jubilee comes, the owner can again walk on his land, farm it, build on it, and dwell on it. The barriers are removed. The owner's connection to the land and the land's connection to its owner are reaffirmed and restored.

"When the Jewish people lost their homeland and their Holy City in the first century, the Romans tried to erase every connection between the land of Israel and the people of Israel. They remade Jerusalem into a pagan city and called it Aelia Capitolina. And to further eradicate the connection of the Jewish people to their homeland, they renamed the land of Israel Palaestina, meaning the land of the Philistines."

"Who were the Philistines?"

"Israel's ancient enemies," he said. "The erasing was so successful that for most of two thousand years the land of Israel would simply be known as Palestine. The Jews were even banned from setting foot in their Holy City. So the owner was cut off from his land. And the other powers who would follow the Romans in occupying the land and the city would do similarly, obscuring the connection of the land to its people.

"But when the Jubilee comes, the connection between the owner and the land is restored, and that which was lost is regained. I told you of Charles Warren, the man with the measuring line. But remember, he didn't only measure Jerusalem. In order to map out ancient Jerusalem, he had to dig it up. So he came with more than surveying equipment; he came with shovels and pickaxes."

"The pickax in my vision."

"He uncovered the walls of the ancient city, ancient gates, and chambers. He uncovered what was hidden under the Temple Mount. But it was something else...something he didn't plan on, something he would stumble upon...that would end up being his most dramatic discovery.

"It happened while he was crawling through one of Jerusalem's rock chambers with his assistant. He stumbled upon a shaft."

"The shaft in my vision."

"The shaft would lead to the discovery of an ancient city, a city hidden in the dust for two thousand years."

"The city in the vision that rose up from the earth. What city was it?"

"Jerusalem," said the Oracle.

"But I thought Jerusalem was already there."

"It was, and it wasn't. For ages everyone thought that the biblical city of Jerusalem was inside the walls we see today."

"It's not?"

"Some of it was. But the original city of Jerusalem, the biblical core, was not even inside the gates we know today but outside them."

"Where?"

"Where Warren found it. He literally uncovered the core and biblical city of Jerusalem that had lain hidden for nearly two thousand years, the city of David and Solomon, Isaiah, and Jeremiah."

"And nobody knew about it for two thousand years?"

"In the mystery of the Jubilee what has to take place?"

"That which is lost," I said, "must be found. So the Jerusalem that was lost was found again."

"Yes, and what else must happen in the Jubilee?"

"The land must be restored to its original owner."

"So this was the beginning of the restoration of Jerusalem to the Jewish people. And according to the mystery of the Jubilee, the original connection between the owner and the land, biblical Jerusalem and the Jewish people, was renewed. The shaft that Warren discovered linked up with Jerusalem's ancient water system."

"Why is that significant?"

"It was through Jerusalem's ancient water system that King David's soldiers first entered Jerusalem and thus by which the nation first came into possession of the city. Warren's discovery thus renewed that ancient connection."

"When did it happen?" I asked. "When was ancient Jerusalem discovered?"

"The shaft was uncovered in 1867."

"1867," I replied, "the same year as the visit of the stranger, the same year as the measuring out of Jerusalem...So Jerusalem is hidden in the earth for two thousand years, and of all the years to begin emerging...it happens in 1867...the same year everything else happens!"

"Remember the prophecy," said the Oracle. "The stranger comes to the land, and then what happens?"

"The return," I replied, "the regathering."

"Yes, so this was all part of the return. The land was being readied. And the discovery was in the autumn of 1867."

"Why is that significant?"

"Because it was in the autumn of 1867 that the stranger came to the land...and to the city...and dwelt in the same dwelling place as Warren. In fact after two thousand years of lying in the dust, ancient Jerusalem was discovered less than thirty days after the coming of the stranger...It would ultimately be a sign...and a foreshadowing."

"Of what?"

"That Jerusalem would be restored...that Jerusalem would again become a living city filled with the children of Israel."

"But if the land was under the rule of others, how would that happen?"

"The ancient prophecy foretold it," said the Oracle. "So it had to come about one way or another."

"Through what?"

"Through the next mystery, a mystery that would ultimately change the course of world history."

"And what would you be shown?"

"The meaning of the woman in the vineyard."

"So the next mystery began in a cage."

"No. The next mystery began with a star."

Chapter 13

THE SULTAN'S CODE

WHEN I RETURNED to the mountaintop, I couldn't find the Oracle. He was sitting on another side of the summit, overlooking the desert. Finally I found him and joined him there."

―――――――

"Who was the woman I saw in the vineyard?" I asked.

"According to the law of Jubilees," he said, "the people must return to the land, and the land also return to the people:

> In the Year of the Jubilee *the field shall return* . . . to him to whom the possession of the land did belong.[1]

"The land has to be returned to the one to whom it belongs. So the one who occupies it must relinquish his control so that the return can take place. Therefore, the Jubilee is the time of the relinquishing and releasing of the land."

"But how would that happen?" I asked. "The only ones who would relinquish land would be those following the ordinances of the Jubilee. But that doesn't work for world history. Nations don't give up their land because of ancient ordinances."

"Exactly," he replied. "So how could it happen? The land of Israel had been taken over by enemies of the Jewish people, one kingdom after the next, until it lay in the hands of the Ottoman Empire, an Islamic power that was not about to relinquish anything to the Jewish people. And they certainly weren't observing the law of Jubilees. But the mystery applies to the entire world, to believer and unbeliever alike. The mystery causes all things, all events, even the rise and fall of kingdoms, to move in the course that will fulfill the appointed purposes. According to the ancient ordinance, the land must be released to its original owner. So the mystery must manifest one way or another."

"So how did it happen?"

"Through the star of Bethlehem," he said. "It all began in the Church of the Nativity in Bethlehem with a conflict between the Greek Orthodox and Latin clergies that oversaw the sanctuary. It involved a metal star that had mysteriously disappeared. The Russian government sided with the

Orthodox clergy, while the Ottoman Empire, along with France, Britain, and Sardinia, sided with the Latin clergy. The conflict would lead to the Crimean War. The war would prove a turning point for the Ottoman Empire. In the course of the conflict, the empire would enter into massive loans with its European creditors, the first of several that would lead to financial disaster, bankruptcy. Two years after the end of the Crimean War, the sultan enacted the Ottoman Land Code. All land now had to be registered."

"Why?"

"So it could be taxed," he replied. "So he could raise money. It would open the door for the large-scale buying and selling of Ottoman land...including the Holy Land. But according to Ottoman law, no land could be sold to foreigners, those outside the empire."

"But then how could it have any effect on the mystery?" I asked. "If the Jewish people were scattered throughout the world, they would be considered foreigners and wouldn't be allowed to purchase land."

"But the mystery," said the Oracle, "ordains that the land must be transferred back to its original owner. So it must come about one way or another. The registration of the land didn't solve the empire's financial problems. And the situation was critical enough to cause the government to do something unprecedented. Nine years after the first land code, the empire enacted a new law, a new Ottoman Land Code—the land could now be purchased by foreigners."

"Then the land could now be purchased by the children of Israel, by the Jewish people."

"Exactly," said the Oracle. "As in the Jubilee, those who occupy the land must release it...they must relinquish it. The land must return to its original owner. And so it would all happen as it was prophesied. The effect of the law would be almost unnoticeable at first. But in time it would change the history of the Middle East and the modern world. Jewish people would begin purchasing their ancient land, at times through third parties and unknown to the Ottoman authorities. When the authorities realized what was happening, they tried to stop it. They placed a ban on Jews buying land in Palestine. But the prophecy could not be stopped. The release of the land would continue nonetheless and would prepare the way for the return of the exiles."

"And it only happened because of the Ottoman Land Code. And the Ottoman Land Code only happened because of the Ottoman debt. And the Ottoman debt only happened because of the European loans. And the European loans only happened because of the Crimean War. And the Crimean War only happened because of the missing star!"

"Yes," said the Oracle, "all events are part of the mystery. The mystery doesn't cause the events but causes all things to work together for the appointed purposes."

"What about my vision? What did the man and the woman in the vineyard have to do with what you just told me? I don't see it."

"Because you're only seeing it as a man and a woman. But what you saw was more than that. They were symbols. The man stood for the people of Israel; the woman, the land of Israel."

"The woman was chained and in a cage..."

"As the land of Israel was for ages held captive by its invaders. And as the woman was cast down, wounded, and crippled, so was the land abused by those who occupied it, crippled, parched, and withered...a land of sorrow and despair. And as the man came to the woman, so the people of Israel began coming to the land. But they found it parched and barren. As the man tried to revive the woman, so they tried to revive the land. But it would be slow at first to respond. He gave her water. So they brought water to the land. Step by step and slowly it began to bear. The deserts would blossom. The long-withered land would again become beautiful."

"What about the canopy?"

"The huppah," he said. "It's the Hebrew wedding canopy under which the bride and groom are married. So it was written,

> No more shall your land be called Desolate....Your land
> shall be called Married.[2]

"Before Israel's first exile in Babylon, God gave a word to the prophet Jeremiah foretelling the return of the exiles to the land. It would foretell as well what would take place in the return of modern times:

> 'Men will buy fields for money, sign deeds and seal them...in
> the cities of Judah...I will cause their captives to return,' says
> the LORD."[3]

"Was the timing of the land's release significant?"

"I would think so," he replied.

"When did the release begin?"

"In 1867."

"1867! Of all the years in history...the land is released in the same year! The year of the stranger's visit...the man with the measuring line...the unearthing of biblical Jerusalem! Everything happened in that same year?"

"Remember," said the Oracle, "when is it that you measure out a land?"

"When you want to build on it...or when the land is to be transferred."

"So the land must be transferred. And what must happen after the stranger's journey?"

"The Jewish people must come back from their exile to the land."

"So then the land must be made ready for their return. So in accordance with ancient ordinance, the Ottoman Empire begins to release the land; the one occupying the land must release it. The stranger's journey began on June 8, 1867. Do you know when the release began? On June 10, 1867. So of all the years and days of human history, the relinquishing of the land begins two days after the stranger's journey begins."

"Did the Oracle ever tell you if there was a reason why everything was happening in the same year, in 1867?"

"He did. And the key was already there in the visions."

"Which one?"

"The man in the white turban."

Chapter 14

THE SEVENTH JUBILEE

I RETURNED TO THE Oracle the next morning. It was a windy morning, as was the night before. And on the mountaintop the gusts were even stronger. The Oracle's robe fluttered against the rock on which he sat."

"The man in the white turban with the sword and the red flag…what did he represent?"

"You wanted to know why everything happened to happen at the same time."

"Yes, and why at *that particular* same time," I replied.

"The timing is determined by the mystery."

"What does that mean?"

"In the Jubilee the land must be released at the set time. And who is it that must relinquish it?"

"The one who *isn't* the original owner but who occupies it."

"And what if the land has changed hands more than once after the original owner has lost it? Who must then relinquish it at the set time?"

"The last one who occupies it."

"That's correct," he replied. "The Jubilee undoes the last transaction, but in doing so, it undoes all of them. By restoring the land to its original owner, the Jubilee undoes all the transactions of all those who have occupied it. So who was it that occupied the Holy Land at the time when all these things took place, the stranger's return, the man with the measuring line, the lost city?"

"The Ottoman Empire."

"And it would be in the days of that empire that the return of the land to its original owners would begin. They would be the last occupiers of the land before the return. So the Jubilee would undo the last transference of the land, its transference to the Ottoman Empire. How did the Ottomans come into possession of the land in the first place?"

"I have no idea."

"In AD 70 the armies of Rome destroyed Jerusalem, drove the Jewish people into the nations, and occupied the land. Then, when the empire divided in two, the Byzantines occupied the land. Then, in the seventh century, the armies of the Muslim caliph Umar occupied the land. From then on the land, with the brief exception of the Crusader kingdom, would be occupied by various Muslim rulers and warring factions...up until the occupation of the Ottomans."

"So what did I see in my vision?"

"The last acquisition," said the Oracle, "the last taking of the land by the last occupiers before the time of the restoration."

"And who was the man in the red cloak?"

"That would be Selim."

"Selim?"

"Selim I, Selim the Grim, an Ottoman prince who defeated his father and brothers to ascend the throne as sultan. Soon after his accession he challenged the Persian shah Ismail in battle and defeated him. Next he turned his armies against the Mamluk Sultanate, an Islamic empire centered in Cairo, Egypt, and, at the Battle of Raydaniyah, defeated it. Selim now became the master of all the lands that had been ruled by the Mamluks. One of those lands was Israel, and one of those cities was Jerusalem."

"So the Mamluks were the last occupiers before the Ottomans."

"Yes."

"So what I saw in my vision..."

"Was the Ottoman conquest of the land under Selim I," said the Oracle, "the last transference."

"So when did the Ottomans come into possession of the land?"

"Not long after the days of Columbus. They would occupy it through the Reformation, the American Revolution, the Industrial Revolution, and into the twentieth century."

At that he paused and looked into the distance before speaking again, before asking me a question.

"So according to the ordinance, when does the Jubilee take place?"

"In the fiftieth year," I replied. "But there would have been several Jubilees from that time to modern times."

He gave no response...but remained silent as if waiting for my next question.

"The Battle of Raydaniyah...what year was it?" I asked.

"1517," said the Oracle.

"The mystery!" I exclaimed.

"What is the mystery?" he asked.

"1517...the last transference of the land. If the Jubilee is every fifty years, then it will lead you to a specific year."

"And what year is that?"

"1867! The year everything happened!"

He let me ponder that for a few moments before speaking again.

"There is a number given in the Scriptures," he said, "to signify completion, ending, the ending of an interval of time, a period, an age—the number
seven. The last transference of the land began in 1517. Then, in 1867, the final
transference, the releasing of the land back to the children of Israel, was set
in motion. So how many years was it from the beginning of the Ottoman
conquest, from the last transference of the land, until the year 1867?"

"Three hundred fifty years."

"So what was the year 1867?"

"The seventh Jubilee."

"The seventh Jubilee," he repeated, "the year of completion, the year of
the beginning of the end. And that's why after two thousand years everything began in that particular year. That's why the stranger had to undertake his journey in that particular year. That's why the land had to be
measured out in that particular year. That's why the ancient city lying in
the dust for two thousand years had to be found in that particular year.
And that's why the land had to be released at that exact time. It all had to
happen in 1867 because 1867 was the year of Jubilee, the year of measuring,
of transferring, of uncovering, and of relinquishing and release. It all happened in the year of the Jubilee, and in the seventh Jubilee, the Jubilee of
ending."

"And nobody planned it. No one was aware of the timing."

"Again," said the Oracle, "the mystery is beyond anyone's planning. Mark
Twain had no idea that his dark witness of the Holy Land would be the
fulfillment of ancient prophecy. The Ottoman sultan had no idea that his
attempt to relieve his debt would be critical in bringing about the return
of the Jewish people to the land. None of them, not even Charles Warren,
who would later catch a glimpse of the larger picture, could fathom the
ancient mystery that would cause their lives and actions to be joined to the
ancient purposes appointed for that exact moment in time. And it wasn't
just them. It was the course of kingdoms and the repercussions of empires.
That too was required for these things to take place as and when they did.
It was the entire world that was required…and that would be required."

"Would be…as in what was still to come?"

"Yes. The seventh Jubilee would mark the end of one era and the beginning of another, the first Jubilee of restoration, the Jubilee of seeds, of
sowing, of planting, and of the setting in motion of ancient purposes. The
seeds of the seventh Jubilee would begin germinating and would come to
their fruition in their appointed times. Some would be revealed sooner,
and some later. But in time the entire world would see it."

Chapter 15

FRUITION

T HAT WOULD BE the last of the mysteries of the first door, the last of
the first stream of visions. It was then that the Oracle began speaking
as if to seal up what had been revealed up to that point and to tell me
more…what would happen next."

"The Jubilee," said the Oracle, "represents the setting in motion of God's
purposes. It sets the stage. It inaugurates the course. It sets in motion the
train of events that must take place in the coming period."

"The coming period…"

"The time until the next Jubilee."

"So then what took place in the Jubilee of 1867 would set in motion a
train of events."

"A train of prophetic purposes that, with the passage of time, would
become increasingly manifest…the fruition of the seeds."

"How so?"

"Let's start with the stranger. The ancient prophecy foretold the very
words he would speak. He had to bear witness. So Mark Twain's destiny
was to bear witness through his words. And so he did. And the words
of his witness had to go forth to the world. And so they did. While still
journeying, he would send his reports of the land back home, where they
would appear in newspapers throughout America. But the witness of the
stranger would go beyond that. Shortly after he returned from his journey,
he was approached by a publisher to convert the reports of his journey into
a book. The book would be released in 1869. It would be called *The Innocents Abroad*. The book was the fulfillment of the ancient prophecy."

"How was it received?"

"It would become a best seller. And because of it, the witness of the
stranger would go forth not only to the nation and to the world and to
his generation but to the generations that would follow. It would continue
to bear witness long after his death. And of all the books he would go on
to write, it was *The Innocents Abroad* that would, in his lifetime, outsell
the rest. It was this book that would establish him as an author and cata-
pult him to international fame. So his career as an author would begin

and always be interwoven with an ancient mystery, the fulfillment of a prophecy given by Moses."

"You said that he is considered the father of American literature. So then could it be said that American literature came into existence because of the fulfillment of an ancient prophecy?"

"It could be said."

"What about the man with the measuring line, Charles Warren?"

"His life would also follow the course set forth by the ancient mystery. He would be called the pioneer of Jerusalem archaeology. He would lay the foundation for the uncovering of ancient Jerusalem. And with each uncovering, the connection between the Jewish people and the land would be revived, restored, and renewed.

"His measuring and mapping out of Jerusalem would prove so successful that it would open the door for a greater mission. The next decade would thus see the mapping out of the entire land. The survey would cover the area from Dan to Beersheba, the same borders given in the Bible to identify the land of Israel. And as they measured and mapped out the land, they discovered long-lost places, sites, and cities of Bible times. And with every discovery the connection between the Jewish people and the land was further restored and strengthened. All this would in turn be part of the building of momentum for a greater restoration that would take place in the following century.

"When you told me your vision of the angel with the measuring line, I told you that the prophet Zechariah saw the same thing and that in his vision the angel wasn't there just to measure Jerusalem but to give a prophetic word. The word would concern the restoration of Jerusalem, a call to the exiles of Israel to return to the land and to the blessings that would await them there. So the man with the measuring line is the one who issues a prophetic call."

"But Charles Warren was an engineer, not a prophet."

"But he was also the man with the measuring line, and the man with the measuring line is the one who issues a prophetic call."

"So did it happen?"

"After measuring Jerusalem and uncovering its ancient pathways, Warren returned to England. There he would be led to write down a vision concerning the land and its future. It was not only a vision but a specific plan on how the vision could come to fruition. It was called *Land of Promise*. Keep in mind the state of the land when Warren penned his words. It was the time of the stranger and the barren, grassless desolation. That makes what he wrote all the more prophetic and stunning."

"What did he write?"

"He wrote that the debt incurred by the Ottoman Empire could be used to bring about the return of the Jewish people to the land. He envisioned the Jewish people again learning how to farm the land. He believed the land could be watered and that the planting of trees would change the land's ecosystem. The deserts, he wrote, could be made to blossom.

"In his vision Warren foresaw the return of the Jewish people from exile and that their return would lead to the birth of a nation. He envisioned the nation of Israel resurrected from the dead, a Jewish state. He saw the great powers of Europe involved in its resurrection. He even believed that America would be the best guarantor of the Jewish nation's rebirth—though he couldn't see how that would come about.

"Where Twain could barely see how the land could support the most meager of populations, Warren wrote of a future where the land could accommodate millions of Jewish people. And yet even with such numbers, he believed that the new Jewish nation could attain a standard of living equal to that of the most advanced nations.[1] With the return of the Jewish people and the blessings of God, the land known to the world as Palestine could again become the 'land flowing with milk and honey'[2] as in the days of the Bible. Warren's vision was amazingly prophetic and, in the year and decades that followed, would come to pass."

"Did he know the biblical prophecies of Israel's rebirth?"

"He did," said the Oracle. "It was those prophecies that gave him the confidence to envision what seemed otherwise unimaginable. And by so doing, he would pen what is considered the first detailed vision and plan for the establishment of a Jewish state in the land of Israel. And it would be written over twenty years before a similar vision and plan would be penned by a Jewish hand."

"You said that the Jubilee sets in motion the purposes of God. Did anything happen concerning the Jewish people in the years after 1867?"

"Yes," he replied, "the Ottoman Land Code of 1867 would set in motion a series of events that would lead to Israel's restoration. By the early twentieth century large tracts of the land had been purchased for the return of the Jewish people, the fruition of what was sown in 1867."

"When were the changes first evident?" I asked.

"Soon after that year," he answered. "When Twain and Warren came to Jerusalem in 1867, the Jewish people constituted a minority in that city. But within just a few years they had become the majority. Then just three years after Twain's visit and one year after the publishing of his book came the founding of Mikveh Yisrael. Mikveh Yisrael was the first school established to teach Jewish people how to farm the land. It was the first time in nearly two thousand years that Jewish people were being taught how to sow and reap the Promised Land, the first sign of a redemption that would transform the country.

"That same decade would see the founding of the first Jewish agricultural settlements in the land since ancient times. And just after that a massive persecution of the Jewish people in the Russian Empire would begin and bring about the fulfillment of the ancient prophecies. It would cause many Jewish families and individuals to seek refuge in other lands and would begin the first massive waves of returning exiles that would continue into the twentieth century."

"And nobody involved in the land's restoration could have planned for it or known that it was coming."

"The prophecies are beyond any plan or effort of man," said the Oracle. "All history moves to bring them to fruition, every event, every life, and every path, all woven together. So it was for the stranger."

"More than what you've already told me?"

"In the latter part of his life his path would be woven together with that of a European journalist and playwright. It was unlikely that two people so diverse and from such diverse backgrounds would become friends, but they did. And as there was a mystery to Mark Twain's life, so there was a mystery to the life of his European friend, who likewise would play a part in an ancient prophecy. He would undergo a transformation that would alter the course of his life and lead him on a mission that would alter the course of the modern world."

"Who was he?"

"His name was Theodor Herzl. He would become the founder of political Zionism."

"Zionism…"

"From the word *Zion*, the ancient name for Jerusalem and its land. Zionism was the movement for the return of the Jewish people to the land and restoration of the nation. Herzl would be called the father of the Jewish state. So of all the people on earth, the paths of the two people so joined to the mystery would intersect. Remember what was written in the Book of Deuteronomy, the prophecy of the stranger leads into the prophecy of the nation's regathering. Twain would be linked to the first prophecy, and Herzl to the second. So as the two prophecies were joined together, so also were the two lives."

"When did Herzl's transformation take place?"

"Herzl himself would identify the time and place. It happened in the city of Paris in 1894. It was then and there that his transformation into the visionary and 'father of the Jewish state' began. It was a significant convergence of time and space."

"A convergence?"

"Because the paths of Twain and Herzl converged in that same city and that same year. The two were brought together in the very place and at the very moment that Zionism was born."

"I wonder what Twain would think if he could come back and see what happened to the land he called desolate. I don't think he would use that word anymore."

"There is a prophecy," said the Oracle, "that foretells the restoration of Zion and says that very thing, that no more will the land be called desolate. I told you of the Scripture appointed to be read on the very day the stranger completed his journey in the land, the prophecy of the stranger journeying to the land. There was another prophecy also appointed to be read on that same day and that would have been chanted in Jerusalem on the day that Twain walked through the city."

"What was it?"

"It was that same prophecy, a prophecy of Israel's restoration. It said this:

> It will no longer be said to you, 'Forsaken,' *nor to your land will it any longer be said, 'Desolate'*; but you will be called, 'My delight is in her.'"[3]

The Oracle got up from the rock and approached me.

"The first stream of mysteries is now completed. The next one lies beyond the second door."

"And you're sure I'll find them?"

"I don't believe you came this far not to. But you will also find me in another place."

"Another place?"

"There's more than one place. And in this way it will help you to remember."

"And what will I find behind the second door?"

"The shaking of nations," he said, "the wings of God...a land of wells...a mystery coin...the fall of a kingdom...a day of lights...a book of hidden prophecies...and more."

"And all these are part of the same mystery that I've been shown so far?"

"Yes, they are its next manifestation. What you've seen thus far will now increase until it touches the entire earth...until it shakes the world."

THE SECOND DOOR

Chapter 16

THE SECOND DOOR

THE SUN WAS setting. I was sitting on a rock at the base of the mountain by which my tent was pitched. And the vision began.

"I was back in the Hall of the Seven Doors. In front of me was the second door. At my side was the Oracle. He handed me the second key. I put it inside the lock, the door opened, and I stepped inside. I was now standing on the pinnacle of the same mountain where I had seen the first ram. And there was Moses in his red robe. By his side was a ram, different from the first. Its body was covered with armor, its neck, its hooves, the top of its head, its horns, everything except for its face. Around its neck was a chain, from which hung a metal pendant, on which was a symbol, the same as on the second door.

"It made its way down the mountain and into the wilderness. I followed behind. As it journeyed, the sky darkened and was soon filled with black clouds and then smoke. I heard what at first I took to be thunder but then realized was the sound of war. The ram was now passing by trenches, mounds of earth, and ruins. Then it stopped and turned its gaze to the right. I turned as well…and saw the first of the visions within the vision."

THE RIDERS

"I saw what appeared to be a British officer from the First World War on horseback, riding through a series of varied landscapes. In his upraised right hand was a rolled-up document. But it wasn't just the landscapes that were changing; it was the rider. He was now wearing a red cylindrical hat, dressed as a Turkish soldier. After that he took on the appearance of other soldiers of other armies and ages, each with varied garments, armor, and weapons. Finally he took on the appearance of a Roman soldier. He arrived at his destination, dismounted his horse, then read the document out loud as if issuing a proclamation. Planted in the ground beside him was a pole crowned with a golden eagle. He pulled it out of the ground…at which moment, he vanished."

The Old Man and the Boy

"The ram resumed the journey, then stopped and turned again. I did likewise. I saw an old man with a white beard and arrayed in colorful ancient garments. Next to him was a little boy in a dark brown coat, a black cap, and shiny black shoes. The two of them were sitting in the middle of a raging battlefield. The old man was holding a little scroll and reading words to the boy. After he finished reading it, he turned to the boy and said, 'It is now time for you to go home.' At that they rose to their feet and began walking hand in hand through the battlefield and then away from it, where they disappeared over the horizon."

The Girl by the Well

"I turned again and saw a row of ancient-looking wells in the middle of a barren desert. Sitting by one of the wells was a little girl, weeping. 'They've sealed up our father's wells,' she said, 'so that none of us can draw from them.' It was then that I saw that each well had been filled to its brim with sand. But then suddenly there came the sound of gushing waters. Then all at once the wells exploded with fountains, or rivers, of water shooting up at the same time. The waters then coalesced into a rushing river flowing away into the distance. 'This is how it begins,' said the little girl. 'The rest will follow.'"

The Fliers

"I turned again and saw a flock of colossal birds flying in the sky above an army as it marched into war. As the birds approached the battlefield, a transformation began. Their bodies began turning to metal, their tail feathers to rudders, their claws to wheels, and their wings to the wings of early twentieth-century airplanes, which is what they, in essence, became. Each aircraft still bore the head of a giant bird but now of solid metal. They flew into battle, engaging the enemy in warfare. I heard a voice. 'So by this,' it said, 'shall the deliverance come.'"

The Angel's Coin

"I was standing on the bank of a river. To my left was a man in a radiant white robe, an angel. He opened his right hand to reveal a coin. 'What do you see engraved on it?' he asked. 'A number,' I answered. 'What number?' '1,335. What does it mean?' I asked. 'It's the number of the end,' he said. 'By this, that which obstructs shall be removed.' In the distance stood a mustached man dressed in gold regalia, with a red cylindrical hat and a gold ornamental sword. The angel approached him and placed the coin in his hand. 'And now you've been paid for your time,' he said. 'So now you must go.' With that the man in the golden regalia departed."

THE MASTER OF THE CELEBRATION

"In the last of the visions I saw a large public square filled with men, women, and children dressed in the formal evening wear of the early twentieth century. It was night. Overlooking the square was a balcony on which stood a man in a black jacket, tails, and a tie. 'Ladies and gentlemen,' he said, 'as the master of the celebration, I appreciate your patience. I know it's been a long wait, but the celebration will begin at its appointed time.' On the wall above the man was a colossal clock. Suddenly the clock chimed out as it struck what I took to be the appointed time. It was somewhere around half past nine. The multitude broke out in celebration, in singing, dancing, and loud rejoicing. And everything was suddenly illuminated by the light of oil lamps."

"The ram continued its journey until it reached the same city on the mountain as did the first ram. But now there were officials lining its path inside the gate. The ram walked through the gate and made its way up to a stone platform. Planted on the platform was an enormous pole bearing a massive red flag. Then, with a force that couldn't be explained by its size, the ram charged into the pole, which began tottering until finally crashing down to the earth. At that moment, the dark clouds began to dissipate. Then the sun broke through. And the vision ended."

Chapter 17

THE YEAR OF THE GEZERAH

T HE NEXT MORNING I awoke with the light of the sun shining into my tent. The curtains of its entrance were slightly ajar. I made myself ready for the day, then went outside. There, about three feet in front of the tent, was the boy, the same boy who had led me to the Oracle. He had been sitting there the whole time, not making a sound, just waiting for me to wake up.

"He smiled as if to greet me, then rose to his feet and motioned for me to again follow him through the desert. So I did. He led me for several minutes through a narrow, winding canyon. At its end it opened up to reveal a waterfall cascading down the mountain rock into a pool of water. The pool was surrounded by reddish-golden rock, the same rock that made up the canyon, and the green of desert vegetation, grass, bushes, and small trees…an oasis. There, across the water, sitting on one of the rocks, was the Oracle."

"This," he said, "will be our new meeting place. Remember the way. It will be here that we open up the mysteries of the second stream."

I joined him on the other side of the water and told him the vision.

"The ram," he said, "as the one before it, represented a specific year of Jubilee. The ram was dramatically different from the first; so too would this Jubilee be dramatically different from the one that preceded it. Between the two Jubilees, what had taken place?"

"The Jewish people," I said, "began returning to the land, and the land started coming back to life."

"And what caused their return?"

"The dream of living in their land."

"That and the persecution that broke out against them in the lands of their exile. So the return that began with a trickle soon became a stream and then a river. They planted fields, vineyards, and forests and built roads, houses, and towns, a culture, the beginning of a nation. What was sown in that first Jubilee of 1867 would come to fruition…and increase. Even world leaders would begin to take notice. But it was still only a dream.

And there was no way that such a dream could come true. The land had been under Ottoman rule since the days of Martin Luther."

"But what about the Ottoman Land Code and the release?"

"It would play a central part in the fulfillment of the prophecies, in the return of the land to its people. But a land isn't a nation. And the Ottoman Empire would not allow the birth of a Jewish nation."

"But the mystery requires the transference of the land to its owner."

"So then what would we expect to take place in the next Jubilee?"

"The transference of the land?"

"Yes, to its original owner," he said. "So the Jubilean cycle that began in 1867 would see the first waves of Jewish exiles returning to the land, the beginning of the restoration, and the founding of Zionism. But it would take another event to fulfill the mystery. That event would come just three years before the next Jubilee."

"What event?"

"The First World War."

"The dark clouds and trenches of my vision."

"So then," he said, "according to the mystery, which year would be the next year of Jubilee?"

"It would have to be the year 1917."

"Then, according to the mystery, we would expect 1917 to be the year of return and restoration and the transference of the land."

"And did it happen?" I asked.

"It happened," said the Oracle, "at the exact appointed time and would come through war and through the *gezerah*."

"The what?"

"The symbol on the second door and on the ram, it was the Hebrew letter *gimmel* and the first letter of the Hebrew word *gezerah*."

"And what does it mean?"

"The decree."

"So what was the next revelation?"

"That of a paper that would alter modern history."

"And how was it revealed?"

"Through the mystery of the rider."

Chapter 18

THE WORD OF KINGS

I RETURNED TO THE oasis. There was no one there. I sat down on a rock by the water, waiting for almost an hour. Then I saw him in the distance making his way to the pool. He sat down beside me."

"You do understand I have other things I need to attend to," he said.

"Of course," I replied, though I couldn't imagine any of them.

"Then let's begin."

"The rider," I said, "or riders...who were they, and what was the document they were carrying?"

"When we last spoke, what did we say would take place in the coming Jubilee, according to the mystery?"

"Those who had possession of the land would have to relinquish it. The land would have to return to those to whom it belonged."

"And I've told you that all events would be woven together to bring about the appointed end ordained by the mystery."

"You have."

"On June 28, 1914, the heir to the Austro-Hungarian throne, Archduke Franz Ferdinand, was riding in a motorcade through the city of Sarajevo when he was assassinated by a Bosnian Serb nationalist. In response to the assassination, the Austro-Hungarian Empire began mobilizing for war against Serbia. Within a month the Russian Empire began mobilizing for war in support of Serbia. Germany in turn began mobilizing for war against Russia, as did the Austro-Hungarian Empire. France in turn entered into war on the side of Russia. In an attempt to defeat France, Germany invaded Belgium. Belgium in turn appealed to Britain. Britain in turn declared war against Germany. By August 1914 the First World War had begun.

"The Ottoman Empire was not openly allied with any of the European powers, though in August it had signed a secret treaty with Germany. But on October 29, 2014, Ottoman warships, acting under the orders of the newly appointed German admiral of the Ottoman navy, launched a surprise attack on Russian ports in the Black Sea. On November 2 Russia declared war on the Ottoman Empire. On November 5, France did the same, as did Britain.

"So the two empires, the British and the Ottoman, were drawn into the conflict on opposite sides of the war. Each was destined to play a part in the fulfillment of prophecy. By the autumn of 1914 it was all in place."

"And the Ottoman Empire," I added, "was the possessor of the land. And if you remove any of those events…it doesn't happen."

"Yes."

"So God was behind those events?"

"Man was behind those events. But God works all things together, the good and the evil, all the pieces of the puzzle, for the purpose of redemption. But there were other pieces in the mystery…smaller ones. One of them was born in the Russian Empire in 1874 to a Jewish family, the third of fifteen children. He had a passion for science and as a young man had moved to Germany to study chemistry. But he had a deeper passion, the dream that his people would one day return to their ancient homeland. And while still pursuing his studies, he attended the Second Zionist Congress convened by Theodor Herzl."

"What was his name?"

"His name was Chaim Weizmann. In 1904 he moved to Britain and was employed by the Chemistry Department of the University of Manchester. Not long after taking up that post, Weizmann's path happened to cross with that of a renowned British politician and member of Parliament who at that time happened to be representing the same district in which Weizmann lived. His name was Arthur Balfour. Balfour was a man of deep Christian faith. His encounter with Weizmann left a lasting impression and a growing conviction concerning the return of the Jewish people to the land.

"Then came the events that would lead to the First World War, which in turn would lead to Weizmann's appointment to the British Admiralty laboratories and as an adviser to the newly established Ministry of Munitions, the head of which was David Lloyd George. Lloyd George's knowledge of the Bible had predisposed him to the dream of a Jewish homeland in Israel. But it was Weizmann's impact on Lloyd George that would be critical in the events that followed.

"At the time of Weizmann's appointment, British and Allied forces found themselves in the midst of a crisis over the shortage of a chemical vital for the war effort, acetone. Weizmann came up with a process of producing the substance in mass quantities. It would prove a key factor in helping the Allies attain victory. But it was another chain of events that would lead to one of the most critical moments in two thousand years of Jewish history.

In December 1916 the government of the British prime minister H. H. Asquith collapsed. The man who succeeded him was David Lloyd George. For his foreign secretary, Lloyd George appointed Arthur Balfour. So the two men who were in favor of a Jewish homeland were suddenly lifted to the heights of world power at that critical moment. If Asquith's government had not collapsed just when it did, what was about to happen would never have taken place. You see, Asquith was against the idea of a Jewish homeland. And it was only in that small window of time that these things could have come about."

"So his government had to crumble," I replied.

"Yes," said the Oracle, "and had to crumble just at that moment."

"Why then?"

"Because it was the very end of 1916. 1917 was coming. And 1917 was the year of Jubilee. And it just happened to be the same year that the British Empire would be placed in the position of determining the future of the land of Israel. And as the Jubilee concerns the return of one's ancestral land, so world history would now turn to the Middle East and to the land of the ancient inheritance.

"As the year of Jubilee began, members of the British government held a conference concerning Palestine. By the middle of the year Balfour called for a draft to be made for a public declaration concerning the land. By autumn the British Cabinet was in discussion over the form the declaration would take.

"But it was determined that the plan wouldn't proceed unless it had the support of the American president. On October 16, 1917, the British government was informed that the president, Woodrow Wilson, was in favor of the declaration. On October 31 the declaration was approved by the British War Cabinet. Two days later, on November 2, it went forth in the form of a letter penned by the foreign secretary, which included a single sentence that would come to be known as the Balfour Declaration. It declared,

> His Majesty's Government view with favour the establish-
> ment in Palestine of a national home for the Jewish people,
> and will use their best endeavours to facilitate the achieve-
> ment of this object..."[1]

"It's the Jubilee declaration," I said, "the return of the land to the original owner."

"Yes," said the Oracle, "and it must return in the fiftieth year. So it had to happen in that year, 1917. And so it did, and just in time, as the year neared its end. And in the Jubilee the transference is a matter of law. It has to be recognized in some way by the reigning authorities. And so it was the British Empire, a reigning authority, that issued the recognition. That recognition would be both momentous and historic. It was the first such declaration of any major power since ancient times, the first since the Roman Empire drove the Jewish people out of their land two thousand years earlier."

"My vision ended with a Roman soldier..."

"Yes, and it began with a British officer riding with a document. The document was the Balfour Declaration."

"And the other riders?" I asked.

"They represented the powers that had taken the land and occupied it in the two thousand years when the Jewish people were in exile...the Ottomans, the Mamluks, the Crusaders, the Byzantines, the Romans."

"So it went back to the beginning, to the Roman soldier. And then he disappeared."

"Yes, just as the Jubilee undoes the occupations of those to whom the land does not belong."

"You said it was the first time that any major power had supported the return of the Jewish people to their land since ancient times, since the time of Rome. But Rome never supported the Jewish people coming back to the land."

"No," he said, "Rome scattered them."

"Was there ever another power that did support their return?"

"One other," he said, "only one...two and a half thousand years ago, when the Persian emperor Cyrus allowed the Jewish people to leave their exile and go back to their homeland."

"Was there a declaration to that as well?"

"Yes, the Cyrus decree. From ancient times God has used the words of kings, world rulers, to confirm His purposes, to establish them, and to inaugurate what is yet to come. In both cases, the ancient and the modern, the declaration would lead to a massive change in the years that followed it.

"So the Jubilee of 1917 was the year of the *gezerah*, the decree. In the Jubilee the land must be returned to those to whom it belongs, and the return must be given legal authority. So it came about in the year of Jubilee, 1917, that the land of Israel was returned, by proclamation, to the Jewish people, those to whom it belonged, and the return came with the legal authority of the world's preeminent empire.

"It was the fiftieth year from the Jubilee of seeds, and that which had been planted in that first Jubilee came to its fruition in the second. In 1867 the release of the land began. In 1917 the release came to its fulfillment. In the first Jubilee the land was measured. In the second it was transferred. And even the man who measured it, Charles Warren, would be a sign. He was a British soldier, a representative of the British Empire, the same power that would bring about the transference in the next year of Jubilee.

"The world was oblivious to what took place in the first Jubilee. But with the second Jubilee the whole earth would see it. The world would be shaken. And through war and the fall of kingdoms and empires, that which was ordained by the ancient mystery would come to pass."

"So everything worked together to produce the declaration."

"The declaration," said the Oracle, "was only the beginning. Each Jubilee sets in motion a new cycle, opens up a new era, unleashes the appointed purposes."

"And what did this Jubilee open up?"

"The Balfour Declaration gave the Jewish people the tangible hope of a homeland. With that hope they came from the ends of the earth back to their ancestral possession, and in greater and greater numbers...as it was decreed in the ancient ordinance, 'Each shall return to his own possession.'"

"There was more to the mystery."

"Meaning?"

"Meaning there was another word appointed to converge at that exact moment in history. And that word would speak to world events in the voice of God...from an old man in a Middle Eastern tent to the rise and fall of empires."

Chapter 19

THE PROMISE

I FOUND THE ORACLE in the oasis, sitting on a rock at the edge of the pool. I joined him there."

"The old man and the little boy on the battlefield...what did they signify?"

"In the year of Jubilee," he said, "what is it that must be invoked and reaffirmed for each to return to his ancestral possession?"

"The original owner's right to the land."

"And what is your right to your ancestral possession based on?"

"On your ancestors' ownership of that land."

"And what does that go back to?" he asked.

"Your ancestors coming into possession of the land."

"So in the Jubilee of 1917 what must be reaffirmed?"

"The ancestral right of the Jewish people to their land."

"Which means it must go back to their ancestors coming into possession of that land. Who is the ancestor, the forefather of the Jewish people?"

I paused for a moment to think. "Abraham?"

"Yes. And in your vision he was the old man with the boy. The right of the Jewish people to return to the land goes back to Abraham, to the moment he received the promise of the land and the moment he entered it. Both of those things appear in the section of the Bible that begins with Genesis 12. It's there that Abraham was called to leave the nations and come to the land that God would show him. It's there that God's first words concerning the land are recorded. And it's there that Abraham receives the promise and enters the land. God would give the land to Abraham and to his children."

"To the Jewish people."

"Yes. The same portion of Scripture beginning with Genesis 12 contains the specific promise giving the land to his descendants, the Jewish people."

"It guess it would be harder to find a stronger title deed than that."

"I would say. So it's here where it all begins and wherein lies the right of ownership and the right to return...to be manifested in the year of Jubilee.

"But for nearly two thousand years," he said, "the world rejected that promise and that right. Empires, armies, and occupiers, one after the other, laid claim to it, while the land's rightful heirs were treated as strangers. But in the Jubilee of 1917 it would all be undone."

"But you said that in the Jubilee the right of ownership, the ancestral right, has to be invoked and recognized. Was it?"

"It was the last Sabbath before the week that would change Jewish history, the week the British War Cabinet approved the Balfour Declaration. Do you remember what I told you about the parashas?" he asked.

"The Scriptures that were appointed in past times to be read on specific days, on the Sabbaths."

"So on that last Sabbath before the declaration that would usher in the return of the land to Abraham's children, there was a Scripture appointed to be read."

"And what was it?"

"It was *Genesis 12*."

"The Scripture that establishes the ancestral right."

"For in the year of Jubilee the right of the original owner must be invoked and affirmed. The word was this:

> Now the LORD had said to Abram: "Get out of your country, from your family and from your father's house, *to a land that I will show you…*"[1]

"And the very first mention of the children of Israel:

> I will make you a great nation…[2]

"And the words by which God gave the land to the children of Israel:

> Then the LORD appeared to Abram and said, "*To your descendants I will give this land.*"[3]

"In that same word, appointed for the week in which the Balfour Declaration would give the land back to the Jewish people, the ancestral right was proclaimed again and again:

> …for all the land which you see I give to you and your descendants forever.[4]

> Arise, walk in the land through its length and its width, for I give it to you.[5]

> I am the LORD, who brought you out of Ur of the Chaldeans, to give you this land to inherit it.[6]

> On the same day the LORD made a covenant with Abram, saying: "To your descendants I have given this land."[7]

> Also I give to you and your descendants after you the
> land...as an everlasting possession.[8]

"It was thus given to the Jewish people '*forever*' as an '*everlasting possession.*'"

"In the vision Abraham was reading from a scroll. Did that signify the Scriptures that were appointed for that moment?"

"Yes. And he read from it in the middle of a battlefield, as it all came to fulfillment in the midst of war. In the midst of the gunfire of the First World War the ancient prophecies were being chanted and proclaimed throughout the British Empire, the power that would bring them to pass...and throughout the Ottoman Empire, the power that would crumble so that the prophecies would be fulfilled, and in every land of the Great War, from Western Europe to America to Russia...throughout the entire world."

"At the end of the vision the old man and the boy left the battlefield. They were returning home."

"Once the ancestral right is affirmed, the heirs may return to their inheritance, the land to the people, and the people to the land."

"Who was the boy?"

"The child of Abraham, the generation of Abraham's descendants that would receive back the land, the Jewish people alive in the days of the declaration, those who would return. And even that could be seen foreshadowed in the words appointed to be recited at that time."

"What words?"

"The very first prophecy ever to speak of the return of the Jewish people to the land. It was also recited on the last Sabbath before the declaration:

> ...they shall return here..."[9]

"But there was another piece to the puzzle, without which the ancient prophecies would never have been fulfilled."

"And that was the Oracle's next revelation?"

"Yes, after the next vision."

"A vision of...?"

"A place where water flows in the middle of the desert, a land of seven wells."

Chapter 20

THE LAND OF SEVEN WELLS

I FOUND THE ORACLE sitting by the waterfall, right at the point where it poured into the pool of water. I joined him there."

"The wells that I saw in the desert...what was that about?"

"Have you ever heard of a place called Beersheba?" he asked.

"It sounds familiar. But I don't know anything about it."

"When the Bible speaks of Israel's borders, it uses the phrase 'from Dan to Beersheba.' Beersheba was Israel's southernmost border, where the nation began...in space as well as time."

"In time?"

"Beersheba was central to Israel's beginning. The nation began when Abraham had a son, Isaac. Isaac grew up in Beersheba. And Abraham was instrumental in Beersheba's founding. Abraham was the one responsible for its name."

"How?" I asked.

"It was there that Abraham dug a well."

"The wells of the vision. And the little girl called it 'our father's wells.' Abraham was the father of the Jewish people."

"In Genesis 21 it's recorded that men of the Philistine king Abimelech took possession of Abraham's well. Abraham approached the king to contend for its return. And Abimelech returned it. So the two made a covenant concerning the land. And the place was called the Well of the Oath. In Hebrew the word for *well* is *beer*, and the word for *oath* is *sheva*. So together it becomes *Beersheva*, or *Beersheba*. In your vision how many wells did you see?"

"I counted seven."

"Do you know what the Hebrew word for *seven* is? *Sheva*, the same word that means oath. So Beersheba is also known as the Land of the Seven Wells."

"So my vision was about Beersheba. Why?"

"The Jubilee," he said. "Beersheba is about Abraham losing his property and then having it returned to him. The very name comes from its loss and return...the essence of the Jubilee. Beersheba is also the first place in the

Promised Land to which Abraham laid claim, the first possession, the first loss, the first appeal for return, and the first restoration. After the giving of God's promise, it was the well, the covenant, and the name *Beersheba* itself that constituted Israel's first legal right and title in the Promised Land."

"But what does all this have to do with the Jubilee of 1917?"

"We left off with the issuing of the Balfour Declaration. But there was one problem. The British Empire didn't have the land to give. It was in the hands of the Ottoman Empire. So according to the mystery, something else would have to take place.

"The chain of events triggered by the assassination of Archduke Ferdinand had drawn the two empires into opposite sides of the same war. In the Middle East, British forces were stationed in Egypt. From Egypt the British military hoped to launch a campaign against the Ottoman Empire in Palestine. But after two attempts to take the city of Gaza and two resulting defeats, that hope was looking less and less likely to be fulfilled. But that would soon change.

"A boy was born into a devout Christian home. From childhood he was immersed in the stories of the Bible and in particular the accounts of the Hebrew Scriptures that his father used to read to him each morning. He learned of the Promised Land, of its heroes, Joshua, David, Elijah. He would remain an avid student of the Bible his entire life. Though he never desired it, because of closed doors and less-than-ideal circumstances he ended up in the army.[1] He would later be known as General Edmund Allenby, another instrument in the outworking of the mystery.

"In the summer of 1917 Allenby was chosen to replace General Archibald Murray as commander of the British-led forces in Egypt. He spent the remainder of that summer preparing his troops and strategizing for the coming campaign. While Murray had focused on Gaza, Allenby placed his focus on a different city: Beersheba.

"So in the autumn of that year, British forces began heading to Beersheba with the Australian Light Horsemen. It appeared to be a battle against the odds. But all these things happen against the odds. By that evening the British-led forces had gained Beersheba. News of the victory spread across the world. It was a watershed moment. It was Britain's first major victory in the Middle East and, some would say, of the war itself. It would also be the breakthrough event that would lead to the restoration of the Jewish people to the land."

"It had to be," I said. "In the year of Jubilee the land has to be restored to its original owner, and it was the British Empire that issued the declaration of restoration. So the British Empire had to be given the land so it could be given back to the Jewish people."

"Yes. And just as Beersheba was intrinsic to Israel's beginning, so it would again be intrinsic to the beginning of Israel's restoration. As it was the first place in the land to be claimed for Abraham and his children, the first to be taken away by others, and the first to be restored...so after two thousand years of exile Beersheba would also be the first place to be reclaimed and returned to Abraham's children. And it all took place in the year of Jubilee, when what is lost must be restored to the original owner. But now the mystery operates on a global scale."

"When exactly was Beersheba regained?" I asked.

"On October 31, 1917."

"Does that date have any significance?"

"October 31, 1917, was the same day that the British War Cabinet approved the Balfour Declaration. So after two thousand years the promise of the land and the beginning of its transference took place on the exact same day. As for the Sabbath that sealed the week Beersheba was regained, there was an appointed Scripture."

"What was it?"

"It was this:

> Therefore he called that place *Beersheba,* because the two of
> them swore an oath there."[2]

"On that very week! That very Scripture!"

"Yes," said the Oracle, "the very Scripture that marks the very first time the name *Beersheba* appears in the Bible or anywhere...the account of Abraham's regaining of Beersheba."

"So the word appointed to seal the week of the regaining of Beersheba was the Scripture that spoke of the regaining of Beersheba."

"And the words were proclaimed throughout the world. For in the year of Jubilee the right of the original owner to his ancestor's land must be reaffirmed. So Beersheba constituted the first legal title given to the Jewish people concerning their right to the land."

"And it just *happened* to happen to be appointed for that week."

"Appointed long before anyone involved with those events was born...the fingerprints of God."

"Amazing."

"In the Jubilee the ancestral land must be relinquished by the one occupying it. And so it all begins in that year with the relinquishing of Abraham's city, Beersheba. The victory would lead to the ultimate relinquishing of the ultimate ancestral possession—Jerusalem. And so in the year of Jubilee, with only twenty-two days left in that year, would come the liberation of the Holy City, Jerusalem. The city would be given to the empire that had just issued the declaration decreeing the return of the land to its people. Two days later General Allenby would enter its gates, ascend a platform, and declare a new beginning for the city and the land."

"As the ram in my vision entered the gates and ascended the platform."

"Yes," said the Oracle, "and so the little boy who had read of the heroes of the Promised Land had now become one of them. And the Bible student who never wanted a career as a soldier was now the vessel through which the ancient prophecies would be brought to their fulfillment."

"It was not only Jerusalem's liberation that fulfilled the ancient prophecies but its preservation."

"You mean that the city was preserved in the midst of war?"

"Yes."

"And was that part of a mystery?"

"Yes...the mystery of the birds."

Chapter 21

THE BIRDS

W HEN I RETURNED to the Oracle, I found him sitting on one of the ledges on the mountain rock surrounding the oasis. I joined him there. I had come to ask him about the birds in the vision. And there were now birds circling over our heads. I asked my question."

"In my vision I saw a flock of giant birds heading to a battlefield and transforming into airplanes. What did it signify?"

"The Holy Land," he said, "is the most contested piece of property on earth, and Jerusalem, the most fought-over city. But in 1917 something appeared over the land and the city that would mark and separate that war from all the wars that had ever been waged over that soil.

"Soon after Allenby arrived in Egypt, he sent word to the British War Cabinet that he needed a revitalized air corps, new planes, better planes, and many more planes. When Allenby took up his command, the skies of the Holy Land were dominated by enemy forces. German airmen, supporting Ottoman troops, had attained total supremacy in the air.[1] If the British were to successfully take the land and the city of Jerusalem, they had to change that. They had to overtake their enemies in the air.

"In the summer of 1917 the revitalization of the British air corps was well underway. New brigades and squadrons were formed; new planes, deployed; new pilots, commissioned. The tide began to turn. The British soon gained supremacy of the skies over the Holy Land. The planes proved to be critical to Allenby's campaign. The British pilots flew reconnaissance missions and would report on enemy strength, enemy movement, and enemy strategy. It was the enemy who was most familiar with the land, not the British. But the intelligence that the air force provided changed all that. But it wasn't just the intelligence. The planes would also provide cover for British troops on the ground in the midst of battle. They would wage war, bombing enemy positions and strongholds. Allenby's integration of air and land forces would become a model for future warfare and would be critical in his success.

"But it wasn't just what Allenby's air force did but what it stopped from happening. It prevented the enemy aircraft from going on bombing missions, from providing cover for enemy troops, and from providing reconnaissance intelligence to enemy headquarters. The British pilots in effect drove the enemy out of the sky. The end result was that the Ottoman and German soldiers were forced to fight blindly. And by this Allenby's forces were able to maximize the element of surprise. All these factors helped enable the British-led forces to ultimately drive the Ottoman Empire out of the land.

"But Allenby's air force played a part as well in a more specific objective, the liberation and protection of Jerusalem. The last thing the British War Cabinet wanted was for Jerusalem to end up in ruins. But by driving the enemy from the skies, the chance of the city suffering massive destruction was greatly minimized. And on December 9, the central day of Jerusalem's liberation, even in bad weather the No. 14 Squadron managed to take the air to patrol the skies and run missions against the enemy.[2] Even after the British entered Jerusalem, Ottoman forces were ready to fight to take it back. So there remained a danger that Jerusalem would again become a battle zone. Allenby's air force would perform a critical function in helping to defeat the Ottoman army in the days following Jerusalem's liberation as well. Thus, in the end, for a site so zealously contested, more than any other in the world, Jerusalem emerged from the war largely unscathed.

"There is a Scripture," he said, "that prophesies of Jerusalem's being kept safe, preserved, and delivered on a day of war. The immediate context of the Scripture is that of a war involving the Assyrian Empire. But the word of God is such that one Scripture can hold several levels of meaning and application, and God can work and act in modern times according to biblical patterns and templates."

"So the prophecy, or the biblical template, speaks of Jerusalem being preserved intact in the midst of war…which happened in the war of its liberation by the British."

"Yes," said the Oracle, "but it's more than that. The Scripture mentions the means by which Jerusalem would be protected and preserved. It would come about this way:

> As birds flying, so will the LORD of hosts *defend* Jerusalem; *defending* also he will *deliver it; and passing over* he will *preserve* it."[3]

"As birds flying," I repeated.

"He could have given those words to speak of the protection of a mother bird to her nest, to give assurance to that generation. But God's knowledge stretches forth to all ages, to every event, every situation, every danger, and every war yet to come. He would certainly know that after two thousand years of hostile occupation Jerusalem would be delivered in that war.

"Beyond that is the prophecy's unique imagery, 'as birds flying.' God's preserving and deliverance of Jerusalem will come 'as birds flying.' In all the ages of its long history Jerusalem had seen countless armies, swords, chariots, horses and horsemen, archers, siegeworks, and warriors—but never a war in which vessels appeared in the skies 'as birds flying' to help bring about its preservation and deliverance...until the war of 1917.

"You know of the parashas," said the Oracle, "the appointed words read from the scrolls on the Sabbath day. But there are other appointed words, other appointed Scriptures. And they aren't found in scrolls but in a book—*The Book of Common Prayer*. The book was originally written in the sixteenth century for the Anglican Church. It contains Scriptures appointed not only for each week but for every day, every morning, and every night. So for whom were those Scriptures appointed?"

"For those of the Anglican Church, I would assume."

"And which army would be filled with those of the Anglican Church?" he asked.

"The army of General Allenby, the British army."

"Exactly. And undoubtedly many of the soldiers in that army would open up that book every morning to read the appointed Scripture. It was December 8, 1917, the last full day of fighting in the battle for Jerusalem. When the fighting was over, Jerusalem would be preserved and delivered. There was a Scripture in *The Book of Common Prayer* appointed hundreds of years earlier to be read on the last day before Jerusalem's deliverance. Do you know what it was?"

"What was it?"

"It was this:

> As birds flying, so will the LORD of hosts defend *Jerusalem*;
> defending also he will deliver it; *and passing over he will preserve it.*"[4]

"The deliverance of Jerusalem," I said, "as birds flying, appointed for that very day!"

"And read that day throughout the British Empire, all over the world, and by the British soldiers who were about to deliver Jerusalem."

"A Jubilee of wings."

"And those who flew over the Holy Land at the time of its deliverance were of the No. 14 Squadron. The squadron had a motto. Do you know what it was?"

"No."

"It was:

> *I spread my wings and keep my promise.*[5]

"And yet there's more," said the Oracle. "On December 9, 1917, the day of Jerusalem's liberation, there was another word appointed in *The Book of Common Prayer.*"

"What was it?"

"It was a prophecy that speaks of a day when distress will come to Jerusalem, when the city will be threatened with warfare. But the prophecy foretells that Israel's enemies will be defeated. They will flee the land. Jerusalem will be delivered. And His people will dwell there, inside its walls, in peace. On the day it was appointed to be read, Jerusalem was delivered, the Ottoman Empire was defeated, the Ottoman soldiers would flee the city, and God's people would dwell inside the walls in peace. The appointed word included this verse:

> Look upon Zion, the city of our appointed feasts; Your eyes
> will see Jerusalem...[6]

"*Zion* is another name for Jerusalem. The word speaks of seeing Jerusalem. So on the morning of the appointed word British soldiers in the land of Israel opened up *The Book of Common Prayer* to find the appointed word telling them to look upon the city of Jerusalem. And it was on that day that it would come true. They would enter its gates for the first time and behold the city.

"The next day, December 10, was a day of rejoicing and comfort, not only for Jerusalem's liberation but for the fact that Jerusalem's warfare had ended. The word appointed for that day was an ancient prophecy from the Book of Isaiah, words that foretold a day of God's comforting His people and His city when Jerusalem's warfare has come to its end...

> "*Comfort...comfort my people!*" says your God. "*Speak comfort to Jerusalem,* and cry out to her that *her warfare is ended.*"[7]

"And so it was appointed to be read on the very day that Jerusalem's warfare had ended."

"When I saw the Oracle again, he would reveal to me the number of the end."

"The end of...?"

"The end of an age."

"Did it come from the prophets?"

"Yes, but it would be given to those who had never read the prophets."

"How?"

"Through a coin."

Chapter 22

THE NUMBER OF THE END

I RETURNED TO THE Oracle to ask him for the meaning of the angel who stood by the river with the coin."

———————

"The prophet Daniel," he said, "was also taken to the bank of a river, where he saw a man much like the one who appeared in your vision. The man told him of things yet to come and of that which concerned the end. And he gave him a number, actually more than one number, but it is the final number that concerns us here."

"A number having to do with what?" I asked.

"The time that the Temple Mount would be given into the hands of strangers, the time that God's purposes would be obstructed."

"The time until that which obstructs is taken away," I said. "The strangers would be occupiers. And if they have the Temple Mount, they would also have Jerusalem. And if they have Jerusalem, they would also have the land. So it also had to do with the time that Jerusalem and the Holy Land would be occupied by enemy forces. Did it come true?"

"Centuries after Daniel was given that prophecy, foreigners invaded the land. They took possession of Jerusalem. They prevented the Jewish people from worshipping on the Temple Mount."

"So it was fulfilled?"

"Yes and no," he replied. "Some parts of the prophecy were fulfilled in ancient times. Other parts were reserved for the future. So Daniel was given a prophetic number:

> Blessed is the one who waits, and comes to the one thousand three hundred and thirty-five days."[1]

"1,335. The number in my vision."

"1,335 is the number signifying the end of the occupation of Jerusalem and the Temple Mount."

"And blessed is the one who waits for that day, because that's when that which holds back the purposes of God is removed."

"Yes," said the Oracle, "when hostile powers must leave the Holy City and God's people can return. It's the number of restoration."

86

"And what does it have to do with the mystery?"

"As the end of the Ottoman occupation of Jerusalem drew near, a sign began appearing."

"A sign…?"

"The number that signifies the end of the occupation—*1,335*. The number *1,335* began manifesting in the Middle East."

"Where in the Middle East?" I asked.

"In the land of Egypt, the place where Allenby started the campaign that would drive the Ottoman Empire out of the Holy Land, the campaign that would end the occupation. The number appeared on an Egyptian coin."

"As in my vision. So when did it begin appearing?"

"Just as the year 1917 was approaching and then throughout that year."

"So it appeared in the year of Jubilee," I said. "The number that signified the end of the occupation appeared in the Jubilee, the year that the one occupying the land has to relinquish it."

"Yes."

"How did they come up with that particular number?"

"It turned out that on the Islamic calendar the year happened to be 1335. It was 1,335 years from the rise of Islam. But in the Bible the same number is linked to the liberation of Jerusalem. And it all converged in the year of Jubilee, 1917."

"So was that the fulfillment of the prophecy?"

"It's not that it was the fulfillment of the prophecy but rather the playing out of a biblical template. The prophecy speaks of days, but the significance here is the pattern, or template. One thousand three hundred thirty-five is the number given to the Jewish people to speak of the end of foreigners occupying the land, inhabiting the holy places, the end of the obstruction of God's purposes."

"So the Islamic calendar just happened to mark the year 1917 with the same number given in the Hebrew Bible signifying the ending of an occupation…and in the process pinpointing the year of Jubilee!"

"Yes. And the number wouldn't have appeared only on the coins."

"No, it would have to have appeared all over the Islamic world…in the year 1917."

"Which powers," he asked, "occupied the land of Israel for most of the two thousand years when the Jewish people were in exile?"

"Islamic powers?"

"Yes. So the occupation of the land that began with the first Islamic empire, or caliphate, with the rise of Mohammad would end 1,335 years later with the defeat of the last Islamic empire in 1917."

"The man in the red hat who had to leave, he represented the Ottoman Empire. It was the Ottoman Empire that was constraining the purposes of God."

"And yet there's still more to the mystery," said the Oracle. "The British government was not going to proceed with the Balfour Declaration until getting approval from the American president, Woodrow Wilson. They were notified of that approval on October 16, 1917. And do you know what October 16, 1917, was?"

"No."

"It was the very day that sealed the year 1335. The occupation would thus end, the restoration would begin, and blessed would be those who waited for that day."

"Amazing."

"One more number," he said. "If in the Bible seven is the number of completion and ending, then eight is the number signifying a new beginning. The Ottoman Empire came into possession of the Holy Land in 1517. So when would be the eighth Jubilee?"

"The eighth Jubilee would be 1917."

"And so after four hundred years the Ottoman Empire's rule over the land comes to an end. The eighth Jubilee becomes the Jubilee of new beginnings."

"There would be one more mystery to be revealed before the closing of the second door and the opening of the third."

"A mystery concerning...?"

"A day and a night, each waiting to come for over two thousand years."

"And how was it revealed?"

"Through a celebration."

Chapter 23

THE DAY AND NIGHT OF KISLEV

I RETURNED TO THE Oracle to seek the meaning of the last vision."

"The people in the square, the clock, the celebration…what did it mean?"

"When the Jewish people returned from their first exile, their captivity in Babylon, the return didn't come about at once but in waves. And the rebuilding of Jerusalem and of the nation would likewise happen over a long period of time. And they encountered much resistance and many obstacles, so many that at one point the work came to a standstill. It was then that God sent them a prophet to encourage them. His name was Haggai. Do you know what *Haggai* means?"

"No."

"Celebration."

"The celebration in my vision. The 'master of the celebration'…so was he the prophet Haggai?"

"A representation of the prophet, yes."

"But in the vision the gathering didn't take place in ancient times but in modern times. It had to have been the early twentieth century."

"And yet the prophet was speaking to them. Why do you think?"

"Haggai spoke to those who returned to the land in ancient times. But his words would now speak to those who had returned to the land in modern times."

"Yes."

"Did the modern restoration of Israel parallel the ancient restoration?"

"As in ancient times," said the Oracle, "the modern restoration came in waves, waves of Jewish exiles returning from the nations, one after the other. They had begun returning in the nineteenth century and were still not a nation at the eve of the First World War, nor could they lay claim to Jerusalem. So too the modern return encountered countless obstacles. So what was it that the master of the celebration said to the gathering?"

"He said that he knew they had been waiting a long time but that the celebration would begin at the appointed time."

"So the Jewish people had been waiting for two thousand years…and those in the land had likewise been waiting. In ancient times Haggai encouraged those who had returned to the land by telling them of the nation's future blessings. And in one of his prophecies he even told them when the blessing would come. He gave them a date. He said this:

> On the twenty-fourth day of the ninth month...the word of the LORD came by Haggai, "...Now, carefully consider from this day forward....Consider now from this day forward, from the twenty-fourth day of the ninth month....But from this day I will bless you."[1]

"The twenty-fourth day of the ninth month," said the Oracle. "Everything centered on that day. From that day forward everything is to change. On the twenty-fourth day of the ninth month the blessing will come and God's purposes will be fulfilled."

"What is it about that day that's so important?" I asked.

"It's a mystery," he replied. "No one really knows. The prophecy speaks of things never fulfilled in Haggai's own day.

> I will overthrow the throne of kingdoms; I will destroy the strength of Gentile kingdoms....[2]

"So the twenty-fourth day of the ninth month is appointed for the ending of a curse, the beginning of blessing, the overthrowing of kingdoms, and the restoration of Jerusalem and the nation."

"So when is the twenty-fourth day of the ninth month?"

"I can tell you when it was in the year of Jubilee."

"When?"

"*December 9, 1917*...the day Jerusalem was liberated."

"The day the Jewish people were waiting for...for two thousand years!"

"The day appointed for the ending of a curse, the day that the occupation of two thousand years of hostile powers came to its end."

"And it said, 'I will overthrow the throne of kingdoms; I will destroy the strength of the Gentile kingdoms.'[3] So the rule of hostile powers would be overthrown."

"Yes, and so the Ottoman Empire would be overthrown."

"The clock!" I said. "That's what it struck. It was 9:24, the twenty-fourth day of the ninth month...December 9, 1917."

"And when," asked the Oracle, "did the twenty-fourth day of the ninth month begin?"

"What do you mean?"

"The Hebrew day always begins at sundown the night before. So it began at sundown on the night of December 8. The night of December 8 was when the Ottoman soldiers gave up the city and fled through its gates. So just as the twenty-fourth day of the ninth month began, the Ottoman soldiers departed the city and two thousand years of hostile occupation came to an end, and a new era began for the Jewish people. And it all happened on the day ordained in the Bible to end the curse and begin the days of blessing."

"What about the oil lamps that ignited in the midst of the celebration? Did that have any significance?"

"There was one other time when Jerusalem was liberated and restored to the Jewish people. It happened in between the writing of the Old and New Testaments. A foreign power, the Seleucid Empire, occupied the land of Israel and the city of Jerusalem and launched a persecution against the Jewish faith. But by a miracle the people of Israel drove out the invaders, regained Jerusalem, and rededicated the Temple. From that victory came the celebration of Hanukah. Hanukah is the Festival of Lights, when the Jewish people commemorate the dedication of the Temple and the restoration of Jerusalem and the land by lighting the lights of the menorah, the oil lamps."

"But why were there oil lamps in my vision?"

"Jerusalem was liberated on December 9, 1917. But December 9 encompasses two Hebrew days: the day that ends at sunset and the day that begins at sunset. The city was liberated from Ottoman rule. And then the sun set. The moment the sun set, it was no longer the twenty-fourth day of the ninth month but the twenty-fifth day. The twenty-fifth day of the ninth month is the Feast of Hanukah. So December 9, 1917, was the beginning of Hanukah. So on the evening of the day that Jerusalem was liberated, all over the world Jewish people lit the lights of Hanukah to celebrate the rededication of the Temple and the ending of the foreign occupation of Jerusalem."

"So the night that sealed Jerusalem's liberation and the ending of its occupation happened to be the start of the ancient holiday that celebrates Jerusalem's liberation and the ending of its occupation."

"Yes. And there's a special word appointed to be read on the Sabbath of Hanukah. And so on the Sabbath of the week that sealed the liberation of Jerusalem, this was the word proclaimed all over the earth:

> The LORD *will take possession of Judah* as His inheritance in
> the *Holy Land, and will again choose Jerusalem.*[4]

"And so in the closing days of 1917 the Lord again took possession of Judah as His inheritance in the Holy Land...and had again chosen Jerusalem.

"We have seen," said the Oracle, "the ancient mystery manifest on a global scale, on the stage of world history, moving through all events, obscure and overt, the lives of individuals, the courses of nations, a world war, the rise and fall of empires. And as in ancient times, when God ended the Babylonian Empire and raised up the empire of Persia to accomplish His purposes, so now the Ottoman Empire collapsed and the British Empire was raised to unparalleled heights. And another nation was likewise being readied for purposes yet to be revealed…America. But that will be for another time. We have now completed the mysteries of the second door."

"And what happens now?" I asked.

"What happens now," said the Oracle, "if the revelations are to continue, is that you will open the third door and unlock the mysteries that lie behind it. And in that event you'll find me in another place."

"So you opened the third door…"

"Yes."

"And what mysteries did it hold?"

"The revelation of a Jubilee unlike the others…a mystery of skeletons, a hidden parchment, the secret of a president that began thousands of years before he was born, someone who was and was not and then was again, a twentieth-century event encoded in the law of Jubilees…and much more."

"So you saw a vision."

"How did you guess?"

THE THIRD DOOR

Chapter 24

THE THIRD DOOR

BEFORE ME WAS the third door. The Oracle handed me the key. I placed it in the lock, pushed the door open, and walked through. I was now standing near the top of a high mountain, but a different mountain than before…something out of the Swiss Alps. And there was no sign of Moses. Instead, there stood a man with a long black beard dressed as if for a festive event, in a black jacket, tails, and a tie. At his side was a ram, white with black spots. Around the ram's neck was a chain with a pendant, on which appeared the same symbol I had seen on the third door.

"The man placed his hand on the ram's back. The moment he did, the black spots began moving, shifting, merging, and spreading until, except for its head and underside, its body was entirely black. It was as if the ram's coloring was mimicking that of the man's clothing. The man then sent it forth down the mountain. It was then that I realized I had seen the man before. It was Herzl.

"I followed the ram down the mountain and through a dark battlefield of trenches and distant explosions."

"Sounds like the imagery of your other visions, the First World War."

"Yes. And then it led me through the streets of a European-looking city. Around us was chaos—raging fires, burning buildings, smashed storefront windows, men, women, and children being herded out of their homes. The ram's coloring now changed to dark brown. It turned back to look at the devastation. In between the ram's shoulders, against the brown coloring, was a yellow star."

"A yellow star…"

"It was then that I noticed yellow stars on the coats and jackets of the people being rounded up. The ram's coloring now changed again. Its body was now covered with black stripes on a white background, and on one of its front legs was a series of numbers, as if someone had branded it. We were now walking along a barbed wire fence, passing others dressed in similar striped clothing with yellow stars. Some were just staring, motionless, but others began following the ram. At the end of the fence was an open gate. The ram passed through the gate, as did the multitudes behind it. The procession ended up at the harbor of a large sea, in which ships were waiting. The ram led the multitudes onto the ships, which then set off from the harbor. As the ships approached their destination, the shores of another land, there were cheers, celebration, and weeping. I followed the ram off the ship, where he led me along the seashore for some time. It was then that I saw the other visions."

"The visions within the vision…of the mysteries to be revealed."

"Yes. The ram paused and turned his gaze away from the sea, inland. I did likewise."

The Arena

"I saw a bearded man in ancient dress in the middle of an ancient Roman arena. He was engaged in combat with a man larger than himself, also bearded but with red hair, and more threatening. Around the arena's inner-most ring sat men in dark suits and ties watching the combat. Just when it seemed that neither of the two contenders could prevail against the other, the larger man was transformed. He was now clothed in white and radiant. He motioned to the men in their seats, as if seeking a decision. The majority stood up, while a minority remained seated. The man in white then blessed his opponent, who then rose up from the sand and with baggage at his side departed the arena. The ram continued walking the shore of the beach, then again stopped and turned his gaze inland. I turned as well."

The Goat

"I turned again and saw a goat in the desert walking along the side of a small mountain in which was a cave. The goat entered the cave. I followed it inside. But once inside there was no sign of the goat, only total darkness. In my hand were three stones. I could feel the inscription of a word on each rock but couldn't see what it said. I threw one of them into the darkness and heard the crash of pottery. I proceeded a few steps deeper inside and threw a second stone. Again there was the crash of pottery. I went a few steps deeper and threw the third stone. But instead of a crash, there was an explosion, a giant flash of light. Suddenly I was surrounded by swirling stars and galaxies enveloping me. It was as if I were watching the birth of a universe. And then I was back on the seashore behind the ram."

The Skeleton Lady

"When the next vision began, I had no idea what I was seeing…massive objects scattered over a vast landscape, moving, colliding into each other. I watched as a structure emerged. It was a gigantic skeleton lying on its back. I estimated that the rib cage alone had to have been around two hundred feet high. I watched as sinews and muscles appeared on the skeleton, then skin, and then hair, long, wavy black hair. It had assumed the form of a colossal woman in a robe of blue and white, beautiful but lifeless. Suddenly she opened her eyes."

THE KING IN THE WHITE HOUSE

"I turned again and found myself standing in front of the White House. I watched as an old bearded man in a long black coat and a skullcap entered through its front doors. He made his way to the Oval Office. I followed him there. In the center of the office sat a bearded king with a crown of corrugated gold, a scepter, and a robe of white, purple, and yellow. 'Are you the one,' asked the man in black, 'anointed to set the captives free?' 'How could I be,' said the king, 'and not know that I was?' At that the king rose from his throne, walked over to the desk, opened its drawer, and took out a clay cylinder covered with symbols. He then walked outside the Oval Office, where a large golden eagle awaited him. The moment he stepped outside, his appearance changed. It was now that of a man with short cropped hair, a light-colored suit, a light-colored hat, and glasses. He placed the cylinder in the talons of the eagle, which then flew away. 'Will you look at that!' he said as he watched the eagle in the sky. He then came back inside and sat down on the throne. His appearance reverted to that of the king. 'I am he,' said the king."

THE BOY OF THE ARCH

"I continued following the ram along the shore. I looked to my left and saw a boy with dark, wavy hair, dressed in clothes from the turn of the century. 'Come,' he said. 'It's going to begin.' In the distance ahead was some sort of monumental arch, so close to the ocean that the waves were crashing against its base. He took my hand and led me over to it. 'Look,' he said. On the arch were engraved images. As I watched, the images began to move. It was telling the story of the siege of a city and destruction of a land. 'Now watch what happens,' said the boy. The images then changed from destruction to restoration and life, mothers with children, people planting, farming, and rebuilding. And then the engravings became still again. 'Who are you?' I asked the boy. 'One who was, who was not, and was again,' he said. I looked away to make sure I could still see the ram. Then I turned back. The boy was gone. I looked again at the engravings on the arch. And then I saw him...on the arch...the boy. He was now an engraved image in the scene of restoration...just smiling."

The Man in the Purple Robe

"I looked again and saw a bearded man in a purple robe sitting on the shore, turned away from the sea. Around him were broken branches of all different kinds and sizes. He was wearing a crown. He was a king. As I approached him, he spoke. 'I built a house,' he said, 'but the waves destroyed it. And I have no one to help me rebuild it.' Just then another man appeared and approached him. 'I am the bearer of burdens,' he said. 'I will help you to rebuild it.' So the two began piecing together the branches until a structure emerged, a shelter or house of branches. The moment it was completed, five white flowers sprung up from the sand in front of its entrance. And the vision ended."

The Four Jeweled Keys

"In the last of the visions I saw a man in a dark-brown cloak. In his hand was a large ring, from which hung four keys. But they were unlike any keys I had ever seen. At one end of each key was a precious stone of different colors. At the other end, the part that was to be inserted into a keyhole, were shapes or symbols. One resembled an X; another, something of a Y; another had three prongs; and another I couldn't liken to anything I had ever seen before. I watched as the man wandered across the earth and through the ages, searching for the doors his keys would open. He journeyed to ancient temples, medieval cathedrals, and the buildings of modern cities. But no door would open. Finally I saw him standing on the shore, overlooking a modern-looking city. He approached one of its buildings and inserted one of the four keys—the door opened. He walked inside and came to a second door, inserted a second key, and the door opened. He did the same with a third door and finally a fourth. When the fourth door opened, it revealed a room filled with people gathered for what appeared to be an official event. A man with white hair was speaking. On seeing the man in the dark-brown cloak enter the room, he said to him, 'And so it is as it has been written; by these keys you shall return.' And the vision ended."

"The ram continued its journey until it reached a city by the shore. It was the same city I had just seen in the vision of the man in the brown robe. The ram's appearance had now returned to what it had been at the beginning, on the mountaintop, white with black spots. It turned away from the sea and headed toward the city, where it disappeared. And the vision ended."

Chapter 25

HERZL'S COUNTDOWN

I SAW THE VISION at night. The next morning, he appeared at my tent...the boy. He smiled at me, then motioned for me to follow. He led me on a path along the side of a small mountain chain, gradually ascending until we came to a cave. He then urged me to go inside, ahead of him. So I did. I looked back, and he was gone.

"Slowly I made my way through the darkness until coming to a chamber illuminated by the reddish-golden light of ancient-looking oil lamps. There, sitting by the wall, was the Oracle. I joined him."

"I hope you don't mind caves," he said.

"No."

"It will be here that we will open the next of the mysteries, those of the third door. Now tell me your vision."

So I did.

"Did you notice that it was different? When you saw the ram in the other visions, it was Moses who sent it down the mountain, and the mountain was in the desert. But now it happened on a very different landscape and with a different person."

"I did notice. Why was it different?"

"Because this vision would reveal a Jubilee unique from the others."

"Not connected to them?"

"Very much connected but of a different nature and of a different cycle and timetable."

"Not based on a fifty-year cycle?"

"Very much based on a fifty-year cycle but on its own. It would be a Jubilee of the political realm and of the domain of nation-states."

"A political Jubilee?"

"In a sense. Did you recognize the man on the mountain?"

"Herzl, the founder of Zionism. Why was he dressed that way?"

"Because that was the clothing of the First Zionist Congress, the gathering he convened in Basel, Switzerland, to begin the political movement that would lead to the creation of a Jewish state. It was an unlikely movement, based on faith as much as anything else."

"Switzerland...That would explain the landscape."

"Herzl sent the ram down the mountain because he was the one who set the movement in motion. He would spend the remaining seven years of his life laboring for that cause, dying exhausted at the age of forty-four." The Oracle paused before continuing. "There was a boy who had a dream in which the Messiah lifted him into the clouds, where they encountered Moses. The Messiah said to Moses, 'It is for this child that I have prayed!' Then he turned to the boy and said, 'Go and declare to the Jews that I shall come soon and perform great wonders and great deeds for my people and for the whole world!'"[1]

"Why did you share that?" I asked.

"Because the boy was Theodor Herzl. He had the dream when he was twelve years old, long before the idea of Zionism would enter his mind. In biblical prophecy the regathering of the Jewish people to the land of Israel is ultimately linked to the coming of the Messiah.

"At the time of Herzl's death the idea of a reborn Jewish nation was still just a dream. You saw the ram walking through the battlefield...the First World War, the Jubilee of 1917, the Balfour Declaration, and the liberation of Jerusalem and the land."

"And then I followed it through a city of burning buildings, smashed windows, chaos, and violence."

"That represented what took place in the 1930s," said the Oracle. "That was *Kristallnacht*, the Night of Broken Glass, when the Nazi fury against the Jewish people exploded in Germany and before the world. The satanic forces that Adolf Hitler and the Nazi party embodied had now overtaken a nation and would soon overtake a continent. The Jewish people were now in danger of annihilation. They needed a refuge. And so it was just before that darkness began to rise in Europe that a homeland was given to them, a refuge, the land of Israel. It all happened at the same time."

"As if it was known in advance that these things would take place."

"It *was* known," he replied. "Thousands of years before these things took place, as far back as Moses, it was prophesied. The people of Israel would be scattered to the ends of the earth and *persecuted*. But it was also prophesied that God would gather them back. And it would all be fulfilled, just as it was foretold, on the stage of modern history.

"In the Book of Jeremiah a prophecy was given as to how it would come about. First would come the fishers, and then the hunters. What are fishers?" he asked. "Those who draw in. The Zionists were fishers. They were the ones who called the Jewish people to come back to the land before calamity would overtake them. They fished for them. Then came the hunters. Hunters pursue; they drive away. The Nazis were hunters.

They hunted them. They came second. And it was that very persecution that caused thousands upon thousands of Jewish people to return to their homeland in the largest waves of return up to that moment. Even in a modern and secular age, all things, both good and evil, are worked together to fulfill the ancient prophecies."

"And when the ram walked behind the barbed wire and to the harbor..."

"The Holocaust," said the Oracle, "and the survivors on their journey back to the Promised Land."

"Herzl never could have imagined how it would all come about...through two world wars and the shaking of the world."

"No, but he could prophesy it."

"What do you mean?"

"Herzl founded Zionism at the First Zionist Congress in Basel, Switzerland. A few days after the congress had ended, he penned in his journal a prophecy. He wrote:

> At Basel, I founded the Jewish State. If I said this out loud
> today, I would be answered by universal laughter. Perhaps in
> five years, *certainly in fifty, everyone will know it.*[2]

"He gave a deadline to his prophecy—*fifty years*, the *time period of the Jubilee*. So Zionism was birthed with a Jubilean prophecy, just as it was a Jubilean movement—the return to the ancestral land."

"So when was the First Zionist Congress?"

"It happened in 1897...So if we add the fifty years of Herzl's prophecy, the fifty years of the Jubilee, it takes us to the year..."

"1947...So did anything happen that year linked to the mystery?"

"In the years following the Second World War, the British government turned the issue of Palestine over to the newly formed United Nations. This would lead to the fulfillment of prophecy. It all converged on the year 1947, the fiftieth year, the year of Herzl's prophecy.

"So the United Nations set up a committee to address the matter: the UN Special Committee on Palestine. The committee worked on the problem for several months. Finally it came up with a solution. The solution would be known as the Partition Plan. It would alter the course of modern history. According to the plan, the British occupation would come to an end and the land would be divided in two—a Jewish state and an Arab state. If approved, it would mean that there would be a Jewish nation in the land of Israel for the first time in two thousand years.

"The plan then took the form of a resolution to be put to a vote before the United Nations General Assembly. It required that those occupying the land, the British, relinquish it, and those to whom the land belonged return to it."

"It was a Jubilean resolution," I said.

"It was the fulfillment of the First Zionist Congress. The day on which that congress concluded was August 31, 1897. So what happens if we add fifty years, to *the exact day*? When would the exact day of its Jubilee fall?"

"August 31, 1947."

"So could the mystery be pointing us to that day? Was there anything significant about that day connected to Israel's restoration?"

"Tell me."

"The Partition Plan, which would give the land back to the Jewish people and bring Israel into existence, was completed on *August 31, 1947.*"

"Fifty years to the exact day!"

"Yes, the Jubilean document was born on the *exact day* of the Jubilee. In fact it was on that very same day, August 31, 1947, that a special event was taking place in Basel, Switzerland."

"The place where the First Zionist Congress convened."

"It was the commemoration of the event that began Zionism. They called the Jubilee…the Jubilee of the First Zionist Congress. One of the leaders attending the event was Chaim Weizmann. As he addressed the gathering, Weizmann actually made reference to what he believed was taking place that same day on the other side of the world—the completion of the plan. He even stated that the event could signal *the beginning of the redemption.*[3] So on the same day that the Jubilee was being celebrated in the place where Zionism began, the plan that would fulfill the ancient prophecies of redemption and the dream that was birthed fifty years earlier was completed—fifty years to the exact day."

"Amazing."

"After its completion the plan was officially received and recorded by the United Nations General Assembly. That took place on September 3, 1947."

"Was that significant?"

"The day that Herzl penned his prophecy was September 3, 1897."

"Fifty years to the exact date!"

"The prophecy foretold that within fifty years everyone would know it. Fifty years later brings us to the exact day that the rebirth of Israel would become known to the representatives of the United Nations. Herzl recorded his prophecy in writing and marked it with the date *September 3.* The United Nations General Assembly recorded the plan that would fulfill Herzl's prophecy fifty years later and would mark its opening page with the exact same date, September 3.[4]

"The representatives of the United Nations had no idea that they were all part of the fulfillment of prophecy and the outworking of an ancient mystery:

> And you shall consecrate the fiftieth year.... It shall be a Jubilee for you; and each of you shall return to his possession..."[5]

_____

"The Oracle would next reveal to me the mystery that lay behind one of the most critical events of the modern world, a realm of two brothers, an ancient word, a mystery name, and an angel."

"And how was it revealed?"

"Through two men in an arena."

Chapter 26

THE RETURN OF JACOB

I FOUND THE ORACLE in the cave, in the same chamber as before."

"The two men in the arena," I said, "who were they?"

"In the beginning of the twentieth century," he said, "the Ottoman Empire stood against the restoration of the Jewish people to the land and so, against the prophecies. Therefore, it collapsed. The British Empire stood in favor of that restoration and of the establishment of a Jewish homeland. Therefore, it was lifted to the apogee of its power and would replace the Ottoman Empire as possessor of the Holy Land.

"But in the years in between the two world wars, the British Empire would change its policy and turn against the return it had once championed. The empire would block ships carrying Jewish refugees from the Holocaust to the land of Israel. It was now warring against the return, the prophecies and the mystery. Therefore, in a short time the largest empire the world had ever seen would collapse into near nothingness. And it would be forced to relinquish the Promised Land. Another power would then stand in favor of Israel's restoration and the return of the Jewish people—America. Therefore, it was at that moment that America was raised up to a position of power, expanse, and influence unparalleled in world history.

"It was during this transition of power that the British government turned over the issue of Palestine to the United Nations. The resulting Partition Plan could only go into effect if approved in the General Assembly. The vote took place on November 29, 1947, the very end of the fiftieth year from the birth of Zionism. In order to pass, the plan needed to be approved by a two-thirds majority. The outcome was in doubt up to the last days before the vote. But again the history and powers of the world would conform to the purposes of the ancient mystery.

"The Soviet Union, the world's chief atheistic power, was certainly not in favor of fulfilling biblical prophecy. It would soon become Israel's archenemy. But in 1947 an unlikely set of factors came together. The Soviet leader Joseph Stalin saw the birth of Israel as a way to weaken and roll back the British Empire while increasing Soviet influence in the Middle East. The solidification of Soviet control over Eastern Europe in the summer of

1947 ensured that the nations of eastern Europe would vote in favor of the resolution.[1]

"The American State Department had positioned itself against the resolution. But the American president was in favor of it. In this was another case of world history coalescing around the ancient purposes. Had the former president, Franklin D. Roosevelt, been in power in that window of time, it is questionable whether he would have sanctioned Israel's rebirth. But in his last campaign for the presidency he would choose a new running mate—Harry Truman. Truman was sworn in to office as vice president on January 20, 1945. Less than three months later Roosevelt died. Truman, a man with deep sympathy for the sufferings of the Jewish people, was suddenly catapulted to the most powerful position on earth—at the precise moment of world history most critical for Israel's rebirth. He would support and work for the passage of the resolution that would bring about Israel's resurrection.

"On November 29, 1947, in Lake Success, New York, the United Nations General Assembly took up the vote. The final count was thirty-three votes in favor, thirteen votes against, and ten abstentions. The resolution passed. Israel would again become a nation."

"I see the connection to the Jubilee," I said, "but not to my vision."

"You saw two men in an arena wrestling. The first was Jacob, patriarch of the Jewish nation. The Jewish people are so identified with him that the entire nation is often referred to simply by the name *Jacob*. Jacob was also called *Israel*. And, as would his descendants, Jacob would spend a good part of his life in exile from his homeland. But then God called him to return. On his return he encountered a man who wrestled with him through the night and to the break of day."

"And who was his opponent with the red hair?"

"The word for *red* in Hebrew is *adom* or *edom*. *Edom* was another name for Jacob's brother, Esau. For a good part of their lives the two brothers were in conflict. But the man in your vision only *looked like* Esau. In the biblical account the man who wrestled with Jacob was an angel. When neither of the two prevailed, the angel touched Jacob's hip and crippled him. But Jacob didn't give up. Finally the angel gave him a blessing. Jacob then returned home. In your vision Jacob represented the Jewish people. So what you saw concerned the return to the land of Jacob's children, the Jewish people."

"But in my vision it happened in an arena before an audience."

"So the return of Israel happened before the world…and before the United Nations, those men in suits and ties. The majority of them stood up, but the minority stayed seated."

"So they were voting on the return of Israel?"

"Yes...but there's more to the mystery. You see, when the nations of the world gathered to vote on the rebirth of Israel, it was a Saturday...*the Sabbath*. So there was a Scripture appointed for that day."

"What was it?"

"It was *the return of Jacob to the land*."

"And *Jacob* is another name for Israel. So on the day the United Nations voted for the return of Israel to the land, the appointed Scripture was the return of Israel to the land."

"Yes," said the Oracle. "And that appointed portion of Scripture contains a command:

> *Return to your native land...*[2]

"Behind the words *native land* are two Hebrew words. One is *eretz*, or *land*. The other is *moledet*. *Moledet* refers to the place or land of your birth. So the word is also translated as 'ancestral land,' 'birthplace,' or 'homeland.' The land of Israel is the place where the Jewish nation was birthed. It is their *moledet*. Thus the Scripture long appointed to be read on the day the United Nations would vote Israel back into existence could be rendered,

> Return to the land of your birth, to your ancestral land, to
> your homeland."

"And when did Israel actually come into existence?"

"Just over five months after that vote. It would be ushered into existence by a declaration. The first words of that declaration were 'The Land of Israel was the *birthplace* of the Jewish people.'[3] But the Hebrew word used in that declaration for *birthplace* was *moledet*, the exact word that appeared in the appointed Scripture."

"What about Esau? What did he have to do with Israel's rebirth?"

"Jacob's return to the land revived an old conflict. When the two brothers were young, Jacob managed to obtain their father's blessing, the birthright. The birthright had to do with the inheritance and the right to the land. Esau believed it belonged to him and vowed vengeance. So as Jacob returned to the land, he prepared for the worst.

"The conflict between the two brothers was also part of the Scripture appointed for the day of the United Nations vote and would be prophetic. The return of the Jewish people to the land would likewise revive an ancient conflict of two brothers, the Jews and the Arabs. And the United Nations vote involved them both. As for Esau, his bloodline ran through the Arab nations, the nations that would wage war on the day of Israel's return. And as did Esau, so they vowed the death of their brothers and the destruction of Israel. And as did Jacob, the Jewish people began preparing for the attack to be launched against them on the day of their return. And it was all set in motion on the day of the appointed Scripture that spoke of Jacob's return and the conflict of the two brothers."

"And what happened to Jacob and Esau?"

"They would be reconciled. But it was prophesied that the children of Esau and the children of Jacob would be in conflict down through the ages. And so the war would continue into the time of Israel's return. But on the day when the world assigned a homeland for the children of Jacob, the appointed word contained an ancient prophecy given to Jacob and specifically concerning his descendants:

> *To your descendants, I will assign this land.*"[4]

"What about the angel in my vision?"

"That," said the Oracle, "is another mystery. In the Partition Plan, voted on at the United Nations, there was no name given to the future Jewish state. The name would only come on the eve of the nation's rebirth the following year. Several different names were proposed, among them Judah and Zion. But it was another name that would be chosen. And on the day of the nation's birth the name would be announced to the world. The new nation would be called Israel.

"In the ancient account, at the end of his wrestling, Jacob pleads with the angel for a blessing. The angel blesses him with a new name: *Israel*. He only received that name as he returned to the land. So too it was only when the children of Jacob were returning to the land that they received the name *Israel*.

"The angel's blessing constitutes the very first appearance of the name *Israel* in the Bible. On the day the United Nations voted the Jewish nation back into existence without a name, do you know what the Scripture appointed for the day contained?"

"What?"

"The name *Israel*...the very first appearance of the name *Israel*."

"How does it appear?"

"It appears in the words,

> *You shall be called "Israel."*"[5]

"So on the day that the United Nations gathered to vote the Jewish nation back into the world, the appointed Scripture was '*You shall be called "Israel"*'?"

"Yes."

"Amazing."

"Now, *Jacob's* birth was recorded in an earlier portion of the Bible. But the angel's words represent *the birth of Israel*. So on the day the United Nations voted for the birth of Israel, the Scripture appointed for that day was that which recorded...the birth of Israel. Therefore, when the nations of the world gathered together to vote on the birth of Israel, all throughout the world the birth of Israel was being proclaimed and chanted from the scrolls of the appointed word. And as the account spoke of the changing of Jacob into Israel, so the resolution passed on that day would lead to the changing of the children of Jacob into the nation of Israel."

"When I next saw the Oracle, he would open up the mystery of an appointed word of a very different nature, one hidden away for two thousand years to be revealed at the exact moment when an ancient prophecy was to be fulfilled."

"And through what vision would it be revealed?"

"The vision of the goat."

Chapter 27

THE DAY OF THE SCROLLS

I RETURNED TO THE cave to find the Oracle sitting in a chamber of clay vessels, cylindrical jars of reddish, brown, and white clay, taller than they were wide, ancient, and crowned with cylindrical lids. I sat down beside him and asked him to tell me the meaning of what I had seen in the cave at the end of the vision."

"The swirling stars and galaxies," I said, "what was that about?"

"The universe," he said.

"But what did it mean?"

"You threw a rock into the darkness," said the Oracle. "On the rock was a word. From the rock came a universe. Before the world...was the word. It was the word that brought the creation into existence. So when God creates, He begins with the word. He spoke to Abraham of a nation that would become as numerous as the stars. He spoke of it before it existed. First the word, then the reality, the nation.

"And before that nation could be established in the Promised Land, the children of Israel were brought to Mount Sinai to be given the word—again, first the word, then the kingdom. Centuries later, when the Jewish people mourned in exile in Babylon, they were given visions and prophecies of their nation's restoration. Seventy years later the word would be fulfilled. And when the remnant of that exile returned to the land, a man called Ezra would gather them together to read to them the Scriptures... Again, the word and then the restoration."

"And with the rebirth of Israel in modern times..."

"Over two thousand years before it happened, it was foretold in the word, in vision and prophecy. As it was for the creation, so it was for the creation of Israel. Before God creates, He sends forth the word. And so the restoration of the word is linked to the restoration of the nation. And when God restores the nation, He always restores the word."

"But what does this have to do with the vision?"

"A bedouin shepherd was searching for a stray goat."

"The goat in my vision."

"The shepherd climbed up the side of a small mountain and noticed the opening of a cave. He threw a stone into it."

"As I did."

"And as you did in your vision," said the Oracle, "so too he heard the crashing of pottery. He would enter the cave with a friend, and they would explore it together. Inside they found clay jars. They removed the lids that covered the openings. Inside the jars were rolls of parchment with writing on them. They brought the parchments to a merchant in Bethlehem.

"At that time the Hebrew University's head archaeologist was Eliezer Sukenik. Upon being told of the existence of the parchments, Sukenik decided to go to Bethlehem to see for himself. The Bethlehem merchant allowed him to take the scrolls and examine them in the privacy of his home.

"Upon arriving home, Sukenik began unrolling the parchments, his fingers trembling at the prospect that what he was about to see was unprecedented. The words on the parchments were in Hebrew. The writing was ancient, going back thousands of years. It would represent the beginning of what has been called the greatest archaeological discovery of modern times...the Dead Sea Scrolls. The scrolls had remained hidden and miraculously preserved for two thousand years.

"But it was not only that ancient texts lay hidden in the caves. Hidden as well was the word of God. The Dead Sea Scrolls contained the Hebrew Scriptures. Up to their discovery, the oldest surviving copy of the Hebrew Scriptures, or most of the Bible, came from the Middle Ages. Any biblical manuscript from before that time had either been lost, destroyed, or unable to survive the passage of time.

"But with the uncovering of the Dead Sea Scrolls, the world was now in possession of a Bible penned a thousand years earlier, from ancient times, from the time of Jesus. The discovery was momentous. The scrolls not only confirmed, in ink and parchment, the ancient origins of the Bible but also its accuracy. The text of the ancient parchments amazingly matched the modern text of the Bible. In two thousand years the word of God remained unchanged. Contained in the scrolls themselves was the ancient prophecy 'The grass withers, the flower fades, but the word of our God endures forever.'"[1]

"When did all this happen?"

"The Dead Sea Scrolls were discovered in the year 1947."

"1947! The same year everything else happened...the fifty-year prophecy, the Partition Plan, and the UN resolution that would bring forth the rebirth of Israel."

"In the year of restoration comes the restoration of the word."

"So the people of Israel came back to the land, and God restored the word to them."

"Yes," said the Oracle. "And when did the nation of Israel actually come back into the world?"

"The following year."

"First the word and then the creation."

"So first the scrolls and then the nation."

"And the scrolls themselves would speak of the nation's restoration. The most celebrated of the Dead Sea Scrolls was the scroll of Isaiah. It was there in that very first cave and was preserved in its entirety. Israel would build an entire sanctuary to house it, the Shrine of the Book. It was that scroll that contained some of the most powerful words of comfort ever given to Israel and some of the most beautiful prophecies of its future restoration. Several of these would come true in the twentieth century with the gathering of the Jewish people back to the land:

> He will…assemble the outcasts of Israel, and gather together
> the dispersed of Judah from the four corners of the earth.[2]

"But the mystery joining together the nation and the word would go even deeper. On the first night when Sukenik sat in his study deciphering the Dead Sea Scrolls, when after two thousand years their ancient secrets would for the first time be revealed, something else was happening. In the next room Sukenik's youngest son, Mati, was listening to the radio. Mati would rush back and forth to tell his father what he was hearing."

"Why?"

"The day that Sukenik brought the Dead Sea Scrolls back to his home, the day he unrolled them, and the day their words first came to light was November 29, 1947. November 29, 1947, was the day that the United Nations was assembled in New York to vote on the resolution that would bring Israel back into existence."

"The word and the nation on the same day!"

"When Sukenik's son rushed into his office that night to give him the last report, his father was deeply absorbed in the ancient words coming to life before his eyes. His son shouted the news: the United Nations resolution had passed. Israel would again become a nation."

"The lost possession," I said, "the word that was lost for two thousand years, was now restored, and the nation that was lost for two thousand years was now restored…at the same time."

"Yes," said the Oracle, "in the very same year, on the very same day, on the very same night—at the very same moment."

"The next mystery would come from a vision that startled me more than any of the others I had seen up to that point. And it was in that vision that I learned the meaning of the letter on the third door and on the ram."

"Which vision was that?"

"The skeleton lady."

Chapter 28

RESURRECTION LAND

I FOUND THE ORACLE sitting in the same chamber as before, surrounded by the clay vessels. He lifted up one of them, opened its lid, reached inside, and removed a rolled-up piece of paper."

"This is the declaration," he said, "that proclaimed to the world that the nation of Israel had returned."

He handed it to me. I noticed the date, May 14, 1948.

"*The* declaration?" I said.

"This is what was published by the Provisional Government at the moment of Israel's return. But there's something strange about it."

"What?"

"Words you would not expect to appear on any such document and that have never appeared on the founding document of any other nation. Look at the bottom, the bottom left. Read it."

"'Prophesy over these bones.' What on earth does that mean?"

"What you saw on the ram and on the third door is the Hebrew letter *tav*. It stands for the word *tikumah*. It was the year of *tikumah*. *Tikumah* is the Hebrew word for *resurrection* and in this case for the year of resurrection. So it was the year of the *tikumah*."

"What does resurrection have to do with the Jubilee?"

"Everything," he said. "What is it that the Jubilee brings?"

"Return and restoration."

"And what is resurrection but the ultimate restoration and the ultimate return, the return to what once was…but was lost. The words on the declaration are ancient. They come from a vision given to the prophet Ezekiel. He was taken to a valley of dry bones. There he heard the Lord say to him, 'Prophesy over these bones.'[1] So he did. The bones started moving together until they formed skeletons, a great multitude of skeletons. Then sinews came upon them, then flesh…And then they came alive."

"Which is what I saw in the vision. What did it mean?"

"The dry bones were Israel, the ruins and hopelessness of a destroyed nation. But it was a prophecy of hope. God would gather them back together and raise them from the dead. He would resurrect them."

"But in my vision there was only one resurrection. Why?"

"Ezekiel saw the resurrection of the *people* that made up the nation. But what you saw was the resurrection of the nation as a *whole*. The woman you saw lying on the ground wasn't a person but the nation itself. You see, it wasn't only that the *people* of Israel would be resurrected; it was that the *entire nation* would follow the pattern of resurrection. The nation itself would rise according to the template of the dry bones."

"So that's why she was so big," I said.

"Yes. Nations," he said, "follow the course of nature. They're born. They grow; they become larger, stronger, and more complex. But a resurrection is the *reversal* of nature, the reversal of death, just as the Jubilee is the reversal of loss. The birth of nations is a natural phenomenon. But what happened to Israel was not natural. It appeared to be a birth. But it was ultimately a resurrection.

"A resurrection brings back, restores, and raises up what was dead. In AD 70 the nation or kingdom of Israel died. Death brings disintegration, the scattering of elements. So ancient Israel disintegrated, so much so that its remnants, its culture, its citizens, and its people were scattered in pieces throughout the earth. To disintegrate is natural. But to come back together is not. But against the laws of nature and history, the scattered pieces of ancient Israel began gathering back together again...the scattered bones of your vision, assembling piece by piece. So from the ends of the earth, the remnants of the ancient nation, the scattered people of Israel, began coming together: resurrection."

"And then the bones began to form skeletons."

"So too in the resurrection of Israel, the bones began to form a skeleton. The nation was first manifested in skeletal form, a skeletal culture, a skeletal government, a skeletal army, the framework of what was yet to come.

"With birth," said the Oracle, "one grows into what one has not yet been. One develops from childhood to maturity. But a resurrection is different. One doesn't begin from one's beginning; one begins from one's end, from the fully formed state of that which had once been. One becomes what one once was. So Israel wasn't born as other nations but resurrected into the fully formed pattern of what it had once been in ancient times, an ancient nation coming back into the modern world."

"And the sinews and skin that formed around the skeleton?"

"The skeletal nation began taking on flesh and blood. The pattern and framework took on flesh-and-blood reality. Israel was becoming a fully formed nation. So it all happened in reverse, as in a resurrection, as in a Jubilee."

"How exactly did it happen in reverse?"

"In the world," he said, "nations give birth to national anthems. But in Israel the anthem appeared when the nation was nothing more than a dream. The nation didn't give birth to the anthem—the anthem gave birth to the nation. In the world a settlement becomes a town and then a city and is given a name. But in Israel the names of the cities came first, before the city existed. And then they came into existence or back into existence...as it was written, 'And the city will be rebuilt on its ruin.'[2]

"In the world," said the Oracle, "languages develop over time. But with Israel its native language, Hebrew, had been dead for ages. Then a young Jewish man from eastern Europe heard a voice saying, 'the resurrection of Israel on its ancestral soil.'[3] A resurrected nation would need a resurrected language. So he made his life's mission the resurrection of the Hebrew language. The rest of his years would be spent creating a massive dictionary of a language that had been dead since ancient times. In the world languages give birth to dictionaries. But with Israel and with Hebrew it was the dictionary that gave birth to the language. And in the world it is the parents who teach the children the native language. But in Israel it was the children who taught the native language to the parents...everything in reverse...resurrection.

"Even the land itself was resurrected. Forests were planted and sprung up where ancient forests had once stood. Vineyards, olive groves, and fields of grain rose up where vineyards, olive groves, and fields of grain had once flourished but died. It had been ages since the land had seen Israeli farmers, sowers, and reapers. But a resurrected land needed to be tended. So there came another resurrection. After two thousand years resurrected Israeli farmers and vineyard keepers appeared in the land to farm and tend its resurrected fruits.

"The last Israeli soldiers died in battle against the Roman Empire, then vanished from the earth. So another resurrection began. After two thousand years the Israeli soldiers reappeared on the earth to protect the nation that had likewise died and reappeared on the earth."

"Has anything like this ever happened before?"

"The total resurrection of a nation? Never has a nation been so completely destroyed and so come back to life...or vanished from world history for thousands of years, only to reappear in modern times. And never have any people been so driven from their homeland, then gathered back together from every corner of the earth.

"Nations exist," he said, "and then are spoken of. But the Israel that was to rise from death was spoken of, prophesied of, and dreamed about for thousands of years *before* it existed. Such things have no precedent. Nor has any such thing ever been foretold thousands of years before it happened. But from ancient times it was prophesied, 'I will cause them to return to the land that I gave to their fathers, and they shall possess it.'"[4]

"When I next saw the Oracle, he would reveal the ancient mystery that lay behind an American president."

"A modern American president?"

"A twentieth-century American president."

"And it went back to ancient times?"

"It went back to an ancient king."

Chapter 29

THE PERSIAN

To find the Oracle this time, I had to walk through several of the cave's chambers. Without the light of the oil lamps it would have been impossible. I found him sitting in a chamber of stone artifacts, what you might imagine finding in the storage room of some archaeological museum. He lifted up a cylinder of hardened clay."

"That was in the vision," I said, "that exact object."

"The cylinder is an edict of King Cyrus," he said. "It's a replica, but everything's the same. Cyrus issued it soon after he conquered Babylon and assumed the throne of a world empire. He was the king you saw in your vision of the White House. It was Cyrus who allowed the Jews to return from their exile to rebuild their nation and their Holy City. There would only be two exiles in Jewish history and two returns, the first in ancient times, the second in modern times. Critical to the first return was the existence of an ancient world leader to support and sanction it, Cyrus. Likewise critical to the second return was the existence of a modern world leader to support and sanction it."

"Who?" I asked.

"The president of the United States," he replied, "Harry S. Truman. Thus the question: Could the two world leaders be linked, joined together in a mystery? Could the return of the Jewish people in modern times under Harry Truman have followed the pattern of the return in ancient times under Cyrus? And is it possible that behind a modern American president is the mystery of an ancient Persian king?"

"Is that what the vision was revealing? The man in the Oval Office was King Cyrus? And the man he became, the man in the light suit and hat, was President Truman?"

"The rise of Harry Truman to the most powerful position on earth was one of the many quirks of converging events required by the mystery. He was the most unlikely of men. It was only after failing in business that he ended up in the political realm. And remember what I told you about how he was catapulted to the presidency."

"He was made vice president just before the former president died."

"Less than three months before he died. And Truman was a student of the Bible, having read it several times through by the age of fourteen. He knew well the connection of the Jewish people to the land. And he held a deep sympathy for the plight of the Jewish people and realized their need for a safe refuge. Just as Cyrus was thrust to the pinnacle of world power to sanction the return of the Jewish people to their homeland and the nation's rebirth, so too was Truman thrust to the pinnacle of world power at the exact moment that the second return of Israel into the world was about to take place.

"Without Cyrus' support and sanction the rebirth of the Jewish nation would never have taken place. In modern times it was Truman's support and sanction that would be critical for the rebirth of the Jewish nation. And it would come through much struggle. Truman's backing of the future Jewish state was fiercely opposed by his own State Department, which appeared resolved to thwart his will on the matter at every turn. Despite this he persevered and would be pivotal in the passage of the UN resolution that would bring Israel back into existence. And then, at the moment of Israel's resurrection, it was because of Truman that America would become the first nation to grant recognition.

"And yet there are other connections between the American president and the Persian king. Cyrus began governing around the year 560 BC. He continued to reign until his death in 530 BC. So his time in government spanned…"

"Thirty years."

"Truman entered his first governmental office in January 1923. His time in government would come to an end with the end of his presidency in January 1953. Thus Truman's time in government spanned…"

"Thirty years…the same as Cyrus'."

"The seminal moment in Cyrus' rise to power came in the autumn of 539 BC. It was then that he defeated Nabonidus, the last king of the Babylonian Empire. With that the age of Babylon came to an end and the Persian age began. Cyrus was now the ruler of the largest empire ever established up to that time, the 'king of the four corners of the earth.'[1] Most scholars place Cyrus' birth between 600 and 599 BC. That would mean that when he ascended to the pinnacle of world power, he would have been around sixty years of age.

"The seminal moment in Truman's rise to world power came in the spring of 1945 when he assumed the office of the presidency. It happened at the same moment that America was assuming the mantle of world superpower. Truman was now the leader of the strongest military, political, cultural, and economic power on earth. When he came to that position of world power, he was…sixty years old. So Cyrus, at the age of sixty, ruled at the dawn of the Persian age and empire, and Truman, at the age of sixty, ruled at the dawn of the American age and superpower.

"The return of the Jewish people in ancient times took place in the aftermath of war. So too the return of the Jewish people in modern times took place in the aftermath of war, World War II. It was after emerging victorious in his war against Babylon that Cyrus issued the decree for the Jewish people to return to their land. So too it was after America emerged victorious from the Second World War that Truman began taking action that would lead to the return of the Jewish people to their land and the nation's resurrection."

"In my vision the president gave the cylinder to the eagle, which then flew away with it. What did that represent?"

"The golden eagle was a symbol of the Persian Empire and of Cyrus himself. It was Cyrus who issued the decree that opened the doors for the Jewish people to return home and rebuild their nation. In the modern world Truman would do the same.

"After Cyrus conquered Babylon, he declared the right of those who had been exiled and displaced from their lands to return home. That's what's written on this cylinder. It's been called the world's first charter of universal human rights. There exists one other document known by such words, the Universal Declaration of Human Rights. Do you know who a key champion of that declaration was? Harry Truman.

"The document specifically proclaims the right of everyone to 'return to his country.'[2] Thus in all of world history there are two leaders associated with a declaration of universal human rights and specifically the right to return to one's homeland: King Cyrus and President Truman. The date of the ancient declaration was 539 BC, the same year that Cyrus gave his sanction for the return and restoration of Israel. The date of the modern declaration was 1948, the same year that Truman gave his sanction for the return and restoration of Israel.

"Cyrus issued his decree to allow the rebuilding of Israel at the end of a critical seventy-year period of Jewish history. Is it possible that President Truman was also connected to a critical seventy-year period of Jewish history connected to Israel's rebirth? The restoration of the modern nation of Israel began in the late 1870s with the establishment of the first Jewish settlements in the land. It marked the beginning of the land's revival and the return of its people. What happens if you add seventy years to the late 1870s?"

"It takes you to the late 1940s."

"Which is the time of Truman's presidency."

"Do we know the exact year those first settlements were established?"

"Yes. It all began in the year 1878. Now add the seventy years…"

"1948!" I replied. "The year of Israel's rebirth. So Cyrus issued his decree sanctioning Israel's return at the end of seventy years, and Truman issued *his* decree sanctioning Israel's return at the end of seventy years."

"And yet," said the Oracle, "the mystery goes even deeper. Cyrus not only recognized and supported the rebirth of the Jewish nation; he specifically issued a decree to release the Jewish exiles from captivity and allow them to come home. And that all took place in his first year of world power. So is it possible that Truman followed the mystery of Cyrus in this as well? Could there be a parallel to Cyrus' word to release the Jewish exiles, and could it have taken place in the first year of Truman's presidency?

"Less than thirty days after Truman became president, the Second World War ended in Europe. The continent was now filled with those displaced by the war. Foremost among them were Jewish refugees, many of them held in camps behind barbed wire and armed guards. The British refused to let them return to their homeland.

"In the summer of 1945 the US State Department commissioned Earl Harrison to investigate the conditions of the camps and issue a report. The result, the Harrison Report, was a scathing document that likened the treatment of the Jewish refugees in the detainment camps to the treatment given them by the Nazis.[3] The report was sent to Truman in late August. One week later Truman wrote to British Prime Minister Clement Attlee citing the findings of the report with the urgent request to release one hundred thousand Jewish refugees and allow them to return to their homeland.[4]

"Attlee responded with resistance and warning. Truman in turn responded by releasing the results of the report publicly. Soon after that he authorized the release of the letter he had sent to the British prime minister. The resulting pressure forced the British Empire to begin the release of Jewish exiles to return to the land. Thousands of Jewish exiles, survivors of the Holocaust, would return to the shores of their ancient homeland. In all of history only two world leaders have issued such a word to bring about the mass return of Jewish exiles to the land: King Cyrus and President Truman. And both Cyrus and Truman would issue that word in their first year of world power.

"Truman's letter would have another consequence. The pressure of the return of the Jewish exiles to the land would ultimately lead the British Empire to end its occupation of the land, which would in turn lead to the nation's rebirth. Cyrus had brought about the end of a seventy-year exile;

Truman would ultimately bring about the end of a two-thousand-year-old exile. It was that letter that set it all in motion."

"When did he send it?" I asked.

"He sent it on August 31, 1945. It was a Friday."

"When the Sabbath begins. So there would have been an appointed Scripture sealing that day. Was it significant?"

"I would say so," the Oracle replied. "The word appointed for August 31, 1945, the day that Truman sent word to release the exiles to return to their homeland, was this:

> The LORD your God will *bring you back from captivity*, and have compassion on you, *and gather you again from all the nations* where the LORD your God has *scattered* you. If any of you are driven out to the farthest parts under heaven, from there the LORD your God *will gather you*, and from there *He will bring you*. Then the LORD your God *will bring you to the land which your fathers possessed, and you shall possess it.*[5]

"It's the prophecy of Moses," said the Oracle, "the very first prophecy to foretell Israel's regathering, the first word in Scripture to speak of the return of the exiles from captivity to the land God had given them."

"So then," I said, "on that Friday as the president sent forth the call for the exiles to return to their land, the ancient prophecy foretelling the return of the exiles to their land was being read and chanted throughout the earth."

"Yes, and Truman's letter to the British prime minister was at that time confidential. The nations had no idea it existed, but all over the world the ancient prophecy foretelling the release and return of the exiles was being proclaimed."

"Was that prophecy from the end of Deuteronomy," I asked, "from Moses' last words to Israel?"

"Yes," said the Oracle. "And do you remember what comes just before that first prophecy of the return to the land?"

"The prophecy of the stranger coming from a faraway land."

"The stranger…he would also have a part in Israel's rebirth."

"Mark Twain? But he had to have been long gone by then."

"Yes, but the mystery is not limited by death. When Truman was wrestling over whether to support the rebirth of the Jewish nation, it was the words of a quote he had kept in his office in the White House that sealed his decision."

"What was it?"

"It was 'Always do right. This will gratify some people and astonish the rest.'⁶ Truman would later recount that it was those words that were pivotal in his decision."⁷

"And..."

"They were the words of the stranger, Mark Twain. So years after his death, the stranger was still playing a part in the mystery. It was the prophecy of the stranger that led to the prophecy of Israel's return, and so it would be the stranger's own words that would lead to the prophecy's fulfillment."

"So it all had to be just as it was," I said. "Truman, the one who would follow the template of Cyrus, had to become president at that exact time, at the moment of Israel's resurrection, at the Cyrus moment. So then the Jubilean mysteries determined who would become the president of the United States."

"Yes," said the Oracle, "as they do everything else."

"In my vision the king didn't seem to realize who he was or how he was used for the purposes of God until the end. Did Truman ever realize the role he played in the mystery?"

"In the spring of 1949, a year after Israel's birth, Israel's first chief rabbi, Isaac Herzog, came to America to visit the president."

"Would he have looked like an Orthodox Jew?"

"He would have."

"Was he the man in the vision who entered the White House?"

"Yes. The rabbi told the president that when he was still in his mother's womb, the Lord had called him to be the instrument to bring about the rebirth of Israel after two thousand years. He told him that the Lord had given him the mission of helping the Jewish people at a time of despair and bringing about the fulfillment of the promise and prophecy of their return to the Promised Land.⁸ But the rabbi would become even more specific. He told Truman that in ancient times a similar mission had once been given to the leader of another great nation...Cyrus. The rabbi told Truman that Cyrus had also been given the mission of helping to redeem the Jewish people from their exile and restore them to their ancestral land. And then he read to the president the words of the ancient Persian king:

> The Lord God of heaven hath...charged me to build Him an
> house at Jerusalem, which is in Judah.⁹

"The president asked the rabbi if the hand of the Almighty was in his actions toward the Jewish people. The rabbi responded that Truman had been given the task once fulfilled by King Cyrus and that he, like Cyrus, would hold a place of honor in the history of the Jewish people.

"The president was so overcome with emotion at the rabbi's words that tears began welling up in his eyes and streaming down his cheeks.[10]

"King Cyrus began several of his inscriptions with the words 'I am Cyrus.' The words would be engraved on his tomb. Years after his encounter with the rabbi, Truman was attending a gathering in New York City. It was then that he would utter the words that would sum up the mystery of his life and his part in the Jubilean mysteries."

"What did he say?"

"He said...

I am Cyrus."[11]

"When I next saw the Oracle, he would open the mystery of another reappearance."

"What do you mean?"

"Cyrus wasn't the only ancient figure to 'reappear' on the modern world stage. There would be another mystery and another person."

"Who?"

"One just as fascinating. One who was, who was not, and who would be again."

"And how was it revealed to you?"

"Through the boy I met on the seashore, the boy of the arch."

Chapter 30

THE MAN WHO WAS

I RETURNED TO THE cave. The Oracle was sitting by its entrance. I joined him there."

———————

"The arch on the shore...what was that?" I asked.

"That would be the Arch of Titus," he said. "Titus was the Roman general who destroyed Jerusalem and the nation of Israel in AD 70. He would later become emperor. After his death an arch would be built in his honor, the Arch of Titus."

"Why was it in my vision?"

"Because on the Arch of Titus are engraved images depicting the destruction of the Jewish nation."

"That's what I saw...and then the images of restoration."

"Images of Israel's resurrection."

"What about the boy?" I asked. "What did he represent?"

"What did he tell you about himself?"

"He said, 'I was, was not, and was again.'"

"There's a prophecy of the Bible that when the nation of Israel is reborn, they will have as their leader a man called David. Ultimately it's a prophecy of the Messiah, who will come from the line of David. But it's worthy of note that when Israel was reborn, its first leader happened to be a man named David. The nation's first prime minister was David Ben-Gurion. That was the boy in your vision. That's what he looked like as a child. It was Ben-Gurion who would proclaim Israel's resurrection to the world."

"But what does he have to do with the arch?"

"The arch commemorates Israel's death. Your vision was ultimately about its resurrection, the reversal of that death. If a nation's land is resurrected, and its cities, its language, its soldiers, and its farmers, should not then its leaders be resurrected as well?"

"Its leaders resurrected? What does that mean?"

"Before the Jewish nation was destroyed in AD 70, a provisional government was formed of its leaders to guide the nation in its war against Rome. This would be its last unified government before its destruction. Among the most prominent of these was a man who would be revered in the ages to come as a hero and martyr in that final and ill-fated war. Do you know who that leader was?"

"No."

"Ben-Gurion."

"Ben-Gurion?"

"Yes."

"What do you mean?"

"It's the Jubilean mystery of reversal and return. In the last days before its destruction the Jewish nation was led by a man named Ben-Gurion. Therefore, in the first days after its resurrection the Jewish nation was led by a man named Ben-Gurion."

"How did that happen?"

"Israel's first prime minister wasn't born David Ben-Gurion. He was born David Grün. When he was a boy, a tall man with dark hair and a long, dark beard visited his home city of Plonsk, Poland. The man was Theodor Herzl. Ben-Gurion was enthralled by the visitor and made it his goal to one day stand on the shores of his ancient homeland. In 1906 he returned. In his first few years in the land he worked in agriculture. But in 1910 he reluctantly accepted a job working as a journalist at his friend's Zionist journal. He decided to choose a pen name. In Hebrew the name *Grün* was very similar to the name *Gurion*. He also knew that in ancient times a man named Ben-Gurion was prominent in leading the Jewish revolt against Rome. So he would sign his articles with the pen name Ben-Gurion. It would end up becoming his official name. So a young man, unsettled on his career, just happens to pick as his pen name the same name as the nation's ancient leader in the days of its end...and by a multitude of the twists and turns of personal, national, and world events, nearly forty years later he would become the nation's first leader in the days of its resurrection.

"The ancient Ben-Gurion was appointed leader in Jerusalem. The modern Ben-Gurion became Ben-Gurion when he began dwelling in Jerusalem. The ancient Ben-Gurion's full name was Joseph Ben-Gurion. The modern Ben-Gurion was born with a middle name, Joseph. So he was now David... Joseph Ben-Gurion.

"The ancient Ben-Gurion was appointed leader in a council that constituted the Judean provisional government. The modern Ben-Gurion was appointed leader in a council that constituted Israel's provisional government. The ancient provisional government proclaimed the existence of a sovereign Jewish nation to Rome. The modern provisional government proclaimed the existence of a sovereign Jewish nation to the world.

"The ancient Ben-Gurion was in charge of his people's military defense. The modern Ben-Gurion was not only Israel's first prime minister but the one in charge of its military defense, Israel's first minister of defense. The ancient Ben-Gurion helped lead his people in a war that would result in his nation's destruction. The modern Ben-Gurion helped lead his people in a war that would result in his nation's resurrection."

"What happened to the ancient Ben-Gurion?"

"The ancient Ben-Gurion would be seen as a moderate and a unifying force. But in the course of the revolt, extremist militant factions rose up against him and those who governed with him. He would be killed in that uprising."

"Was there any parallel to the modern Ben-Gurion?"

"The modern Ben-Gurion would also be seen as a moderate within the Israeli political spectrum and a unifying force. In the resurrection of Israel there would likewise arise extremist militant factions. And their existence would likewise be a challenge to Ben-Gurion's authority and government. But it was now the time of reversal. So what happened next would be the reversal of what happened in ancient times. Ben-Gurion would forcibly disarm the militant factions and unify the nation's military forces.

"As for ancient Israel, the rise of the extremist factions would lead to chaos, the destruction of Jerusalem, and the nation's end. But the rise of the modern Ben-Gurion would lead to the reverse, unity, national rebirth, and ultimately the restoration of the nation's government in Jerusalem."

"So the ancient Ben-Gurion disappears," I said, "and then the Jewish nation likewise disappears. But in the modern world Ben-Gurion reappears, and then the Jewish nation likewise reappears."

"Yes," said the Oracle. "That which disappeared with the ancient Ben-Gurion—the Israeli soldier, the Israeli government, the Jewish nation— would all reappear with the reappearance of Ben-Gurion in the modern world. Or you could say that the transformation of a man in the modern world named David Grün into a man from the ancient world, Ben-Gurion, would lead to the transformation of a people in the modern world into a nation from the ancient world. And it would all be crystallized on May 14, 1948, as a short and stocky man with a halo of white hair read the words of a hastily written document into a cluster of microphones before the world. Those hearing his words had little idea that the speaker himself was the embodiment of the mystery manifesting before the world. The man who announced the resurrection of the ancient nation was himself a living resurrection of what had perished in ancient times.

"The event was the reversal of what had taken place in the war of the ancient Ben-Gurion. The Jewish people had lost their government, their citizenship, and their nation. Now, as the modern Ben-Gurion spoke, all those things came back into the world. In the aftermath of the war waged by the ancient Ben-Gurion, the Jewish people were taken captive and exiled to the ends of the earth. But in the aftermath of the war waged by the modern Ben-Gurion, the gates would be open for the exiles to return home from the ends of the earth."

"Ben Gurion," I said, "was following the Jubilean ordinance."

"Yes," said the Oracle, "but how do you mean that?"

"The one who is separated from his land must return to it. So in ancient times Ben-Gurion was separated from the Jewish nation... But after two thousand years Ben Gurion returned to it... each to his own possession."

"So he did."

"And his declaration," I said, "would be answered from across the world by President Truman—two world leaders, each living out the template of a leader from ancient times, and each fulfilling their part in the ancient mystery... and the world had no idea."

"No, the world had no idea," he replied. "But, nevertheless, its future would be determined by it."

"The next mystery would open up one of the most amazing of ancient words ever given concerning an event that would take place in the modern world. It would comprise another prophetic convergence of time and space."

"And how would it be revealed?"

"Through a prophet... and a king I met while walking."

Chapter 31

THE DAY OF AMOS

WHEN I FOUND the Oracle, he was sitting in one of the chambers of the cave I had never before entered, a small chamber, illuminated by the light of oil lamps. There was nothing of note within it except a short, wide stone platform, upon which rested an open scroll, the text of which I took to be Hebrew."

"The king on the seashore," I said, "and the man who helped him build the house of branches...who were they?"

"The king you saw was David, the founder of the nation's royal dynasty."

"And the man who helped him rebuild?"

"The bearer of burdens. In Hebrew the name *Amos* means burden bearer. It was the prophet Amos."

"And the house of branches?"

"In Hebrew a house or shelter of branches is called a *sukkah*, or tabernacle. The house of branches belonged to the king. The vision concerned the tabernacle of David."

"The tabernacle of David?"

"The phrase appears several times in the Scriptures. It has many layers of meaning, but it certainly refers to David's kingdom and thus the nation of Israel. In your vision it was fallen. So in ancient times the kingdom of Israel had collapsed. The tabernacle of David had fallen."

"The man offered to help the king raise it up. What did that mean?"

"It was Amos through whom the most famous prophecy concerning the tabernacle of David was given, a prophecy that would foretell the raising up of the fallen tabernacle. In the modern world that tabernacle was raised up on May 14, 1948, the day of Israel's birth, a day of prophecy. The nation that had closed its eyes in ancient times in a war of flaming arrows and siegeworks now opened them in an age of atomic weapons and superpowers."

"What was the prophecy?"

The Oracle leaned over to examine the scroll. Using his hand to find the place, he began to read, or rather to translate, the ancient words:

"On that day I will raise up the tabernacle of David, which has
fallen down.[1]

"The kingdom of David, the nation of Israel, had fallen. But in the end
times God would restore it. So in the birth of Israel in 1948 the tabernacle
of David was raised up; the nation that had once stood in ancient times had
been destroyed but was now being resurrected. The prophecy continues:

And I will repair its damages; I will raise up its ruins.[2]

"So the nation that had been broken for two thousand years and a land
that had been covered in ruins would now be repaired."

"What does that mean, to raise up the ruins?"

"The ancient cities that now lie in ruins would be rebuilt. The fallen
buildings of the land would rise again. And on the ruins of a civilization
that had fallen, a new nation would rise. The prophecy goes on:

...and rebuild it as in the days of old.[3]

"The new nation was to be rebuilt 'as in the days of old.' So Israel would
be rebuilt as it had been in ancient times. Its language would be rebuilt as
in days of old, its people, its land, its army, its government, its culture, the
nation itself. The prophecy continues:

I will bring my people Israel back from *exile*.[4]

"The regathering of the Jewish people began in the days before the nation
was born, but its greatest fulfillment would come after its birth as Jewish
people began returning in unprecedented numbers from the far corners of
the earth.

They shall build the waste cities and inhabit them.[5]

"Which is exactly what happened as the Israelis built new cities on the
ruins of the ancient ones. The prophecy goes on:

They shall plant vineyards and drink wine from them; they
shall also make gardens and eat fruit from them.[6]

"So the prophecy foretold what would happen to the land that had for
ages been barren desolation. Those who would return from exile would
plant the barren land. It would blossom and bear fruit."

"Amazingly accurate."

"Yes," said the Oracle, "but there's more to the mystery. In the declaration that Ben-Gurion read on May 14, 1948, are the words 'Sabbath eve.'[7]
That's when the declaration was read."

"So it happened on a Friday."

"The declaration went forth on Friday, late afternoon, at the approach of the Sabbath. And then at the stroke of midnight the British occupation came to an end and the nation was born. The Sabbath begins at sundown Friday night and lasts until sundown Saturday. Israel came into existence in that exact space of time, as Friday night turned into Saturday. The nation was born on the Sabbath."

"So then there was a Scripture appointed for the day of its birth."

"Yes, it came from the haftarah scroll."

"What's that?"

"The scroll of the prophets. Its appointed word consists of much shorter passages, most often just a handful of verses. On the day Israel was reborn, there was a word from the prophets appointed from ages past to be proclaimed at that very moment, from sundown Friday night to sundown the next day, the very space of time in which the ancient nation was raised back to life."

"So what was the word appointed for May 14, 1948?"

"It was this:

> On that day I will raise up the tabernacle of David, which has
> fallen down."[8]

"The appointed word was the very Scripture that speaks of what took place on that exact day! The appointed word on May 14, 1948, the day the tabernacle of David was raised up, was the word that speaks of the day that the tabernacle of David would be raised up!"

"Yes," said the Oracle, "Israel's birth took place on the day appointed for the prophecy of Israel's birth...the fingerprints of God."

"So as Ben-Gurion was announcing the raising up of the ancient nation, the appointed word was that which spoke of the raising up of the nation of Israel."

"Yes. And the appointed word would foretell not only what would happen to Israel but what would be proclaimed to the world that day.

"The ancient word appointed for that day prophesied,

> I will bring my people Israel back from exile.[9]

"So the declaration proclaimed that Israel would be open for...

> ...the Ingathering of the Exiles.[10]

"The ancient word appointed for that day had prophesied,

> They shall build the waste cities and inhabit them.[11]

"So the declaration of that day proclaimed that the exiles had…

> …built villages and towns, and created a thriving community.[12]

"The appointed word prophesied the exiles would plant the land that had been a barren devastation and make it blossom:

> They shall plant vineyards…they shall also make gardens.[13]

"So the declaration spoke of the planting of the land by the returning exiles:

> They made deserts bloom…[14]

"And note," said the Oracle, "when Israel's birth was announced to the world, there was by no means any assurance that it would survive. On the following day, when the surrounding Arab nations launched the war intended to uproot the Jewish nation at the moment of its birth, many doubted that there would still be an Israel at the war's end. But the last words of the prophecy appointed for that day contained a promise:

> "I will plant them in their land, and no longer shall they be pulled up from the land I have given them," says the LORD your God.[15]

"All these things were contained in that one prophecy, the raising up of the fallen tabernacle, the rebuilding of the ruins, the restoring of the cities, the planting of the land, the survival of the nation, and the ending of the exile…and all of them were appointed for the day that Israel's exile would come to an end."

"At the end of my vision five white flowers blossomed in front of the rebuilt tabernacle. What did that mean?"

"In Hebrew the word *iyar* means blossom. May 14, 1948, was the fifth day of the Hebrew month of Iyar."

"Who decided that Israel would be born on that particular Sabbath?"

"It just happened to be the day set for the British to depart from the land. You see, even empires must follow His purposes.

"And so on the day of Israel's resurrection, all around the world the ancient prophecy was being chanted in Hebrew. They chanted the raising up of David's tabernacle, the rebuilding of its cities, the ending of its exile, the planting of its soil, and its survival against all odds by the hand of God. And so the ancient exile came to an end and the nation was reborn as the appointed prophecy foretelling the end of the exile and the nation's rebirth was recited throughout the earth."

"There would be one more mystery to be revealed before the mysteries of the third door would be finished and the mysteries of the fourth door could be opened. It was a mystery unlike the others, something of an ancient code, a cipher embedded into the Jubilean ordinance itself."

"And how was it revealed?"

"Through the keys of the wandering man."

Chapter 32

THE JUBILEAN CODE

THE ORACLE WAS sitting in the same chamber in which I found him the first time I entered the cave. 'This,' he said as I sat down beside him, 'will be the last time we meet in this place. And this will be the last revelation of the third door, the third stream of the mysteries.'

"I had come to find the meaning of the man with the four keys. I brought a paper on which I had written the shape of each key as best I remembered it. I had shown it to him when I first shared the vision, but I thought it wise to remind him."

"So what was the meaning," I asked, "of the four jeweled keys?"

"When Israel came back into the world," he said, "the nation's gates were opened wide for the return of the Jewish people in numbers never before witnessed. From every corner of the globe they returned to the ancestral land. 1948 was the year of Israel's return and the return of her children. When was it," he asked, "that the nation was first given the command to return?"

"In the Book of Deuteronomy?" I replied.

"That was the first *prophecy* of the return, but when was the *command* to return first given?"

"In the Jubilee?" I replied. "In the Jubilee they were commanded to return."

"Yes. It first appears in the law of Jubilees. It's there where the command 'you shall return' was first given in the plural to the many, to the entire nation. That's the first thing to understand. The second is that in Hebrew, numbers are represented by letters. For example, the first letter, *aleph*, denotes the number 1. The second letter, *beit*, denotes the number 2. Other Hebrew letters stand for tens, hundreds, and thousands. And the third is that Hebrew years are different from the Western years. For example, on the Western calendar the year 1900, up until the autumn of that year, was the Hebrew year 5660.

"So if you were going by the Hebrew calendar, how would you write out the year 1900?"

"As 5660."

"Yes, except in Hebrew, letters are used to represent numbers."

"So then I would use letters that add up to 5660."

"That's right," he said, "except it's simpler than that. In Hebrew dating, the millennium is taken for granted. So the letter representing the millennium is either absent or written separately from the other letters. So you only need to use the Hebrew letters that add up to 660, and by that the year 1900 would be identified."

"If every Hebrew letter represents a number," I said, "then every Hebrew word has a numerical value."

"Technically, yes. And there are those who seek numerical meaning for every word. But this is something else. This is simply the standard way of writing out or identifying a year in Hebrew.

"Now we can open up the mystery. In the Jubilean ordinance in Leviticus 25 it is written: '*You shall return*, each one to his own family.'[1] Three verses later it is written, '*You shall return*, each one to his possession, his ancestral land.'[2] The words *you shall return* are the translation of just one Hebrew word: *tashuvu*."

"*Tashuvu*."

"*Tashuvu* is the Jubilean command contained in one word. Hidden in that one Hebrew word is a secret that spans the ages, a mystery of four Hebrew letters."

"Four Hebrew letters," I said. "They were the four keys, the four symbols in my vision. The four keys were the letters of *tashuvu*."

"Yes," said the Oracle. "It was all there in your vision at the end when the man was told that by these keys *you shall return*. He was referring to the Jubilean command. *You shall return* is *tashuvu*, and the word is made of four Hebrew letters."

"But I didn't recognize the keys as Hebrew letters."

"The symbols you showed me," he said, "*were* Hebrew, just a different kind of Hebrew, the most ancient of Hebrew scripts, Paleo-Hebrew. In your vision the wandering man represented the Jewish people in the wanderings of their exile. The man was continually trying to unlock the doors of his exile. So the Jewish people in their wanderings continually longed to return to their homeland."

"But the man couldn't open any of the doors."

"And the Jewish people couldn't open the doors of their return until the appointed time."

"If the keys are letters," I asked, "then are the letters also keys? Does the Hebrew word for *you shall return* itself contain the mystery concerning the return of the Jewish people to the land?"

"The four Hebrew letters of *tashuvu* are the letter *tav*, the letter *shin*, the letter *beit*, and the letter *vav*. And remember, each letter is also a number. *Tav* is the Hebrew number for *400*. *Shin* is the Hebrew number *300*. *Beit* is the Hebrew number *2*. And *vav* is the Hebrew number *6*. 400, 300, 2, and 6. What number does the word *tashuvu* come out to?"

"708," I replied.

"708. That's correct. Now tell me," he said, "what year do those Hebrew letters and that word pinpoint on the Western calendar?"

"If the Hebrew letters for 660 stand for 1900," I said, "then 708 is…48 years later. So the Hebrew letters stand for…the year…1948!"

"Yes," said the Oracle, "the word *tashuvu* pinpoints the year 1948."

"1948! The year Israel came back into the world."

"The year of the return."

"Amazing! And so the Hebrew word that means *you shall return* contains the secret of the time when the nation of Israel would return! The ancient Jubilean ordinance actually identifies the year of Israel's return!"

"And in what command does that Hebrew word appear? The command to return to your possession, to your ancestral land. So the Jewish people returned to their ancestral possession in 1948."

The Oracle paused for a moment, then spoke.

"And there's more to the mystery. Further on in the Bible the word *tashuvu* is written differently, with a second *vav*; so too in modern Hebrew. But in Leviticus 25 it appears without the second *vav*. It's all the more striking since it is this particular spelling that appears in the Jubilean ordinance at the mystery's inception. But remember what I told you about Hebrew dates: one letter or numeral is kept either absent or separated from the others."

"The letter that represents the millennium."

"Yes, so in the case of *tashuvu* the missing or separated letter is already identified—the Hebrew letter *vav*."

"So then could it stand for the millennium?" I asked.

"The full Hebrew year was 5708. And the number 5 would commonly be used to represent the millennium. But which millennium actually was it? In which millennium of the Hebrew calendar did Israel actually return?"

"It was in the sixth millennium."

"So the missing or separated number, the number of the millennium, would be 6. And what Hebrew letter stands for the number 6?"

I was silent.

"The letter that stands for 6 is the *vav*. And the *vav* is the *missing* or *separated* letter of *tashuvu*. So the return of the nation would take place in the year 708 of the sixth millennium. Or, in other words, the 6 would indicate how many times the number 708 would recur in the Hebrew calendar. On its sixth recurrence they would return...which comes out to the year 1948."

"At the end of my vision the man opened the fourth door and entered a room filled with people. It was the room in which the declaration of Israel's birth was proclaimed, wasn't it?"

"Yes. And at the very end of that declaration and document appears the Hebrew year, 1948, when Israel returned home.

"So it was all there in the ancient law of the Jubilee, in the command to return to your ancestral possession. It was all there from the very beginning of the mystery! It was all there from the beginning in the very words they were given in the desert: 'You shall return.'"

"That was the final mystery the Oracle revealed to me in the cave. Now I would wait for the vision that would lead me to open the next door, the fourth door."

"And what mysteries would it hold?"

"A Jubilee of lightning, a song of prophecy, the shaking of nations, the man with the trumpet, the return of the priests, a mystery of lions, a man called the Nazir, a time code hidden on a mountaintop, a day two thousand years in the making, and much more."

"So you opened the fourth door..."

THE FOURTH DOOR

Chapter 33

THE FOURTH DOOR

I T WAS A cold night. I was bundled up in my tent when the vision began. I stood in front of the fourth door with the Oracle at my side. I opened it and walked through. I was again on top of the desert mountain, and there again was the old man in the red robe, Moses. At his side was a ram. There was nothing especially distinctive about it except that it was younger and thinner than the other rams I had seen. Around its neck was a chain and pendant, on which was a symbol that matched that of the fourth door.

"The ram made its way down the mountain and across a desert plain. I followed. It turned its gaze to the right. I did likewise, and the visions began."

TEN MEN WITH TORCHES

"I saw a band of men with torches, journeying through the desert by night. There were ten of them, including their leader, a man in a fedora. They arrived at a mountain. In its base was an opening, a shaft. They entered it. Guided by the light of their torches, they made their way through stone chambers, stone steps, and stone passageways. Finally they came to an entranceway that was sealed with a large boulder. They rolled it away and entered a circular chamber. All around the chamber were openings, ten of them, the entrances to ancient-looking tombs. The ten men approached the tombs, holding up their torches to see what appeared to be an engraving in the rock face over each entrance. Engraved above each tomb was the image of an ancient soldier. The face of each soldier matched the face of the man viewing it. Then I heard a voice. 'You have returned,' it said, 'and have opened up your own tombs.'"

THE WILLOW AND THE HARP

"The ram resumed its journey, then stopped again and turned its gaze. I turned as well. I saw a bearded man in a ragged, dust-covered robe. He was sitting under a tree by a river. Hanging above him on the branches was a harp. He stood up, pulled it out, and sat down again, now with a harp in his lap. He began plucking its strings and singing. It was a song of mourning and longing. As the song continued, the sky began to darken

139

and the sound of war grew louder and louder. When the song ended, there was silence. In the sky above a distant mountain was a blinding radiance, as if from a thousand suns."

THE CLOUD PROCESSION

"I turned again and saw a great procession of men in white robes and white cloth hats moving through the desert. Those in front were bearing on their shoulders a tent. Above the tent was a cloud that appeared to move as they moved, or they moved as it moved. Finally they reached the gate of a city, the doors of which had been removed and were lying on the ground. In front of the gate was what appeared to be a gathering of ancient warriors. The warriors parted to the sides to allow the procession to pass through the gate. Then they passed through as well and, as they did, were transformed. They were now dressed in modern army fatigues of olive green, holding guns and radio transmitters. The procession now began ascending a mountain inside the city walls. The men in white and the soldiers who flanked them were now illuminated by the cloud that moved above them and that was now bursting with light."

THE CHARIOT RIDER

"In the next vision I saw a man standing in a stationary chariot. He was arrayed in an ornate robe and had Middle Eastern features, black curly hair, and a full black beard. 'Come,' he said, 'and I'll take you to the city. I know the way. I've been there before.'"

"He said that to whom?"

"To me. So I stepped into the chariot, and we rode away. 'It's not far,' he said, 'only nineteen minutes.' We rode through plains, valleys, and terraced hills. Finally we arrived at our destination, the walled city. I knew it was Jerusalem. 'Who are you?' I asked the man. 'A king,' he said, 'but not of this land...but from the land of two rivers.' I stepped out of the chariot and entered the city."

THE MAN IN THE BLACK ROBE

"I turned again and saw a city on fire and people fleeing it in every direction. In their midst was a man in a black robe with a hood that covered his head—likewise fleeing. The scene changed. I was now standing on a ship filled with slaves in chains. One of them stood out from the rest. It was the man in the black robe. The scene changed again. It now seemed to be something out of the Middle Ages—a procession of men, women, and children, all carrying baggage. Some were crying. In the distance was a burning village. I knew it was their village. And there in the procession was the man in the black robe. Again the scene changed, scene after scene, each of some kind of calamity or sorrow, and departure. And in every scene he was there, the man in the black robe. Finally I approached him. 'Who are you?' I asked. 'My name,' he said, 'is Separation.'"

THE IMAGE OF A SIEGE

"I turned again and saw a bearded man in ancient garments walking along a bas-relief carved in the side of a mountain. It depicted the siege of an ancient city; ancient horsemen, soldiers, archers, and lancers; after that colossal birds; and finally lions just as colossal as the birds. The man turned to the engraved lions and spoke to them. They began to move and then to emerge from the wall. They now stood as giant statues, except they were moving. In the distant landscape a war was raging. The lions set out in the direction of the battle. I watched as they encircled one of its mountains and two of them made their way up to its peak, where one of them roared. When the battle ended, the lions returned to the mountain, where they reentered its side and resumed their original positions in the stone relief."

THE THRESHING FLOOR

"In the next vision I was standing in a meadow. To my right were two angels in the midst of a conversation. 'Who will perform the sounding?' the one asked the other. 'Come,' said the other, 'and I'll show you.' They walked through a meadow until they came upon a little boy sitting on the grass, dressed in the black clothing of an Orthodox Jew. The two angels sat down beside him, one on each side. One of them handed him an object. It was a ram's horn. 'When am I to sound it?' asked the boy. 'At the time of the harvest,' said the angel, 'and in the place of the threshing floor.' The scene now changed. The fields and hills were now filled with workers reaping the harvest. 'It's time!' said the boy. He ascended a high hill and entered the gate of a threshing floor made up of golden stones. He then took out the ram's horn and sounded it. When the people heard the sound, they began converging on the threshing floor with rejoicing and tears."

THE SUNDIAL

"In the last of the visions within the vision, I found myself standing in front of an antiquities store. I went inside and began browsing through its pottery, coins, oil lamps, and other ancient artifacts. 'Can I help you?' asked the man in the store. 'I'm just looking,' I replied. 'You're looking for answers,' he said. 'Come.' He led me over to a square plate of stone covered with markings. Engraved on the plate was the image of two mountains, one on each side of the stone. 'It's a sundial,' he said, 'but no ordinary sundial. Watch what it does.' As I looked, the shadow began moving across its surface from the engraving of the one mountain to that of the other. We were inside, so it had nothing to do with the sun. 'Keep watching,' he said. The shadow now began reversing its motion, moving back from the other mountain to the one. 'This,' he said, 'is the clock of restorations.'"

"The larger vision now moved toward its conclusion. I followed the ram through the desert. I began to hear low rumblings, the sound of war. I could now see armies lining up in the distance on every side. The rumblings were growing louder and louder. The armies were drawing near. I feared for the ram. But just then a transformation began. The ram began increasing in size and appearing more and more lionlike."

"As in the vision of the lions."

"Yes. And whenever the ram moved, it was as if its movements were generating flashes of lightning and peals of thunder. The ram then ascended the mountain of the ancient walled city. It turned its gaze to one of the city's closed gates and began to charge it. As its horns struck the gate, the doors burst open and fell off. The ram then entered the walled city, followed by a great procession. And the vision ended."

Chapter 34

THE YEAR OF THE KIRYAH

I KNEW IT WAS only a matter of time before I would see him."

"The boy..."

"Yes. It was the next morning. I was getting ready for the day. In the corner of my eye I noticed a movement in the tent curtains. I pulled them aside, and there he was. He had grown bolder. He had been peering in to see if I was awake. He smiled and motioned for me to come.

"I followed him through a plain, alongside a mountain, and through a winding canyon. At the end of the canyon was a small valley. In the middle of the valley was something of a garden, hedged in by a low wall of irregular stones, a little over three feet high. He led me through the gate. The garden was filled with all types of trees—olive trees, fig trees, palm trees—and flowers and plants and vines. And there were gardens within the garden, each in a compartment framed by the same low stone wall that enclosed everything. And then I saw him."

"The Oracle."

"He was sitting on a rock surrounded by flowers of different colors and varieties."

"Welcome," he said. "It's a little pleasure of mine, bringing life to the desert. Join me."

So I sat down on a rock beside him and told him the vision.

"The ram you saw behind the third door stood for the Jubilee that was unlike the others and of its own fifty-year cycle. But when you walked through the fourth door, you were taken back to the mountain you had seen at the beginning. Thus you were returning to the larger mystery and the progression, that which began with the Jubilean year of 1867 and continued into that of 1917. What you saw behind the fourth door is the continuation of the larger progression. So the ram you saw behind the fourth door represented..."

"The next Jubilee."

"Yes. Remember, each of the Jubilean years sets in motion the events of the next cycle. So the next Jubilee would seal the cycle begun in 1917."

"What events did the Jubilee of 1917 set in motion?"

"It would set in motion the fall of the Ottoman Empire and ultimately the defeat of the Central Powers in the First World War. The consequences and repercussions of that fall would lead to the Second World War and beyond. The central document of that Jubilee, the Balfour Declaration, would lead to the British Mandate, in which Great Britain would administer the land of Israel in view of a future national home for the Jewish people. Beyond that the declaration would be critical in the rebirth of Israel. It was President Truman's belief in that declaration as an unbreakable promise that strongly influenced his decision to support Israel's rebirth.

"The Jubilee of 1917 would continue to shape the history of the Middle East and the world for decades to come. It would dramatically open the gates for the exiles of Israel to return home in unprecedented numbers. By the mid-1930s the number of Jewish people in the land was over six times larger than what it had been in 1917. At the time of Israel's rebirth it was over ten times larger, and just two years later, over twenty times larger. Before the eyes of a world that had just entered the Cold War and the nuclear age the words of the ancient prophecies were being fulfilled:

> Behold, I will bring them from the north country, and gather
> them from the ends of the earth, among them the blind and
> the lame, the woman with child and the one who labors
> with child, together; a great throng shall return there. They
> shall come with weeping, and with supplications I will lead
> them.... Hear the word of the LORD, O nations, and declare
> it in the isles afar off, and say, 'He who scattered Israel will
> gather him, and keep him as a shepherd does his flock.'"[1]

The Oracle paused, looked into the distance, then turned to me. "So then," he said, "according to the mystery, when would the next Jubilee come?"

"The fiftieth year after 1917..."

"Which is?"

"1967."

"So if the mystery continues..."

"It doesn't have to?"

"The mystery continues as long as He wills it to. So if it continues, the appointed year will be..."

"1967."

"And so the mystery ordains that 1967 will be the year in which a prophetic event will take place. And if we take what the mystery has revealed thus far, what would it tell us about what would happen in 1967?"

"It would involve a return, an event of restoration, the regaining of an inheritance...the coming home of those who were separated from their ancestral possession."

"And what would that regaining and restoration be? In the late 1940s Israel regained its nationhood. But there was still a crucial part of the ancestral possession that was missing."

"Jerusalem."

"Jerusalem," he repeated. "And so in your vision the symbol on the fourth door and on the ram was the Hebrew letter *kof*. It stands for the Hebrew word *kiryah*. It means city. So the coming Jubilee would concern the city."

"Jerusalem."

"So if the mystery continues to manifest, it would ordain 1967 as the year in which an event of prophetic restoration would take place, when that which was lost would be returned to those to whom it belongs...and the event would be connected to Jerusalem."

"Was it?" I asked.

"That," said the Oracle, "we shall see."

"So what did you see?"

"A mountain on which was a prophecy waiting for two thousand years to be uncovered. And the moment it would be uncovered, the prophecy would be fulfilled."

"And how would it be revealed?"

"Through the ten men with torches."

Chapter 35

THE PARCHMENT

I RETURNED TO THE garden. The Oracle was now sitting under a low and wide-spreading tree, something I could picture growing in the plains of Africa. I sat down beside him."

"It's an acacia tree," he said. "It grows in the desert."

"The vision of the men with the torches who entered the mountain and stood in front of the tombs...what did it mean?"

"In the year AD 70 the armies of Rome destroyed the Temple of Jerusalem, the city, and the nation. But there was one last stronghold. It was called Masada. The word means fortress. Masada was a mountain fortress built by King Herod the Great and then taken over by Zealots, Jewish revolutionaries central in Israel's war against Rome. When Jerusalem fell, Zealots, soldiers, and refugees fled the city and joined the resistance in Masada. So the center of the Jewish struggle moved from Jerusalem, now in ruins, to the desert mountain fortress.

"Eventually the Roman army, under the command of Flavius Silva, laid siege to Masada. According to the ancient account, when the Roman soldiers reached the top, they found the fighters and resisters dead, slain by their own hand. Rather than be taken captive by Rome, the soldiers had decided to take their own lives and die as free men. So they drew lots to appoint the executioners, ten men, who in turn drew lots to appoint the final executioner, who would then in turn die by his own hand."[1]

"Ten men, the band of ten men in the vision."

"So Masada," said the Oracle, "was the place of Israel's last stand."

"In the vision there were tombs. Are there tombs in Masada?"

"Masada itself is the tomb...the tomb of ancient Israel and the resting place of the last soldiers of that war. The nation's ancient grave stood abandoned for ages in the desert wilderness as the Jewish people wandered the earth. But after two thousand years the nation that vanished with Masada was resurrected. The last of the ancient Israelis to stand on the mountaintop were the soldiers that had perished in Masada's fall. So according to the Jubilean dynamic of reversal, the first Israelis to return to Masada..."

"Would be soldiers. Did that actually happen?"

"In the first years of the nation's rebirth, Israeli soldiers were drawn to the ancient fortress. They began making pilgrimages to the desert mountain."

"Each shall return to his own possession," I replied. "Masada was the possession of the Israeli soldier. So that's where they returned to."

"And not only these but soldiers in the Israeli army, having completed their basic training, would be taken to the top of the mountain to be sworn in as they vowed, 'Masada shall not fall again.' But Masada wasn't the possession of the Israeli soldiers alone. It belonged to the nation."

"So then Israel had to return to Masada?"

"Yes, and it would happen in the early 1960s. The resurrected nation would return to its ancient grave to excavate it. After two thousand years it would be uncovered."

"So Israel was opening up its own grave...as were the men of the vision."

"The leader of the ancient Israelis on Masada was a military commander. The man who led Israel's return to Masada was also a military commander. His name was Yigael Yadin. He had been a general in the newborn Israeli army, its head of operations in 1948, the war of its birth, and after that its chief of staff.

"So the commander of Israel's last army would be linked to Masada's loss and the nation's end. But the man who led Israel back to Masada would command its first army and be linked to the nation's resurrection. In fact Yadin had been hailed as the architect of Israel's War of Independence, the war that brought Israel back from the dead.[2] And as Masada's last leader was central in the end of Israel's army, Yadin would be instrumental in the resurrection of that army. He would be credited as the creator of Israel's standing and reserve military forces, its resurrected army."

"So the one who was central in the nation's resurrection would be the one to uncover its grave."

"It could be said that he was born to uncover it. His original last name was Sukenik. His father was Eliezer Sukenik..."

"The man who uncovered the Dead Sea Scrolls."

"Yes. And now his son was about to uncover another ancient mystery.

"So in the mid-1960s Yadin led thousands of volunteers from Israel and around the world back to the desert fortress. Central in that expedition was the Israeli army. The military provided Yadin with equipment, support, and men to help with the excavation. The modern Israeli soldiers represented the resurrection of the ancient Israeli soldiers...and they were now returning to their ancient graves to open them up. They had no idea that hidden in the sands of Masada was a mystery that had been waiting for two thousand years to be uncovered. It was buried in the mountain's ancient synagogue. And the one who uncovered it was also an Israeli soldier."

"What was it?"

"The word of God…parchments of Scripture, the most prominent of these being a prophecy…from the Book of Ezekiel."

"What was the prophecy?"

"It came in a vision." The Oracle then began reciting the word hidden for two thousand years on the desert mountain:

> "The hand of the LORD…set me down in the midst of the
> valley; and it was full of bones."[3]

"The valley of dry bones! The prophecy of Israel's resurrection!"

The Oracle continued:

> "And He said to me, 'Son of man, can these bones live?'"[4]

"So hidden in the nation's grave was the prophecy of its resurrection!"

"Yes," said the Oracle, who then continued reciting the words of the ancient vision:

> "So I prophesied as I was commanded; and as I prophesied,
> there was a noise, and suddenly a rattling; and the bones came
> together, bone to bone…and flesh came upon them.…And
> breath came into them, and they lived, and stood upon their
> feet, an exceedingly great army. Then He said to me, 'Son of
> man, these bones are the whole house of Israel.…"Thus says
> the Lord GOD: 'Behold, O My people, I will open your graves
> and cause you to come up from your graves, and bring you
> into the land of Israel…'"""[5]

"And that's exactly what they were doing," I said.

"What do you mean?"

"They were opening up their own graves. And as they did, they uncovered the prophecy hidden in their graves prophesying that God would cause their graves to be opened!"

"Yes," said the Oracle, "and the prophecy had been waiting there for ages just for that moment. From ancient times through the fall of Rome, the Crusades, the Inquisition, the voyages of Columbus, the rise and fall of empires, the persecutions, the Holocaust, two world wars, the modern age…it had been there all the time…waiting.

"So when the Jewish people were led captive into the nations, when it looked as if they would be wiped off the face of the earth, when there was no hope, God had embedded His promise into the sands of their ancient grave. It was all there, waiting for two thousand years, waiting for the day of their resurrection and their return to that place. For when God makes a promise, it doesn't matter if it's a day or a thousand years; He won't forget it. He'll bring it to pass."

"Amazing!" I replied. "So the return to Masada was a Jubilean event. And yet it didn't take place in the Jubilean year. So how does it relate to what would happen in the coming Jubilee?"

"The fall of Masada is part of what the Jewish people lost at the beginning of the age. But it happened only after something else had likewise fallen and was likewise lost."

"Jerusalem... It happened after the fall and loss of Jerusalem."

"Yes," said the Oracle. "But the Jubilee brings the reversal of the loss. So if the loss of Jerusalem led to the loss of Masada, then the return to Masada would lead to..."

"The return to Jerusalem."

"And if the Jewish soldiers of ancient times left the gates of Jerusalem to come to Masada..."

"Then if the Jewish soldiers of modern times return to Masada, then..."

"Then what?"

"Then Jewish soldiers will also enter the gates of Jerusalem. And the Jewish people would return to Jerusalem."

"Yes," said the Oracle. "So as the loss of Jerusalem was followed by the loss of Masada, the return to Masada would be followed by the return to Jerusalem. And it would have to happen in the year appointed by the mystery. It would have to take place in the year 1967."

"It would be in the next mystery that I would be shown how all these things would come to pass."

"And how would it all come to pass?"

"It would all begin with a song."

Chapter 36

THE PROPHET'S SONG

I RETURNED TO THE garden and found the Oracle sitting under a willow tree. I joined him there."

"The song that I heard in my vision, the song of the man with the harp...what did it have to do with the Jubilee of 1967?"

"Everything," he replied. "In the Jubilee everyone is restored to their possession. For the nation of Israel there is one possession in this world above all others—Jerusalem. But in AD 70 Jerusalem was destroyed. And for two thousand years the Jewish people longed to return there. In 1948 Israel returned to the world, but the Jewish people were still separated from their Holy City. Their exile from Jerusalem had never been undone.

"When the United Nations came up with the Partition Plan, Jerusalem was cut off from the newborn nation. The city was to be placed under United Nations control. In 1948 one of the Arab nations seeking Israel's destruction, Jordan, seized the ancient city, along with much of the West Bank. Israel was able to take control of the city's more recently built suburbs, known as West Jerusalem. But its ancient and biblical capital, the walled city, lay in the hands of its enemies. Jewish people were now banned from setting foot in their Holy City, and Jewish holy sites within the city were turned into garbage dumps and urinals.

"But the Jubilee ordains that everyone shall return. So if Jordan was banning the Jewish people from returning to Jerusalem and the word decrees that the Jewish people must return to there, then something would have to happen. One way or another something would have to happen..."

"And it would have to happen in the appointed year," I said, "in 1967."

"Throughout the Bible there appear songs of prophecy, songs of the prophets, songs given by God to reveal His will or to prophesy of future events."

"The man in the vision with the harp...was he a prophet?"

"He was a representation of the prophets, and the song, a representation of the prophet's song." The Oracle paused for a moment, looked up at the willow tree, then continued. "It was springtime and the anniversary of Israel's birth. It was also the time of the Israeli Music Festival. A young Israeli woman, Shuli Natan, approached the festival stage with a song that its writer, Naomi Shemer, had given her. It was the first time the song would be sung in public. But the song was not of celebration but of longing and sorrow. It was called 'Yerushalayim Shel Zahav,' 'Jerusalem of Gold.' It would give voice to two thousand years of Jewish yearnings for the Holy City.

"So she would sing of how the ancient cisterns had dried up...how the ancient market square was deserted...how no one of Israel's children was able to enter the ancient city...and how, unlike in ancient times, no one now ascended to the most holy place in the Jewish faith, the Temple Mount. And around the ancient city were the sounds of desolation, the howling of the wind in the mountain caves.[1]

"It was a song of Jubilee, the longings of the separated for their long-lost inheritance. And it was the echo of a song sung in ancient times. In the sixth century BC, when the Jewish people were taken captive to exile in Babylon with Jerusalem left in ruins, a song of lamentation and longing went forth, the song of the exiles that would become known as Psalm 137:

> By the rivers of Babylon, we sat down and wept when we remembered Zion. We hung our harps upon the willows in the midst of it. For there those who carried us away captive asked of us a song...saying, 'Sing us one of the songs of Zion!'...If I forget you, O Jerusalem, let my right hand forget its skill!..."[2]

"The willow tree," I said, "like this one...and the harp on the willows, as in the vision."

"Yes," said the Oracle. "The ancient lamentation spoke of the songs of Zion, the songs of Jerusalem, so 'Jerusalem of Gold' would specifically refer to the songs of Jerusalem. In the ancient lamentation the writer tells of the Jewish people hanging up their harps. No longer could they sing the songs of Jerusalem. In the modern lamentation the same word appears— *kinor*, the Hebrew harp. The writer writes that she herself has now become the harp yearning to sing the songs of Jerusalem.

"The ancient song contains the words 'Eem eshkakhech Yerushalayim,' 'If I forget you, O Jerusalem.' In the song given to Israel in the spring of 1967 the same words appear, the same exact Hebrew words from the ancient song sung by the Jewish exiles by the rivers of Babylon.

"Psalm 137 was the song of the first exile. 'Jerusalem of Gold' was the song of the second. And it would be a song of prophecy. It would be a sign of what was about to take place. The separation of the Jewish people from Jerusalem had gone on for two thousand years. 'Jerusalem of Gold' was sung on May 15, 1967. Less than thirty days after it was sung, the exile that had begun in ancient times would come to an end. The song's longings would be fulfilled."

"What was the reaction to the song?"

"The audience was transfixed. When it was finished, there came an outburst of thunderous applause that wouldn't stop. The song had struck a deep and ancient chord in the nation's soul. It began rapidly spreading across the land among the religious and nonreligious Israelis alike. Children were humming its melody. Its author began performing it for Israeli soldiers. They had no idea that they would soon be swept up in a colossal whirlwind of events that would bring the song's longings and the nation's ancient prayers to fulfillment.

"In fact, on the very day that 'Jerusalem of Gold' was first sung to the nation, the events that would bring about its fulfillment were being set in motion. Enemy troops were moving across the desert to mass at Israel's borders. The song would be a prophetic harbinger of the colossal events that were about to take place and that would lead to the gates of the ancient city."

"How did it happen?"

"How it happened," he said, "was a manifestation of how the mystery works through all events and powers. One of those powers was the Soviet Union, the atheistic, anti-God, and anti-Israel Soviet Union.

"In May 1967, on the eve of Israel's anniversary, an official of the Soviet Union sent word to Gamal Abdel Nasser, president of Egypt, that Israel was intending to launch an invasion. It was a false report."

"Why did they do it?"

"Perhaps to stir up trouble in the region. Regardless of the motive, the superpower that had declared war on the Bible was about to cause biblical prophecy to come to fulfillment.

"Nasser responded by sending Egyptian troops into the Sinai Peninsula toward Israel's borders. On May 16 Egypt demanded the immediate withdrawal of United Nations peacekeeping troops from the Sinai. The UN complied. The buffer zone between Egypt and Israel was now gone. Tens of thousands of Egyptian troops were now lining Israel's borders. On May 22 Nasser announced the closure of the Straits of Tiran, cutting off Israel's only shipping route through the Red Sea, an act of war. On May 30 Egypt entered into a military pact with Jordan, and an Egyptian general was placed in charge of Jordanian forces. By June well over two hundred thousand enemy troops were massed along Israel's borders.

"Israel was outnumbered on every count. The Arabs had been armed by the Soviet Union with more than twice as many tanks and planes and four times as many antiaircraft guns. Nasser declared, 'Our basic objective will be the destruction of Israel.'[3] His threats of total annihilation were echoed in radio broadcasts and public declarations throughout the Arab world.[4] A sense of doom fell upon the Jewish nation. The government began stockpiling coffins. Public parks were consecrated by rabbis to serve as cemeteries. Many feared it would be a second holocaust and the end of the Jewish state."

"It was the darkening in my vision and the rumbling of war. So what happened?"

"On June 3, 1967, a meeting took place between the Israeli prime minister and the nation's chief political and military leaders to decide what to do. Though it would be brought to an official cabinet vote the following day, it was at that meeting that it was determined that the nation could not afford to wait for its enemies to launch a war of annihilation but had to act as quickly as possible. The decision was made to go to war. One of those involved in that meeting and that decision was Yigael Yadin, the man who uncovered Masada. Yadin had taken part in the nation's return to Masada. So now he would take part in its return to Jerusalem.

"The government would call for a full mobilization of all Israeli men up to fifty years of age."

"Fifty years…the time of the Jubilee."

"Yes. It was of course natural to have an age limit on the mobilization. But since the year was 1967, it meant that the cut-off year was…"

"1917…the year of the other Jubilee…So everyone who fought in that war had to be born in the year of Jubilee or in the years in between the two Jubilees."

"The emergency meeting and the decision to go to war took place on Saturday night, the sealing of the Sabbath day."

"That means there was a Scripture appointed for that Sabbath."

"Yes. It was from the Book of Numbers."

"Was it significant?"

"It was the instructions given to Israel *to prepare for war.*"

"So the Scripture about Israel preparing to go to war was appointed for the day that Israel would decide to go to war."

"Yes. In that appointed Scripture the words appear—*go to war.*"

"So as Israel was preparing for war, the ancient Scripture being recited and chanted and proclaimed all over the world was speaking of Israel preparing for war."

"Yes."

"What did the Scripture tell Israel to do?"

"To number all the adult males who would then be mobilized for war…the very thing Israel was doing at that very moment. And the

Scripture appointed to be read at the *end* of the Six-Day War concerned another kind of conscription, that which applied to the tribe of Levi. Yet it is striking that it was here that an age limit is given—*fifty years of age*."

"The same age limit used in the mobilization for the Six-Day War."

"Two days after that emergency meeting the Six-Day War began. On June 5, 1967, the Israeli air force in a sudden lightning strike destroyed the air force of the surrounding Arab nations."

"Lightning," I said, "like the lightning I saw in the vision, coming from the ram."

"So Israel battled the Egyptian army in the South and the Syrian army in the North. But it was Jordan that occupied Jerusalem. The Israeli government pleaded with Jordan to stay out of the war. Israel was fighting for its life, not for Jerusalem. Had Jordan stayed out of the war, the Holy City would have stayed in Jordanian hands. But it was the year of Jubilee and the mystery decreed that events would have to converge on the ancient city. Therefore, Jordan entered the war.

"The initial focus of the battle with Jordan wasn't Jerusalem. In fact the Israeli soldiers were ordered to stay away from the ancient city. Rather, the fighting centered on a mountain overlooking Jerusalem, Mount Scopus. It was Israel's sole enclave east of the city. On Mount Scopus were Israeli army personnel, an Israeli university, and an Israeli hospital. The soldiers were ordered to rescue the enclave. But even that was part of the mystery."

"How so?"

"The destruction of Jerusalem in AD 70 was connected to one place above all others: Mount Scopus. Mount Scopus was the headquarters of the Roman General Titus. It was from Mount Scopus that the siege of Jerusalem was commanded and from Mount Scopus that Jerusalem was destroyed. It was the base of the Roman legions that destroyed Jerusalem. And as Mount Scopus played a central part in Jerusalem's destruction, so now it would play a central part in Jerusalem's restoration. And as the leaders of the Roman army stood on that mountain, planning the city's destruction, so in the Six-Day War the leaders of the Israeli army, Moshe Dayan, its minister of defense, and other high Israeli officials, now stood on that same mountain after it was secured to speak of the city's liberation.

"Finally the word was given to Colonel Motta Gur, commander of the 55th Paratroopers Brigade, to take the Old City. He led his men to the sealed-up gate on Jerusalem's eastern wall. Gur broke through the gate and entered the Old City. For the first time in two thousand years Israeli soldiers were standing on the streets of Jerusalem."

"The Israeli soldiers left Jerusalem in AD 70," I said. "So now they returned…each to his own possession."

"Yes, and just as Jerusalem was lost when Roman soldiers swept down from the North into the Temple Mount, so now the soldiers of Israel swept down from the North into the Temple Mount. It was at that moment Gur radioed the words that would be heard all over the nation: 'The Temple Mount is in our hands.'[5]

"The soldiers then made their way down to the Western Wall, where some wept, some prayed, some cheered, and some just stood in silent awe, too overcome to speak. And as the Roman soldiers of Titus had sealed the destruction of Jerusalem with the display of the Roman standard, so now Jewish soldiers sealed the city's restoration with the display of the Israeli flag hung by the stones of the Western Wall.

"It was June 7, 1967, the day that the nation's two-thousand-year-old exile from its Holy City came to an end…in the year of Jubilee. And as the Jubilee is the year appointed for return, so the proclamations of Israel's leader would echo that word. Gur would tell his men, 'You have been given the great privilege…of *returning to the nation its capital* and its holy center…'[6] Moshe Dayan would declare, '*We have returned* to all that is holy in our land. *We have returned*, never to be parted from it again.'[7] And the rabbi who accompanied the soldiers to the Temple Mount and the Western Wall would pray, '…We have not forgotten you, Jerusalem, our Holy City, home of our glory.… To Zion and the remnant of our Holy Temple we declare: "*Your sons have returned to their borders.*"'"[8]

"What about the song?" I asked. "It was the song of two thousand years of lamentation, but three weeks after it was first sung, everything changed."

"When the soldiers that liberated Jerusalem found themselves on the Temple Mount, they spontaneously began singing the song they had just learned weeks before. And when Naomi Shemer heard of Jerusalem's liberation, she knew she had to add to the song another set of verses. So she wrote of the children of Israel returning to their ancient city. They had returned, she wrote, to the water cisterns and the market squares. They had returned to the Temple Mount. And the sound of the shofar, she wrote, the ram's horn, could now be heard from the holy place. And all around the city, in the caves she had just described as howling with the wind of desolation, now a thousand suns were shining."[9]

"So it turned into a song of rejoicing."

"In the prophets," said the Oracle, "it was written that in the days of destruction the nation's songs would be turned into mourning and lamentations."

"And that's what the psalm was about…the Jewish people could no longer sing their songs of Jerusalem but hung up their harps and wept. The sound of rejoicing was replaced by lamentation."

"Yes, and 'Jerusalem of Gold' continued where the ancient psalm left off. But in the Jubilee everything is turned around—even that."

"So if the songs of joy turn into lamentation, then in the Jubilee the songs of lamentation will be turned into a song of joy."

"Yes. And the prophets foretold that as well—that the Lord would bring the Jewish people back to the land and would turn their mourning into joy."

"So in the year of Jubilee 'Jerusalem of Gold' turned into a song of joy."

"Yes, the nation's song of lamentation and mourning was turned into a song of rejoicing. And two thousand years of mourning were thus turned into joy. God is like that," said the Oracle.

"What do you mean?"

"It's His will…His heart."

"What is?"

"To turn mourning into joy."

The Oracle was silent for a moment.

"Do you remember," he said, "when I asked you to tell me what would take place that year, before you knew what actually did take place that year, when you had nothing to go on beyond the Jubilean mystery?"

"Yes."

"You said that 1967 would be the year of a prophetic event that would involve a return. And so it was. You said that this event would involve a restoration, the return of something lost, the regaining of an inheritance by the one to whom it belonged. And so it did. You said it would involve the coming home of those who had been separated to their ancestral possession. And it did. And according to the mystery, 1967 would be the year of Jerusalem. And so it was. Those who had left the gates of Jerusalem at the beginning of the age now returned to reenter its gates in the year of Jubilee…and the separation was over."

"I guess I did."

"Yes," said the Oracle, "it would seem you're becoming something of a prophet."

———————————

"The next revelation would involve the secret things that take place in the shadow of world events and of which the world has no idea."

"And what did it involve?"

"The *kohanim*."

"The kohanim?"

"The people of the cloud."

Chapter 37

THE DAY OF THE PRIESTS

I RETURNED TO THE garden and joined the Oracle by the tree under which he was sitting."

"It's an almond tree," he said, "a symbol of resurrection, the first of trees to put forth blossoms."

"The men in white robes in the desert procession...with the cloud... who were they?"

"They were the *kohanim*," he replied, "the priests of Israel, the ministers of God, the keepers of His sanctuary. And the tent you saw, that was called the *tabernacle*. It was in that tent that priests ministered in the days of Israel's journey to the Promised Land. Later on it would become the temple. And the cloud above the tent was the glory of God that led the Israelites through the wilderness."

"They were journeying from the wilderness to the gate. Why?"

"The gate led to the mountain. The mountain was Jerusalem and the place on which God's sanctuary was to rest."

"What's the connection to the mystery?"

"No people were so connected to Jerusalem as were the priests. Unlike the Israelites from other tribes, the priests had no inheritance in the land. Their inheritance was the ministry. And Jerusalem was the city of the ministry. It was there that they officiated over the nation's holy days and festivals and there in His Temple that they performed the sacred rites. Jerusalem was the city of the priests."

"So it was something as the ancestral possession of the priests."

"And if the priests are especially connected to Jerusalem, and Jerusalem is especially connected to the Jubilean mysteries, then the priests would likewise be especially connected to the Jubilean mysteries. Beyond that the priests were the keepers of the Jubilee. They oversaw the Jubilean transactions, the relinquishing of the land, and its restoration. In fact several of the Jubilean ordinances specifically required the priests' ministering. And it was the priests who marked, heralded, and proclaimed the Jubilean year to the rest of the nation.

"The priests were the Jubilean ministers. So if the priests were especially linked to both the Jubilee and Jerusalem, and if the Jubilee of 1967 centered on the return of Jerusalem, then could the return of Jerusalem also involve the return of the priests?

"It was June 7, 1967, the moment of Jerusalem's liberation. Among the first Israelis to enter the walled city was Shlomo Goren, the chief chaplain of the Israeli army, the same rabbi who accompanied the soldiers onto the Temple Mount and then at the Western Wall, and who spoke the first blessings of the first prayer service there.

"As he stood on the ancient holy sites, his mind turned to a relative, his father-in-law. His father-in-law was also a rabbi and was known throughout the nation for his piety and deep yearning for Jerusalem's restoration. And now it had happened. Goren believed that it was right that his father-in-law should be there in the Holy City to witness the moment of its liberation. So he sent his assistant to bring him there. With the road from Jerusalem to the rabbi's house still under enemy fire, Goren's assistant borrowed a military jeep with a recoilless rifle and set out to find the rabbi.

"Upon arriving at the rabbi's home, Goren's assistant told him he had come to bring him to the Holy City. The rabbi was so overcome with emotion that he left his house without putting his shoes on. The assistant then drove with the rabbi to the home of another revered rabbi, also known for his zeal for the redemption of Jerusalem. They found him deep in prayer. They beckoned him to come to the liberated city. The rabbi seemed dazed, as if not comprehending the moment, but went along anyway. Goren's assistant now headed out with the two rabbis in his jeep to bring them inside the walls of the Old City.[1] Now what is it," asked the Oracle, "that must take place in the year of Jubilee?"

"Each must return to his possession."

"And Jerusalem was the city of the priests. Therefore, could the year of Jubilee involve the priests returning to Jerusalem?"

"It couldn't have happened before?"

"1967 was the first Jubilee in which Israel returned to Jerusalem as its own possession. So it was the first time the priests could return in kind. And June 7 was the first day of that return. The man who drove the jeep that day was seeking only to carry out the command of his superior to bless two revered rabbis. But without knowing it, he was taking part in an ancient mystery. Rabbi Goren's father-in-law was Rabbi David HaCohen. *Cohen* comes from the Hebrew word *kohanim*. It means priest. He was a descendant of Aaron, the brother of Moses, a priest of Israel. So in the year of Jubilee, when each is to return to his possession, and on the day of Jerusalem's restoration the priest returned to Jerusalem.

"But then there was the other passenger. He was Rabbi Tzvi Yehuda Kook. Three weeks before the Six-Day War, on the anniversary of Israel's birth, he gave a speech that shocked its hearers. He cried out in pained longing for the restoration of the nation's ancestral possessions, the holy places and cities from which the nation was now separated."[2]

"As in the singing of the song 'Jerusalem of Gold.'"

"Yes. Both prophetic messages went forth at the time of Israel's anniversary, within a day of each other. And less than thirty days after the rabbi spoke, the Six-Day War broke out, and Israeli soldiers would be standing on the very same places of which he had spoken that night. In fact, on the very night on which he spoke those words, Egyptian military forces were mobilized for the first time for the war that would bring it all about.

"But Rabbi Kook was also known as Rabbi Tzvi Yehuda *HaCohen* Kook. He was also a descendant of Aaron. He was also a priest."

"And the priest was to herald the coming of the Jubilee. So in giving that prophetic word, he was heralding the Jubilee."

"Yes," said the Oracle, "and now in a jeep heading to the Holy City, he was witnessing its fulfillment. It was the third day of the Six-Day War. People were hiding in their houses. Gunfire was still in the air. And in the midst of all that one jeep filled with ammunition and a rifle brought back two descendants of Israel's ancient priesthood to their ancestral possession.

"Two thousand years earlier, in the wake of the Roman destruction, the priests of Jerusalem fled the city, were taken captive, or were killed. For two thousand years they lived in exile from their inheritance. But in the year of Jubilee the separation is undone. At the beginning of the age the priests of Israel were taken away from Jerusalem. But in the year of Jubilee, 1967, they returned.

"In ancient times, when Israel returned to the land, the priests were there. When the nation entered the Promised Land under Joshua, the first Israelites to cross the Jordan River and lead the nation in were the priests. When the Jewish people returned to Jerusalem from exile in Babylon, the priests were there, central in that return and leading in the nation's restoration. And so on June 7, 1967, when Israel returned to Jerusalem after its two-thousand-year-old exile, the priests were again present at the moment of return."

"And they would have been the first to return...with the soldiers."

"As in ancient times. The two were connected. It was the priests who sounded the trumpets that summoned the nation to war. And the soldier who drove the jeep that brought the two priests to the Holy City, he was also carrying another mystery. His name was Menachem HaCohen. He too was one of the *kohanim*, a son of Aaron, a priest of Israel."

"It was the day of the priests!" I said.

"So the three priests arrived at the ancient wall of the Temple Mount, where their ancestors had ministered to God in ancient times. It was only after a time that the full weight of what was happening fell on Rabbi Tzvi Kook. He began to weep. As for Rabbi David HaCohen, he approached the wall, leaned against its ancient stones, and stood there frozen for hours, praying and reciting the psalms. The Lord had brought comfort to the priests. And as for their driver, the translation of his name, *Menachem HaCohen*, forms a phrase: 'the comfort of the priest.'

"And so on June 7, 1967, when Israel returned to Jerusalem, the Jubilean ministers came home. Each had returned to his own possession."

"The next mystery would reveal why it all had to happen when it did. And the secret would go all the way back to the days of Babylon."

"And how was it revealed?"

"Through the man in the chariot."

Chapter 38

THE BABYLONIAN CODE

I RETURNED TO THE garden to find the Oracle sitting in a vineyard filled with trees, vines, clusters of purple grapes, and an ancient-looking stone press."

"The man in the chariot who took me to Jerusalem…who was he?"

"A very ancient man," he replied. "What happened in the Jubilee of 1967 was the undoing and redemption of the Roman destruction of Jerusalem in AD 70. But is it possible that what took place was connected as well to a mystery even more ancient?

"When the Assyrian Empire collapsed at the end of the seventh century BC, two powers were left to battle for supremacy, Egypt, under Pharaoh Necho, and the newly ascendant kingdom of Babylon, under King Nabopolassar. With Nabopolassar in ill health, his son, the crown prince, led the Babylonian army to the city of Carchemish. His name was Nebuchadnezzar. In Carchemish he dealt a decisive blow to the Egyptian army. Babylon was now the undisputed supreme power of the Middle East. Nebuchadnezzar and his army now swept southward and eastward, bringing the peoples, lands, and cities of Syria and Israel into subjection and incorporating them into the newly established Babylonian Empire.

"One of the cities brought into subjection was Jerusalem. In the face of the Babylonian onslaught, the Judean king, Jehoiakim, surrendered and became Nebuchadnezzar's vassal. The Scriptures record that Nebuchadnezzar received tribute from the next Judean king, Jehoiachin, treasures from the Temple, and captives from Jerusalem's upper classes and royal families. Babylonian chronicles likewise bear witness to Nebuchadnezzar's taking of Jewish captives back to Babylon. The city of Jerusalem was now under Babylonian sovereignty, and with it the entire nation."

"Was Babylon near two rivers?"

"Yes, the Tigris and the Euphrates."

"The rider in my vision said he was from the 'land of two rivers.' Was he Nebuchadnezzar?"

"He was. So Jerusalem was now a vassal city, and Israel, a territory of the Babylonian Empire. Soon after subduing the city and the land,

Nebuchadnezzar received word that his father had died. He left his army and the business of transporting the captives in the hands of others and rushed back to Babylon to take the throne. Many view this moment as the beginning of the 'times of the Gentiles,' the age when Jerusalem would lie in subjugation to the Gentile kingdoms and empires. It would also mark the beginning of the end."

"The end?"

"Years later, when the Judean king Zedekiah rebelled against Nebuchadnezzar's rule, the Babylonians returned. This time they set fire to the Temple, razed the city to the ground, ravaged the land, took thousands into captivity, and brought the Jewish kingdom to an end. These two events, Jerusalem's subjugation and loss of sovereignty and the destruction of the Jewish kingdom, would open and close a period marking the nation's last days."

"How long was it in between the two events?"

"The answer appears in the Book of Jeremiah and 2 Kings. Both use the same expression to date it. Jerusalem was destroyed in

the nineteenth year of King Nebuchadnezzar."[1]

"The nineteenth year," I repeated. "In the vision the man told me it would take nineteen minutes to get to the city. The nineteen minutes were the nineteen years."

"Yes," said the Oracle, "the key is *the nineteenth year.*"

"So it would be the nineteenth year of Nebuchadnezzar's reign. So when did it begin?"

"Shortly after his troops entered Jerusalem. It was then, after hearing of his father's death, that he returned to Babylon to receive the crown. Nineteen years later he destroyed the kingdom of Judah. So it wasn't just that Jerusalem was destroyed in the nineteenth year of his reign but that the two events took place nineteen years apart.

"We can further pinpoint it. We know that it wasn't long after his victory in the Battle of Carchemish that Nebuchadnezzar swept through the land of Syria and Israel. The battle took place in the year 605 BC. Most scholars place it in May or June. Nebuchadnezzar's father then died in the middle of August. Nebuchadnezzar ascended the Babylonian throne on the first day of the month of Elul.

"Therefore, the window of time for the Babylonians to enter and subjugate Jerusalem falls in between June or July and mid-August 605 BC. Further, the subduing of the cities and lands of Syria could not have happened instantly, and Jerusalem, to the south of Syria, would have fallen in the latter part of that conquest. Thus we can further narrow down the first conquest of Jerusalem to the days between July and mid-August 605 BC.

"Beyond that, when Nebuchadnezzar left the region to return to Babylon, the fighting had apparently subsided, Jerusalem had already been subjugated, and its Jewish captives had already been taken into Babylonian custody. That would have also taken time. These factors point to the subjugation of Jerusalem in July, or the Hebrew month of Tammuz, in the year 605 BC."

"What about the other event, the destruction that came nineteen years later? Do we know when in the year it happened?"

"It happened in the summer, in the Hebrew month of Av. Both events took place in the summer. So from the initial Babylonian invasion and subjugation of Jerusalem to the nation's destruction, it was a full nineteen years."

"But you said the first invasion would have most likely taken place in a different month, the month of Tammuz."

"Tammuz is one month before Av. So the time between the two events would be just over nineteen years, nineteen years and a few weeks."

"So how does all this relate to the mystery?"

"We've looked at two days," said the Oracle, "each of them representing a loss, the loss of sovereignty, and the loss of national existence. But the Jubilee brings restoration, the reversing of loss. So when did Israel's restoration as a nation take place?"

"In 1948," I replied.

"So then," said the Oracle, "what happens if you add the period of Israel's destruction to the start of the period of Israel's redemption? What happens if you add the nineteen years of the mystery to the year 1948? Where does it bring you?"

"To 1967! 1967 is the nineteenth year!"

"Israel was restored as a nation on May 15, 1948. Jerusalem was restored to Israel on June 7, 1967. So the time period between the two events is nineteen years... and a few weeks—the same exact time period of the nation's destruction. And do you remember how the events of 1967 began, what triggered everything to come out at that exact time?"

"It was triggered by the Soviet Union sending a false report to Egypt."

"And when did they do that?" asked the Oracle. "They sent that word on the eve of Israel's anniversary as a nation—the anniversary of the *nineteenth year*. And when Rabbi Kook spoke his prophetic word on Israel's restoration, he did so on the day that marked exactly nineteen years from the day of Israel's declaration of rebirth.

"The time leading up to the war would be known as the waiting period. The period began when Egyptian troops crossed the Sinai and concluded three weeks later with the outbreak of the Six-Day War. On what day did that period begin? On May 15, 1967, the day that marked Israel's *nineteenth year*. And when was the prophetic song 'Jerusalem of Gold' first sung to the nation? On the day that marked Israel's *nineteenth year*. It all began as Israel completed its *nineteenth year*.

"In the ancient cycle the nineteen years concerned the loss and destruction of Jerusalem and Israel. In the modern cycle the nineteen years likewise concerned Jerusalem and Israel. The ancient nineteen-year cycle concerned the loss of sovereignty and existence. The modern nineteen-year cycle concerned the exact opposite, the exact reversal, the regaining of sovereignty, the undoing of loss, and the nation's rebirth. So in the year of Jubilee the nineteen years of loss and destruction become the nineteen years of restoration and rebirth.

"And since the Jubilee is about reversal, what happens," said the Oracle, "if we reverse the nineteen years of destruction? If the ancient nineteen-year cycle *begins* with the soldiers of a Gentile kingdom *entering* the gates of Jerusalem…then the modern nineteen-year cycle will *end* with the soldiers of a Gentile kingdom *departing* Jerusalem and with Israeli soldiers entering in its gates. And so it did in 1967.

"And if the ancient nineteen-year period *begins* with the Jewish nation *losing* its sovereignty over Jerusalem…then the modern nineteen-year period will *end* with the Jewish nation *regaining* its sovereignty over Jerusalem in 1967. And so it did.

"If the ancient nineteen-year period *ends* with the mass *departure* of the Jewish people from the land…then the modern nineteen-year period must *begin* with the mass *return* of the Jewish people from *exile* to the land in 1948. And so it would."

"And," I said, "if the ancient nineteen-year period *ends* with the Jewish nation *disappearing* from the earth…then the modern nineteen-year period must *begin* with the Jewish nation *reappearing* on the earth."

"And so it did," said the Oracle, "in 1948. And remember what I told you about the times of the Gentiles, which many have seen as beginning in 605 BC when the Babylonians first invaded. So then what about that which took place in the corresponding year, 1967, the regaining of Jerusalem? Is it possible that it then could be seen as the beginning of the end of the times of the Gentiles?"

"Is it?"

"Perhaps," he said. "It could be seen as such. And so it was prophesied in ancient times by the rabbi from Nazareth, 'Jerusalem will be trampled by Gentiles until the times of the Gentiles are fulfilled.'"[2]

"The next time I saw the Oracle, he would open up another revelation of the secret things from ancient times that play a part behind the world events of modern times."

"What secret things?"

"A mysterious person I had never heard of before."

"What mysterious person?"

"The man called the Nazir."

"And how would it be revealed to you?"

"Through a man in a black robe."

Chapter 39

THE NAZIR

I FOUND THE ORACLE sitting under a tree filled with fruit, each one red, round, and with what looked like a crown at its bottom."

"It's a pomegranate tree," he said. "Images of pomegranates adorned the Temple of King Solomon."

So I joined him under the pomegranate tree.

"The man in the black hooded robe, whose name was Separation…what was that about?"

"There was an ancient ordinance," he said, "concerning a vow. If an Israelite desired to consecrate himself for the Lord's purposes, he would take a vow of separation. The vow would involve abstaining from wine, from cutting his hair, and from defilement. The vow could be taken for a specific period of time or for life. The one who took the vow was called the Nazir. *Nazir* comes from a Hebrew root word meaning to separate. So the Nazir was the *separated one*, and the time of his vow was known as his *days of separation*. The root word from which *nazir* comes can speak of both separation *to* the Lord or *from* the Lord."

"So the man in the black robe whose name was Separation was the Nazir?"

"A form of the Nazir," he replied. "And when did you see him?"

"At times of calamity, loss, and exile."

"In the days of their separation," he said. "What you saw was the embodiment of Israel's exile, their *days of their separation*. Now, according to the ancient ordinance, the Nazir could only begin his vow and bring it to completion in one place—the sanctuary. In the days of the wilderness he would be brought to the doors of the Tabernacle. In the days of the Temple he would be brought to the Temple Mount. So the days of separation could only end on the Temple Mount. But for most of two thousand years the Temple Mount was in enemy hands and the appearance of a Nazir among the Jewish people was a rare phenomenon.

"But in the days of Israel's rebirth there appeared a Nazir. He abstained from wine and defilement and never cut his hair. He would also take a vow of devotion concerning Jerusalem: he would not leave his dwelling place until Jerusalem was restored to Israel. His vows of separation became so well-known that he would be known as the Nazir or the Nazir of Jerusalem. On June 7, 1967, when Jerusalem was restored to the Jewish people, its restoration would involve the mystery of the Nazir."

"Who was he?" I asked.

"You already know him. He was a rabbi. He was David HaCohen."

"The one who was sent for?"

"Yes, when Rabbi Goren sent for his father-in-law, he was also sending for the Nazir. And when Goren's assistant reached his house, the Nazir found himself in a dilemma. Because of the vow, the Nazir couldn't leave his house. But according to rabbinical law, such a vow could be nullified by the word of three witnesses. So three men stood as witnesses in the Nazir's house to release him from his vow so that he might be taken into the gates of the newly liberated Jerusalem."[1]

"So the jeep," I said, "it wasn't only carrying two rabbis and three priests. It was also carrying the Nazir."

"Yes," said the Oracle, "and so it was part of another ancient mystery. Keep in mind the ancient ordinance: the only way the Nazir could complete his vow was by being brought to the sanctuary or the door of the sanctuary. And ever since the days of King Solomon, that place was in Jerusalem, on the Temple Mount. So in ancient times the vow of separation could only be brought to completion with the Nazir being brought to Jerusalem and to the Temple Mount. On June 7, 1967, the Nazir was taken to Jerusalem, and not only to Jerusalem—but specifically to the Temple Mount. No one planned what took place that day in view of the ancient mystery. It happened because of the battle that forced the driver to take the route he took. They entered the newly opened gate on the city's eastern wall, then turned onto the ancient pavement of the Temple Mount, the holiest place on earth.

"Thus the Nazir had returned to the very same place where the ancient Nazirs had to be brought to fulfill their vows, the place on which stood the doors of the sanctuary and the Court of Nazirs. It was the first known time in two thousand years that such a thing had happened."

"So Jerusalem had returned," I said, "and the Nazir had returned on the same day—to his ancient possession."

"And note, the ordinance didn't say that the Nazir would simply *come* to the sanctuary but specifies that he must be *brought*. So on the day of Jerusalem's liberation the Nazir was literally *brought* to the sanctuary. And who was it in ancient times that would bring the Nazir to the sanctuary? The priest. And who was it on that day that brought the Nazir to the sanctuary? It was Menachem HaCohen, *the priest*. So he was not only driving his fellow priests; he was bringing the Nazir to the sanctuary."

"Is it significant that the Nazir of Jerusalem was himself a priest?"

"It was," said the Oracle. "The priest ministered as the representative of the people of Israel. The Nazir was the *separated one*. And yet he was a priest representing Israel. For it was the people of Israel who had become separated from their land, from their Holy City, and from their ancestral inheritance. It was Israel that had become the Nazir nation."

"That's why the man in the black robe was always with them in their exile."

"But on June 7, 1967, the Nazir was brought to the place where the *days of separation* come to an end. For it was on that day that Israel's days of separation had come to their end. And it was the release of Israel from the days of *its* separation that caused the Nazir to be released from the days of *his* separation…that he could leave his home and come to that place. So the Nazir was brought to the place where the days of separation come to their end on the same day that the two-thousand-year-old days of separation of the Jewish people from Jerusalem also came to their end."

"And it all took place in the year of Jubilee," I said. "And the Jubilee ends the separation. It causes the separated ones to return."

"Yes," said the Oracle, "and yet there's still one more mystery. Do you know on what day the Six-Day War ended? It ended on the Sabbath."

"So there was an appointed Scripture…What was it?"

"It was *the ordinance of the Nazir*."

"No! That's too…"

"But it was."

"How many times does the ordinance of the Nazir appear in the Bible?"

"Only once," said the Oracle, "only in that one passage. And it was that passage that was the appointed word to be read on the Sabbath of the Six-Day War."

"What did it say specifically?"

"It said this:

> Now this *is the law of the Nazir: When the days of his separation are fulfilled, he shall be brought to the door of the tabernacle of meeting.*[2]

"So the appointed Scripture ordained the very thing that took place at the time of its appointing, the bringing of the Nazir to the sanctuary. The command could never be fulfilled until the Six-Day War, when its words were appointed to be read. And so the command to bring the Nazir to the sanctuary was being recited all over the land of Israel and all over the world on the very week that the jeep driven by the priest would bring the Nazir to the sanctuary.

"And so on June 7, 1967, the separated one came home, the Nazir returned to Jerusalem. It was the sign of the Nazir. Remember what it means. When the Nazir is brought to the Temple Mount, the days of separation come to their end. So it was on that day that the two-thousand-year-old days of separation between the Jewish people and Jerusalem came to their end."

"The next revelation began with a mystery revealed to me behind the second door."

"Then it was linked to the year 1917."

"It was a mystery begun in the Jubilee of 1917 but only completed in the Jubilee of 1967."

"And what did it involve?"

"The day of the lions."

Chapter 40

THE DAY OF THE LIONS

I RETURNED TO THE garden and joined the Oracle under a fig tree."

"In my vision I saw lions coming out of a stone relief and going to war. What did it mean?"

"The lion," he said, "is a symbol of power, authority, and royalty."

"They encircled a mountain. Did the mountain represent Jerusalem and their battle, the Six-Day War?"

"It did," he replied. "The battle over Jerusalem began on June 5 when the Jordanian army, despite Israel's warning to refrain from war, began shelling Israeli positions around the ancient city. Jerusalem was about to be drawn into the war.

"In order to cut off the Jordanian forces and stop the shelling, Israel set out to encircle the mountains and roads that surrounded the ancient city. Though it was not the initial or intended purpose, the strategy would lead to the return to Jerusalem. Central in the encirclement of Jerusalem was Israel's Harel Brigade. The brigade's commander was ordered to seize the vital passageways leading to and from the city and to take the mountain ridges to the north and east of Jerusalem. The success of the Harel Brigade would give Israel control of the Judean hills and open the door for the Jubilean event."

"And the lions that went up to the top of the mountain?"

"That would be the 55th Brigade," he replied, "a brigade of paratroopers. On the eve of the Six-Day War the 55th Brigade was being prepared for battle in the Sinai Peninsula. But the war's rapidly shifting dynamics caused a change in plans. The brigade was sent instead to fight in the hills surrounding Jerusalem. On the morning of June 7 the brigade's commander was standing with his men on the Mount of Olives. His intelligence officer received word from the army's chief of staff to take Jerusalem. The commander then told his men of the order. The brigade made its way down the Mount of Olives, up Mount Moriah, and through the gates of the ancient city."

"But why lions?"

"You've asked about the lions," said the Oracle, "but not about the rest of your vision. When the vision began, what did you see?"

"A bearded man, a stone relief of an ancient battle, and birds."

"Birds," he said. "You've seen them before."

"Yes, the vision of the birds...the taking of Jerusalem by the British, the first time in history that a war over the land of Israel and Jerusalem involved the sky...and wings."

"And what Scripture was appointed in *The Book of Common Prayer* to be read on the last day of fighting in the battle of Jerusalem?"

"The prophecy that spoke of the Lord delivering Jerusalem 'as birds flying.'"[1]

"And which prophet spoke those words?"

"Isaiah," I replied. "Was he the man with the beard?"

"Yes. And in your vision he was linked to the stone relief, the siege of the ancient city. Isaiah was there when Jerusalem was under siege by the Assyrians. It was then that he prophesied that the Lord would deliver Jerusalem and that the deliverance would come 'as birds flying.' But there was more to that prophecy. Directly above the verse that speaks of the flying birds, the prophecy speaks of another animal:

> As the lion and the young lion roaring over its prey when a
> multitude of shepherds is summoned against him, he will not
> be afraid of their voice, nor be disturbed by their noise, so
> the LORD of hosts will come down to fight for Mount Zion
> and for its hill.[2]

"So the prophecy foretells the deliverance of Jerusalem as *birds flying* and as *lions roaring*. So if the deliverance of Jerusalem in the Jubilee of 1917 came as *birds flying*, could it be that its deliverance in the Jubilee of 1967 would come as *lions roaring*?

"At the end of your vision behind the fourth door, you saw a young, slender ram transforming into something like a lion. So in the days leading up to the war, many feared for the young nation's survival, just as you feared for the ram. But once the war began, Israel was aroused as a lion. The nation responded to its encroaching enemies with massive force, ferocity, and lightning-like speed. And as the roar of a lion strikes fear in the hearts of its enemies and melts their resolve, so the roar of Israel's might in the Six-Day War struck fear in the hearts of those who had planned its destruction and melted their resolve. And as a lion's roar warns its enemies not to invade its territory, so Israel warned Jordan not to invade its territory. It was the defiance of that warning that would usher in the fulfillment of prophecy.

"The lion is also Israel's symbol of royalty. Jerusalem was the throne from which the kings of Israel reigned. Thus the city itself became identified with the lion and would be adorned with their images. So in the Six-Day War, Israel battled for its royal city, the city of lions."

"So that's why the lions were in the vision."

"For all those reasons," said the Oracle. "But there's more to the mystery. I told you that it was the Harel Brigade that seized the mountain ridges surrounding Jerusalem and that opened the way to Jerusalem's restoration. The commander of the Harel Brigade was Colonel Ben Ari. Do you know what *Ari* means?"

"No."

"It means lion."

"The Lord would fight *as a lion*."

"So in the Six-Day War leading the troops in the battle for Jerusalem was a man named Lion. The prophecy says that the Lord will fight as a lion specifically *for Mount Zion and for its hill*. Mount Zion and its hill stand for Jerusalem, the city set on the mountain of God. Do you know what the name of the Harel Brigade means? *Harel* means the mountain of God. So in battle for Jerusalem you have Colonel Ari and the Harel Brigade...the lion and the mountain of God...So the Lord fought as a lion for Mount Zion.

"There was another leader," said the Oracle, "another colonel who played a central role in the regaining of Jerusalem. He was the operations officer of the army's Central Command. He was the one who directed the battle for Jerusalem. And on the morning of June 7 it was he who gave the critical command to the 55th Brigade to take Jerusalem. His name was Arik Regev. Do you know what the name *Arik* means?"

"No."

"Lion."

"So the battle for Jerusalem was directed by a man named Lion."

"The lion who directed the battle for Mount Zion and gave the order to take its *hill*. And there was another who was central in Jerusalem's return, the man who received the command to take the city, the intelligence officer of the paratroopers brigade. He was the one who came up with the plan that put the paratroopers in place to enter the city gates. His name was Arik Achmon. And his name was also..."

"Lion."

"So the man who gave the command to take Jerusalem and the man who received it were each named Lion."

"And the one who devised the plan that led to the return of Mount Zion was named Lion."

"And then there was the man who, more than any other soldier in the Six-Day War, became famous for his role in the city's liberation. He was also a colonel. He was the commander of the 55th Paratroopers Brigade, the one who charged his men to take Jerusalem, the one who led them into the gate, and the one who took the Temple Mount and then the Western Wall. His name was Motta Gur."

"The name doesn't sound like the others."

"Because the name comes from a different Hebrew root. Do you know what *Gur* means?"

"No."

"Lion cub or young lion. So the man who actually took the city and who led the nation through its gates was also named Lion."

"In the vision I saw two lions made their way to the top of the mountain. Did one of them represent Colonel Gur?"

"Yes," said the Oracle, "and the other, his intelligence officer, Arik Achmon. They were the first two to enter the gates."

"Two lions," I said.

"Do you remember how the prophecy began?

As *the lion and the young lion*…"[3]

"Two lions!"

"One could take the words as poetic parallelism, but the fact is the prophecy specifically identifies two lions in the deliverance of Jerusalem. And what kind of lions does it specifically identify?"

"The lion and the young lion."

"So the two who were the first to take Jerusalem were Arik Achmon and Motta Gur. *Arik* means lion, and *Gur* means young lion, 'the lion and the young lion.'"

"Amazing!"

"And the prophecy says that the Lord will fight *as the lion and the young lion for Mount Zion and for its hill*. The phrase was used to designate Jerusalem and specifically the Temple Mount. And it was Arik Achmon and Motta Gur who were the first to ascend the Temple Mount, the lion and the young lion fighting for Mount Zion and its hill. The prophecy speaks of a lion roaring over its prey, in this case the Lord roaring as a lion, in this case over Mount Zion and its holy hill. So it was Gur, the young lion on the Temple Mount, who roared to Israel and to the world the most famous words of the war: 'The Temple Mount is in our hands.'[4]

"The day after Jerusalem's liberation, the nation's founder and first leader, David Ben-Gurion, walked through the gates of the ancient city. He was at that time an old man. Do you know what the name *Gurion* means in Hebrew?"

"What?"

"Lion cub. So as the two lions and their troops entered the gates of the city, the nation of Israel returned with them. Do you know which gate it was that the soldiers entered through to win Jerusalem?"

I was silent.

"It was the *Lion's Gate*. The lions entered through the *Gate of the Lions*."

"No one could have put all this together."

"No one but One," said the Oracle. "The prophecy says it will be *as* the lion, but it will *be* the Lord. The manifestation of lions in Jerusalem's restoration wasn't about lions. It was the sign from ancient times that behind it all was the hand of God bringing to pass the prophesied return and restoration, the Almighty moving...*as a lion.*"

"The next revelation would center on a man who would play a central part in the Jubilee of 1967. It could even be said that he was born to fulfill that part."

"And how was it revealed to you?"

"Through a boy in a threshing floor. It was through him that I learned the mystery of the Jubilean man."

Chapter 41

THE JUBILEAN MAN

I RETURNED TO THE garden to find the Oracle sitting in the shade of an olive grove. I joined him there."

"What was the central sign of the Jubilee?" he asked.

"People returning to their land."

"Yes, that's what took place. But what was the sign that the Jubilee had come? What was it that heralded it?"

"The sounding of the ram's horn."

"Yes. So it was written in Leviticus, in the Jubilean ordinance: 'Then you shall cause the trumpet of the Jubilee to sound...'[1] The trumpet of the Jubilee is the ram's horn, the shofar. For the Jubilee to begin, the shofar had to be sounded. It was the sounding of the shofar that signaled the year of return and restoration, and release throughout the land.

"Is it possible that in 1967, the Jubilean year that witnessed the most dramatic of returns concerning Jerusalem, the sign of the Jubilee, the sounding of the shofar, could have manifested?"

"In my vision I saw an angel give a shofar to a boy to sound it at the set time."

"The central moment of that Jubilee came as Israeli soldiers entered the ancient city and made their way to their most holy of places. The images of Israeli soldiers returning to the Temple Mount and to the ancient stones of the Western Wall reverberated across the world. It was the defining moment of the war and the embodiment of the Jubilean return. It was at that precise moment that an ancient mystery manifested. In the midst of the soldiers standing at the Western Wall was a man holding a ram's horn. He set it to his mouth and blew. The sound of the Jubilee went forth in the Jubilean year, on the Jubilean day, in the Jubilean place, and at the Jubilean moment. The same sound ordained in ancient times to proclaim the return of the exiled heirs to their lost inheritance now proclaimed to the world the return of the Jewish people to their lost inheritance."

"Did the man who sounded the shofar know the mystery? Did he intend to sound it on the Jubilee?"

"He didn't intend it that way," said the Oracle, "any more than did any of the others intend to fulfill the mystery when they fulfilled it."

"All the more amazing," I said. "And who was the man?"

"Rabbi Shlomo Goren, the same one who sent for the priests and for the Nazir. In your vision he was the child who came to the threshing floor."

"How did it all happen?"

"Goren wasn't born in the land but was one of the exiles who returned from the nations. He was born in Poland. While he was still a young boy, his family immigrated to Palestine, which was at that time under British rule. In the Orthodox Jewish world he was recognized as a prodigy. At the age of seventeen he was ordained as a rabbi. Beginning with Israel's War of Independence he served in the army as a military chaplain. It was Goren's conviction that the return of the Jewish people to the land was central in God's purposes of world redemption.

"In the first days of the Six-Day War, Goren was at the front lines of battle. At his side was a shofar. He had intended to follow the ancient command to sound it in the midst of battle. But in the midst of battle his vehicle was struck by enemy fire, and the shofar was destroyed. Goren then asked his father-in-law if he could borrow his shofar for what could be the liberation of Jerusalem. His father-in-law complied.

"In the days leading up to the Six-Day War, long before Jerusalem was in play, Goren had prophetically spoken of the city's liberation. And on the morning of June 7, 1967, he would be there with the first Israeli troops as they approached the city. As he entered with the soldiers through the Lion's Gate, he set the shofar to his mouth and sounded it. It was the very moment of the Jubilean return. He continued sounding it as he and the troops made their way to the Temple Mount, another prophetic return, the return of the Jewish soldier to the sacred ground lost in the war against Rome in AD 70, and another Jubilean moment two thousand years in the making."

"Each shall return to his own possession."

"And then Goren made his way to the Western Wall for the sounding of the shofar that would reverberate around the world. In ancient times who was it that sounded the shofar of Jubilee? Though the ordinance doesn't specify, it was the priests who were called to mark the holy days of Israel, to sound the trumpets, and to herald the appointed times of God. And the priests were the ministers of the Jubilee.

"Rabbi Goren wasn't born of the priestly house but through marriage had become part of it. His father-in-law, David HaCohen, *was* born of the priestly line. In ancient times it was the shofar belonging to the priests that marked and ushered in the nation's sacred times and holy days. From whom did Rabbi Goren obtain the shofar that would be sounded in Jerusalem's liberation?"

"From his father-in-law."

"And his father-in-law was a priest. So the shofar that was sounded in Jerusalem at the moment of Israel's return to her Holy City was the *priestly* shofar. So as it was in ancient times, so it was on June 7, 1967; the shofar of the priests sounded in Jerusalem to usher in the sacred times of God."

"In the vision the boy was to sound the shofar on the threshing floor. Why the threshing floor? Was it because it's linked to the harvest and the boy was told to sound the shofar at the time of the harvest?"

"And Rabbi Goren *would* sound the shofar in early June, at the time of the wheat harvest. But that's not the reason behind the threshing floor. The reason is part of a deeper mystery.

"In the year of Jubilee, in returning to its first owner, the land returns to its original state. Do you know what the original state of the Temple Mount was?"

"No."

"A *threshing floor*. When the Temple Mount was first purchased by King David, it was a threshing floor."

"So the original state of the Temple Mount was a threshing floor."

"And do you know what the Hebrew word for *threshing floor* is?"

"No."

"*Goren*. In Hebrew *threshing floor* is *goren*."

"Goren! Rabbi Goren!"

"In Hebrew his name means threshing floor. And the threshing floor is the Temple Mount."

"'*Rabbi Threshing Floor*'! So the man who returns to the threshing floor is named Threshing Floor!"

"In the Jubilee the original state of the land is reaffirmed. So Goren's very name manifested the original state of the land and reaffirmed its ancestral connection to the Jewish people. The Temple Mount was purchased by King David when it was a goren, a threshing floor. And it was the man named Threshing Floor whose feet literally stood on the threshing floor, the Temple Mount, to sound the shofar on the day of the threshing floor's redemption."

The Oracle paused to let me take it all in. He wasn't finished.

"Do you know when Rabbi Goren was born?"

"I have no idea."

"He was born in 1917."

"The year of Jubilee!"

"Yes. He was born in the year of the Balfour Declaration, the liberation of Jerusalem from the Ottoman Empire, the year of return and restoration. Each Jubilee is joined to the next. So Goren was born in the one Jubilee to usher in the other. And when he ushered in the fiftieth year, he himself was *fifty years old*. It was the Jubilee of his own life. It wasn't only the shofar that was the sign. It was the man himself. He was its embodiment. He was the Jubilean man. So the Jubilean man sounded the Jubilean shofar in the Jubilean year in the Jubilean place at the Jubilean moment... and as he sounded it, the ancestral possession passed back into the hands of those to whom it belonged."

"Who could have put all that together?"

"Only One," said the Oracle, "only One."

––––––––––

"There would be one more mystery to be revealed behind the fourth door and before the fifth could be opened. And that mystery would begin where another had left off... the mystery of a desert mountain. But the revelation would be taken to another level."

"To another level?"

"To another level of amazing..."

"And what was the mystery?"

"The Masada Algorithm."

Chapter 42

THE MASADA ALGORITHM

W HEN I RETURNED to the garden, I found the Oracle sitting in the same place as in the beginning, under the acacia tree. I joined him there."

"This is the last of the mysteries concerning the fourth door," he said. "Since it begins where another leaves off, we must first revisit the other mystery. Tell me, what is Masada to ancient Israel?"

"Masada was Israel's last stand, where its last soldiers perished, where everything ended. Masada was the nation's grave."

"And what does that have to do with the Jubilean mysteries?"

"The Jubilee is about restoring what was lost and returning to the place you left. And so the people of Israel had to return there; the people resurrected from death had to return to their ancient grave. And so they did. And when they did, they found a word waiting two thousand years to be uncovered—the prophecy of their resurrection. They opened up their grave and found a prophecy that said, 'I will open your graves.'"[1]

"And what was it that fell before the fall of Masada?"

"Jerusalem."

"And so if the Jubilee reverses that which was lost, then what happens if everything is reversed?"

"If the loss of Jerusalem led to the loss of Masada, then in the reversal the return to Masada will lead to the return to Jerusalem. And if in the fall of Jerusalem Jewish soldiers left the gates of the city, then in the reversal Jewish soldiers will again enter its gates. And so if Israel returned to Masada, it would also return to Jerusalem. It would all come to pass in the Six-Day War."

"In your vision" said the Oracle, "you came into an antiquities store and were shown a sundial."

"Yes, why?"

"Because the mystery would now be one of timing. On the sundial were the engravings of two mountains. The two mountains were Jerusalem and Masada. The shadow moved across the sundial from one mountain to the other and then back again. The mystery concerns the timing between the two events. The fall of Jerusalem and the fall of Masada took place in the same decade. So in the restoration…"

"The return to Masada and the return to Jerusalem would take place…in the same decade."

"Yes. And so the return to Masada and the return to Jerusalem would happen in the same decade—the 1960s."

"When *exactly* did Masada fall?"

"Masada was originally assumed to have fallen in AD 73. But that was before the discovery of Latin inscriptions that dated the reign of Flavius Silva, the Roman governor of Judea who laid siege to Masada. The inscriptions ruled out the year 73 as too early. Thus the fall of Masada was determined to have taken place in the spring of AD 74. So how much time passed between the fall of Jerusalem and that of Masada?"

"From AD 70 to AD 74, about four years."

"What happens then," said the Oracle, "if we now apply the mystery? What happens if we take the fall of Jerusalem and Masada and reverse it? Could it foretell the redemption of those events in modern times? Could it reveal the timing between the return of the Jewish people to Masada and their return to Jerusalem?"

"We would have to know the year that Israel returned to Masada," I said, "and then add to it the same period of time between the loss of Jerusalem and the loss of Masada. So when did Israel return to Masada?"

"Israel returned to Masada in 1963.[2] So if we add the four years, where does it bring us?"

"To 1967! It brings us to the year of Israel's return to Jerusalem!"

"So the Jewish people lose Jerusalem in AD 70, and four years later, in AD 74, they lose Masada. In 1963 they return to Masada…"

"And four years later they return to Jerusalem."

"But let's now go deeper," said the Oracle, "to the Masada algorithm."

"The what?"

"The algorithm of Masada," he replied. "When exactly was it that Jerusalem was lost and the exile began? According to the ancient account, the Temple was set on fire on the tenth day of the Hebrew month of Av. It would have been a Sunday. The following morning began the first day that the sun rose on a Jerusalem with no Temple…the first day that Jerusalem was no longer in Jewish hands, the first of the countless days of Israel's exile from its Holy City, and the first day the Jewish people were bereft not only of their Holy City but their holy house, the Temple."

"When did it happen," I asked, "on the Western calendar?"

"The Hebrew date places it forty-nine days before the Feast of Trumpets. The Feast of Trumpets takes place on the new moon that begins the

Hebrew month of Tishri. In the year AD 70 the new moon of Tishri took place on September 24 on the Julian calendar. Forty-nine days back takes us to August 6, the first day of the exile."

"And when exactly did Masada fall?"

"According to the ancient accounts, the defenders of Masada died by their own hand on Passover, the fifteenth day of Nisan."

"And when did it take place on the Western calendar?"

"In AD 74 it fell on March 31."

"Then we have the two dates."

"So what happens if we take the exact number of days between the two ancient dates and apply the mystery of reversal?"

"What happens?"

"Between the loss of Jerusalem and the fall of Masada, the first day of exile and the last day of the resistance, is a time span of 1,333 days."

"So then to reverse it, we would have to find the day that Israel returned to Masada and count 1,333 days forward. But we would have to know the exact date. Do we know it?"

"We do," said the Oracle. "It was the day that Yigael Yadin, Israel's archaeologist general, inaugurated the excavation of the desert fortress. It all began on the morning of October 13, 1963. So we must now take the time period between the fall of Jerusalem and the fall of Masada, the 1,333 days, and add it to the day Israel returned to Masada, and see where it brings us."

"October 13, 1963, plus 1,333 days...brings us to what?"

"June 7, 1967."

"June 7, 1967!"

"The exact date of Israel's return to Jerusalem. So it was 1,333 days from the loss of Jerusalem to the loss of Masada...and 1,333 days from the return to Masada to the return of Jerusalem."

"Down to the exact day! So the Six-Day War had to happen exactly when it did," I said. "And the Arab world had to threaten Israel exactly when it did. And the waiting period had to go on for the exact number of days it went on. And the Soviet Union had to send a false report to Egypt on the exact day they sent it."

"Not only that superpower," said the Oracle, "but the other one as well. It was America that restrained Israel from acting until finally giving the go-ahead just days before the war. Without that restraint and that go-ahead, the restoration of Jerusalem would not have taken place on that exact day."

"And the soldiers," I said, "they had to enter the Lion's Gate on that exact day. They had to return to Jerusalem on the 1,333rd day."

"Yes," said the Oracle, "and nobody planned it. And look at the world in which it happened. It all took place in a time of social upheaval, a war in Southeast Asia, a countercultural revolution, a race to the moon, and a 'summer of love.' It was in the midst of all these things the ancient mystery was moving…as it was the year of Jubilee. And it all came about through the intrigues of an atheistic superpower, the fury of the Arab world, the mobilization of armies, a song that touched a sacred longing, and a war that shook the world and brought an ancient people back to their lost possession. The ancient mystery was working, bringing every event together to coalesce into the appointed purposes…to the exact day."

———————————

"That was the last of the mysteries of the fourth door and the last time I would see the Oracle in the garden."

"And what was waiting for you behind the fifth door?"

"Three mountaintops, the ancient mystery behind a more recent American president, a woman of bronze, the return of an ancient king, the Jubilee of Capitol Hill, a golden man, a mystery of seventy years, a pool of lights…and the magi."

THE FIFTH DOOR

Chapter 43

THE FIFTH DOOR

I WAS STANDING IN front of the fifth door with the Oracle to my left. He handed me a key. I placed it in the lock, opened the door, and walked through. I was again standing on top of the desert mountain."

"The same mountain?"

"Yes, and with the same man in red, Moses, and at his side a ram. Around its neck was a chain, on which hung a white stone, on which was the same symbol as on the fifth door. It was the strangest of all the rams I had seen up to that point. Its appearance was of white marble. Its legs and horns had the appearance of grooved columns; its face, the appearance of chiseled stone; and its hair, the sculptured adornments you'd find on the top of an ancient pillar. And yet it was its torso that was most striking. It resembled a marble cylinder covered with rows of wedge-shaped symbols or letters. And it was in motion, the symbols rolling slowly upward. But it wasn't the cylinder that was moving but the symbols, the letters them-selves, rotating along the cylinder as if they were shadows. But they weren't shadows; they were wedge-shaped engravings in motion. The ram made its way down the mountain and into the desert. I followed. It turned its gaze to the left. I turned as well."

THE WOMAN OF THE DOME

"I saw a statue, a bronze woman almost twenty feet high, on top of a domed building. She had a sword in one hand and a rolled document in the other. She began to move. She descended the dome and walked away from the building. The next thing I knew, I was overlooking the walled city of Jerusalem. It was the very moment of Israel's return in the Six-Day War. But everything was frozen, the soldiers, the rabbi at the wall, everything, as if it had all become a three-dimensional photo-graph. Between my vantage point and the city were dome-covered build-ings. And then I saw her, the bronze woman. She was walking on top of the domes until she arrived at the largest one and made her way to its summit. She unrolled the document and began to read aloud its words. When she finished reading, everything unfroze; the scene resumed its motion. But the woman was now frozen. She was now of the same color and substance of the dome on which she stood…motionless as in the beginning but now overlooking Jerusalem."

The Three Mountains

"I turned again and saw three mountains over which the sun was rising. On each mountain was a robed and hooded figure ascending to its summit. The first was clothed in a robe of red; the second, in a robe of blue; and the third, of blackened gold. The figure in red removed his robe to reveal a mustached man in a military uniform of greenish brown, with loose baggy trousers and an officer's cap. He lifted a ram's horn to his mouth and sounded it in the direction of the other two mountains. Then the figure in blue removed his robe. Underneath was a man dressed in olive green army fatigues, with a netted green helmet and an eye patch. He too set a ram's horn to his mouth and sounded it in the direction of the third mountain. The third figure then removed the robe of blackened gold. Underneath was a woman. It was the bronze woman I had just seen in the previous vision. She too set a ram's horn to her mouth and sounded it facing away from the other two mountains. And then the sun went down on the three mountains."

The Lair

"I turned again and saw a man scaling the side of a mountain. He was clothed as a warrior with weapons strapped to his back. And yet on his head was a crown…a warrior-king. The sky was filled with dark, ominous clouds. The man made his way to an opening in a rock, through which he entered. It led him into a vast chamber illuminated by torchlight and filled with black dragons. They were all assembled in an enormous circle. Each dragon faced outward, away from the circle's center. And each held its wings outstretched and moved to the left so that the circle was slowly revolving. Seated on the ground in the center of the circle was a woman clothed in white garments with blue, purple, and scarlet embroidery. On her head was a white crown adorned with jewels of assorted colors. Around her neck was a metal band held in place by a series of chains stretching outward in every direction and downward to the rock floor, to which they were secured, keeping her from moving. She was the dragon's captive. The warrior reached toward his back to retrieve what I thought would be a weapon—but was, instead, a ram's horn. He set it to his mouth and sounded it into the lair. At the sound of the horn the chains broke off the woman's neck. The dragons went into an uproar, each one taking flight inside the lair and merging with the others to become a dark, frenzied swarm."

The Golden King

"I turned again and saw what appeared to be a small stone house set on top of a pyramid-like pedestal of stone blocks. I was transported inside the house to a chamber lit up by the light of torches set in its walls. There before me was a king seated on a throne. The king, the throne, and nearly everything else in that chamber was of pure glistening gold. The golden king rose from his throne, walked over to a golden chest, and removed a cylinder, which was also of pure gold. He then walked outside, where on top of the stone pedestal was a large eagle, as in the vision of the Oval Office. The moment the king stepped out of the stone house, his appearance transformed. It was now that of a man in a dark-blue business suit, a red tie, and blondish hair. He placed the golden cylinder in the talons of the eagle, which then took off into the sky and disappeared. The man then returned to the stone house, where his appearance changed back to that of the golden king, sat down on the golden throne, and became motionless. It was then that I noticed the words engraved beneath his feet: 'I too am he.'"

The Boy on the Hill

"In the next vision I saw the same two angels from the vision of the threshing floor. The one now led the other through a valley and a meadow and into an enclosed garden. Inside the garden was a little boy sitting on the ground and playing with little stone blocks, building houses. The angels sat down by the boy, one on each side. One of the angels handed him a ram's horn. But the boy showed little interest. The scene now changed. The boy was older and racing with other boys up to the top of a hill. Reaching its summit before the rest, he noticed a small platform of white stone. He stood on it. At that moment, the angel appeared and handed him the ram's horn. 'It is time,' he said to the boy. 'It was for this moment that you were born.' 'How could that be,' asked the boy, 'if I had no idea?' 'Does the trumpet need to know it was appointed,' said the angel, 'in order to sound? It is not the vessel, but He who sounds it.' The boy then lifted the horn to his mouth and sounded it. And on a distant hill an angel lifted a horn of radiant gold and did likewise."

The Pool of Lights

"In the next vision I was standing on a white marble terrace outside of some sort of palace. It was early evening. Around me were at least forty men in white robes and white headpieces and of Middle Eastern features. Everyone was gathered around a large oval pool of water encased in a wall of a stones. In their midst was a man I presumed to be their leader or teacher. His appearance was likewise Middle Eastern but different from the rest. His clothing was different as well, of blue, purple, and scarlet. In his hand was a rod, at the end of which was a fire. As he moved the rod over the surface of the pool, a line of yellow light would appear in the deep blue of the water, remain for a time, then fade away. I watched as he drew two crowns, two lions, and two eyes. 'What is the meaning of the images?' asked one of the white-robed men. 'The crowns,' said the man with the rod, 'stand for kings; the lions, for cities; and the eyes, for the appointed times.'"

THE CYLINDER

"At the start of the final vision it took me a few moments before I could tell what I was seeing. It was a cylinder of stone or clay and covered with wedge-shaped letters."

"Why couldn't you tell what it was?"

"Because it was so colossal. It was several stories high and far wider than it was high. At each of its ends stood guards, bearded, robed, and crowned with ornate headdresses. One of them shouted a command. The cylinder began to roll, slowly at first but with increasing momentum at every turn. I watched as it rolled over plains, valleys, and deserts. Finally, with what was left of its momentum, it rolled up a mountain. On the top of the mountain was a plateau. As the cylinder rolled over the plateau, the engraved words on its surface were imprinted on the ground. And as the sun set, rays of golden light began shooting up from each letter. And then from each pillar of light came other lights, shooting horizontally across the plateau until all the vertical lights were joined together. A structure began to emerge—a building formed entirely of light. Then a man appeared in a dark-blue suit, a red tie, and blondish hair. I had seen him before. He stood in front of the building with a paper, as if about to issue a proclamation. 'I have been charged,' he said, 'to build a house in Jerusalem of Judah. And so it shall be done.'"

"I continued following the ram through the desert and up to the walled city. It entered the city's gate and walked through its streets, squares, and alleys until finally departing through another gate. As it emerged, I noticed that the engravings were gone from its body. It was then that I realized what had happened; the entire city was now covered with engravings. The wedge-shaped letters now covered the walls, buildings, towers, streets, and squares. And just as they had been moving on the ram, they were now moving across the city and rolling up and down its buildings and walls. The ram turned back to watch it all from a nearby mountain. Then he resumed his journey and disappeared over the mountain into the wilderness. And the vision ended."

Chapter 44

THE YEAR OF THE BIRAH

T HE VISION HAD taken place at night. I had expected to find the boy waiting outside my tent the next morning. But there was no sign of him. At midday I went to draw water from one of the desert wells. That's when he appeared. And when I say *appeared*, I mean his head popped up from the other side of the well, smiling, playful, and as mysterious as ever. At times I wished I could speak his language so we could better communicate, but perhaps that was part of the mystery.

"He motioned for me to follow him. So I did. He led me through several valleys until we came to our destination, a mountain, which we ascended. When we reached the top, I saw what looked like the ruins of an ancient Greek or Roman building or temple with pedestals, pillars, and steps and a few odd structures I couldn't identify, everything of white marble. The building had no roof and not enough walls to prevent me from seeing the vast desert landscape that formed the background against which it stood.

"There, sitting on the steps in between two of its massive pillars, was the Oracle. He motioned for me to join him. So I did. I told him the vision."

"The ram," he said, "of course represents the Jubilee. As each Jubilee sets in motion the events of the next era, so did the Jubilee of 1967. The Six-Day War altered the dynamics of the Middle East. The failure of Arab nationalism in that war opened the door for the ascent of radical Islam. It ushered in an era of terrorism, al Qaeda, Hamas, Osama Bin Laden, and 9/11. It gave birth to a new US-Israeli alliance and caused the United States to become the chief arbiter in the Middle East.

"As for the Soviet Union, the defeat of its Arab allies in the Six-Day War caused alarm among its European allies and satellite nations and the weakening of the communist bloc. The Jubilee of 1967 transformed not just the nation of Israel and the Middle East but ultimately the world. Some observers even commented that ever since 1967 the world had been living in the seventh day of the Six-Day War.[1]

"As for Israel, it was now overseeing a land mass several times larger than what it had possessed before the Six-Day War. As for Jerusalem, the city prospered and grew. The Jewish quarter was rebuilt and inhabited. And the words of the prophet Zechariah were fulfilled:

> Old men and old women shall again sit in the streets of Jerusalem.... The streets of the city shall be full of boys and girls playing in its streets.[2]

"The years after 1967 saw more Jewish people coming back to the land than ever before. At the same time, it was in this period more than any other that Jerusalem became the focal point of global controversy. Israel would declare Jerusalem as its capital. And Jerusalem would become the only national capital the world refused to recognize. The symbol you saw on the ram and the door was the letter *beit*, the Hebrew *b*. It stood for the word *birah*. *Birah* means capital."

"What about the ram?" I asked.

"Did it look something like this?" asked the Oracle, pointing to the ruins of the white marble building.

"Yes, like an ancient building. What was this place originally?"

"A house of government and law."

"Is that a clue to the next Jubilee...that it would be connected to government and law?"

"It would be. And what else would this next Jubilee be connected to?"

"How could I know?"

"What are *all* the Jubilees connected to?" he asked.

"Restoration and return, the return of the ancestral possession to its original owner. But that already happened in 1967."

"Perhaps there was more to it," he replied. "So then according to the mystery, in what year would the next Jubilee fall?"

"It would come out to 2017."

"And if the mystery should manifest again, what would we expect to take place in 2017?"

"An event of restoration...an event having to do with the return of a lost possession to those to whom it belonged."

"And what or whom would this event involve specifically?"

"The Jewish people, Israel, Jerusalem."

"Each Jubilee continues that which was begun by the Jubilee that came before it. It restores that which was not restored in the preceding Jubilee. In the Jubilee of 1917 the Jewish people were promised a homeland, but Jerusalem was missing. So in the Jubilee of 1967 it was Jerusalem that was returned. So what was it that was *not* given or restored in the Jubilee of 1967?"

"I don't know."

"Then," said the Oracle, "we will have to find out."

"So the Oracle told you that the next Jubilee would involve government and law…what government?"

"The American government. The Jubilean event would manifest in Washington, DC."

"And how was it revealed to you?"

"Through the woman of darkened bronze."

Chapter 45

THE JUBILEE OF CAPITOL HILL

I RETURNED TO THE mountain to find the Oracle sitting on the top step of the ancient palace, in between two of its white marble columns. I joined him there."

"Tell me," I said, "about the woman of darkened bronze."

"In the year of Jubilee the return of the heirs to their ancestral inheritance must be given legal authority and recognition."

"But the legal authority is in the law of Jubilees itself."

"Yes, for a person living in ancient Israel. But in this case the original owner is not a person but a nation, the nation of Israel itself. Therefore, the legal recognition of its return must come from the nations, from the world, from world rulers and authorities. In the return of the exiles from Babylon that legal authority was given by the greatest world power of that age, the Persian Empire and its emperor, Cyrus. In the Jubilee of 1917 the legal authority came from the greatest world power of that time, the British Empire. And in the return of Israel into the world it came from the greatest of the postwar powers, America.

"But in the return of Israel to Jerusalem in 1967 the world refused to recognize that return or Jerusalem as Israel's capital. And in the Jubilee, if the original owner returns to his possession and the authorities refuse to recognize that return, then the return will not be complete and there will be conflict. And so it was with Israel's return to its ancient capital. Not only did the world refuse to recognize the return but the nations gathered together, over and over again, to condemn that return and to declare it illegal."[1]

"In the United Nations?"

"Yes. It was there that they issued condemnation after condemnation against Israel, more condemnations than they had issued against any other nation, more than they had ever issued against all the nations of the world combined. And many of those condemnations were focused on what happened in the Jubilee of 1967. The world was condemning the return. The world was condemning the Jubilee and warring against the Jubilean restoration."

"But if any nation had a right to any city, it was Israel to Jerusalem."

"The only nation whose title deed to its land and capital was the word of God itself. In all its history Jerusalem had been the capital of only one nation, Israel. And yet the world declared that it had no ancestral right or connection to its ancient capital. But one of the manifestations of the Jubilee is that the heir's return to the land is given legal authority and recognition.

"2017 was the fiftieth year after the return of Jerusalem in the Six-Day War, the Jubilean year. The world's preeminent power was the United States of America. The highest legal or legislative body of the world's pre-eminent power was the United States Senate.

"In the mid-1990s the United States Congress passed a law calling for America's recognition of Jerusalem as the capital of Israel. But the president at that time signed a waiver delaying its implementation. That waiver was renewed every six months by every successive president. It looked unlikely that it would ever become a reality.

"But in 2017 America had a new president, Donald Trump—and it was the year of Jubilee. The waiver expired in late spring. The new president had promised a change in America's policy concerning Jerusalem, but then, as did the presidents before him, he signed the waiver.

"Still, it was the year of Jubilee. And the waiver just happened to be set to expire in June, the month that marked fifty years from the last Jubilean event. In fact it was set to expire during the fifty year anniversary week of that event."

"The Jubilee of the Jubilee," I said.

"Yes. And it was then that something happened. The United States Senate gathered together, and the mystery manifested. The bronze woman you saw in your vision was the Statue of Freedom, the figure that crowns the dome of the Capitol Building. It was in that building that the Jubilean event of 2017 would be set in motion. A resolution was introduced that concerned Jerusalem and the granting of legal recognition to what had taken place fifty years, one Jubilee, earlier, the return to Jerusalem."

"It was the document I saw in the woman's hand."

"Yes," he replied. "The Senate resolution was a Jubilean document. The Jubilee focuses on the return of the ancestral possession to its owner. And that was the exact focus of the Senate resolution. In the year of Jubilee the original owner's sovereignty to the land is affirmed, reaffirmed, and given legal recognition—which is exactly what the Senate resolution called for. The Jubilee joins together two things: the fifty-year time period with the return of the ancestral possession. So the Senate resolution joined together the fifty-year period with the return of the ancestral possession of Jerusalem.

> And you shall consecrate the fiftieth year...[2]

"In the year of Jubilee the fiftieth year is consecrated. So in the year of Jubilee the United States Senate consecrated the fiftieth year. The resolution said this:

> Whereas June 2017 marks the *50th anniversary* of the *Six Day War* and the *reunification* of the city of *Jerusalem*...Whereas, in *1967, Jerusalem* was *reunited* by *Israel* during the conflict known as the *Six Day War*...Whereas *this year marks the 50th year* that *Jerusalem* has been administered as a *united city*.[3]

"After the consecration of the fiftieth year comes the restoration. So after the Senate set apart the fiftieth year, it called for the recognition of the restoration:

> *Resolved*, That the Senate...recognizes the 50th *Anniversary of the reunification of Jerusalem*...reaffirms the Jerusalem Embassy Act...as United States law, and calls upon the President and all United States officials to abide by its provisions.[4]

"In the year of Jubilee every authority in the land, from king to priest to judge and magistrate, was to recognize the restoration of the land to its original owner. So the Senate resolution called for the president and every American official to recognize the restoration of Jerusalem as Israel's capital, to grant the legal recognition to Israel's sovereignty over its Holy City that had been missing for the past fifty years.

"The Senate resolution commemorated the fifty-year anniversary of Jerusalem's return and thus was a proclamation of Jubilee. And it followed the pattern of what was decreed in the Jubilean ordinance. The Jubilee must first be proclaimed. After that its requirements must be implemented. So the resolution began by first proclaiming the Jubilee over and over again, and then after that it called for its implementation. The Senate wasn't trying to fulfill the ancient ordinance. Thus it's all the more striking that the highest legislative body of the greatest of world powers would produce a resolution that was in effect a proclamation of the Jubilee."

"And in the Jubilean year."

"Not only in the Jubilean year," he said, "the Jubilean month and the Jubilean week. In fact the Senate passed its Jubilean resolution on *the day of the Jubilee*…fifty years from the start of the Six-Day War *to the exact day*. The Jubilean resolution went forth on the day of Jubilee."

"And they had no idea?"

"They knew it was fifty years, but they had no idea that they were fulfilling the mystery and that which was ordained in the law of Jubilees."

"The next mystery would involve three events, each separated from the others by at least half a century and yet joined to the others by a series of ancient threads."

"And how was it revealed?"

"By three people, one of them Jewish, one of them Gentile, and the other, not at all human."

Chapter 46

THE DAYS

I RETURNED TO THE ruins of the ancient palace. The Oracle was sitting on one of its pillarless pedestals. There was another one nearby on which I would sit."

"What was the meaning of the three mountains," I asked, "and the three who ascended them to sound the ram's horn?"

"One," he replied, "you've already seen, the Statue of Freedom. As for the second of the three, the man with the eye patch in the army fatigues—have you ever seen him before?"

"He looked familiar."

"That was Moshe Dayan, Israel's defense minister during the Six-Day War and the war's most recognizable figure."

"And the first figure, the man with boots, trousers, and the officer's cap?"

"You haven't seen him before, but you know him. That was General Edmund Allenby. So what do you think it meant?"

"The three Jubilees," I replied. "The Statue of Freedom represented the Jubilee of 2017. The man with the eye patch, Moshe Dayan, stood for the Jubilee of 1967; and General Allenby, the Jubilee of 1917."

"Yes," said the Oracle, "but there's more to it than that. The Senate resolution of 2017 wasn't the central event of that Jubilean year but the opening event. It would set the course that would lead to the central Jubilean event. And what about the previous Jubilee? What was the central event of the Jubilee of 1967?"

"The regaining of Jerusalem."

"Yes. And what was the opening event war that set everything in motion?"

"What was it?"

"The war's opening, the start of the Six-Day War, Israel's surprise attack on the airfields of its enemies. That opening strike was the critical act that began the war and determined its outcome. Within a matter of hours Israel had neutralized the air power of those who had sworn to destroy it and for the rest of the war maintained control of the skies. It was that opening event that would lead to the return of Jerusalem, the central event of that Jubilee. On what day did that event take place?"

"It was in June," I replied.

"It was June 5," said the Oracle. "The opening day of that Jubilee was June 5. And what was the opening event of the Jubilee of 2017?"

"The Senate resolution."

"And on what day did it take place?"

"I don't know."

"On *June 5*, the same day."

"So each Jubilee was set in motion on the same day."

"The two Jubilees began fifty years apart to the exact same day."

"What about the first mountain I saw, the first of the three Jubilees?"

"The Jubilee of 1917. What was the Jubilean event of that year?"

"The Balfour Declaration...and Allenby's liberation of Jerusalem."

"The Balfour Declaration was approved at the end of October 1917, the same time that the war to liberate Jerusalem began. And Allenby's army would enter Jerusalem in the early days of December."

"But with the other Jubilees, the opening event happened in June."

"In the early part of 1917 the British commander of the Egyptian Expeditionary Force was Lieutenant General Archibald Murray. Murray was given orders to launch an offensive in Palestine in the hope of driving out the Ottoman Empire. In March of that year he confronted Ottoman forces in the First Battle of Gaza. But he was defeated. In April he confronted them a second time in the Second Battle of Gaza but was again defeated.

"In London the new British prime minister, David Lloyd George, decided that Murray had to be replaced by a new commander, one with more vision and drive. The man chosen was General Edmund Allenby.

"Allenby immediately set out to revive the morale of Murray's exhausted and demoralized troops. His efforts proved successful. At the end of October Allenby engaged the Ottoman army at the Third Battle of Gaza and won. It was the beginning of the land's liberation and the end of Ottoman rule.

"Without Allenby's campaign the land would not have been liberated, nor would have Jerusalem. And the promise of a national home for the Jewish people in the Balfour Declaration would have been of no effect. It was Allenby's appointment as commander of the Egyptian Expeditionary Force that changed the course of the war and opened the way for everything else that took place."

"So when was the critical moment?"

"In his memoirs of the war Lloyd George revealed the details behind the appointment:

> The War Cabinet came to the conclusion that it was desirable to introduce more resolute leadership into the command

of the Egyptian Expeditionary Force…On *5th June*, 1917,
the War Cabinet decided…that General Allenby should be
appointed as Commander-in-Chief of the British Forces in
Egypt…[1]

"It all happened on *June 5*. The appointment would set in motion the
chain of events that would bring about the liberation of Jerusalem and
the Jewish homeland promised in the Balfour Declaration. It all began on
June 5.

"So the event that opened the Jubilee of 1917 was June 5. The event that
opened the Jubilee of 1967 was June 5, exactly fifty years later. And the event
that opened the Jubilee of 2017 was June 5, exactly fifty years later than the
day that opened up the Six-Day War and exactly one hundred years later
than the day that opened the Jubilee of 1917. All three Jubilees were set in
motion on the same exact day."

"In my vision the one who blew the shofar faced the next mountain."

"Yes," said the Oracle, "because all the Jubilees are bound together. The
Israeli pilots who took to the air on that pivotal morning of June 5, 1967,
did so exactly fifty years to the day after the British War Cabinet made its
pivotal decision to appoint General Allenby to the command of the Egyptian Expeditionary Force. And the members of the United States Senate
who convened on Capitol Hill on June 5, 2017, to pass the Jubilean resolution did so exactly fifty years to the day after the Israeli pilots took to the
air and exactly one hundred years to the day after the British War Cabinet
made its decision.

"Thus the Jubilees not only took place fifty years apart; they took place
fifty years apart to the exact day!"

"Each figure in the vision stood on top of a mountain. Jerusalem is the
mountain of God. So did each mountain represent Jerusalem…the Jerusalem of that Jubilee?"

"Yes," he replied, "as each opening event would lead to Jerusalem. What
began on June 5, 1917, would lead to Jerusalem's liberation from the Ottoman
Empire. What began on June 5, 1967, would lead to the return of Jerusalem to
the Jewish people. And what began on June 5, 2017, would lead to…"

"Would lead to what?"

"Ah," said the Oracle, "I almost went ahead of myself."

"Would lead to what?"

"I believe you will have to *see* what it would lead to…"

"And I would see it…in the next mystery."

"Which would involve what?"

"The words of kings and rulers and how they usher in the purposes of God…just as they had in ancient times. They would again in the Jubilee of 2017, even through the most surprising of vessels."

"And how was it shown to you?"

"Through the dragons' lair."

Chapter 47

THE JUBILEAN DECLARATION

IRETURNED TO THE ruins of the ancient palace. The Oracle was sitting on one of its low walls. I joined him."

"The vision of the dragons' lair...what was I seeing?"

"Remember what I told you about the granting of legal recognition and authority."

"That in the Jubilee it's not just that you return to your land but that the return has legal authority. It has to be recognized."

"Yes. By whom?"

"By the ruling authorities."

"And in Israel's return to Jerusalem in 1967?"

"It was the one thing that was never given."

"And the world's leading power and authority was America. And no president would defy the world to grant that recognition. But 2017 was the first Jubilee after the return of Jerusalem. And one of the manifestations of the Jubilee is the granting of recognition and legal authority to the owner's return to the land."

"But you said that Trump signed the waiver, so there was no recognition."

"He signed it in June. The waiver lasted for six months. So where would that bring us?"

"To December. That would be at the very end of the Jubilean year."

"And so if the mystery is to manifest," said the Oracle, "it would have to manifest then."

"And did it?"

"On December 6, 2017, the president entered the White House Diplomatic Reception Room with an announcement to give to the world:

> I have determined that it is time to officially recognize Jerusalem as the capital of Israel.... Through all of these years, presidents representing the United States have declined to officially recognize Jerusalem as Israel's capital. In fact, we have declined to acknowledge any Israeli capital at all. But

202

> today, we finally acknowledge the obvious: that Jerusalem is
> Israel's capital.[1]

"The president's declaration concerned the Jubilean nation, Israel; the Jubilean city, Jerusalem; and the return and restoration of the ancestral possession to those to whom it belonged, the central issue of the Jubilee. It was the Jubilean event. The fiftieth year had come and again, like clockwork, the mystery of the Jubilee had manifested."

"It was the restoration that had been missing in the Jubilee of 1967—the legal recognition of the return."

"Yes. And as both Balfour and Truman were representatives of the world's leading power of the day, so too was Trump in the Jubilee of 2017."

"The warrior-king in my vision…it was Trump."

"Yes."

"And the woman chained in the center of the dragons, she represented Jerusalem…the royal and holy city."

"Yes. And in the year of Jubilee she was released. The event was momentous. It was the first time an American president had recognized Jerusalem as the capital of Israel…the first time in *modern history* that *any* world leader or nation had ever recognized Jerusalem as the capital of Israel, or even as belonging to Israel. And it was the first time *any* major power had recognized Jerusalem as the capital of Israel *since ancient times*.

"To find any other instance of such a recognition, one would have to go back at least two thousand years. And to find any instance of a world power actually supporting the return of the Jewish people to Jerusalem, actively affirming the city as Israel's capital, and issuing a proclamation concerning it, one would have to go back nearly two and a half thousand years to the days of the Persian Empire.

"The prime minister of Israel responded to the Jerusalem Declaration by calling it one of the four milestones in the history of Israel's restoration."[2]

"What were the others?"

"The Balfour Declaration, the founding of the Jewish state, and the liberation of Jerusalem[3]…each one linked to the mystery."

"What about the rest of the world? What was the reaction?"

"The declaration sent the world into an uproar. There were condemnations, demonstrations, threats, and violence."

"The dragons in my vision…when the trumpet was blown, they went into an uproar. Did the dragons represent the nations?"

"No, but the spiritual forces by which nations are driven. You see, the war over Jerusalem is ultimately a spiritual one. And the world's raging over Jerusalem went back to the days of Israel's rebirth. In 1949, after surviving the attack of five armies intended to annihilate it, Israel managed to gain possession of West Jerusalem. It wasn't the biblical city of Jerusalem but the modern suburbs that had sprung up around its walls. But even this was too much for the world. The nations gathered at the United Nations to pass a resolution attacking Israel's right to West Jerusalem and calling for immediate action."

"What kind of immediate action?"

"To forcibly drive Israel out. It was the first time that the world would specifically attack Israel's sovereignty over its ancient capital and the first time it would call for action to separate Jerusalem from the Jewish nation. The resolution would seal the world's course for years to come. It was passed on December 9, 1949.[4] It's a noteworthy date. December 9 was the anniversary of the Jubilean event of 1917, the day Jerusalem was liberated from the Ottoman Empire."

"Did they plan to do it on the same day?"

"No," said the Oracle, "the war over Jerusalem is a spiritual one and one that transcends anyone's planning. Now, on the world's calendar the resolution was passed on December 9. But on the biblical calendar it happened on a different date—the eighteenth day of Kislev."

"And is that significant?"

"President Trump issued the Jerusalem Declaration, recognizing Israel's sovereignty over Jerusalem and Jerusalem as Israel's capital...on *the eighteenth day of Kislev, the exact same day.* So on the anniversary of the day the world issued its declaration that Jerusalem was *not* the capital of Israel, the president issued the Jerusalem Declaration, proclaiming that Jerusalem *was* the capital of Israel."

"And no one planned it that way."

"No, no one but One. But that wasn't the only mystery to manifest in the Jubilee of 2017. The Senate resolution went forth in June at the fifty-year mark, the Jubilee anniversary week of Jerusalem's liberation in the Six-Day War. The president's declaration went forth in December, at the one-hundred-year mark, the double Jubilee anniversary week of Jerusalem's liberation by General Allenby."

"Did the president choose to issue the Jerusalem Declaration at the hundred-year anniversary of Jerusalem's liberation?"

"No. It just so happened that the presidential waiver lasted from the beginning June to the beginning of December...from the fifty-year anniversary week of the one Jubilee to the one-hundred-year anniversary week of the other. Nobody intended it. Nor did they intend this: four days before Trump issued the declaration, the appointed Scripture that was recited throughout the world was that which spoke of the *return of Jacob*, the *return of Israel*, to his *ancestral possession*."[5]

"The focus of the declaration."

"And that wasn't the only appointed Scripture," said the Oracle. "From the scroll of the prophets the appointed word spoke of how the Jewish people had been removed from their Holy City...how it was taken by the peoples of the region to whom it did not belong. It declared that Jerusalem was the possession of the Jewish people...and how they would again return to that mountain...to Jerusalem.

"So the year of Jubilee had come and the Jubilean event had again been displayed before the entire world. For the first time in two and a half thousand years a proclamation had gone forth sanctioning the return of the Jewish people to Jerusalem...the return of each to his own possession."

"The next time I saw the Oracle, I would be shown a mystery that lay behind a modern American president."

"What kind of mystery?"

"An ancient one...a two-and-a-half-thousand-year-old mystery."

"And how was it revealed to you?"

"Through the tomb of a king."

Chapter 48

THE RETURN OF THE PERSIAN

I RETURNED TO THE ancient building on the mountaintop but saw no sign of the Oracle. Finally I heard his voice. 'In here,' he said. The reason I hadn't seen him was because he was sitting inside the building's only enclosed chamber. I'm sure there had once been other chambers, but it was the only one left. I went inside. There were several openings in its walls, through which came shafts of sunlight. The Oracle was sitting on a stone slab. There was another one to his right. I sat down on it."

"I saw a stone house on a pyramid of stones, and in the house, a golden king. I know it was connected to Cyrus, but what did it all mean?"

"Twice," he said, "the nation of Israel was sent into exile, the first time to Babylon, the second, to the ends of the earth. And twice they returned, once in the ancient world and once in the modern. Who was the king who issued the decree concerning their ancient return?"

"Cyrus."

"And so in the modern return, in the regathering of the Jewish people in the twentieth century, we saw the replaying of that mystery in a Cyrus of the modern world."

"In the presidency of Harry Truman."

"Yes, in his sending word for the exiles to return, in his working for the resolution that brought Israel back into the world, and in his recognition of the nation at the moment of its birth.

"But Israel's regathering and restoration didn't end with Truman. It went on, just as did the Jubilees. So as one Jubilee and one restoration led to the next, could the one American Cyrus have led to another? If the return and restoration were to continue, is it possible that the template of Cyrus could manifest a second time? Could there be another to arise in whom the ancient mystery would manifest?"

"Was that what my vision was about?"

"Yes," said the Oracle, "the building you entered wasn't a house—it was a tomb. You entered the tomb of King Cyrus."

"A tomb in which a king came back to life."

"As there would be a second American Cyrus, one who would replay the mystery and who would begin where the first had left off."

He paused to give me time to ponder his words before going on.

"If each Jubilee leads to the next, and if in each Jubilee the seeds are sown for the one that follows, is it possible that in the days of the first American Cyrus the seeds were planted for another?"

"Seeds for another? What does that mean?"

"It was in the presidency of Harry Truman, in the days of the American Cyrus, that the next Cyrus would be born."

"And the child was named..."

"*Donald Trump*," he replied.

"Donald Trump...Not the most likely person to fulfill a biblical calling."

"It is the least likely who are often used. He was born in the year 1946, the second year of the Truman administration. His birth came right in the midst of that period when Truman was working to open the doors for the Jewish exiles to return home and setting the events in motion that would lead to the rebirth of the Jewish nation—the template of Cyrus. So it was in the days of the first American Cyrus that the second was born."

"But Truman had been a student of the Bible. I don't believe you could say that of Trump. His life was not..."

"In that way he only all the more fits the template of Cyrus. In the Book of Isaiah it was prophesied of Cyrus, '...*you have not known Me*.'[1] Though Cyrus *hadn't* known God, he was used to fulfill God's purposes.

"It was in March of 2017, Trump's first year as president, that he issued a statement from the White House on the occasion of *Nowruz*."

"What's Nowruz?"

"It's the New Year's day celebration of *ancient Persia*. In the president's statement he actually spoke of King Cyrus. And he did more than speak of him. His statement contained a quote. It wasn't the words of the quote that were most significant but their context. It was an apocryphal saying attributed to the ancient king. The president said this:

> Cyrus the Great, a leader of the ancient Persian Empire, famously said that "freedom, dignity, and wealth together constitute the greatest happiness of humanity."[2]

"It was not only that the president had issued a public statement in which he spoke of Cyrus but that he spoke words attributed to the ancient king. In other words, he wasn't only speaking *of* Cyrus; he was now speaking *as* Cyrus. The president and the king were joined together. And this took place *before* the act that would manifest the mystery of the two leaders before the world."

"The Jerusalem Declaration."

"The Book of Ezra opens up with these words:

> Now in the first year of Cyrus king of Persia, that the word
> of the LORD by the mouth of Jeremiah might be fulfilled, the
> LORD stirred up the spirit of Cyrus king of Persia, so that he
> made a proclamation...[3]

"This is the setting in which Cyrus would issue the decree concerning the return of the Jewish people to their land. So according to the Scripture, when does the proclamation go forth?"

"In the first year." I replied. "So when was Trump's first year?"

"He became president on January 20, 2017. So his first year would extend to January 20, 2018."

"So then, according to the template, he would have to issue a proclamation in that period."

"The president issued his proclamation on December 6, 2017. Thus with forty-five days left the proclamation went forth *in the first year.*

> The LORD stirred up the spirit of Cyrus king of Persia, so that
> he made a proclamation throughout all his kingdom, and
> also put it in writing...[4]

"The president likewise first made a verbal proclamation to the world and after that sealed it in writing as he signed a written proclamation, which he then held up for the world to see."

"The prophet Isaiah," I said, "declared that Cyrus was called by God to do what he did. And the chief rabbi of Israel told Truman that he too was called, as Cyrus was to do what he did. What about Trump? Was he ever told of the calling of Cyrus?"

"Yes," said the Oracle, "more so than all his predecessors. It was spoken *before* he fulfilled it, by people of faith, Christian leaders. And it was spoken before he even became president."

"So Trump was the appointed Cyrus for America."

"Trump was the Cyrus *of* America but a Cyrus *to* Israel. His significance *to* America would follow another paradigm."

"The cylinder in the tomb and the cylinder on the ram would represent the Jubilean declaration."

"Yes," he replied, "the king's proclamation and the president's proclamation. Note, the king's proclamation spoke not only of the return of the Jewish people to their land but of their sovereignty over their Holy City, Jerusalem. Note the words in Cyrus' declaration:

> Jerusalem which is in Judah...[5]

"'Jerusalem which is in Judah...' means Jerusalem is part of and belonging to Judah. Judah is the Jewish nation. So the president's declaration likewise recognized Jerusalem as part of and belonging to the Jewish nation. Cyrus' proclamation recognized Jerusalem as the capital of the Jewish nation. The president's declaration did the same.

"Cyrus' proclamation decreed that the Jewish people were now permitted to 'go up to Jerusalem.'6 Thus it specifically affirmed their right to return to their Holy City. The president's proclamation likewise affirmed the right of Israel to return to its Holy City. And therein lies another mystery behind the president and that declaration. Listen again to the Scripture:

> Now in the first year of Cyrus king of Persia, *that* the word
> of the LORD by the mouth of Jeremiah might *be fulfilled*, the
> LORD stirred up the spirit of Cyrus king of Persia, so that he
> made a proclamation..."7

"What was the word," I asked, "that Cyrus fulfilled?"

"It was a prophecy given to Jeremiah revealing how long Israel's exile would last:

> For thus says the LORD: *After seventy years* are completed
> at Babylon, I will...perform My good word toward you, and
> cause you to return...8

"After *seventy years*,'" said the Oracle. "The key is seventy years. It was the king's proclamation that allowed the Jewish people to return to Jerusalem after seventy years. So Cyrus is connected to an interval of seventy years. Is it possible, then, that the same interval of time, seventy years, could have a part in the replaying of the mystery in the American president and his declaration?

"Cyrus ascended to world power at the end of the seventy years. When Donald Trump ascended to world power, how many years had he lived? For *seventy years*. Thus, as with Cyrus, he ascended to world power *after seventy years*. And that rise began as he announced his candidacy for the presidency just two days into the start of his *seventieth year*. His life was, itself, the embodiment of the seventy years. And as for the ancient Cyrus, the period of seventy years would likewise be central to his life. He would live for seventy years."

"So the modern Cyrus began where the ancient Cyrus left off."

"You could say that."

"What about Israel?" I asked. "The seventy years of the prophecy were connected to Israel. So could the president's proclamation be connected to a seventy-year period having to do with Israel?"

"If the seventy-year period," he replied, "ends with the proclamation, then we would have to go back seventy years from that proclamation to see if it brings us to any significant event. The proclamation took place in 2017. So going back seventy years would lead to…"

"1947!"

"1947. The year that Israel was voted into existence at the United Nations. So the seventy years began with Israel's conception. In the ancient case it was at the end of a critical seventy-year period in Israel's history that Cyrus ascended to world power. So the template would reveal that after a critical seventy-year period in Israel's history we would see the rise of a world leader who would issue a proclamation concerning Israel. So the modern seventy-year period ended in the year 2017, the very year that a new Cyrus, Donald Trump, rose to world power and just happened to issue a proclamation concerning Israel…"

"Which has to be issued in the seventieth year."

"And when he issued that declaration, he made special mention of another president. He spoke of the other Cyrus, Harry Truman. And his declaration contained the phrase that would link the modern declaration to the ancient—the phrase *seventy years*. He said this:

> It was *70 years* ago that the United States, under President
> Truman, recognized the State of Israel.[9]

"So the proclamation itself makes note that the proclamation is itself going forth at the end of a seventy-year period."

"And there's another connection," I said. "The two presidents who walk in the template of Cyrus are connected not only to a critical seventy-year period in Israel's history but a seventy-year period with regard to each other. The two presidencies take place seventy years apart from the other. Trump leads America seventy years after Truman led America. And as the reign of Cyrus framed the seventy-year period, so each of the two American presidents frame the modern seventy-year period, the first at its beginning and the second at its end. And the seventy-year period they frame has to do with Israel's restoration."

"Very good," said the Oracle. "Now, note the parameters of the Scripture. The declaration goes forth at the end of the seventy years, *and, at the same time*, in the first year of the king's reign as world leader. In President Trump both parameters converge; the seventieth year with regard to Israel is also the first year of his presidency…and on top of that it all converges in the year of Jubilee."

"And for all of it to converge as it did," I said, "Trump had to assume the presidency at the end of the seventy years—at the exact time he did. And for that to happen, an American presidential election had to take place at the end of seventy years—the exact time it did. And the election had to result in his victory. The timing and the voting, everything, it all had to be part of the mystery."

"Yes," said the Oracle, "presidential elections and their outcomes are also part of the mystery."

The Oracle got up from his seat. I did as well. He led me over to the steps of the ancient building.

"I'll speak of an ancient king," he said. "And you'll speak of a modern president."

I didn't say anything, as I wasn't sure what he wanted me to do.

"And so it came to pass that at the end of Israel's seventy years, a new king came to power..."

"And it came to pass at the end of Israel's seventy years," I replied, "that a new president came to power."

"And in the first year of his reign he issued a proclamation..."

"And in the first year of his presidency he issued a proclamation."

"The king's proclamation recognized the right of the Jewish people to Jerusalem..."

"And the president's proclamation recognized the right of the Jewish people to Jerusalem."

"And of Jerusalem as Israel's capital..."

"And of Jerusalem as Israel's capital."

"The king's proclamation granted legal authority and sanction to the return of the Jewish people to Jerusalem by the greatest power of the ancient world..."

"And the president's proclamation granted legal authority and sanction to the return of the Jewish people to Jerusalem by the greatest power of the modern world."

"Well done," said the Oracle with a smile. "Soon you'll have no need of me."

"What was the next mystery?"

"One that would go back further than Cyrus...and in which the law of Jubilees would determine a presidential election and an American president...and a word appointed for the day of his birth."

"And how was it revealed?"

"Through an angel and a boy on a hill."

Chapter 49

THE TRUMPET MAN

I RETURNED TO THE ruins of the ancient house. The Oracle was standing beside one of the pillars. I approached him."

"Look at that," he said, gazing up at one of the ornamental curves on its capital. "It almost looks like a ram's horn. '*You shall cause the trumpet of the Jubilee to sound...*'[1] The trumpet, the ram's horn, lies at the center of the mystery. Without it there's no return and no restoration. Without it there's no Jubilee. In fact the Hebrew word for *Jubilee* is *Yovel*. And *Yovel*, or *Jubilee*, literally means the trumpet, or ram's horn. For the Jubilee to come, the trumpet must be sounded."

"And it *was* actually sounded," I said, "in the Jubilee of 1967, at the moment of Jerusalem's return."

"Yes, by Rabbi Goren," he said. "It was the central act of that Jubilee, and he was its central figure, its embodiment. But what about the following Jubilee? What was its central act?"

"The Jerusalem Declaration."

"And who was its central figure?"

"It would have to be the president."

"In your vision of the boy and the angel, the boy represented the president. And the race up the hill was the race for the presidency. In each of your visions of the two angels and the boy, the boy represented the central figure of that Jubilee. Do you remember the mystery of the rabbi's name?"

"Yes, Goren. It means threshing floor."

"And the central ground of that Jubilee was the threshing floor, the Temple Mount. But the name *Goren* was of European origin, and in its original European context it held a different meaning. And yet in Hebrew, the language of the land in which the Jubilean event took place, it meant *threshing floor*. So what about the central figure in the next Jubilee? Is it possible that his name also holds a mystery?"

"Trump?"

"In his ancestor's native language the name has been taken to mean drum. But in English, the language of America, where the Jubilean event would take place, the name holds another meaning."

"What?"

"He who sounds the trumpet."

"The Jubilee!" I said. "Trump was the one who made the declaration, who sounded it...It was Trump who sounded the trumpet in that year of Jubilee!"

"*'You shall cause the trumpet of the Jubilee to sound...'*"[2]

"So the central figure in the Jubilee of 2017 was Trump, which means he who sounds the trumpet. And the central figure of the Jubilee of 1967 was he who sounded the shofar, the ram's horn...which is also a trumpet."

"And the president's name," said the Oracle, "holds another meaning, similar, but slightly different. The word *trump* refers not only to the one who sounds the trumpet but to the trumpet itself. In the King James Bible the *last trumpet* is called the 'last *trump*.'[3] And when speaking of the Messiah's second coming, it prophesies that it will come about with the '*trump* of God.'[4] *Trump* means trumpet."

"What's the word in the original language that the word *trump* stands for?"

"*Trump* is the biblical translation of the Greek word *salpinx*. When the Jubilean ordinance in Leviticus was translated into Greek, the word *salpinx* referred to the shofar, the ram's horn, the trumpet of Jubilee. In other words, 'In the year of Jubilee you shall sound the shofar, the salpinx, the trump.' So in which year does the trump sound?"

"In the fiftieth year," I replied, "the year of Jubilee."

"And the fiftieth year was 2017. And the year of Jubilee must be the year of the trump. The year must be marked by it. And so 2017 *was* the year of the Trump. It was the year especially marked by the Trump, the year he came to power. In the Jubilee the trump sounds. So in the year 2017 the Trump sounded. And the law of Jubilees specifically commands that the trumpet '*shall sound throughout all your land.*'"[5]

"So the Trump sounded throughout the land."

"And what kind of sound does it make? The sound of the shofar is loud and jarring."

"And so the sound of the Trump was loud and jarring."

"Think about it," he said. "In the year of Jubilee the trump leads all things. So in the year of Jubilee America's leader and the world's most prominent leader was named Trump. In the year of Jubilee the Trump must lead."

"And the Jubilean event of 2017 would begin in America...So in the year of Jubilee Trump led America."

"Yes. And when does the Trump *begin to sound*?"

"At the beginning of the Jubilean year."

"The presidential election took place at the end of 2016. So Trump was given the platform of the presidency to sound in January of 2017, at the *beginning* of the Jubilean year. The ancient law ordains, '*You shall cause the trumpet of the Jubilee to sound…*'[6] So America had caused the Trump to sound in the year of Jubilee."

"It's almost a play on words."

"Such things are used in the Scriptures. And the names people are given often reveal the purpose for which they were born and appointed. The president was appointed to be a trumpet to sound in the year of Jubilee."

"A most unlikely instrument," I said. "And he had no idea."

"So in your vision," said the Oracle, "the angel told the boy that the trumpet doesn't need to know it was appointed to sound…that it wasn't about the vessel but the One who sounded it. It's not even about what the vessel does before or after its appointed time of sounding."

"And so it only matters that the trump sounds at the appointed time…and the appointed time was 2017."

"More specific than that," he said. "Do you remember what the United States Senate did in the middle of that year?"

"The Jubilean resolution."

"They passed a resolution recognizing the fiftieth year and the return of the original owner, Israel, to the ancestral possession and that, as in the Jubilee, official sanction be given to that return. But according to the law of Jubilees, for that to happen, the trumpet must sound. So on the exact date that marked the Jubilee, fifty years to the day the Six-Day War began, the Senate called for the president to recognize the right of the Jewish people to their ancestral possession, Jerusalem. They called for *the Trump to sound*. For when the trump sounds in the year of Jubilee, the original owners receive the right to their ancestral possession. So the Trump sounded in 2017, the year of Jubilee, and the original owners, the Jewish people, received the right to their ancestral possession, Jerusalem."

"Amazing."

"Shall I tell you another mystery?" asked the Oracle.

"Please."

"Do you believe that God weaves together every event with every other event?"

"I've come to believe in that," I replied.

"Donald Trump came into the world on June 14, 1946. It was a Friday, sealed with the setting of the sun, the Sabbath."

"So there was a portion of Scripture appointed for the day of his birth."

"Yes."

"And was there anything in that portion that was significant?"

"There was."

"What was it?"

"It was the section of the Bible that focuses on...the trumpet."

"So Trump was born on the day the Scripture spoke of the trump?"

"Yes," said the Oracle. "And the Scripture specifically speaks of how to produce the trumpet."[7]

"How to produce the trump," I said. "So on the day when the appointed Scripture spoke of producing the trump...the Trump was produced!"

"It wasn't that the Scripture was appointed for that one sole event, but all events and words are woven together by the hand of God."

"So the Scripture ordained the birth of the trump on the day of the Trump's birth."

"And the appointed Scripture went on to speak of the different times and ways the trumpet was to sound. It would sound to call the people, to summon its leaders, and to move the nation forward."

"And at any other times?"

"It was to sound during the appointed and sacred times of God."

"One of those appointed and sacred times of God," I said, "is the Jubilee. So on the day of Trump's birth the appointed Scriptures spoke of the trump being made to sound at God's appointed times...Trump was born to sound at the appointed time, in the year of Jubilee."

"The very year he came to power and began sounding."

"Does it say anything else about the trumpet?"

"Yes, that it would also sound to call for God's help, for the nation's deliverance. It would sound the call to war. In fact it was this very passage of Scripture, the ordinance of the trumpet, that led Rabbi Goren to sound the shofar on the day of Jerusalem's liberation."

"So the Scripture of Trump's birth led to the central moment in the Jubilee of 1967. And that key moment was the moment Israel returned to Jerusalem. And Trump's key moment in the next Jubilee was connected to that same moment. Trump's declaration would be the sealing of that return and that moment."

"Yes," said the Oracle, "the sounding of the second trump would seal the sounding of the first."

"Speaking of Rabbi Goren," I said, "you told me that in Hebrew his name meant threshing floor, but you never told me what his name meant in the original language."

"His family's original name was Gorenchik."

"So what does *Gorenchik* mean?"

"Are you sure you're ready?" asked the Oracle.

"Yes."

"Horn...*Gorenchik* means horn."

"*Horn!*" I replied. "As in *trumpet?*"

"Yes, as in *ram's horn, shofar, trumpet*...and *trump.*"

"So the man who sounded the horn at the Western Wall was named Horn?" I almost shouted.

"Yes."

"Rabbi Horn? So the central figure in the Jubilee of 1967 was Rabbi Horn! And fifty years later the central figure in the Jubilee of 2017 was President Trump!"

"And in biblical Hebrew *horn* and *trump* are the same word: *shofar.* So you shall cause the shofar of Jubilee, the horn of Jubilee, the trump of Jubilee, to sound."

"So one Jubilee is ushered in by a rabbi named Horn, and the other by a president named Trump! It's too much!"

"Are you surprised?" said the Oracle. "Did you not think that God had a sense of humor?"

"When I saw the Oracle again, he would take me even deeper into the realm of appointed times and the mystery that lay behind the events of modern times."

"And how was it revealed to you?"

"Through the waters of the magi."

Chapter 50

THE SEVENTY-YEAR MYSTERY

IRETURNED TO THE ruins of the ancient house to find the Oracle in the same place as in the beginning, sitting on its front steps in between two of its pillars. I sat down beside him."

"The men in white robes and hats and the pool of lights…who were they, and what did it mean?"

"As to where you were," he replied, "in the context of the mystery, it would have been the palace of a Babylonian or Persian king."

"And the men in white robes?"

"They would have been the *wise men* of the royal court, the magi."

"The magi, as in the wise men of the Christmas story?"

"Something like that. The magi were a priestly caste in ancient Mesopotamia believed to be endowed with divine wisdom. Their worship involved the elements of nature, fire and water."

"And the man with the rod?"

"Their leader, a Middle Eastern man but of an appearance different from the rest—that would be the prophet Daniel."

"What would the prophet Daniel be doing with the magi?"

"Daniel lived in the Babylonian exile, in the royal court of Babylon, and then of Persia. The Bible records that Daniel was made chief of the wise men of Babylon."

"And the images of the lions?"

"The city represented by the lion is Jerusalem."

"But there were two of them."

"Signifying two Jerusalems," said the Oracle, "one that was lost to Israel and the other that was restored."

"And the two crowns that represented two kings…what two kings?"

"One was ancient and the other was not."

"And the eyes?"

"The pool of water was a well. In Hebrew the word for *well* is *ayin. Ayin* is also the Hebrew word for *eye*. The letter *ayin* has a numerical value of seventy. It stood for the appointed times."

"Seventy," I said, "as in the seventy years. But what does it have to do with Daniel?"

"Daniel lived at the time of the exile of seventy years. And he was shown a mystery linked to the number seventy and having to do with years...seventy sevens of years...a countdown to the coming of the Messiah."

"And what was this telling me?"

"That concerning the seventy years in the revelation you were shown, the mystery goes deeper, there's more to be uncovered."

"So let's go deeper," I said.

"At the end of seventy years in Babylon, Cyrus came to world power, the proclamation went forth to restore Jerusalem and the land to the Jewish people, and the exiles began to return. So in the modern case what happened at the end of the seventy years?"

"At the end of seventy years," I replied, "a man in the pattern of Cyrus came to world power, and a proclamation went forth concerning Jerusalem and its restoration to the Jewish people."

"In the ancient case Israel was restored to Jerusalem under Cyrus seventy years after its exile from Jerusalem began under Nebuchadnezzar. So the end of the seventy years saw the restoration of what was lost at the beginning of the seventy years—the nation's separation from Jerusalem."

"In other words, the seventy-year period specifically had to do with the nation's separation from Jerusalem...and then the end of that separation."

"Yes."

"So is there any parallel in the modern case?"

"The separation of the Jewish people from Jerusalem goes back two thousand years. And yet there is a modern equivalent. When the United Nations passed the Partition Plan, dividing up the land, it was a double-edged sword. On one hand, it would bring about the rebirth of Israel. On the other hand, it would cut off the newborn nation from its Holy City. It would declare Jerusalem a "corpus separatum," a city separated, under the sovereignty and control of the United Nations—and thus separated from the Jewish nation.[1] There now was to be a nation of Israel in the world—but an Israel cut off from its ancient capital. So the same resolution that brought Israel into the world also began a period of separation, the nation from its Holy City.

"That separation would last until the Jubilee of 1967, when Jerusalem was restored to Israel. But with regard to the world and the realm of nations, authorities, powers, sovereignties, resolutions, and laws, the separation would continue until the Jubilee of 2017. It was only then that the world's unanimously upheld severance of Israel and Jerusalem was broken.

"So the period began when the United Nations decreed that Israel was legally separated from Jerusalem and ended when the United States nullified that decree by declaring that Jerusalem was legally joined to Israel—from 1947 to 2017. How many years?"

"Seventy years."

"But your vision was telling us to go deeper. The seventy years began when the United Nations voted on the Partition Plan, on Saturday, November 19, 1947. But on the biblical calendar it was a different date—the sixteenth day of Kislev. And on the biblical calendar the new day begins at sundown. The vote was taken after sundown—the beginning of the next day. The resolution was passed on the seventeenth day of Kislev.

"We have our first marker. The seventeenth day of Kislev constitutes the beginning of the seventy years. And when do the Scriptures say that Cyrus issued his decree?"

"*After seventy years.*"

"If we take those words literally, on what day would the *after seventy years* begin? What day would constitute the definitive beginning of the *after seventy years*? The day after. Seventy years later on the day after the seventeenth day of Kislev—the eighteenth day of Kislev."

The Oracle paused for a moment, gazing into the distance, then spoke.

"The president issued the Jerusalem Declaration on December 6, 2017. Do you know what that was?"

"What?"

"The *eighteenth day of Kislev.*"

"The day *after the seventy years!*"

"The *exact* day after the seventy years. In 2017 the eighteenth of Kislev fell on December 6, the day the Jerusalem Declaration went forth—on the exact day that constituted the *after seventy years.*"

"And nobody planned it that way?"

"I would doubt," said the Oracle, "that the president, when he planned his announcement, was studying the original Hebrew. It all just came together. The six-month legal waiver concerning Jerusalem happened to expire the first week of December. It was in that week that the eighteenth day of Kislev fell. Had the president made his announcement at night, after sunset, instead of in the daytime as he did, the declaration would not have gone forth on the eighteenth day of Kislev. But as with everything else, it just happened to fall into its exact appointed place at the exact appointed time…from one declaration to the other…seventy biblical Hebrew years—to the day."

———————————

"There would be one more revelation concerning the mysteries of the fifth door before the sixth door could be opened."

"And it would involve…"

"A cylinder."

"The cylinder covered with wedge-shaped letters?"

"Yes."

"You saw it in the earlier visions."

"Yes, but never like this."

"What did it reveal?"

"The house of the return."

Chapter 51

THE HOUSE OF RETURN

Whuse I returned to the mountain, I found the Oracle standing by a pillar at one of the building's four corners. There, at its base, we sat down."

"Isaiah was a prophet of Israel," I said, "and he spoke of Cyrus as an instrument of God. The one who came to the White House and told Truman that he was an instrument of God, as was Cyrus, came from Israel to tell him that. He was the chief rabbi of Israel. Did anything like that happen with regard to Trump...I mean with someone coming from Israel...or representing Israel?"

"Yes," said the Oracle, "something did. After the president recognized Jerusalem, a visitor came to Washington, DC. As with the rabbi, he came from Israel and came with a word for the president, a word to be given in the White House. It was Israel's prime minister, Benjamin Netanyahu. He said this:

> I want to tell you that the Jewish people have a long memory.
> So we remember the proclamation of the great King Cyrus
> the Great—Persian King. Twenty-five hundred years ago, he
> proclaimed that the Jewish exiles in Babylon can come back
> and rebuild our temple in Jerusalem."[1]

"So the modern leader of Israel identified the modern Cyrus."

"Yes," said the Oracle, who then paused before continuing. "So now you've come to learn the meaning of your last vision."

"The vision of the colossal clay cylinder that rolled across the earth..."

"As in your other visions," he said, "it represented the proclamation."

"The proclamation of Cyrus or of Trump?"

"Both," he said. "The proclamation of Cyrus declared the right of the Jewish exiles to return to the land. Beyond that it gave sanction for the rebirth of the Jewish nation. Both of these things, that right and that sanction, were fulfilled in the modern world by the first American Cyrus, President Truman. Truman was central in the release of the post-Holocaust

Jewish exiles in Europe and their return to Israel, and after that in America's recognition of the resurrected Jewish nation.

"But Cyrus' proclamation had another dimension and focus as well—the city of Jerusalem. Specifically it identified Jerusalem as belonging to the Jewish people, recognized the city as the nation's capital, and affirmed the right of the Jewish people to return there. Those three things were never fulfilled by Truman. They would wait for another Cyrus to fulfill them."

"That would be President Trump and the Jerusalem Declaration."

"Yes, but there was yet another component to the ancient declaration. It said this:

> All the kingdoms of the earth the LORD God of heaven has ·
> given me. And He has commanded me to build Him a house
> at Jerusalem which is in Judah.[2]

"The proclamation was linked to a house. It specifically directed the *construction of a house*; it decreed a building to be built in Jerusalem. So if the American president is following the template of the ancient king, could his declaration follow that of the ancient proclamation? Could it likewise decree that a house be established, a building be built, in Jerusalem? Listen to what the Jerusalem Declaration decreed:

> That is why, consistent with the Jerusalem Embassy Act, I am
> also directing the State Department to begin preparation to
> move the American embassy from Tel Aviv to Jerusalem.[3]

"As in the proclamation of the ancient king, the president's declaration ultimately focused on a house. An embassy is not a temple, but it is nevertheless a house, a building. And likewise the president specifically directed that the house would stand in Jerusalem. The house that Cyrus decreed was specifically linked to the return of the Jewish people to the city—so too would be the house that the president decreed. The house that Cyrus decreed would manifest the recognition of Jerusalem as the capital of a resurrected Israel by the world's foremost power of the time—so too would the house decreed by the president. The ancient king's declaration would specify the means needed to accomplish the building of the house:

> Let him go up to Jerusalem which is in Judah, and build the
> house...which is in Jerusalem....Let the men of his place
> help him with silver and gold, with goods and livestock,
> besides the freewill offerings for the house of God which is
> in Jerusalem.[4]

"The president's declaration to the world would likewise specify the means needed to accomplish the building of the house:

> This will immediately begin the process of hiring architects, engineers, and planners, so that a new embassy, when completed, will be a magnificent tribute to peace.[5]

"The Jerusalem Declaration would constitute the first declaration of any major power since the days of Cyrus to specifically affirm Jerusalem as belonging to the Jewish people, Jerusalem as the capital of Israel, the right of the return of the Jewish people to their Holy City, and the establishment of a house in Jerusalem to seal and embody all these things.

"But there was more to the template. Just as important as was the declaration was what happened in its wake. The building of an embassy would typically take years. But the president decided to dramatically speed up the timetable by taking an already existing building and converting it to become America's first embassy in Jerusalem. So instead of taking years, it took months. That president's decision would cause everything to converge on one particular day."

"On what particular day?"

"On May 14."

"The day Israel came into existence."

"The day its rebirth was proclaimed to the world. And at the stroke of midnight of that day, the moment it returned to the world."

"Which was when the other Cyrus, Truman, recognized its return. So the two American Cyruses are joined by the same date—May 14."

"Yes. And in America, where Truman issued his recognition, it was before the stroke of midnight. It was May 14. So the recognition of each Cyrus was manifested on the same day. The first American Cyrus recognized Israel as a nation; the second recognized Jerusalem as its capital. And on the day when that which was set forth in the Jerusalem Declaration was fulfilled, the president spoke to those gathered for the inauguration of the new embassy. And the very first words that came from his mouth contained the name of his forerunner in the ancient mystery:

> The United States, under President Harry Truman, became the first nation to recognize the state of Israel. Today we officially open the United States embassy in Jerusalem."[6]

"So the president himself was connecting the two events…and the two Cyruses…and the two dates."

"And more than by the same date," said the Oracle. "The president's words went forth, and the new *house* was inaugurated on May 14, 2018.

The words of his predecessor went forth, and the new nation of Israel was inaugurated on May 14, 1948. How long between the two events?"

"Seventy years."

"It happened again at the end of seventy years…and again on the exact same date. And at that very moment, the seventy-year mystery was manifested before the world as Israel's prime minister, Netanyahu, said this:

> *Exactly 70 years ago today*, President Truman became the first world leader to recognize the newborn Jewish state. Last December, President Trump became the first world leader to recognize Jerusalem as our capital. And today, the United States of America is opening its embassy right here in Jerusalem.[7]

"'*After seventy years*' comes first the decree and then the restoration. Cyrus first issued his decree. After that came the restoration. The decree that brought Israel back into the world was issued at the end of 1947. The restoration, and the realization of that resolution, came five months later with Israel's rebirth. Seventy years later the decree recognizing Jerusalem and the authorization of the house came with the president's Jerusalem Declaration at the end of 2017. The restoration, and the realization of that declaration, would come with the inauguration of the Jerusalem embassy—likewise…five months later."

"So in each case," I said, "you have a decree and a restoration. And between the decree of 1947 and the decree of 2017 are seventy years. And between the restoration of 1948 and the restoration of 2018 are seventy years, each ending on the exact same date, May 14."

"And what happened on May 14, 2018, the inauguration of the American embassy, the house in Jerusalem, was the fulfillment of the Jubilee—the fulfillment of the president's Jubilean declaration that had gone forth in the year of Jubilee. It was the manifestation of the legal authority and recognition given to Israel's return to Jerusalem, the original owner to his ancestral possession—the Jubilee. Two days before that inauguration and the completion of the seventy years of separation was the Sabbath."

"And what was the appointed Scripture?"

"The portion of Scripture appointed to be recited in America, the nation that had decreed these events, and around the world, was called Behar-Bechukotai. It was the portion that contained these words:

> You shall make the trumpet to sound throughout all your land….And each of you shall return to his possession…"[8]

"The Jubilean ordinance!" I said. "So everything came full circle. The trump of Jubilee had sounded throughout the land, and the possession was returned to its original owner."

"And all on the day that ended the seventy years."

"A question," I said. "Since in the ancient decree *the house* was the Temple, could what happened in 2018, the establishment of *the house* in Jerusalem, be a foreshadowing of a future rebuilding of the other house, the Temple?"

"It could," he said. "Remember, each Jubilean event is only the beginning and sets in motion the course for the next Jubilean cycle. So the Jubilee of 2017 had set in motion a course of events. A world ruler had issued a decree concerning the restoration of Israel, as the ancient world ruler had done in the days of the first return."

"And as did the world ruler, Truman," I said, "at the moment of Israel's birth, in the second return."

"Yes," he replied. "God has always used world rulers. He uses them to grant recognition, to bestow authority, and to confirm and inaugurate His purposes." He paused after that as if pondering whether to tell me something. And then he did.

"We've spoken of the name *Trump* but never of his first name, Donald. And yet the name *Donald* also carries significance."

"What does the name *Donald* mean?"

"*World ruler.*"

Chapter 52

THE STREAMS

THE ORACLE ROSE from his seat and began walking away from the ancient house. I followed him. He led me over to the other side of the mountain's summit, to a ledge overlooking a landscape even more vast than that which I had seen from the ruins."

"Over there," he said, pointing to a distant mountain, "that's where we first met. And there," he said, pointing to an expanse to the mountain's right, "beyond that valley is the garden. And there, along the ridge of that mountain, is the cave. To its right is a vast plain. On the far side of the plain is the ravine that leads to the oasis. And over there, that's where the tent was." He paused to let me take it all in. "Before we move forward, a question: What did you expect to find when you came here?"

"Nothing even remotely similar to what I found...to what I was shown."

"How so?" he asked.

"An ancient mystery that determines the course of world history...I never would have thought that anything like that could be possible...but it's real...and it touches everything from kings, to presidents, empires, superpowers, down to the most minute details...And everything happens to happen in the exact way, at the exact place, and at the exact time. And no one's orchestrating it, no one on earth. And those who play a part in one Jubilee are gone in the next...but the mystery keeps moving forward..."

"Yes," said the Oracle. "One Jubilee prepares the way, sets the stage, and leads to the next. Take just one of its streams, the return of Jerusalem. In the Jubilee of 1867 Charles Warren begins the mapping out of the parameters of biblical Jerusalem and in the process accidentally uncovers the ancient city. In the next Jubilee Allenby liberates Jerusalem. To wage his campaign, he uses the maps of the land that were drawn up as the result of Warren's mission in the previous Jubilee. Fifty years later Israeli soldiers enter through the gates of the Old City and Jerusalem is restored to the Jewish people. And fifty years later that return is given legal sanction and Jerusalem is recognized as Israel's capital for the first time since ancient times.

"Or take another stream, the return of the land. In the Jubilee of 1867 the Ottoman Empire enacts the law that begins the release of the land. In the next Jubilee the Ottomans themselves are released from the land and the land is released to the Jewish people. Fifty years later, in the Six-Day War, comes the most dramatic release of the land in Jewish history. And do you know when that release was completed?"

"No."

"The day the Six-Day War came to an end—on June 10, 1967. And do you know when the release of the land began, when the Ottoman Land Code was enacted?"

"No."

"On June 10, 1867, two Jubilees, exactly one hundred years, earlier...on the same exact day.

"Or take another stream," he said, "that of the political realm. At the end of the First Zionist Congress, Theodor Herzl writes that he founded the Jewish state and everyone would know it in fifty years. The United Nations finishes the plan that will bring Israel into existence fifty years later to the exact day. And on that exact day, the Jubilee of Zionism is being celebrated across the world in Basel, Switzerland."

"So as one Jubilean event is commemorated, the next is set in motion."

"Yes, and it happened more than once. In 1967 Israel planned to celebrate the Jubilee of the Balfour Declaration in 1917. But before the celebration could begin, the next Jubilean event, the Six-Day War, had begun. And in 2017 celebrations were planned to commemorate the Jubilee of Jerusalem's return in 1967. But again, as the one Jubilean event was being celebrated, the next was being set in motion, in this case by the resolution of the United States Senate. And in that same year another Jubilee was being celebrated, Allenby's liberation of Jerusalem from the Ottoman Empire. And on the very week of its commemoration, Jerusalem's one-hundred-year double Jubilee, the next Jubilean event was breaking forth from the White House with the issuing of the Jerusalem Declaration. Every Jubilee is connected to every other Jubilee in ways of which we have spoken...and in ways of which we have not."

"Of which we have not? What do you mean?"

"I'll give you an example in just one life. The phenomenon of Jewish soldiers fighting in the land of Israel had been gone from the world since ancient times, since the days of the Roman Empire. But if what was lost is to be restored, then part of the mystery must be the return of Jewish soldiers to the land. At the beginning of the age the armies of Rome warred against the last of the Jewish soldiers, killing them or driving them out of the land and thus beginning two thousand years of foreign occupation. So what would the reverse of that be?"

"The return of Jewish soldiers to the land and the driving out of the occupying power…which in modern times would be the Ottoman Empire."

"John Henry Patterson was born in Ireland to a Protestant father and a Catholic mother. He grew up with the Bible, reading of Israel's ancient heroes and warriors. When he was seventeen, he joined the British Army. Before retiring from the military, he would attain the rank of lieutenant colonel. But it was the role he played in the First World War that would bring him into the mystery.

"While stationed in Alexandria, Egypt, he met two Jewish men from Russia, Joseph Trumpeldor and Ze'ev Jabotinsky. They envisioned the creation of a Jewish fighting force. Patterson became the needed champion of that vision. Through his efforts the Zion Mule Corps, a band of Jewish fighters, was formed in 1915. The corps was disbanded shortly after fighting Ottoman forces in Gallipoli, Turkey. But Patterson's ultimate dream was to lead Jewish soldiers back into the land of Israel, to fight for its liberation. At the swearing in of new Jewish volunteers to the corps, he implored them: 'Pray with me that I should…be divinely permitted to lead you into the Promised Land.'[1]

"His dream would come true when the British Army approved the formation of the *Jewish Legion*. The Jewish Legion would constitute the first Jewish band of soldiers to fight on the soil of the Promised Land since the days of the Roman Empire. And they would fight not only *in* the land but *for* the land, for its return."

"So when did the Jewish Legion come into existence?"

"1917."

"The year of Jubilee!"

"The Jewish Legion came into existence in the summer of 1917, the same summer in which Allenby was preparing to take the land. In the Jubilee the heir comes back to the land and the one occupying it has to depart. And if the one occupying the land refuses to leave, then the transfer must happen by force. And so it did. After nearly two thousand years, the heir, in the form of the Jewish soldier returned to the land to drive out the one occupying it, the Ottoman Empire. So in the year of Jubilee the Jewish soldier returned to his own possession."

"Did the Jewish Legion actually fight with Allenby's army?"

"By the end of the campaign, it is estimated that one out of every six soldiers in his army belonged to the Jewish Legion."

"And what was John Patterson's part?"

"He was its commander. So the first Jewish legion to enter the land of Israel since ancient times was led by an Irish Christian.

"But Patterson would play a part in yet another central event of that Jubilee. He would bring Jabotinsky to London for a critical meeting with a member of parliament, Leo Amery. Amery would become a critical voice in the British government not only for the creation of the Jewish Legion but for the most important document in Jewish history since ancient times, the Balfour Declaration. He would be central in its passage and the penning of its words.

"But Patterson's role in Israel's resurrection would go still further. Without a military force Israel would never have become a nation or remained in existence for more than a moment. His Jewish Legion would serve as the prototype and forerunner of the Israeli army. In fact Patterson would be called 'the godfather of the Israeli army.'[2]

"And yet his role would extend still further. By bringing the Jewish Legion into existence, Patterson created the training ground for Israel's founders and its first generation of leaders. Members of the Jewish Legion included Yitzhak Ben-Zvi, Israel's second president; Yaakov Dori, first chief of staff of the Israeli Defense Forces; Eliyahu Golomb, architect of the Haganah, Israel's underground defense force; and David Ben-Gurion, Israel's first prime minister and the nation's founding father.

"Patterson would continue to labor on behalf of Israel's restoration for the rest of his life, which would come to its end in another critical year, 1947, on the eve of the nation's birth, the year Israel was voted back into existence. And yet his impact would extend beyond his life. In the Jubilee of 1967 Israel's prime minister was Levi Eshkol. Eshkol was the ultimate overseer of the Six-Day War, by which Jerusalem was regained. But Eshkol's preparation for that war began fifty years and one Jubilee earlier, when he served as a young man as a member of Patterson's Jewish Legion.

"And there was yet another connection. In the days of the Second World War Patterson would befriend and partner with a young Jewish man to advocate for the creation of a Jewish army. The friendship was so deep that the man would name his firstborn son after Patterson. A year before his death Patterson would bless the new family as godfather at the child's circumcision. The child would later become one of Israel's revered heroes, giving his life to save Israeli hostages. His death would in turn lead his younger brother to go into public life—and later become the prime minister of Israel. The family name was Netanyahu, and the younger brother was named Benjamin. Benjamin Netanyahu would be Israel's prime minister in the Jubilee of 2017, the year that saw the first recognition of Jerusalem as the capital of Israel since ancient times and that marked the one-hundred-year anniversary of Patterson's leading of the first Jewish army into the land of Israel since ancient times."

"I see another connection."

"Tell me," said the Oracle.

"The Jubilee of 1917 was the year that the Jewish soldier first returned to the land of Israel. Fifty years later, the Jubilee of 1967, was the year that the Jewish soldier returned to Jerusalem."

"Yes. Every Jubilee is connected to all the others, each fulfilling another part of the same mystery. So all these events had their origins in the Jubilee of 1917 with the unlikely soldier from Ireland. But what about *his* origins? When was he born?"

I was silent, having no idea of the answer.

"He was born," said the Oracle, "in *the year of Jubilee*."

"In 1867?"

"Yes, in the first Jubilee of Israel's restoration, in the Jubilee of the stranger and the man with the measuring line and the releasing of the land. So the man who birthed all these things was himself birthed in the year of Jubilee."

"That would mean that 1917 was his *fiftieth year*."

"Yes. He was born in the Jubilee of 1867 to play a central role fifty years later in the Jubilee of 1917...when another child would be born, Shlomo Goren, to play a central role fifty years later in the Jubilee of 1967.

"And do you remember Eliezer Sukenik?"

"The man who discovered the Dead Sea Scrolls on the day Israel was voted into existence."

"Yes. He too was a soldier in Patterson's Jewish Legion. Sukenik had a son."

"Yigael Yadin, the man who unearthed Masada."

"Yes, and the head of operations in the war of Israel's rebirth. Yadin was also born in the Jubilee of 1917. And when he turned fifty years old, he would likewise play a central part in the next year of Jubilee, 1967...in the Six-Day War."

"In the meeting with the prime minister when the decision to go to war was made."

"Yes, and in his serving as the prime minister's counsel throughout the war. So in each case the child of the one Jubilee ushers in the next. Everything is joined together in the mystery. Everything and everyone, even their words."

"Even their words...What does that mean?"

"At the central moment of the Jubilee of 1967, the moment of Jerusalem's liberation, Rabbi Goren stood with the soldiers in the Holy City and spoke the word of an ancient prophecy. It was from Isaiah: "*Comfort my people.*

Comfort them," says the Lord your God.'[3] The prophecy goes on, *'Speak comfort to Jerusalem, and cry out to her, that her warfare is ended...'*[4]

"The rabbi had no idea that fifty years earlier, at the central moment of the Jubilee of 1917, in Allenby's liberation of Jerusalem, the word from *The Book of Common Prayer* appointed for that moment was the prophecy: *'"Comfort, yes, comfort My people!" says your God. Speak comfort to Jerusalem, and cry out to her, that her warfare is ended...'*[5]

"The morning after Rabbi Goren uttered those words would mark the first time the sun had risen on a Jerusalem under Jewish sovereignty in two thousand years. It was June 8, 1967. If you remember," he said, "the mystery began as the steamship *Quaker City* set out from the harbors of New York with a young American journalist on board."

"Mark Twain," I said, "the stranger."

"Yes, the stranger's journey. And when did it all begin? It all began on *June 8, 1867.* Thus it was all set in motion one hundred years earlier *on the exact same day.*"

The Oracle was silent for a few moments. Then he spoke.

"Now," he said, "I believe we're ready for the sixth door."

"There's something I don't understand. 2017 was the last of the Jubilean years. It hasn't been fifty years since then. And yet there are more doors."

"To each vision," he said, "was a mystery. Each mystery in turn was the puzzle piece in a larger mystery, represented by each door. But the mystery represented by each door is part of a yet larger mystery. What lies behind the sixth door concerns that larger mystery."

"How could it be larger than what you've already shown me?"

"The sixth door will take you behind everything you've seen thus far, and then beyond it...to where it all leads...to the end."

"So the sixth door would be different from the others."

"Yes, it would reveal the other Jubilees...Jubilees of other natures and realms...and where it was all heading."

"Where?"

"To the end."

"And what exactly would you see behind the sixth door?"

"That which is and is yet to come...the dark jubilee, a stained-glass woman, a Jubilee of spirit, the awakening dragon, and ultimately the return of all returns...the missing and final piece of the mystery."

THE SIXTH DOOR

Chapter 53

THE SIXTH DOOR

I OPENED THE SIXTH door. There on the mountain was a ram of gold."

"Gold, as in the color or as in the metal?"

"Both. It was as a statue of pure gold come to life. Around its neck was a golden chain with a golden pendant, on which was a symbol that matched that on the sixth door. It made its way down the mountain and through the wilderness. I followed behind. The path it took was different from that of the other rams. There was no familiar landmark. We were walking through a desert plain surrounded by hills. The ram stopped and looked to the left. I did likewise, and the visions began."

THE STANDARDS

"I saw two men riding on horseback in Roman military dress and armor, a middle-aged man and a younger man. Behind them was a massive army. Behind the army was a desolate landscape of scattered fires and smoldering ruins. The two dismounted their horses and began planting a series of golden poles topped with golden eagles, Roman standards, into the ground. I didn't realize it at first, but they were arranging the poles to form Roman numerals, an *X*, a *V*, an *L*, and more than one *I*. When they finished, they remounted their horses and led their army onward. The standards then began to sink into the earth. The land then lay desolate for what seemed to be ages. Then I noticed a change, the beginning of a slight greening. And then from out of the ground where the standards had sunk came sprouts. The sprouts then became small trees, then larger trees. The trees were growing in the same formation as that of the standards and the Roman letters. And then they began to put forth leaves, fruits, and flowers."

THE SANDAL

"In the next vision I found myself standing in a harbor where countless people were departing the shore in ships. I made my way inland against the flow of the multitudes fleeing the land until I came to a mountain. Multitudes more were coming down from the top of the mountain. I began ascending it against the downward flow until I reached the top. I couldn't at first make sense of what I was seeing. Towering over a giant expanse was a structure of colossal arches, but not quite arches, giant looping structures made up of ancient stones. I walked back and forth, trying to make sense of it. And then it hit me. The stone structure I was trying to make sense of was built to resemble a colossal sandal. Standing at my side was a man in white. 'What is it?' I asked.

"'The sandal of departure,' he said. 'If the one departs, so must they all.'"

THE CHURCH OF THE RABBI

"In the next vision an angel led me to a city by a river and into a massive domed cathedral, through its ornate interior, and over to a stone table. On top of the table were bones, each one aglow with white radiance. 'Can these bones live?' he asked. Just then a wind blew open the cathedral's massive doors, and the bones began moving together, connecting one to the other until a skeleton was formed. Then came muscles and skin and then garments, just as in the earlier vision. Lying on the platform was now a bearded man, who by his overall appearance could have passed for an ancient rabbi. He opened his eyes, left the table, and walked over to an olive tree that was growing in the center of the sanctuary. Several of its branches had been broken off and were lying on the floor. The man picked them up and reattached them, at which point they came alive and began putting forth leaves and olives. At that the cathedral began to transform, its interior taking on the simple and ancient appearance of hewn stone, oil lamps, and scrolls. 'For God,' said the bearded man, 'is able to graft them back into their own olive tree.'"

THE AWAKENING OF THE DRAGON

"I turned and saw a hooded figure in a robe of dark crimson. He was walking through the ruins of an ancient city of marble pillars, arches, domes, temples, and statues. Jutting out from the top of a nearby hill was a line of spikelike objects. I didn't realize it at first, but what I was seeing were the scales of a dragon, a colossal dragon of white stone. The dragon was partially submerged in the earth, lying still, dormant. The hooded figure ascended the hill, approached the dragon's head, and spoke. 'It is time for you to return as well.' At that the dragon opened its stone eyes and began breathing, the white of its stone now turning dark crimson. It then roused itself from the earth and began walking through the ruins, breathing on them. Wherever it breathed, there came the sound of rumbling. The statues were now moving, stepping down off their pedestals and out of their temples, gods and goddesses and the ancient leaders who worshipped them...all following the dragon. Then it breathed on an ancient stadium, and I heard the sounds of cheering and screams. There was now a cacophony of sounds rising up from the ruins of the ancient city, drums, festivities, laughter...and those screams."

THE STAINED-GLASS WOMAN

"I turned again and saw a donkey walking through the gate of a walled city, across a large plaza, and into an elaborately decorated cathedral. I took it to be St. Peter's Basilica. It approached a stained-glass window, on which was the image of a woman seated on a throne, adorned with gold and arrayed in a purple cloak. She had light skin, auburn hair, and a regal gaze. The woman began to move, rising from her throne and stepping out of the window. She was still of stained-glass but now of three dimensions. She sat down on the donkey and was carried out of the cathedral and away from the plaza, then through villages, mountains, and a multitude of diverse landscapes. As she journeyed, her appearance began changing...from European to Middle Eastern and Jewish; her hair, from auburn to black; and her garments, from ornate to simple and ancient. And then the colored glass began breaking off until she was no longer an image but a person, beautiful, young, and full of awe. Finally she arrived at her destination, the gate of an ancient city, Jerusalem. She dismounted the donkey and approached the gate, where seven women in white were waiting for her. They clothed her in the radiant white robe of a bride and ushered her through the gate."

THE HOMECOMING

"I was back in the harbor of the earlier vision where everyone was fleeing the land. But now they were returning, in ships, boats, and on foot, clothed in the garments of diverse lands and ages. Again I journeyed inland. Streams of people were converging from every direction to the same place—the mountain. It was then that I recognized a figure walking among the others in the streams of people. It was the stranger. Then I saw the man with the measuring line and the woman in the vineyard and the old man walking hand in hand with the little boy. Then I saw King David and Ben-Gurion, Herzl and Allenby, the prophet Amos, Rabbi Goren, Truman, the man in the black hooded robe, Cyrus, the magi, people from all different times and places...and visions...all now part of the procession converging on the mountain and ascending it. I didn't go up with them but stayed behind so I could see it all from a distance. At the end of the multitudes was the white-haired man in a red robe with a staff...Moses. The mountain's summit was now bathed in golden light. In the midst of the radiance, and partly obscured by it, was the looping structure I had seen earlier, a second colossal sandal but this one of pure radiant gold. The man in white was now again standing at my side. 'And if the one returns,' he said, 'so shall they all.'"

"That was the last of the visions within the vision. I continued following the golden ram through the wilderness. Along the journey we came upon the fifth ram, the ram of white marble. He followed behind the golden ram. Then we came upon the fourth ram, then the third, the second, and the first. They all joined the procession. In the distance ahead was the same mountain as in the last vision, with streams of people still ascending it and Moses at the end. The rams approached and began ascending it as well. They were soon just behind Moses. He led them, as a shepherd would lead his sheep, up to the mountain's summit. I watched as the procession came to its end, and all the ascenders entered into the golden radiance on the mountaintop. And the vision ended."

Chapter 54

THE ORACLE'S TENT

"I T WAS AN especially hot day. I decided to go to the oasis to cool myself in the waters of the pool. I was floating on my back with my eyes closed when I heard a noise. I looked up. And there he was."

"The boy?"

"The boy…standing on the rock at the edge of the water, looking down at me with a smile. How he found me, I have no idea. So I got out of the water, changed my clothes, and followed him. I was taken again through scenery I had never seen before. Much of the sand in the desert was hard and crusted. But he now led me into a valley where the sand was soft and loose, what you would expect to find on a beach. It was in that valley that I first saw the tent."

"The tent."

"The Oracle's tent. I had expected something much more ornate. From the outside there was nothing to distinguish it, just coarse black and brown cloth. Cautiously I parted the curtains of its entrance."

―――――――

"Welcome," said the Oracle. "Come in."

So I did. It was on the inside that it looked more like what one might expect of a desert chieftain's tent, with carpets, pillows, and cushions all covered in Middle Eastern embroidery, along with household vessels of molded clay and beaten metal, oil lamps, ornamented chests, old books, and other miscellaneous items too numerous to mention. He offered me some tea and refreshments. And I told him the vision.

"So," he said, "behind the sixth door you saw not only the sixth ram but all the others. The sixth door is unlike the doors before it. It concerns all of their mysteries, their origins and ends."

"Their ends?"

"That to which they lead…and that which they bring about in the end."

―――――――

"The next time I saw the Oracle, he would reveal the secret behind all the Jubilean years I had been shown. He would open up their matrix."

Chapter 55

THE MATRIX OF YEARS

I RETURNED TO THE Oracle's tent. It was mid-afternoon. He was sitting in the shade just outside the curtains that formed the tent's entrance. He beckoned me to join him inside. So we entered the tent and sat down on its embroidered cushions."

"Is it possible," he asked, "that behind everything we've seen, all the Jubilean manifestations, lies a mystery that binds them all together?"

"You mean beyond Leviticus and the mystery of the Jubilee itself?"

"Yes. What is it," he asked, "that the Jubilee undoes?"

"The loss of one's ancestral possession, one's land."

"And what loss was it that lay behind everything we've seen?"

"The land of Israel and Jerusalem."

"Which happened when?"

"In AD 70 with the destruction of Israel."

"Yes and no," he replied. "The loss and the destruction began earlier than that. It all began in AD 66 when the Jewish people in Judea revolted against Roman rule. In response the Roman governor Cestius Gallus invaded the land to end the revolt. After a nine-day siege of Jerusalem that ended in failure, Gallus withdrew his army. In the midst of that withdrawal his troops were ambushed and suffered heavy losses. The Roman forces were driven out, and a revolutionary provisional government was set up in Jerusalem.

"It was then that the Roman emperor Nero sent one of his generals, Vespasian, to crush the revolt. Vespasian entered the land from the north and focused first on the land of Galilee. In the subsequent months he and his son, Titus, waged a military campaign of destruction, obliterating rebel strongholds and decimating the civilian population."

"Those were the two men I saw on horseback, Titus and Vespasian."

"Yes. So Galilee was the first of lands to be lost to the Jewish people. The nation's destruction would begin there. It was there that those who resisted Roman rule were first crushed and where the survivors were first taken prisoner and led captive into the nations. The coming two thousand years of Jewish exile began in Galilee. So in terms of the Jubilee, Galilee was the first of Israel's ancestral possessions to be lost. Do you remember what I told you about Israel's first settlements?"

"Before it became a nation?"

"Long before it became a nation. The first Jewish settlements in the land, the beginning of the nation's restoration, were established in 1878. One of the settlements established that year was called Petah Tikvah, or the Door of Hope. But the very first was called Gei Oni, or the Valley of Strength. It was founded in the spring of that year. Later it would be revived and renamed Rosh Pinah, meaning the Cornerstone."

"And it's significant because..."

"That very first settlement was planted in northern Galilee, the very first land lost to the nation in Vespasian's campaign. So the restoration of the land began in the same place where the land was first lost."

"The Jubilean reversal."

"Yes," he replied. "But it's not only a matter of where, but *when*."

"When the land was lost?"

"Yes. When was the ancestral land first lost? It was that loss that determined everything that followed. And all the Jubilean restorations would be joined to that loss. So when did it take place?"

"When Vespasian invaded the land."

"Yes, but when?"

"I don't know."

"Vespasian invaded the land in AD 67. It all began in that year."

That's when it hit me.

"The formation of the standards," I said. "It was LXVII. It was the Roman numeral 67!"

"The armies of Vespasian began their campaign in AD 67. It was that campaign that began the removal of the Jewish people from the land and the land of Israel from the people, the separation of two thousand years."

"The separation that the Jubilee undoes."

"It was that event in AD 67 that would determine the timing of everything else. In which year does the Jubilee take place?"

"The fiftieth year."

"The fiftieth year after AD 67 is what?"

"117."

"Yes. The timing of the Roman invasion plus the fifty-year cycle of the Jubilean mystery will determine that the years of restoration will end in the number *17*. Tell me, when was the land transferred for the last time before the time of restoration?"

"When it passed to the Ottoman Empire."

"And that took place in the year 1517...a year ending in the number 17—the twenty-ninth Jubilee from the year of Vespasian's invasion. And in what year did Allenby drive the Ottoman Empire out of the land and liberate Jerusalem, and was the promise of a national homeland given to the Jewish people?"

"In 1917."

"Another year ending in 17—the thirty-seventh Jubilee from the year of the invasion. And when, for the first time since ancient times, did a major world power restore legal sanction to Jerusalem as the capital of Israel?"

"In 2017, when America recognized Jerusalem."

"Another year ending in 17—the thirty-ninth Jubilee from the ancient invasion.

"But a mystery beginning in AD 67," said the Oracle, "and made up of fifty-year cycles will ordain that the key Jubilean events will also take place in years that end in the number 67. Tell me, in what year did the stranger and the man with the measuring line come to the land? And in what year did the release of the land begin?"

"In 1867."

"A year ending in 67—the thirty-sixth Jubilee from the first loss of the ancestral land. And when, after two thousand years, did Jewish soldiers enter the gates of Jerusalem?"

"In 1967."

"Another year ending in 67—the thirty-eighth Jubilee from when it all began. So with the exception of the political Jubilee, which began in the fiftieth year of Zionism, every Jubilean event manifests in a year ending with the number 17 or the number 67: 1867, 1917, 1967, and 2017...the timing of each one determined by the invasion of AD 67, the year in which the destruction began."

"What season was it when it all began?"

"Springtime," said the Oracle, "as in your vision. The invasion began in the spring of AD 67. Vespasian began his attack in the month of May. And the greatest and defining siege of that first campaign and of the entire war apart from Jerusalem, the siege of the city of Yodfat, began in the early days of June.

"And so it just happened to happen that the Jubilean redemption began in the spring. It was in the late spring of 1867, at the start of June, that the stranger began his journey. And it was in that same month that the release of the land began. And in the Jubilee of 1917 it was also in late spring, in the beginning of June, that Allenby was appointed commander of the campaign that would liberate the Promised Land. And in the Jubilee of 1967 the events that would set in motion the Six-Day War began in May and the beginning of June. And in the Jubilee of 2017 it was at the beginning of June that the United States Senate passed the resolution that would lead to the Jerusalem Declaration. And that first Jewish settlement that began Israel's restoration was inaugurated in May, the month of the destruction. And in that same month, in May of 1948, the nation of Israel was reborn."

"So the timing of the ancient calamity," I said, "determines the timing of the restorations."

"Or the timing of the restorations," he said, "is joined to the ancient calamity. Each Jubilean event is the redemption of that which began in the spring of AD 67."

"And it was all there from the beginning."

"What was the next revelation?"

"The secret that lies at the center of the age... and that sets the stage for the end."

"And what is it?"

"The mystery of the sandal."

Chapter 56

THE RETURN

I RETURNED TO THE Oracle's tent on a windy afternoon."

_____

"In my vision where everyone was fleeing the land, there was a sandal on top of the mountain. What did it mean, and what did it have to do with everything else?"

"If you had to sum up the Jubilean mystery," he said, "in one word, its essence, its power, and its consequence, what would it be?"

"Return," I said, "and restoration."

"Those are two words, but let's focus on the first: _return_. The Jewish people return to their ancient land; the priests return to their Holy City; the soldiers return to their ancient fortress; the farmers return to their ancient fields; the Nazir returns to his ancient court; each returns to his own possession."

At that he took out a piece of parchment. I knew enough now to recognize the writing on the parchment as Hebrew.

"The Jubilean ordinance," he said, "Leviticus 25. And this," he said, pointing to one of the words on the parchment, "is the central command in Hebrew, _tashuvu, you shall return_. It comes from the Hebrew root word _shuv_...which begins with the letter _shin_. That's what you saw on the sixth door and on the golden ram. The word _shuv_ is filled with meaning. It can be translated as 'to return, to turn back, to recover, to reverse, to recur, to relinquish, to receive back, to restore, and to come home.'"

"All those things describe what happened in the Jubilean years."

"Yes," said the Oracle, "and yet there's a deeper dimension to the word and to the mystery. According to the ancient covenant, if the people of Israel remained joined to God, they would remain joined to the land. But if they departed from God, they would depart from the land. The physical realm was bound to the spiritual. Physical separation from the land would be a manifestation of a spiritual separation from God.

"But it was also written in that same covenant and foretold by the prophets that if they returned to God, they would likewise return to the land. So then their physical return to the land would be connected to a spiritual return to God.

"Do you know what the word _shuv_ also means?"

"No."

"*To repent.*"

"The same word for *return* also means repent?"

"That's the point," he replied. "For to repent is to return…and to come home…and to be restored. For the people of Israel it's all joined together. So then, we have a mystery," he said. "According to the Law and the Prophets, if the nation turned away from God, the people would be taken into exile and scattered to the ends of the earth. And it happened exactly as it was prophesied. The Jewish people were led captive into exile and scattered to the ends of the earth.

"But according to the covenant, before a physical departure of such magnitude could have taken place, there had to have been a spiritual departure. But then what was it? It would have had to have taken place at the time of the physical departure, thus in the first century, when the exile of two thousand years began."

"So there had to have been a spiritual departure," I said, "colossal enough to have transformed Jewish history. So what was it?"

"The Scriptures prophesy that at the end of the age, the Jewish people will return not only physically to the land but spiritually to God. In the Book of Hosea it is written:

> The children of Israel shall abide many days without king or prince.…Afterward the children of Israel shall return and seek the LORD their God and David their king.[1]

"According to the prophecy, after a long period of time without a kingdom or nation-state, the Jewish people will return, not just to their land but to 'their God and David their king.' You can only return to that which you've departed from or been separated from. So according to the prophecy, there would be a separation between the Jewish people and 'David their king.'"

"Who is 'David their king'?"

"When the prophecy was given, David had been dead for centuries. But the name David was used by the prophets to speak of the Messiah, the royal descendant of King David."

"So then it's saying that at the end of the age the Jewish people will return not only to the land but to the Messiah…But how can they *return* to their Messiah unless they first…?"

"*Left their Messiah*," said the Oracle, "You can only return to that which you first left."

"'Left,' I said, "another word for *departure*."

"And that is exactly what the mystery is pointing to…a spiritual departure. And when would that spiritual departure have taken place?"

"Somewhere around the time of the physical departure, when the Jewish people left the land…in the first century."

"Can you think of any phenomenon that appeared in the first century…something spiritual, something major, something history changing and involving the Jewish people in the land of Israel?"

"Jesus?"

"Jesus," said the Oracle, "something major, history changing, spiritual, involving the Jewish people, and taking place in the first century and in the land of Israel. It would fulfill every requirement."

"But Christianity," I said, "is foreign to the Jewish people."

"It's only foreign," said the Oracle, "because it became foreign. And it only became foreign because it was departed from. But that only fulfills the requirement. It must be that which was departed from and two thousand years ago."

"It's not a different religion?"

"It was never called Christianity in the beginning," he said, "And the word simply means the movement of the Messiah. And there's only one people that are waiting for the Messiah."

"Are you saying that Christianity is Jewish?"

"A faith named after the Messiah and concerning an Israeli Jewish man called Rabbi? It was and will always remain a Jewish faith. His real name wasn't Jesus but the Hebrew *Yeshua*. In the Hebrew Scriptures it was prophesied that the Messiah of Israel would be born in the city of Bethlehem; ride a donkey into Jerusalem; be rejected, scourged, beaten, and delivered to death as a lamb to the slaughter; and give his life as a sacrifice for sin. He would overcome death to bring redemption, forgiveness, and salvation to all who would receive it.[2] And all this had to take place before the second Temple was destroyed…in other words, before the year AD 70."

"Everything you just said describes Jesus…There's no one else."

"No," said the Oracle, "there's never been another candidate. And his first name, Yeshua, or Jesus, just happens to means salvation, and his second name—Messiah. And he just happens to be the central figure of human history and at the same time the only one who fulfilled the ancient prophecies of the Jewish Messiah."

"But then why didn't they accept him?"

"It's the opposite," he replied. "If they had accepted him, then he couldn't have been the Messiah. The prophecies required that the Messiah of Israel be rejected by his people…until the appointed time."[3]

"But those who were not of Israel did accept him."

"And that too was prophesied—the Jewish Messiah would become the 'light to the Gentiles.'[4] But even though Israel as a nation didn't receive him, many within the nation did. All the first believers were Jewish, all the first disciples. There were thousands upon thousands of Jewish believers. It was Jewish believers who gave to the world this faith and who, by so doing, changed the course of human history.

"From the beginning Israel was called to be a light to the nations, to give the world the word of God, to teach the world the ways of God, to bring forth the Messiah, and to spread salvation to the ends of the earth. And only once in human history did this ever take place. Only once did the word of God go forth from Jerusalem to all the earth. Only once and only in the name of this one called Messiah. This was Israel's calling and inheritance...the nation's spiritual possession."

"So what happened?"

"After the first century the Jewish apostles, disciples, and believers began disappearing. And their disappearance would seal the separation between the Jewish people and their Messiah. And it would all happen at the time of the other separation, the separation of the Jewish people from their land. And in the ages to come the children of Israel would become estranged from the land of Israel. It became foreign to them and the possession of strangers. Yet it was their homeland. In the same way, in the days of separation they became estranged from their Messiah. He became as foreign to them and as the possession of strangers. And yet he was in reality their Messiah...their ancestral possession."

"But the Jubilee," I said, "is about ending the separation. And if the separation from the land is already ending, then what about the spiritual separation? Shouldn't it likewise be coming to an end? And if so, when?"

"At the time of the return," he said, "at the time of the end."

"There's a missing piece..."

"Yes," said the Oracle, "actually more than one...Find them...and you'll complete the puzzle."

"The puzzle, as in the entire mystery?"

"Yes. Find them...and the mystery will be finished."

"So what was the next revelation?"

"One of the missing pieces of the puzzle...And it was all there from the beginning."

"From the beginning?"

"In the prophecy of Moses. I just didn't see it until then. It was the other side of the mystery."

"And how was it revealed?"

"Through the church of the rabbi."

Chapter 57

THE OLIVE TREE RESURRECTION

W HEN I RETURNED to the Oracle's tent, it was midday. The curtains of its entrance were ajar. I looked inside. He was sleeping. I
was determined not to make a sound. But it was as if he sensed
my presence. He opened his eyes, sat up, and motioned for me to come in.
I sat down on one of the embroidered pillows by his feet. He handed me a
small wicker basket of figs. I took one and asked my question."

"What I witnessed in the cathedral, the bones, the resurrection, and the
man who looked like an ancient rabbi…what did it mean?"

"Do you remember what I shared with you in our last meeting, what was
ordained in the law of Israel concerning the connection of the physical
realm to the spiritual realm?"

"Yes," I replied, "that if the nation of Israel departs from its land, it would
have to be connected to some kind of spiritual departure."

"Yes, then if they return to the land…"

"It would have to be connected to some kind of spiritual return."

"Yes."

"So which comes first;" I asked, "the physical return or the spiritual?"

"The Scriptures speak of both," he replied. "On the one hand, it is prophesied that there would have to be a spiritual return among the Jewish
people *before* a physical return to the land could begin. On the other hand,
it is also prophesied that *after* they return to the land, there will come a
spiritual return, Israel's complete, national, and final return to God at the
end of the age. So then it would come in stages: first an initial spiritual
return involving a remnant, or portion, of the nation. This would then set
in motion the physical return to the land. And after that physical return
would come Israel's final and national return to God. It was all there at the
beginning of your visions, in Moses' last words to Israel."

"In the Book of Deuteronomy?"

"Yes, it was there, right after the prophecy of the stranger's visit to the land."

"Which was fulfilled in the Jubilee of 1867."

"Just one chapter later comes the first prophecy ever given of the regathering of the Jewish people to their land. But listen carefully to what it says:

> Now it shall come to pass, when all these things come upon
> you…and you call them to mind among all the nations where
> the LORD your God drives you, *and you return to the LORD
> your God…that the LORD your God will bring you back* from
> captivity, and have compassion on you, *and gather you* again
> from all the nations where the LORD your God has scattered
> you.…Then the LORD your God will *bring you to the land*
> which your fathers possessed, *and you shall possess it.*[1]

"According to the prophecy, a spiritual return of some form must first take place among the Jewish people before the physical return to the land can begin. It will trigger that return. But to return, one must go back to that which one has left. So there would have to be a spiritual return to that which was departed from in the beginning."

"The prophecy of Hosea," I said. "It foretold that in the last days the Jewish people would have to return to *David their king*, the Messiah…thus a return to the Messiah they had once left. And it would have to be one that they left from in the first century when they left the land. And there's only one who fits the requirement—Jesus…or Yeshua."

"In two thousand years there has been no other."

"What about the olive tree that I saw and the branches that were broken off and reattached?"

"In the Book of Romans the apostle Paul writes of the faith as an olive tree, an olive tree linked to the Jewish people but to which the Gentiles were now being grafted in. But he adds that the Jewish people, the natural branches, though separated from the tree, will, in the end, be grafted back in, reattached."

"So then there would have to be some sort of spiritual return among the Jewish people, a return to the Messiah. There would have to be an initial spiritual return before the return to the land could begin. Did such a thing ever take place?"

"It did," said the Oracle. "In the nineteenth century a spiritual revival took place among the Jewish people. And it was exactly that, a return to that from which they had departed two thousand years earlier."

"A return to Jesus?"

"To their Messiah, Yeshua. And it was only after the spiritual return began that the physical return to the land was set in motion. The two returns were joined together, just as had been the two departures. Each return represented the reclaiming of a lost possession, the physical return to Israel's physical possession, and the spiritual return to the nation's spiritual possession."

"Where did the spiritual return take place?"

"According to the prophecy, it would take place among the nations where the Lord had driven them. It would begin in Europe, in the British Empire. The same empire that would later play a central role in the Jewish people's physical return would first play a central role in their spiritual return. And both returns would center on the same city."

"London?"

"Yes, and it would center on one specific event."

"A specific event?"

"In the first century, in the days of the Book of Acts, a gathering took place of Messianic Jewish believers, disciples, apostles, and leaders in Jerusalem. It was from that gathering that the door of faith would be opened to the nations. The gospel would go forth beyond the land of Israel to the nations. And the Gentiles would now come in. That gathering would change the course of world history.

"But as the first century neared its end and the days of the Book of Acts drew to a close, such gatherings of Jewish believers disappeared from the world. But in the days of return that which disappeared..."

"Must reappear," I said. "So was there another gathering?"

"Yes," he replied. "It would be the first such gathering in two thousand years, the first such council of Messianic Jewish believers since the days of the disciples. They came from the nations, teachers, leaders, and emissaries, to the city of London. There they worshipped, prayed, shared, declared their identity, agreed on their purpose and mission, and arrived at a resolution. The gathering established the first known alliance of Messianic Jewish believers since the first disciples gathered in Jerusalem two thousand years earlier. One of the speakers at the event reminded the assembly of its ancient origins. He said this:

> There was a meeting a long time ago, when Jews from every nation were gathered together, and the Lord poured out His Spirit upon them: that was the first Hebrew-Christian Alliance...[2]

"The council that convened in Jerusalem at the beginning of the age resulted in the faith going forth from Israel to the nations, from Jew to Gentile. So the council that now convened in the nations, in London, would represent the reverse, the beginning of the return of the faith to the Jewish people and the Jewish people to their Messiah."

"The city by the river that I saw in my vision with the cathedral—was it London?"

"It was."

"And the man who was resurrected from the bones, who looked like an ancient rabbi, was he a Jewish believer...an apostle?"

"Yes, the Jewish apostle after whom the cathedral was named."

"But would the spiritual return of just a remnant of Jewish people be enough," I asked, "to usher in a physical return to the land?"

"With the purposes of God," said the Oracle, "the issue isn't numbers. It only takes a remnant. It was only a remnant of Jewish believers in the first century that changed the course of world history. And remember, the spiritual return comes at first only in part but triggers the beginning of the physical return, the return to the land. And the return to the land would begin in the exact same way, with just a remnant of people."

"So if the spiritual return triggers the physical return, was the return of the Jewish people to the land spoken of at that gathering?"

"At the time of the gathering it hadn't happened yet," he said. "So it could only have been spoken of prophetically."

"So was it spoken of prophetically at that gathering?"

"It was. One of those who addressed the assembly said this:

> Israel shall abide many days without a temple, and without a sacrifice, but that afterwards *they shall return to their own land*...[3]

"The original prophecy simply says, 'They shall return.'[4] But the speaker added, 'They shall return to their own *land*.' As far as when the return of the Jewish people to the land would take place, he added,

> ...of Israel's restoration...the time appears to be drawing near.[5]

"His words were prophetic. The return of the Jewish people to the land and the restoration of Israel would soon begin. Another leader at that gathering would likewise speak prophetically of what was yet to come:

> Our nation will be restored to its own land."[6]

"Was the timing of the gathering significant?" I asked.

"You never asked me when it took place."

"When did it take place?"

"In the year...*1867.*"

"1867! The year it all began!"

"It *had* to be that way. First must come the spiritual return, a return to the Messiah. Then the return to the land can begin."

"So that's the reason why the mystery began in 1867."

"It's the reason why everything began in 1867. It was that gathering in London that constitutes the first Jubilean event, the first return."

"When in 1867 did that gathering convene?"

"It happened in the spring, in the month of May."

"May? Wasn't that the same month in which the destruction of Israel began, when the Roman armies invaded the land?"

"It was."

"So in the same month that the destruction began, so did the restoration. And how long was it after that event that everything else began... all the other Jubilean events?"

"Less than thirty days after that gathering a ship set sail from the harbors of New York, bound for the Promised Land, and the journey of the stranger began. Two days later, after two thousand years, the release of the Promised Land began as the Ottoman Land Code became law. Less than five months later, after being hidden for fifteen hundred years, the ancient city of Jerusalem was uncovered. And then would come the first school to teach Jewish people to farm the land... and then the first settlement... and then the return of the exiles.

"So when the land was liberated in 1917 and the promise of a Jewish homeland given, it took place on the fifty-year Jubilee of that gathering and that spiritual return. And when Jerusalem was restored to the Jewish people in the Six-Day War, it took place on the hundred-year Jubilee of that gathering."

"You told me the month of the gathering," I said, "but not the day."

"The day," he replied, "held another mystery."

"What day did the gathering take place?"

"May 14."

"May 14! The same date on which Israel would be reborn!"

"Yes," said the Oracle, "the spiritual return foreshadowed the physical return." He paused for a moment before continuing. "I will tell you of two more mysteries concerning these things.

"When Jerusalem was destroyed in AD 70, it altered not only the course of Jewish history but the history of Christianity. Up to that time everything had been centered in Jerusalem. Jerusalem was the home of its leadership, the 'mother church.' But when Jerusalem was destroyed, the faith was cut off from its Jewish leadership, its spiritual fathers. So the end of Jerusalem would usher in the ending of the age of Jewish disciples.

"But in the Jubilee of 1967 everything was reversed. Jerusalem was restored to the Jewish people. So what would happen?"

"If the disappearance of Jerusalem ushered in the disappearance of Jewish believers" I said, "then the restoration of Jerusalem would mean... the reappearance of Jewish believers."

"Yes," said the Oracle. "And so the Jubilee of 1967 would mark not only the return of Jerusalem but the beginning of an age of spiritual revival among the Jewish people. The return of Jerusalem would usher in a massive return of Jewish people to their Messiah, to Jesus, and the reappearance of Jewish believers and disciples in numbers not seen since the first century. Many of these revivals and movements would trace their beginnings to the year 1967. Others were born of the Jesus Movement. The Jesus Movement was birthed in the Summer of Love. And the Summer of Love began in 1967."

"And in the year of return," I said, "the year of Jubilee. And when in that year did the Summer of Love begin?"

"It all began in the month of June, the same month of the Six-Day War and the return of Jerusalem. Both returns and restorations began, after two thousand years, the same year, the same month."

"You said you would tell me *two* mysteries. What was the other?"

"The other has to do with the man who convened the gathering of Jewish believers in 1867. His name was Carl August Ferdinand Schwartz. It has to do with his origins."

"His origins?"

"When he was born."

"When?"

"In the year 1817."

"1817...that would be the year of Jubilee...before the other Jubilees. So the mystery goes back even further."

"Yes," said the Oracle. "So in 1817 a child is born, destined to play a key part in the Jubilee of 1867, his fiftieth year...during which another child is born, John Patterson, destined to play a central part in the Jubilee of 1917, *his* fiftieth year...during which a third child is born, Shlomo Goren, destined to play a central part in the Jubilee of 1967, *his* fiftieth year...each one a piece of the puzzle...of the mystery...the mystery of return—where everything returns to the state in which it was at the beginning of the age—a Jewish land, a Jewish capital, a Jewish nation, Jewish soldiers, Jewish farmers..."

"And Jewish disciples."

"Yes," said the Oracle. "Everything returns...but not all returns are by nature good."

"What do you mean?"

"There is another return that has not yet been revealed to you, a return of a very different kind and nature."

"What other return?"

"The dark Jubilee."

"The next time we met, he would reveal it."

"The dark Jubilee? It almost sounds scary."

"A Jubilee unlike all the others."

"And how was it revealed?"

"Through the awakening of a dragon."

Chapter 58

THE DARK JUBILEE

I WOULDN'T HAVE MADE the journey at the time I did if not for the vision, if not for its disturbing and ominous nature. It was near sunset when I reached the Oracle's tent. And it was at night, by the light of the campfire just outside his tent, that we spoke."

"The dragon," I said, "the red dragon in the ruins…"

"Yes," he said, "That will take us into another realm, that of the dark Jubilee."

"The dark Jubilee—what is it?"

"A Jubilee that follows the same pattern as that which God gave to His people…and yet is not of God."

"I don't understand."

"A Jubilee that parallels the Jubilee of Israel and that corresponds to it but is of the opposite nature, an anti-Jubilee, a Jubilee of darkness."

"I still don't understand."

"The fate of Israel and the fate of the world are bound together. Israel is a microcosm of the world, and the world, the macrocosm of Israel. And so if Israel's destiny is determined by the Jubilean mysteries…"

"Then so too the destiny of the world?"

"Yes. The repercussions of the Jubilean mysteries always go beyond the borders of Israel and the Jewish people. They involve nations, world leaders, world events, world wars…"

"But how do the Jubilean mysteries *determine* the world's fate?"

"Two thousand years ago," he said, "the center of Western civilization and world history was the Roman Empire. Into that empire came the word of God, the message of Messiah, the gospel. The empire was transformed, its faith, its culture, its institutions, its ethics and values, its worldview. The word that went forth from Jerusalem altered the course of Roman history, Western history, and world history. Western civilization would rest on a biblical foundation. It would become a civilization that aspired to biblical values, embraced biblical faith, and held to a biblical worldview. And as Western civilization expanded to become more and more synonymous with world civilization, its biblical underpinnings became part of world culture."

"But how does this relate to the Jubilean mysteries?"

"In the Jubilee you return to the place from which you left. You return to your original state. So the Jewish people returned to their original state, to where they were at the beginning of the age, to a Jewish polity, as in the first century. Now, if the *world's* future is also determined by the Jubilean mysteries, what would that mean?"

"That the world would also return?"

"To what?"

"To the state in which it existed at the beginning of the age?"

"Each shall return to his own possession," said the Oracle. "If Israel returns to the state in which it existed at the beginning of the age, then so too must the world."

"So the world must return to the state in which it existed at the beginning of the age. What exactly is that state?"

"The state of Rome. A state devoid of biblical foundations and alien to Judeo-Christian values and faith."

"So then, according to the mystery, Western culture will become increasingly non-Christian?"

"It means we will witness the departure of Western civilization from its biblical foundation, a departure from the faith that defined it, a departure in spirituality, in morality and ethics, in culture, and worldview..."

"What you just describe is already happening."

"Yes," said the Oracle. "It's all part of the mystery of return, which in this case means a civilization dislodging itself and separating from the foundation on which it once rested.

"There have been times when such departures have taken place by force and rapidly, as in the case of the Soviet Union or Nazi Germany. But more often it happens step by step, the disestablishment of biblical authority, the unhinging of ethical moorings, the dechristianization of culture, the removal of God's word, the overturning of values, the purging of God's name. And do you know when this phenomenon became unmistakably manifest?"

"No."

"In the days of the return, in the same era that saw the return of the Jewish people to Israel. So as Israel was returning to the state in which it existed at the beginning of the age, the world around it was doing the same, returning to its original state. And that original state was not only *non*-Christian but *pagan*."

"So the mystery would reveal a return to pagan civilization."

"Yes, to a modern version of it. When a civilization departs from biblical values, it will return to pagan ones. It will celebrate its new values as enlightened, secular, progressive, revolutionary, or just new, but they remain what they are.

"In the pagan world of the first century, children were killed in their mothers' wombs. So as modern culture departs from its biblical foundations, it returns to the same pagan act. And as modern culture departs from its biblical foundations, it returns to pagan views and practices concerning sexuality, gender, and marriage."

"It's already happening," I said.

"Yes," he replied, "and now you know why."

"In my vision the dragon breathed on the stadium, and I heard cheers and screams. What did that represent?"

"The first-century civilization that surrounded Israel was not only non-Christian but *anti-Christian*. It warred against the faith and persecuted those who upheld it."

"So if the modern world is returning to what it was at the beginning of the age, then will it turn increasingly anti-Christian?"

"Apart from divine intervention, it will again war against the faith and the word. And those who hold true to that which is biblical will be increasingly marginalized, delegitimized, ridiculed, vilified, and finally persecuted."

"A return to Rome."

"In a sense," said the Oracle. "And Rome was not only an anti-Christian civilization but an anti-Israel civilization as well. So the Scriptures prophesy that in the end times the issue of Israel and Jerusalem will be the center of world controversy and the nations will gather to war against them."

"So end-time prophecy is Jubilean."

"It is," he said, "but why do you say that?"

"Because the return is central to everything. Everything returns to where it was. And everything centers on the return even when it wars against it, as in the return of Israel."

"Yes," said the Oracle, "each shall return to his own possession—even the world itself."

"A dark return," I said. "Is there anything good that comes out of all this?"

"Most certainly."

"What?"

"A return of a different nature."

"What return?"

"That," said the Oracle, "would be another mystery."

"And that's what you were shown next...the good."

"Yes."

"And what was it?"

"Another manifestation of the mystery, another return, very different from what I had just been shown me...and yet related to it."

"And how was it revealed?"

"Through a stained-glass woman."

Chapter 59

THE STAINED-GLASS METAMORPHOSIS

I T WAS LATE afternoon when I arrived at the Oracle's tent. I had calculated that there would be enough time to share and then return to my tent before nightfall. But it didn't turn out that way. When I entered his tent, he offered me a cup of tea and a plate of dried fruits. We spoke of everything but the vision. He asked me to share the story of my life. So I did. Before I knew it, the sun had set. Outside the tent the wind was picking up, beating against the curtains. But inside it was peaceful. He kindled clay oil lamps, seven of them, and distributed them evenly throughout the tent, I sensed that he was now ready to speak about the vision."

"The stained-glass woman who journeyed to the ancient city...who was she, and what did it mean?"

"The city was Jerusalem," he said. "Two thousand years ago the faith that would go out to all nations was birthed in the land of Israel and the city of Jerusalem...a universal faith and a Jewish faith at the same time, born of Jewish soil, founded on the Jewish hope, built on the Jewish Scriptures, and centered on the Jewish Messiah. It was a radical faith, a revolutionary faith. It had no governmental sanction, no cultural support, and virtually no earthly resources. It had nothing to do with the status quo of its time but was a phenomenon separate, distinct, and contrary to the world. And the status quo waged war against it. It was born in persecution.

"And yet it was this form, as recorded in the Book of Acts, the original, most radical, most Jewish, least established, and most revolutionary form of what would become known as the Christian faith, that would overcome an empire and change the course of human history.

"The faith was never to have stayed inside the borders of its homeland. It was born to transcend them and go out to the world. So Jesus sent His disciples to all peoples and lands. But as it went out from Jerusalem and into the nations, something happened. The branches became increasingly estranged from the roots, and the roots from the branches. With the destruction of Jerusalem, the disappearance of Jewish believers, and more and more non-Jewish people becoming believers, what would be known as the church began to lose its connection to Israel, to it Jewish roots, to its ancestral heritage.

"And as the church departed from its ancestral land, its roots, and its origins, the power and glory recorded of the first believers likewise began to depart. At the same time, the church began gaining acceptance from the surrounding culture. And thus another transformation began. What was by nature a radical faith began moving increasingly toward the status quo, merging with the world, and losing the revolutionary power of its origins for the power of establishment.

"In time the church became an established part of Roman and Western civilization and all the more estranged from its Jewish origins and the Jewish people. What was born in Jerusalem was now joined to Rome, and what was birthed in the Spirit was now increasingly bound to the world."

"So the departure from its Jewish roots and the departure from its radical nature happened at the same time."

"Yes," said the Oracle, "all part of the same departure from what had been in the beginning, the Book of Acts, the church's long-lost possession."

"So it was an exile," I said, "the exile of the church from its ancestral possession."

"And it paralleled the exile of the Jewish people. As the Jewish people became increasingly separated from their land, the church became increasingly separated from its ancestral roots. You see, the church is an Israel of spirit. The two are bound together. When one departs, so does the other."

"What does the Jubilean mystery have to do with the church and the Christian faith?"

"Each shall return to his own possession. So the church must also return. It must return to that from which it departed at the beginning. If Israel is coming home, so too must the church, so too must the faith."

"When?"

"The two departed together in the beginning," he said, "and so together they must return in the end."

"But if Israel is already returning, what does that mean for the church?"

"It means the church must increasingly return to its original form and nature. It means that the two-thousand-year-old separation between the church and Israel must come to an end. It's already beginning. And just as in ancient times the destruction of Jerusalem sealed the separation of the two, so the restoration of Jerusalem in modern times has ushered in their reconciliation. Never since the first century have believers in Jesus and the nation of Israel been more closely joined together or the faith more strongly bound to its Jewish roots. It is also part of the mystery. It is the church's Jubilean return."

"Everything returning to where it was in the beginning."

"Yes. In the beginning of the age there was an Israel in the world, and the faith was joined to it. And so there is again now an Israel in the world, and again the faith is returning to it. In the beginning of the age, in the gatherings of believers, Jesus' true Hebrew name, Yeshua, was spoken. It is being spoken again. In the beginning of the age Jewish and Gentile believers were as one in Messiah. They are so again. And as the faith once turned from Jerusalem to Rome, so it now turns back to Jerusalem. The branches are returning to their roots and the roots to their branches, each to its own possession."

"The stained-glass woman in my vision, she was the church."

"Yes. And her journey and metamorphosis represented the return of the church to its roots, to Jerusalem."

"So will it involve the whole church," I asked, "and every Christian?"

"Not all who are called by those names...but the true, the remnant."

"And what about the other loss," I asked, "the church's departure from the revolutionary state of its origins?"

"There is a return to that as well," he replied.

"How so?"

"The mystery of reversal," said the Oracle. "It was as the church became established, a part of the status quo, and joined to the world that it lost its radical nature and its revolutionary power. So in order to return to what was lost, it must be separated from the status quo and disestablished from the world."

"How?"

"It's already happening," he replied. "In the same era in which the Jewish people began separating from the nations to return to their homeland, a parallel phenomenon took place, the separation of the faith from mainstream culture, the disestablishment of the church, and the dechristianization of Western civilization."

"In the vision, as the woman returned to Jerusalem, she lost her jewels, her riches, and ornamentations, and ended up clothed in the simple garments of Bible times. So it's the opposite phenomenon of what took place at the beginning."

"Yes, the return of the faith to its original state. What you saw was the woman leaving the trappings of two thousand years to come home."

"You said that the church was born in persecution. Does that mean persecution is part of the return?"

"It does."

"But that's *not* a good thing."

"Yes and no," he said. "It is another double-edged sword, a necessary part of the mystery, the ushering in of the return. The church must decrease in worldly power that it might increase in the power of God. For all things must return to the state in which they were at the beginning of the age, the Jewish people, the world, the faith, and the church."

"And so that means...?"

"It means the return to the Book of Acts...the return of true disciples, apostles, and messengers of God, the return of the radical and revolutionary witness that once stood distinct from the world and shined into the darkness the light of God. It means the return of the power that once broke down ancient walls, made kingdoms shake, opened prison doors, set captives free, turned the world upside down, changed the course of human history, and overcame all things. That," said the Oracle, "is the ancestral possession of this faith. That is its inheritance and its Jubilean return. Each shall return. So too the faith...So too it must return to its own possession."

"The best of times and the worst of times."

"Yes," said the Oracle, "the times when gray disappears, when the dark grows darker and the light shines all the brighter...And for those who choose to shine, it is the time of greatness."

He was quiet after that, as was I, until I finally broke the silence.

"So is this the final piece of the puzzle?"

He paused before responding.

"There is one more," he said.

"And which piece is that?"

"The piece around which every other revolves and falls into its place."

"Which piece?"

"The last piece," he said, "the mystery of the age."

"And what was it?"

"It was that which all the Jubilees were leading up to...the mystery of the end."

"And how was it shown to you?"

"Through a vision in which all the other visions came home."

Chapter 60

THE LAST PIECE

I RETURNED TO THE Oracle's tent at midday. He was sitting on an ornately decorated cushion of gold and azure. He motioned for me to join him. So I did, taking my seat on a cushion of gold and crimson. He turned to his left to retrieve a small stool-like table of sand-colored stone. On its surface was a large assortment of colored glass pieces."

"What is it?" I asked.

"A puzzle."

"Of what?"

"Put it together," he said, "and you'll see."

It took me most of an hour to put it all together. I expected that it would have the feel of a stained-glass window, but it more closely resembled an ancient mosaic.

"What do you see?" asked the Oracle.

"A sandal…as in the visions."

"And so it is."

"The last time we were together, you spoke of a missing piece around which all the other pieces revolve. Is it one of these pieces?"

"No," he replied. "The missing piece is the puzzle itself…a puzzle of mysteries within mysteries."

"The missing piece around which everything centers is a sandal?"

"What is it that the mystery centers on?"

"Return."

"And what is the return based on?"

"On the departure, the loss."

"And what does the departure center on?"

"On the land of Israel," I replied, "and Jerusalem."

"And when did the departure begin?"

"Two thousand years ago."

"Yes, the departure of the Jewish people from the land and the city in AD 70. But that followed an earlier departure, that of the disciples, and the going out of the faith from the same land and city. Could there have been another?"

"Another departure?"

"Yes, before all the others, a departure from which all the other departures proceed and around which they all revolve. Could all the departures have begun with one? And if so, where would it have taken place?"

"From Jerusalem?"

"Yes," he said, "it would have to have been a departure from Jerusalem. But it would have had to have taken place before that of the Jewish people and that of the disciples."

"That's what the sandal represents...that departure."

"Yes."

"The sandal belonged to whom?"

"The Messiah."

"The missing piece is the sandal of the Messiah?"

"The missing piece is the Messiah. He's the missing piece of everything...and the centerpiece. Everything revolves around him...the world, history, the counting of years, and the marking of every human event...The entire age revolves around the Messiah...and his departure."

"When did it happen?"

"At the end of the gospel account, after the resurrection, he stands on the Mount of Olives with his disciples. After charging them to go forth to the world as his witnesses, he's taken away... taken up into the heavenlies. The event will be known as the ascension.

"It was the first departure, that from which all the others begin. And what was it that He departed from? The land of Israel and the city of Jerusalem. Everything else will follow. If Messiah departs from Jerusalem..."

"Then everything will depart from Jerusalem...the disciples, the faith, the church..."

"And the Jewish people, the nation of Israel. Messiah is the King of Israel, and a nation must follow its king."

"Even if it doesn't follow its king?"

"It still follows. If the king departs, so too must the kingdom, so too must his people. The age begins with the departure of the King from Jerusalem...and then his people."

"But what's the connection between Messiah's departure and the Jubilee?"

"The Jubilee involves the separation of what?"

"The ancestral possession from the one to whom it belongs."

"And to whom does the land of Israel belong?"

"To the nation of Israel."

"Ultimately to the King of Israel, the Messiah. And to whom does the city of Jerusalem belong?"

"To the Messiah?"

"Yes, to the King. Jerusalem is the city of his throne. The Jubilean mysteries begin with separation. So the first separation of the age, and that from which the others come, is the separation of the King from the kingdom, from his land and his royal city."

"And from his people?"

"Yes, his people. The Jewish people are his first possession. And Messiah is first the possession of the Jewish people. The one belongs to the other. But for two thousand years the one has been separated from the other, Messiah from his people, and the Jewish people from their Messiah."

"The sandal," I said, "as his feet leave the land, so the feet of his people must leave the same land."

"Yes, and so begin the days of separation, for the Jewish people and for the Messiah. It was all there in the Hebrew Scriptures. The prophets foretold that the Messiah would be cut off from his people, and yet he would become a light to the nations."[1]

"So it's the mother of all departures and all separations."

"Of the age, yes. Messiah departs Jerusalem, and so does everything else...each to the ends of the earth. And through each of these departures a stream of countless repercussions have poured into the world. In this way alone the Jubilean mysteries have determined the history of the world."

"But there's still a missing piece," I said, "without which they aren't the Jubilean mysteries."

"And what would that be?"

"The return," I replied. "Each shall return to his own possession. Therefore the Messiah has to return to his own possession. If he left the nation of Israel, then he has to return to the nation of Israel. And if he departed from Jerusalem, then he has to return there."

"Yes," said the Oracle, "and it was all foretold from the beginning, on the Mount of Olives, in the midst of his departure:

> And while they looked steadfastly toward heaven as He went up, behold, two men stood by them in white apparel, who also said, "Men of Galilee, why do you stand gazing up into heaven? This same Jesus, who was taken up from you into heaven, will so come in like manner as you saw Him go into heaven."[2]

"And so too was it foretold in the Hebrew Scriptures:

> And in that day His feet will stand on the Mount of Olives...[3]

"In all of world history there was only one who departed from the Mount of Olives. And thus only one can return there."

"The two sandals I saw on the mountain, one in each vision…they were had to do with the two comings of Messiah."

"Yes."

"And the second one was of gold because the second time He comes as King. The first sandal was of the departure, and the second, of the return."

"Yes," said the Oracle, "it is *from* the one departure that come all other departures. And it is *to* the one return that all the other returns proceed. To that return all the other returns are heading."

"So then all the Jubilean mysteries, all the Jubilean years and events that led to the return of Israel, they're all ultimately leading up to the ultimate return…the return of Messiah."

"Yes, the return of the Jewish people, the return of Israel, the return of Jerusalem, the return of the church, of Rome, of Masada, of the Israeli farmers, of the Israeli soldiers, of the Jewish disciples, and all the other returns…all of them are leading up to the ultimate return.

"It is the ultimate reversal of the Jubilee. He left the land, so then did the Jewish people. But in the reverse the Jewish people return to the land that he might likewise return. The King must be restored to the kingdom, and the kingdom to the King…the mystery of the age."

"And that's why I saw them all coming, the people of Israel and the people from the visions all gathering together up to the mountain. It was the final homecoming."

"The return of *all* things," said the Oracle.

"Does 'all things' include more than what you just shared?"

"He departed not only from the city but from the world itself. It's the world that is the ultimate possession…of him to whom it belongs."

"What do you mean?"

"To whom does the world, the creation, belong?"

"To God?"

"And in that is the ultimate mystery and the ultimate Jubilee…the mystery that begins with the separation of God and the creation. It is from that separation that come all the other separations, before and beyond that of Israel."

"What do you mean?"

"It is from the separation between the Creator and the creation. From that separation comes all loss, all sorrows, all other separations, all pains, all evils, all darkness. But…in the Jubilee all is restored. And so God will return to the world, and the world to God. Thus at the very end of the Bible it is written, 'The kingdoms of this world have become the kingdoms of our Lord and of His Messiah…'"[4]

"It's the final transference," I said, "the final transference of ownership."

"And 'the Lord shall reign over all the earth.'[5] And 'they shall beat their swords into plowshares, and their spears into pruning hooks; nation shall not lift up sword against nation, neither shall they learn war anymore.'[6] And the lion shall lay down with the calf. And peace will cover the earth. And all things will be as they were meant to be from the beginning...as in the Jubilee. All things will return to their own possession."

The Oracle then lifted the stone table and the puzzle of colored glass and returned it to the place from which he had earlier retrieved it. He was silent for a few moments. Then he spoke.

"And yet...there is still more."

"I don't understand. How could there be anything more after the end?"

"But there is," he said, "just as there's more of Heaven above the clouds. You have yet to uncover the Jubilee's final mystery."

"Is that...?"

"Yes," he said, "it is that which lies behind the seventh door."

"I don't understand either. If he showed you the end, what could possibly come after that?"

"Only that which comes after the end."

"But if it comes after the end, then the end isn't the end."

"I know. It's a paradox. But behind the seventh door was the mystery that went beyond everything else, beyond every border, beyond the limits of the mystery...and to the Jubilee beyond the Jubilee."

"I don't understand."

"That which transcends the Jubilee...and yet fulfills it...the last Jubilee...the most cosmic and yet the most personal...and the meaning of it all."

"So the seventh door opened to..."

"The ultimate mystery."

THE SEVENTH DOOR

Chapter 61

THE SEVENTH DOOR

I WAS STANDING IN front of the seventh door. I was more apprehensive about opening that door than all the others that had preceded it. I couldn't imagine what was waiting on the other side or what more there could possibly be that hadn't already been revealed. I turned the key and opened it. What I saw upon opening it surprised me more than anything I had seen upon opening the other six. There was no mountain, no wilderness, and no landscape. I found myself in a room. It was night. There was a crib against the wall, and a baby in the crib."

"Why did that surprise you more than anything else?"

"Because it was *my room*."

"Your room?"

"The room of my first home, my first room. And the baby in the crib, it was me."

"You?"

"Yes. And the baby was crying. And then I saw the ram, a ram of pure white, standing not far from the crib and gazing at the baby. Around the ram's neck was a chain, from which hung a pendant of pure white. On the pendant, as with all the other pendants, was a symbol that matched that which was on the seventh door. The ram turned its gaze toward me, then walked out the doorway. I followed it. Suddenly I found myself standing in a field on a warm summer day. I saw a little boy lying on the grass, looking up at the clouds. It was again me, now as a little boy."

"Do you remember ever doing that, lying there, and what you were thinking?"

"I do. I remember wondering if there was a Heaven and what it was like. And then I saw the ram on the grass in the distance. It turned its gaze in my direction, then walked out the opening in the fence. I followed it. Suddenly I was standing in a playground on a cold, windy day. There was a boy by himself, leaning against the fence with his eyes closed."

"And it was you."

"Yes."

"Do you remember it?"

"Yes. I was praying to God at that moment, asking Him, 'Why?' Then I saw the ram walking through the playground and heading to the gate in the fence. I followed it out. The ram was leading me through varied scenes and moments of my childhood, and then of my teenage years, and of my adulthood, and of my life."

"What was the connection? What was it that connected all the scenes and moments together?"

"In every scene I was seeking or asking…or crying out or question-ing…or searching…or wondering…or longing…That was the thread running through all of them. I followed the ram through each scene and moment until I found myself back in the wilderness."

"In the vision?"

"Yes, still in the vision, but as if it were reality, as if I were in the present moment. The ram was now in front of me, looking directly into my eyes. Then it turned away but didn't move. It knew it was waiting."

"For what?"

"For me to get on its back. So I did. It took me through the wilderness. And then the city on the mountain appeared in the distance."

"Jerusalem."

"Yes, just as in my other visions. We ascended the mountain, approached the city walls, and entered through its gate. But that's where things took a different path.

"As we moved through the streets, I felt a strange sensation, as if the road had been pulled away from under me. I looked down. We were flying. And the ram was now radiant, otherworldly, and winged. The streets receded beneath us and then its buildings as we kept ascending higher and higher and higher and finally into a cloud.

"It was when we emerged from the cloud that I saw it…a city of daz-zling radiant light. I had never seen or imagined anything so majestic or beautiful. The ram took me through the gate, through the streets, and to a river of water unlike any water I had ever seen. I dismounted and just stood there taking it all in.

"Everything was saturated in radiance and permeated with an over-whelming and tangible presence of peace, love, and awe. I couldn't describe what I was seeing or hearing or feeling except that I knew it was the presence of God and that I had never experienced anything like it.

"It was then that I noticed some sort of being standing to my right. The light around me was so bright that I couldn't tell anything beyond the fact that it was a being, that it was standing to my right, and that its brightness matched the intensity of the surroundings. And then it spoke in a voice that was something like that of a man.

"'Do you know where you are?' he asked.

"'No.'

"'You are in the place where the mystery ends...and begins...and always is.'

"'What does that mean?' I asked.

"'It is here,' he said, 'that each returns to his own possession.'"

Chapter 62

THE FINAL MYSTERY

I T WAS THE first time the boy came so early to wake me up, a long time before the dawn."

"How did he wake you?"

"He whistled. He just kept whistling outside my tent until I woke up. I quickly put on some clothes and followed him. I didn't recognize the way, but I couldn't tell if it was because it was actually unfamiliar or because I could barely see it. But the darkness had little effect on the boy, who kept up a brisk pace with no hint of any hesitation. He knew exactly where he was going. We journeyed for some time until we came to a high mountain, higher than any of the mountains I had ascended during my time in the wilderness. He led me up one of its steep trails. We walked partway and climbed the rest."

"Still in the dark?"

"Yes. And beyond how dark it was, there was a cloud just below the mountain's pinnacle. So as we ascended the mountain heights, we found ourselves inside a mist that made it nearly impossible to see anything that wasn't immediately in front of us. Still, the boy seemed unfazed by it all. I stayed as close to him as I could.

"It was only after we emerged from the cloud that I saw the first traces of twilight. We approached the mountain's summit. And that's when I saw him."

"The Oracle."

"Yes, sitting on a rock. It was much the same as when I saw him for the first time, except the mountain now was higher, and below us was a cloud. And as in the beginning he motioned for me to sit on a rock opposite that on which he was sitting. So I did."

"There are no more doors," I said.

"No."

"So will that be my last vision?"

"Time will tell," he said. "But this will be our last time together. You've been shown many things. It is time now that we seal them."

"Tell me," said the Oracle, "in all that's been revealed to you, what have you learned?"

I didn't answer him right away. I didn't think there was any way I could. There was too much to sum up. But then I attempted it.

"I've learned...that God is real."

"And you didn't know that before?"

"I did, and I didn't. At times I felt it, and at times I didn't. But it's beyond that now. It's not a matter of feeling. God is real, and more than real...more real than the world."

"And why do you say that?"

"There's no way that all these things could have happened apart from the reality of God. The prophecies alone...to foretell human events from ancient times and against all odds of their coming true, and yet thousands of years later they come true. Even in the modern world, with all our technology, we still can't foretell such things. And yet thousands of years ago it was all foretold by shepherds and farmers, simple people with nothing, and it all came true...that fact alone. And all the other dimensions of the mystery, all the details, all the precise quirks and twists and turns...all happening at the exact appointed times, in the exact ways, in the exact places...all brought to their appointed times and places by an unseen hand over the course of millennia...No one but God could have done it, and nothing but His reality can explain it."

"And what does it tell you about the word, the Scriptures?"

"The word is real...and also more real than the world."

"And you say that because of what?"

"Because the world changes, but the word remains. And in the end the world and everything in it conforms to the word and to its purposes."

"What else does it reveal?" asked the Oracle.

"That nothing is an accident...If the veil wasn't removed, you could miss it. And it could appear as if there was no purpose. But it was all there. Nothing is an accident, the world, history...life...It's not random. It has a purpose, even when you can't see it. It means something. It has meaning and purpose."

"Yes," said the Oracle, "a purpose not just to the world and not just to history and not just to life, but to *each life*. No life is an accident. No life is without meaning. To each is a purpose...to yours."

"To mine..."

"To yours."

"Specifically…"

"To yours specifically…Even when it seemed to be without meaning and purpose, even when you couldn't make any sense of it…there was a reason and a purpose…just as there was in the mystery. The hand of God was there, moving all things for the purpose and hope of redemption…even when you asked why and found no answer."

"Even as I asked why, that was in my vision. But I haven't told it to you yet."

"It was not just in your vision," he replied, "but in your life. You asked God why, but you didn't hear an answer. There was a reason and a purpose. And so it is written, "'I know the plans I have for you,' says the LORD, "plans of peace and not of calamity, to give you a future and a hope.'"[1]

"That's in the Scriptures?"

"Yes, and that promise is also more real than the world and than all the circumstances of your life."

At that he became silent. He looked into the distance to the cloud resting beneath us, now accented with the orange-golden radiance of the rising sun. And then he spoke.

"Did you ever wonder," said the Oracle, "why all these things?"

"What do you mean?"

"Why the Jubilean mysteries?"

"I don't know what you mean."

"Why everything revolves around them, prophecy, revelation, world history? Why this particular mystery and not another?"

"Why?"

"What is the Jubilee about?" he asked.

"Return and restoration."

"And you can only return to that which you've left and only be restored to that which you've lost."

"And the Jewish people left their land and lost their ancestral possession…but they would return and be restored."

"That's only the *beginning* of the mystery," he said. "The mystery concerns more than the Jewish people."

"Who else then?"

"Everyone," he replied. "The Jewish people stand for all peoples. What happens to them has to do with all."

"To the world."

"Not just to the world," he said, "and not just to all…but to each. Everything you've been shown, every one of the Jubilean mysteries, has to do with each one, each life."

"But everyone hasn't left their land or lost their ancestral possession."

"And yet everyone has. Therein is the mystery. Everyone *has* departed. And everyone *has* lost what belonged to them."

"I don't understand."

"Because you were born into it and haven't known anything else."

"Born into what?"

"A world of separation...a world fallen and separated from that which is perfect...and pure...and good, a world estranged from the purpose for which it was created...a world fallen into darkness and evil...fallen from the light. And so everyone born of this world is a child of separation, separated from God by the darkness...by sin. Remember," he said, "with the nation of Israel, what happens in the physical realm speaks of the spiritual."

"So the physical exile speaks of a spiritual exile."

"Yes, but it speaks of an exile that has to do with everyone."

"An exile from what?"

"As the children of Israel dwelt in exile from the Promised Land, so the children of this world dwell in exile from a spiritual Promised Land."

"Which is what?"

"An exile from the life you were created to know..." he said, "the life you long to live, a life of fullness and purpose, of blessings, of joy. *That* is your inheritance...and the inheritance of all those created in His image...the life they were born to know and live...their ancestral possession."

"But how can something be your ancestral possession or your homeland if you've never been there?"

"The same way the Promised Land was the homeland for generations of Jewish people who had never been there. But they knew that they could never truly be at home apart from it. So it is for those of this world."

"What does that mean?"

"Tell me," said the Oracle, "why is it that you never feel at home?"

"At home where?"

"In this world...when you were lying on the grass, looking up at the sky, longing for Heaven...when you knew in your heart that there had to be more to life than what you found in this world, when you cried out in your tears...you and every child of this world.

"Did you ever think it strange," he said, "to spend your entire life in this world, to know nothing else but this world...and yet to never feel at home within it?"

"Why is that?"

"Because it *isn't* home. So no matter how long you live in it, and no matter how familiar it becomes, your heart can never be fully at peace within it. How could you feel at home in a world of sorrows and pains and fears and rejections and broken dreams and tears and heartbreaks and losses and failures and sins and shame and evil and emptiness? You could never feel at home in this world because it's not your inheritance. It's not your land. And it's not what you were created for. That's why you feel what you feel. That's why you always sense something missing…you and everyone else in this world. Everyone senses it…because something *is* missing. That's why you're always longing for something more and searching for something better…for the good, the perfect, the pure, the right, the true, and the beautiful."

"We search for it because it's what we were created to find?"

"Yes," he said, "that's why you came here. You didn't come here seeking only for the meaning of the vision…You came here searching for what was missing."

"And what was missing?"

"What the mystery is all about."

"And what is the mystery all about?"

"Redemption," he said. "At the center of the mystery is redemption. Who is it that the Jubilee is for? For the exiled, the separated, the broken, the fallen, the one who has lost. So to a world separated from God, a world of fallen lives and broken people, what is the Jubilee? It's the ending of the separation. It's the love of God reaching out to those in exile…to restore the broken, to raise up the fallen, to bring back the lost. What is that? It's redemption," he said, "to be restored, brought back, healed, and saved…It's redemption. It's the missing piece."

"How so?"

"In Hebrew the word for *salvation* is *yeshua*. From that same word comes the Hebrew name *Yeshua*, the real name of Jesus. If all loss begins in separation from God, then all redemption begins with the ending of that separation. That's the meaning of *Yeshua*. It's through him that salvation comes. So it was foretold in the Hebrew prophecies that Messiah, through his death, would make atonement for our sins and cleanse us from iniquity. If you make an end of sin, then you end the separation…then the exile is over…then *our* exile is over.

"There was only one day in the Hebrew year on which the Jubilee could come—on Yom Kippur, the Day of Atonement. That was the day that the sacrifice was offered up to atone for sin, to end the separation between man and God. It's the sacrifice that ends the separation and ushers in the Jubilee. Messiah *is* the sacrifice. So from him comes the Jubilee and the power of restoration."

"The power of what restoration exactly?" I asked.

"All restoration," he replied, "the restoration of each life to God...the resurrection of each life to God."

"Resurrection. That was central in the mysteries."

"Because it's the ultimate restoration. So the sacrifice of Messiah leads to resurrection. You were shown the mystery of Israel's resurrection. But who is it that a nation follows?"

"Its king. A nation follows its king."

"And the King of Israel is the Messiah. Thus Israel is the resurrected nation...because its leader is the resurrected King."

"So from him is all restoration."

"And all the blessings of the Jubilee. In him the outcast are received back; the defiled are made pure; the broken are restored; the condemned, forgiven; the sick, healed; and those in bondage, set free."

"All this has to do with the restoration," I said, "but what about other part of the Jubilee? What does it have to do with the return?"

"What is salvation about?" he asked. "It's about coming home. It's the prodigal son returning to his father. It's about finding forgiveness and restoration in the love of God and the arms of the Father."

"So salvation is also a Jubilean mystery."

"Of course," he replied. "To be saved is to be no longer separated from God, to leave your exile...to return...to come home."

"What if one never returns to God? What if one chooses not to?"

"Then one remains separated, in spiritual exile. And as the soul is eternal, so too then is the separation. But that's not the will of God. He isn't the God of exile but of return, the God of Jubilee. So He calls each of us to return."

"Is there anyone so separated, so far from God, that they're beyond redemption, beyond hope...beyond the love of God?"

"Is there any sin so great," he said, "that God's love is not greater still? Consider what you've been shown. The Lord brought back the children of Israel from the ends of the earth. It didn't matter how far away they were. He gathered them as a shepherd gathers his flock. They were gone for ages, but He never forgot them. He never gave up on them. And He never forgot His promise. Even after thousands of years He kept His word. He restored them. So what was hopeless to the world was not hopeless to God.

"The answer to your question is no. There is no one so far away that His arms aren't longer still, no sin so great that His love isn't stronger still, and no life so hopeless that His redemption isn't greater still. And if He didn't forget His ancient people, neither will He forget you. And if He didn't give up on them, neither will He give up on you. And if He kept His word to them, so too will He keep His word to you. 'For with God nothing will be impossible.'"[2]

"So how do you return?"

"It's all in the mystery," he said. "In Hebrew to return is to repent, and to repent is to return. So how do you return? You repent. You turn to God. You come back. You open your heart to His love and His forgiveness, and you come home."

"But how?"

"It can begin with a simple prayer. You ask for mercy, for cleansing and forgiveness, for redemption and restoration. And you find it in the love, the hope, the sacrifice, and the name of Messiah."

"So the Messiah is the doorway to the Jubilee."

"Messiah *is* the Jubilee."

"And then what?" I asked.

"Then you live it."

"And what does that mean?"

"Then you live in the power of the Jubilee, the power of restoration."

"And the power of the Jubilee is...?"

"The power to leave the darkness, and the ways of separation, and the life you were never meant to live...and the person you were never meant to be. It's the power to break free of the past and of every chain of bondage. It's the power of new beginnings...the power to walk in newness and to become the person you were created to become...a beloved child...of Heaven. And it is the power to regain your inheritance and the blessings you were born to know."

"How?"

"The same way you would regain inheritance in the year of Jubilee. You stand in the authority of your redemption and you enter it. You dispossess the darkness. For in the power of the Jubilee the darkness has no more authority over your life, no sin, no fear, no bondage, no addiction, no failure, no shame, nor any other darkness. Every dominion is broken. By the power of Jubilee you dispossess it and enter your inheritance."

"And yet," said the Oracle, "there is more."

"More?"

"One last revelation."

"What is it?"

"The final one."

"I thought what happened at the end of the age was the final revelation."

"That was only the end. But the final revelation is what takes place *after* the end."

"What takes place after the end?"

"The final Jubilean mystery, the final return, and the final restoration. The final mystery is revealed in the very last pages of the very last book of the Bible, the Book of Revelation. There, at the very end, everything returns to the beginning."

"To the beginning of the age?"

"To the beginning before the beginning of the age, to the beginning of the beginning. You see, in the final Jubilee, at the very end, all things return to the very beginning. To before the fall, before the darkness, before the entrance of evil…and sorrow, before the separation from God…to the way it was in the beginning…to Paradise."

"Paradise—is that the ultimate ancestral possession?"

"Yes, our original possession…and the long lost inheritance. The final Jubilean mystery is the return to Paradise. Do you know what Messiah said while dying on the cross? He said,

> I say to you, today you will be with Me in *Paradise*.[3]

"And what was it that was lost in Paradise? The Tree of Life, the embodiment of eternal life. Now listen to what reappears in the very last pages of the Scriptures:

> And he showed me a pure river of water of life, clear as crystal, proceeding from the throne of God and of the Lamb. In the middle of its street, and on either side of the river, was the *tree of life*…[4]

"What is it that the Jubilee ends?"

"The separation, the exile."

"And in the beginning there was no separation. God and man dwelt together. So of the end it is written:

> And I heard a loud voice from heaven saying, "Behold, the *dwelling of God is with men, and He will dwell with them*…"[5]

"In the final Jubilee it will be as it was always meant to be, as in the beginning. There were no tears, no pain or sorrow. Now listen to what is written of the end:

God will wipe away every tear from their eyes; there shall
be no more death, nor sorrow, nor crying. There shall be no
more pain, for the former things have passed away."[6]

"So the ultimate land of the Jubilee...is Heaven?"

"Yes."

"And the Promised Land a shadow of Heaven?"

"Yes, of Heaven and Paradise."

"So the return of the Jewish people to the Promised Land, is it a shadow
of entering Paradise, entering Heaven?"

"Yes. It is appointed for every child of God to enter the Promised Land."

"What then?"

"Then all will be Jubilee. Then the exile will be over. And we'll be home."

"So Heaven is our ultimate ancestral land?"

"Heaven," he replied, "is home."

"What about Jerusalem?" I asked. "Jerusalem was at the center of all the
Jubilean mysteries and at the center of the return. His people always returned
to Jerusalem. So does Jerusalem have any place in the final mystery?"

"It does," said the Oracle. "And so in the very last pages of the Bible, it
is written:

> And he carried me away in the Spirit to a great and high
> mountain, and showed me *the great city, the holy Jerusalem,*
> descending out of heaven from God, having the glory of
> God....The city had no need of the sun or of the moon to shine
> in it, for the glory of God illuminated it. The Lamb is its light."[7]

"So Jerusalem is also a shadow of Heaven?"

"It is. As the earthly Jubilee centers on an earthly Jerusalem, the final
Jubilee centers on the heavenly Jerusalem. And it is written that within
that Jerusalem...

> They shall be His people. God Himself will be with them and
> be their God.[8]

"Who is it in the Jubilee," he asked, "that everything returns to?"

"The original owner."

"And who is the original owner *of everything*?"

"God."

"So in the last Jubilee everything will return to Him to whom it belongs.
'*They shall be His people. God Himself will...be their God.*' In other words,
we will be His, and He also will be ours. He will be our possession."

"So the ultimate mystery of the Jubilee, the ultimate possession, isn't so
much a land or a kingdom...it's God...Himself."

"Yes," said the Oracle, "the ultimate exile is not to be separated from a land—but to be separated from God. So too the ultimate return is not a return to a land—but to God. The first possession lost will be the final possession restored. In the end our ultimate possession is God Himself. He's the missing piece, apart from which everything else is empty…and without which nothing else has meaning…not even life…not even Heaven itself."

"So the ultimate return is the return of God to us and us to God."

"Yes. Each is the missing possession of the other. And in the Jubilee each shall return to his own possession. We shall be His, and He shall be ours."

"And what happens after that?"

"Did you see anything in your vision after the seventh door?"

"There was no other door."

"There was no other door because there is no *after that*. On the seventh door was a symbol. It was the Hebrew letter *ayin*. *Ayin* begins the Hebrew word *olam*. *Olam* stands for that which is everlasting, eternal, forever. The last Jubilee is of the *olam*. It has no end. It has no *after that*. The last Jubilee is forever."

"I have a question."

"Ask."

"If the Jubilee is the time that each returns to his possession, then if one returns to God now, then the Jubilee can in a sense begin now?"

"Yes," said the Oracle, "for those who return to God, the Jubilee for them begins here and now."

"When one returns to God."

"Not when *one* returns, but only when a specific one returns to God."

"What do you mean?"

"Do you know who that particular one is?"

"No."

"It's *you*. That particular one is *you*. It is only when *you* return to God that the Jubilee can begin. And do you know the only place that this one can return to God?"

"No."

"Here."

"Here?"

"In whatever *here* that particular one is…here, and as you are. That's the only one and the only place. And do you know the only time in which it can happen?"

"When?"

"Now," he said. "Never another time. Never tomorrow. You can only come to Him when the time is now. No other time is real. So the only one who can come is you…the only place is here…and the only time is now.

"And so the voice of God would now call to the one who is here and now and to each one who would hear His voice wherever and whenever they are…The voice of God would say to you this…

> I have known you from the beginning, from before you took your first step, before you breathed your first breath, before you were even conceived. I have seen all your tears and have known all your sorrows and wounds and pains, all your longings and hopes, all your fears, your dreams and heartbreaks, your burdens and weariness, your times of asking Me why, your cries of loneliness and emptiness, your times of separation, your mourning for what was lost, your weaknesses and failings, your wanderings, your sins and shame…And I have still loved you with an everlasting love…
>
> And now I call you to leave the darkness and all that is passed and all that I never willed or purposed for your life…that the days of your separation would come to an end. It is time now to return. It is time to come home…to enter the inheritance of blessing you never knew but were born to enter. It is time for your Jubilee.
>
> Come to Me. And I will not turn you away but will receive you. And I will wipe away all your tears. I will forgive all your sins. I will heal all your wounds. And I will turn all your sorrows into joy. And you will forget your days of darkness and wandering, the days of your separation. And I will make all things new.
>
> And I will bring you into a land where the crippled walk, where deserts bloom, where the blind see, where the defiled become pure, and where that which was lost is found again. I will bring you to a place you have never known and yet have always longed to be, to your Promised Land. And I will never leave you. And you will never again know what it is to be lost. For in that day, you will have come home. You will be Mine, and I will be yours…forever."

"He didn't say a word after that. Nor did I. I couldn't. It was enough to just take it all in. And there was nothing I could think of to say that wouldn't have sounded inappropriate or inadequate in the wake of what had been spoken. There was nothing else to say.

"So we just sat there in silence as the wind swept over the mountaintop and as the light of the rising sun broke through the cloud beneath us."

Chapter 63

AFTER THE END

SO THAT WAS the last time you saw the Oracle?"

"Yes."

"Did you ever go back to that mountain?"

"No. I knew if I did, I wouldn't find him there."

"What about his tent?"

"I did go back once to look...but it was gone. He had moved on."

"Where do you think he is?"

"I have no idea but somewhere receiving revelations or giving them."

"And what about you? The revelations weren't just about the big and cosmic things; they were also personal...to you."

"And to each."

"Yes, but also to you."

"If you mean, did I come to God? The answer is yes."

"And you never went back home?"

"Not yet."

"What about the visions? Did they continue?"

"No. I don't believe they were supposed to. I saw what I was meant to see, and I was shown what I was meant to be shown."

"But you can't just keep it to yourself. It's too big, and it involves the world...and everyone."

"No, I don't believe it was just for me. I wrote it all down. And now you know it as well."

"But it was given to *you*. You were the one who came here seeking truth and the meaning of the vision that started it all."

"But you came here seeking truth and revelation as well."

"Yes, but I didn't actually come here to discover what I discovered. I never expected to be shown what you revealed to me. But once you began, I knew I had to hear everything."

"Then why did you actually come here?"

There was silence for a moment. He hesitated to answer.

"Actually..."

"Yes?"

"Actually..." he paused again, "I had a vision..."

The statement produced a silence much longer than that which had preceded it. The traveler waited anxiously for a response from the man on the mountain, who was now looking out into the distance, as if deliberating in deep thought. Finally he spoke.

"So then," he said, turning his gaze away from the distance and toward the one awaiting his answer, "where shall we begin?"

NOTES

CHAPTER 2

1. 2 Samuel 16:23, emphasis added.
2. Romans 3:2.

CHAPTER 6

1. Deuteronomy 28:64, emphasis added.
2. Leviticus 25:10.
3. Deuteronomy 30:3.

CHAPTER 9

1. Deuteronomy 29:22–23, author's translation.
2. Deuteronomy 30:3.
3. Deuteronomy 29:22, emphasis added.
4. Mark Twain, *The Innocents Abroad* (Hertfordshire, UK: Wordsworth Editions Limited, 2010), 362, https://www.amazon.com/Innocents-Abroad-Wordsworth-Classics/dp/1840226366.
5. Deuteronomy 29:23.
6. Twain, *The Innocents Abroad*, 320, emphasis added.
7. Twain, *The Innocents Abroad*, 313, emphasis added.
8. Twain, *The Innocents Abroad*, 396, emphasis added.
9. Deuteronomy 29:23, NASB, emphasis added.
10. Deuteronomy 29:22–23, CEV, emphasis added.
11. Twain, *The Innocents Abroad*, 387, emphasis added.
12. Twain, *The Innocents Abroad*, 393, emphasis added.
13. Twain, *The Innocents Abroad*, 309, emphasis added.
14. Deuteronomy 29:23, NASB.
15. Twain, *The Innocents Abroad*, 311, emphasis added.
16. Twain, *The Innocents Abroad*, 326, emphasis added.
17. Twain, *The Innocents Abroad*, 311, emphasis added.
18. Deuteronomy 29:23, emphasis added.
19. Twain, *The Innocents Abroad*, 396, emphasis added.
20. Twain, *The Innocents Abroad*, 391, emphasis added.
21. Twain, *The Innocents Abroad*, 309, emphasis added.
22. Deuteronomy 29:23, AMP.
23. Deuteronomy 29:23, NLT.
24. Twain, *The Innocents Abroad*, 350.
25. Deuteronomy 29:27, NASB, emphasis added.
26. Twain, *The Innocents Abroad*, 396, emphasis added.
27. Twain, *The Innocents Abroad*, 397, emphasis added.

CHAPTER 10

1. Zechariah 2:1–2.
2. Zechariah 1:16–17.

CHAPTER 11

1. Deuteronomy 29:22–23, author's translation.
2. Al Hamichya (Blessing After Certain Foods).

Chapter 13

1. Leviticus 21:24, KJ21, emphasis added.
2. Isaiah 62:4, author's translation.
3. Jeremiah 32:44.

Chapter 15

1. Charles Warren, *The Land of Promise; or, Turkey's Guarantee* (London: George Bell & Sons, 1875), https://books.google.com/books?id=1YH7CkC5RgMC&q.
2. Warren, *The Land of Promise*, 3.
3. Isaiah 62:4, NASB, emphasis added.

Chapter 18

1. Arthur James Balfour, letter to Lord Rothschild, November 2, 1917, http://avalon.law.yale.edu/20th_century/balfour.asp.

Chapter 19

1. Genesis 12:1, emphasis added.
2. Genesis 12:2.
3. Genesis 12:7, emphasis added.
4. Genesis 13:15.
5. Genesis 13:17.
6. Genesis 15:7.
7. Genesis 15:18.
8. Genesis 17:8.
9. Genesis 15:16.

Chapter 20

1. Earl Wavell, *Allenby, A Study in Greatness: The Biography of Field-Marshall Viscount Allenby of Megiddo and Felixstowe* (n.p., Pickle Partners Publishing, 2016), chapter 1, https://books.google.com/books?id=rlJvCwAAQBAJ&pg.
2. Genesis 21:31, emphasis added.

Chapter 21

1. John Mordike, "General Sir Edmund Allenby's Joint Operations in Palestine, 1917–18," Commonwealth of Australia, 2008, http://airpower.airforce.gov.au/APDC/media/PDF-Files/Working%20Papers/WP06-General-Sir-Edmund-Allenby-s-Joint-Operations-in-Palestine-1917-18.pdf.
2. Walter Raleigh, *The War in the Air: Being the Story of the Part Played in the Great War by the Royal Air Force* (Oxford, UK: Clarendon Press, 1935), 248, https://archive.org/details/warinairbeingsto05rale/page/248.
3. Isaiah 31:5, KJV, emphasis added.
4. Isaiah 31:5, KJV, emphasis added.
5. "14 Squadron," Royal Air Force, accessed June 5, 2019, https://www.raf.mod.uk/our-organisation/squadrons/14-squadron/, emphasis added.
6. Isaiah 33:20.
7. Isaiah 40:1–2, emphasis added.

Chapter 22

1. Daniel 12:12, author's translation.

Chapter 23

1. Haggai 2:10, 15, 18–19.

2. Haggai 2:22.

3. Haggai 2:22, emphasis added.

4. Zechariah 2:12, emphasis added. Note that the haftarah for the first Sabbath of Hanukah, Zechariah 2:14–4:7, uses Masoretic verse numbering. Zechariah 2:12 is Zechariah 2:16 with Masoretic verse numbering.

CHAPTER 25

1. Jerry Klinger, "The Messiah and Theodor Herzl," Jewish American Society for Historic Preservation, accessed June 6, 2019, http://www.jewish-american-society-for-historic-preservation.org/images/The_longing_makes_the_Messiah.pdf.

2. Theodor Herzl, as quoted in Evelyn Gordon, "Warping Herzl's Legacy on Legitimacy," *Jerusalem Post*, February 3, 2014, https://www.jpost.com/Experts/Warping-Herzls-legacy-on-legitimacy-340205, emphasis added.

3. Chaim Weizmann, "Fifty Years of Zionism" (speech, Jubilee of the First Zionist Congress, Basel, Switzerland, August 31, 1947), https://ufdc.ufl.edu/UF00072101/00001/1j.

4. United Nations Special Committee on Palestine, "Report to the General Assembly," vol. 1, September 3, 1947, https://unispal.un.org/DPA/DPR/unispal .nsf/0/07175DE9FA2DE563852568D3006E10F3.

5. Leviticus 25:10.

CHAPTER 26

1. Laurent Rucker, "Moscow's Surprise: The Soviet-Israeli Alliance of 1947–1949," Cold War International History Project, accessed June 6, 2019, https://www.wilson center.org/sites/default/files/CWIHP_WP_461.pdf.

2. Genesis 32:9, author's translation, emphasis added.

3. Declaration of the Establishment of the State of Israel, May 14, 1948, https://www. knesset.gov.il/docs/eng/negilat_eng.htm.

4. Genesis 35:12, author's translation, emphasis added.

5. Genesis 32:28, author's paraphrase, emphasis added.

CHAPTER 27

1. Isaiah 40:8, author's translation.

2. Isaiah 11:12.

CHAPTER 28

1. Ezekiel 37:4, NASB.

2. Jeremiah 30:18, NASB.

3. Eliezer Ben-Yehuda, as quoted in "The History of Eliezer Ben-Yehuda Hebrew," Lev Software, accessed June 25, 2019, http://www.levsoftware.com/history.htm.

4. Jeremiah 30:3.

CHAPTER 29

1. Written on the Cyrus Cylinder is "I am Cyrus, king of the world, great king, legitimate king, king of Babylon, king of Sumer and Akkad, king of the four corners of the earth..." As cited in William J. Duiker, Jackson J. Spielvogel, *World History* (Boston, Cengage Learning, 2016), 31, https://books.google.com/books?id=hqKaBAAAQBAJ&pg.

2. "Universal Declaration of Human Rights," Article 13, United Nations, December 10, 1948, https://www.un.org/en/universal-declaration-human-rights/.

3. Earl G. Harrison, "Report of Earl G. Harrison," August 24, 1945, https://www.ushmm.org/exhibition/displaced-persons/resourc1.htm.

4. Harry S. Truman, "Letter to Prime Minister Attlee Concerning the Need for Resettlement of Jewish Refugees in Palestine," August 31, 1945, https://www.truman library.org/publicpapers/index.php?pid=481&st=&st1=.

5. Deuteronomy 30:3–5, emphasis added.

6. Mark Twain, "Note to the Young People's Society, Greenpoint Presbyterian Church," February 16, 1901, http://www.twainquotes.com/Right.html.

7. "Truman Recognizing Israel," December 6, 1964, https://www.c-span.org/video/?c4010891/truman-recognizing-israel.

8. Michael T. Benson, *Harry S. Truman and the Founding of Israel* (Westport, CT: Praeger, 1997), 190, https://books.google.com/books?id=jmoab5xc9ogC&pg.

9. Benson, *Harry S. Truman and the Founding of Israel*, 190, quoting Ezra 1:2, KJV.

10. Benson, *Harry S. Truman and the Founding of Israel*, 190.

11. Benson, *Harry S. Truman and the Founding of Israel*, 189.

Chapter 31

1. Amos 9:11.

2. Amos 9:11.

3. Amos 9:11.

4. Amos 9:14, NIV, emphasis added.

5. Amos 9:14.

6. Amos 9:14.

7. "Scroll of Israel's Independence," May 14, 1948, http://makomisrael.org/wp-content/uploads/2011/10/talkspace-Israel-Full-Session-Line-up-03-03-08.pdf

8. Amos 9:11.

9. Amos 9:14, NIV.

10. "Scroll of Israel's Independence."

11. Amos 9:14.

12. "Scroll of Israel's Independence."

13. Amos 9:14.

14. "Scroll of Israel's Independence."

15. Amos 9:15.

Chapter 32

1. Leviticus 25:10, author's translation, emphasis added.

2. Leviticus 25:13, author's translation, emphasis added.

Chapter 34

1. Jeremiah 31:8–10.

Chapter 35

1. Josephus, *The Wars of the Jews*, 7.10, http://sacred-texts.com/jud/josephus/war-7.htm.

2. Hugh Orgel, "Yadin Buried as Herzog Calls Him 'Architect of War and of Peace,'" *Daily News Bulletin*, July 2, 1984, http://pdfs.jta.org/1984/1984-07-02_125.pdf?_ga=2.223402332.637821424.1559914138-1078271779.1559914138.

3. Ezekiel 37:1.

4. Ezekiel 37:3.

5. Ezekiel 37:7–8, 10–12.

Chapter 36

1. Naomi Shemer, "Jerusalem of Gold," 1967, http://www.tousauxbalkans.net/Yerushalayim_Shel_Zahav.

2. Psalm 137:1–3, 5.

3. Gamal Abdel Nasser, as quoted in David Remnick, "The Seventh Day," *New Yorker*, May 21, 2007, https://www.newyorker.com/magazine/2007/05/28 /the-seventh-day.

4. "Arab Threats Against Israel," CAMERA, accessed June 7, 2019, http://www.six-daywar.org/content/israel.asp.

5. "The Six-Day War: Background & Overview," Jewish Virtual Library, accessed June 7, 2019, https://www.jewishvirtuallibrary.org/background-and-overview-six-day-war.

6. Mordechai Gur, as quoted in "1967: Reunification of Jerusalem," CAMERA, accessed June 7, 2019, http://www.sixdaywar.org/content/ReunificationJerusalem.asp, emphasis added.

7. Moshe Dayan, as quoted in Mitchell Hurvitz, "Column: A Return to the Holy Land," *Greenwich Sentinel*, January 15, 2017, https://www .greenwichsentinel.com/2017/01/15/column-a-return-to-the-holy-land/, emphasis added.

8. *Dream & Destiny* (UK: United Synagogue, 2017), 68, http://docplayer .net/100862975-B-a-l-f-o-u-r-1oo-1-w-w-w-balfour1oo-com.html, emphasis added.

9. Shemer, "Jerusalem of Gold."

Chapter 37

1. Menachem Mendel, "Liberating the Old City of Jerusalem and the Western Wall in 1967," May 8, 2012, http://menachemmendel.net/blog/liberating-the-old-city-and-the-western-wall-in-1967/; Shlomo Goren, "Selections from a Diary of Jerusalem's Liberation," April 2007, https://www.yeshiva.co/midrash/5909.

2. Gil Troy, *The Zionist Ideas: Visions for the Jewish Homeland—Then, Now, Tomorrow* (Philadelphia, Jewish Publication Society, 2018), 244, https://books.google.com/books?id=bVxQDwAAQBAJ&pg.

Chapter 38

1. 2 Kings 25:8; Jeremiah 52:12, emphasis added.

2. Luke 21:24.

Chapter 39

1. Mendel, "Liberating the Old City of Jerusalem and the Western Wall in 1967."

2. Numbers 6:13, author's translation, emphasis added.

Chapter 40

1. Isaiah 31:5, kjv.

2. Isaiah 31:4, author's translation.

3. Isaiah 31:4, author's translation, emphasis added.

4. "The Six-Day War: Background & Overview," Jewish Virtual Library.

Chapter 41

1. Leviticus 25:9.

Chapter 42

1. Ezekiel 37:12.

2. While there was some activity at Masada after the War of Independence and during the 1950s, the full-scale excavation did not begin until 1963.

Chapter 44

1. E.g., Remnick, "The Seventh Day"; Alon Pinkas, "The Seventh Day of the Six Day War," *Jerusalem Post*, June 2, 2011, https://www.jpost.com/Magazine/Features/The-Seventh-Day-of-the-Six-Day-War.

2. Zechariah 8:4–5.

Chapter 45

1. E.g., UN General Assembly, Resolution 66/18, Jerusalem, A/RES/66/18 (January 26, 2012), https://unispal.un.org/UNISPAL.NSF/0/34BE727D1EED7D688525799500 579D23.

2. Leviticus 25:10.

3. Commemorating the 50th Anniversary of the Reunification of Jerusalem, S. Res. 176, 115th Cong., June 5, 2017, https://www.congress.gov/bill/115th-congress/senate-resolution/176/text, emphasis added.

4. Commemorating the 50th Anniversary of the Reunification of Jerusalem, emphasis of *Resolved* in original, other emphasis added.

Chapter 46

1. David Lloyd George, *War Memoirs of David Lloyd George* (London: Ivor, Nicholson & Watson, 1934), 1830, 1834, https://archive.org/stream/in.ernet.dli.2015.211123/2015.211123.War-Memoirs_djvu.txt, emphasis added.

Chapter 47

1. Donald J. Trump, "Statement by President Trump on Jerusalem," White House, December 6, 2017, https://www.whitehouse.gov/briefings-statements/statement-president-trump-jerusalem/.

2. Benjamin Netanyahu, "‏ראש הממשלה נתניהו: אנחנו מעלים את ירושלים על ראש שמחתנו!‏," Facebook, December 7, 2017, 10:33 AM, https://www.facebook.com/Netanyahu/videos/10155206821047076/; see also Alexander Fulbright and Raphael Ahren, "Netanyahu Likens Trump's Jerusalem Speech to Israel's Founding," Times of Israel, December 7, 2017, https://www.timesofisrael.com/netanyahu-likens-trumps-jerusalem-speech-to-israels-founding.

3. Netanyahu, "‏ראש הממשלה נתניהו: אנחנו מעלים את ירושלים על ראש שמחתנו!‏"

4. UN General Assembly, Resolution 303 (IV), Palestine: Question of an International Regime for the Jerusalem Area and the Protection of the Holy Places, A/RES/303 (IV) (December 9, 1949), https://unispal.un.org/DPA/DPR/unispal.nsf/0/2669D6828A26 2EDB852560E50069738A.

5. Genesis 32:4–36:43.

Chapter 48

1. Isaiah 45:5.

2. Donald J. Trump, "Statement by President Donald J. Trump on Nowruz," US Virtual Embassy Iran, March 22, 2017, https://ir.usembassy.gov/statement-president-trump-nowruz/.

3. Ezra 1:1.

4. Ezra 1:1.

5. Ezra 1:3.

6. Ezra 1:3.

7. Ezra 1:1, emphasis added.

8. Jeremiah 29:10, emphasis added.

9. Trump, "Statement by President Trump on Jerusalem," emphasis added.

CHAPTER 49

1. Leviticus 25:9.
2. Leviticus 25:9.
3. 1 Corinthians 15:52, KJV.
4. 1 Thessalonians 4:16, KJV.
5. Leviticus 25:9.
6. Leviticus 25:9.
7. Numbers 10:1–10.

CHAPTER 50

1. UN General Assembly, Resolution 181 (II), Future Government of Palestine, A/RES/181 (II) (November 29, 1947), https://unispal.un.org/DPA/DPR/unispal.nsf/0/7F0A F2BD897689B785256C330061D253.

CHAPTER 51

1. "Remarks by President Trump and Prime Minister Netanyahu of Israel Before Bilateral Meeting," White House, March 5, 2018, https://www.whitehouse.gov/brief-ings-statements/remarks-president-trump-prime-minister-netanyahu-israel-bilateral-meeting-2/.
2. Ezra 1:2.
3. Trump, "Statement by President Trump on Jerusalem."
4. Ezra 1:3–4.
5. Trump, "Statement by President Trump on Jerusalem."
6. Tim Hains, "President Trump Recorded Message for Jerusalem U.S. Embassy Opening," RealClear Politics, May 14, 2018, https://www.realclearpolitics.com/video/2018/05/14/president_trump_recorded_message_for_us_embassy_in_jerusalem_opening.html.
7. Benjamin Netanyahu, "PM Netanyahu's Remarks at the Opening of the US Embassy in Jerusalem," Israel Ministry of Foreign Affairs, May 14, 2018, https://mfa.gov.il/MFA/PressRoom/2018/Pages/PM-Netanyahu-s-remarks-at-the-opening-of-the-US-embassy-in-Jerusalem-14-May-2018.aspx, emphasis added.
8. Leviticus 25:9–10.

CHAPTER 52

1. Israel Zangwill, *The War for the World* (New York: Macmillan Company, 1916), 403, https://books.google.com/books?id=raYqAAAAMAAJ&pg.
2. Benjamin Netanyahu, "Prime Minister Benjamin Netanyahu's Remarks at the Burial Ceremony for Lt. Col. John Henry Patterson's Ashes," Prime Minister's Office, April 12, 2014, http://www.pmo.gov.il/English/MediaCenter/Events/Pages/eventgdodim041214.aspx.
3. Shlomo Goren (quoting Isaiah 40:1), as quoted in "1967: Reunification of Jerusalem," CAMERA.
4. Isaiah 40:2.
5. Isaiah 40:1–2.

CHAPTER 56

1. Hosea 3:4–5.
2. Micah 5:2; Zechariah 9:9; Psalm 118:22; Isaiah 53:3–12.
3. Isaiah 53; Psalm 118:22; Zechariah 12:10.
4. Isaiah 49:6.

Chapter 57

1. Deuteronomy 30:1–3, 5, emphasis added.
2. Abraham Cappadose, as quoted in C. Schwartz, ed., *The Scattered Nation*, vol. 2 (London: Elliot Stock,1867), 158, https://books.google.com/books?id=NS8WAAAAYAAJ&pg.
3. T. Meyer, as quoted in Schwartz, *The Scattered Nation*, 162, emphasis added.
4. Genesis 15:16.
5. T. Meyer, as quoted in Schwartz, *The Scattered Nation*, 162.
6. A. A. Isaacs, as quoted in Schwartz, *The Scattered Nation*, 157.

Chapter 60

1. Isaiah 11:10; 42:6; 53; 60:1–3.
2. Acts 1:10–11.
3. Zechariah 14:4.
4. Revelation 11:15, author's translation.
5. Zechariah 14:9, author's translation.
6. Isaiah 2:4.

Chapter 62

1. Jeremiah 29:11, author's translation.
2. Luke 1:37.
3. Luke 22:43, emphasis added.
4. Revelation 22:1–2, emphasis added.
5. Revelation 21:3, author's translation, emphasis added.
6. Revelation 21:4.
7. Revelation 21:10–11, 23, emphasis added.
8. Revelation 21:3.

ABOUT JONATHAN CAHN

JONATHAN CAHN CAUSED a worldwide stir with the release of the *New York Times* best seller *The Harbinger* and his subsequent *New York Times* best sellers. He has addressed members of Congress and spoken at the United Nations. He was named, along with Billy Graham and Keith Green, one of the top forty spiritual leaders of the last forty years "who radically changed our world." He is known as a prophetic voice to our times and for the opening up of the deep mysteries of God. Jonathan leads Hope of the World, a ministry of getting the word to the world and sponsoring projects of compassion to the world's most needy; and Beth Israel/ the Jerusalem Center, his ministry base and worship center in Wayne, New Jersey, just outside New York City. He is a much-sought-after speaker and appears throughout America and the world.

To get in touch, to receive prophetic updates, to receive free gifts from his ministry (special messages and much more), to find out about his over two thousand messages and mysteries, for more information, to contact him, or to have a part in the Great Commission, use the following contacts.

Check out:	HopeoftheWorld.org
Write direct to:	Hope of the World
	Box 1111
	Lodi, NJ 07644 USA

To be kept up to date and see what's happening:

Facebook:	Jonathan Cahn (official site)
YouTube:	Jonathan Cahn
Twitter:	@Jonathan_Cahn
Instagram:	jonathan.cahn
Email:	contact@hopeoftheworld.org

To find out how you can go to the Holy Land with Jonathan on one of his upcoming Israel Super Tours, write to: contact@hopeoftheworld.org or check online for the coming Super Tours.